THE
ARRIVALS

THE
ARRIVALS
A NOVEL

Naomi Gladish Smith

CHRYSALIS BOOKS

Library of Congress Cataloging-in-Publication Data
Smith, Naomi G.
The arrivals / Naomi G. Smith.
p. cm.
ISBN 0-87785-313-4
1. Survival after airplane accidents, shipwrecks, etc.—Fiction.
2. Aircraft accidents—Fiction. 3. Travelers—Fiction. I. Title.
PS3619.M5923A88 2004
813'.6--dc22
2004000550

Edited by Mary Lou Bertucci,
with thanks to Rachel Glenn
Design by Karen Connor
Set in Caslon by Karen Connor

Printed in the United States of America.

Chrysalis Books is an imprint of the Swedenborg Foundation, Inc.
For more information, contact:

Chrysalis Books
Swedenborg Foundation Publishers
320 N. Church Street
West Chester, Pennsylvania 19380
(610) 430-3222
Or
www.swedenborg.com

To
Bob
for Everything
and
to
Jennifer, Matt, Rachel, and Owen,
my first readers

THE
ARRIVALS

Only a few passengers heard the slight *thwump* that came from the plane's midsection, and just one or two in the first-class section saw Marion Draper's terror when, moments later, she carefully shut the cabin door behind her. In the space of a nanosecond, the flight attendant willed a bland, impersonal smile in place of her panicked grimace.

The gallant attempt at self-control was futile, however, for before Marion could signal her fellow attendants, the plane's nose dipped sharply. The sudden gasps of two-hundred-and-forty-nine passengers became a clamor of cries and shrieks. Then the plane leveled and there was a collective intake of breath as for several heartbeats the laboring plane flew on.

It plummeted again.

"Shit," gasped a man clutching a laptop.

"God help us," murmured the old woman three rows behind.

The scream of a terrified child pierced both prayer and curse, and then all sound was engulfed by the crash of plates and glassware shattering against the bulkhead as the plane's speed accelerated, its frame shuddering.

"Put your head down!" Marion Draper called out, her voice steady. "Put your head between your knees and your—" Her next words were lost as Marion's size-five body slammed against the seatback next to her. A spinning water pitcher sailed inches above her and smashed into the forehead of a white-haired man who, either frozen in fear or defiance, had remained sitting upright. In the moments that followed, though the plane bucked and shivered, there were signs that those in the cockpit continued their struggle for control. Their screaming descent slowed, the plane's nose came up again, and for a few moments, it flew an almost level course. But though the plane advanced through the turgid air, it had not stopped losing altitude. It was still moving forward when it hit the first swell of Lake Huron.

1

Sherwood Prescott's grip on the phone tightened. Surely Phillipa would answer. They must be back from the medical center by now. He stared out the hotel window at the Chicago lakefront where trees bowed before great gusts of wind and scarlet leaves scattered along the wide sidewalks. He heard a click. The answering machine?

"Yes?" His wife's voice was unreadable.

"What did they say?"

"It . . . it's not good, Pres." The silence told Sherwood Prescott more than the words. The diagnosis must be even worse than they'd imagined.

"Is Karen there?"

"She went to bed as soon as we came home. Oh, Pres, the doctor said she may respond to treatment, but even if she does . . ." Phillipa's carefully maintained composure broke, "she may not have long."

"He didn't tell Karen that?" Outrage sharpened Sherwood Prescott's voice.

"She asked. You have to remember, Karen's twenty three, an adult." Phillipa paused. "Pres, I won't be able to go to Brussels with you. Not now."

He knew she couldn't. Of course not. The fact that he'd worked so hard—they'd both worked so hard—for this assignment meant nothing beside this news of Karen. So why did it hurt? Why was the disappointment right there battling with the pain he felt for Karen?

"What did the tests show? Are they still saying it's just some autoimmune disorder, or do they have a name for it?"

"I took notes. Look, why don't we wait and talk when you come home? I'll go over my notes, and we can discuss Dr. Lorimar's suggestions."

How like Phillipa to take notes. Sherwood could imagine his wife in the doctor's office writing it all down, as though by spelling out the words she could contain the terror. "I can't come home, Phillipa. My flight leaves O'Hare at eight tonight."

There was another small silence. "Pres, can't you take another flight? One with a stop in Washington, so you could come see Karen?" And me. Though the last two words were unspoken, Sherwood Prescott heard them.

"You know I can't, Phillipa. The negotiations begin in two days. I have people to contact, meetings to go to before then." He shouldn't have to say it. She knew his schedule as well as he did—better.

"Yes, of course." Phillipa's response came a heartbeat later, and Prescott knew what she wanted to say was "No, no! This is more important than any job, than anything."

But he couldn't respond to the unspoken plea. He had to be on that plane to Brussels. She knew that. They both knew it.

Beatrice Jorgenson put aside the letter she'd been reading. She carefully aligned her fork and knife and, glancing at her daughter, pointedly pushed away her plate. At fourteen, Christine should be shedding her baby fat, but of course Beatrice knew enough not to mention weight to her daughter. Still, making it obvious that one needn't eat more than necessary wasn't nagging. If indeed Christy had even noticed Beatrice's gesture and uneaten lunch. The child didn't notice anything that wasn't under her nose. She sat dreamy-eyed, shoveling in her food, seemingly unaware of what she was eating. Might just as well have been a tossed together hamburger-helper as the gourmet pasta salad Beatrice had ordered.

"Excited about the trip?" Beatrice said, determinedly cheerful.

"Guess so." Christy made a stab at a cherry tomato. It skittered from beneath the fork's prong and bounced off her plate onto the floor where it rolled across the white rug and came to rest against the mahogany leg of the off-white sofa.

Beatrice pursed her lips.

"Sorry." Christy slid from her seat and clumped over to the sofa. But she did not pick up the cherry tomato. Instead, she took a step back and head cocked, regarded the bright red sphere.

"What on earth are you doing?" Beatrice said sharply.

Christine blinked. "Nothing." She bent over and picked up the tomato. She looked up to see her mother's expectantly raised eyebrow and muttered in grudging explanation, "It just looked sort of pretty."

Beatrice gave a dismissive flick of her fingers. "I'm having the limo pick us up at five since it will be rush hour, but even so, you'll have a good four hours to take care of last-minute things. Are you sure you've packed everything you'll need? At least one good sweater—it may be cold in Brussels, and I don't want you in that Nature Center sweatshirt you seem to have adopted as your uniform. And make sure you take your navy suit. You'll need something decent for restaurants and churches."

"Mother, everybody wears jeans everywhere." But the protest was half-hearted. Christy absently spooned another helping of pasta salad onto her plate and withdrew into her own thoughts.

Stuart Casperson swiveled his chair so that he faced the whitecap-flecked lake. This was his favorite perk, this office that looked out over Lake Michigan to the east and the Outer Drive winding north. It was nearly as good as J.K.'s corner one. Too bad he was able to sit and enjoy the view so seldom. He'd almost balked at going on this European trip; when J.K. asked him to join J.K. Jr., Stuart had been tempted to say that eight days back after two weeks of meetings in Taiwan was barely enough time to recover from his jet lag. But he hadn't voiced his objections. First, because the ability to trouble-shoot was why they paid him the big bucks. Rescuing negotiations stalled by J.K. Jr.'s abrasive personality, soothing the resulting wounded sensibilities, and in general putting out Junior's brush fires was getting to be a Casperson specialty. But more importantly, he hadn't objected because it might be better not to be home right now.

Stuart's gut twisted. The look in Janie's eyes when she'd asked him about that letter. Stuart swung his chair around to face his desk. What had possessed Cindy to write to him at his home address? Lucky he'd been able to adjust so quickly his first, shocked reaction to the envelope and Janie believed his explanation. At least that look of questioning hurt had been replaced by one of doubt, then hope. But there would be more questions; he'd have to come up with a better explanation. It was too much like the other time. God, why had he gone back to Cindy? If he had to lose his head, why couldn't it have been to someone who had half a brain instead of a bimbo who could screw up a two-car funeral? The Visa bill incident had nearly wrecked his marriage. Wouldn't have been so bad if Cindy had charged only the lingerie; he could have told Janie it was a present he hadn't yet given her. It was the sportswear that had nailed it. How did you explain golf outfits and a lady's driver to a wife who had never swung a golf club in her life?

No more. He'd promised himself before, but this time he meant it. No reply if Cindy called, wrote, or used a carrier pigeon. He'd had it.

Stuart Casperson cleared his throat and snapped on the intercom. "Lorraine, arrange to have flowers sent to my wife, will you? Roses. Red—no, yellow. A couple dozen."

"Yes, Mr. Casperson."

"And you'll have those files ready by six?"

"I'll bring them to the airport."

"You're coming to the airport?" Stuart's tapping pencil stilled.

"Didn't Mr. Kaufman tell you? He wants me to go with you."

Casperson was out of his chair and across the office before Lorraine had finished speaking. He palmed open the massive oak door and glared at the woman in the alcove outside.

"What did you say?"

As always, Lorraine was seated at the desk with her face turned slightly toward the wall, her eyes almost hidden by blunt-cut, gray hair that fell like curtains on either side of her face. Her sideways glance was calm as she replied, "Mr. Kaufman asked me to get my ticket yesterday. I thought you knew; I thought you'd discussed it when he called you in to talk about the trip."

"No, Lorraine, J.K. didn't happen to mention he was sending my secretary—excuse me, my administrative assistant—along. Any idea why? Did he say it was to help baby-sit Junior or to sooth my fevered brow when I've had a tough day repairing baby boy's screwups?"

Lorraine glanced down the hall to where J.K.'s secretary sat. "I think perhaps Mr. Kaufman wanted someone along who spoke French and German," she said quietly.

"Oh, right. I forgot. You're the lady who has taken so many language courses you ought to own stock in Berlitz," said Casperson.

A flush showed on the part of Lorraine's cheek not screened by the curtain of her hair. "What would you like them to put on the card with the roses?"

Stuart Casperson's momentary pique disappeared. "The usual: 'All my love, Stu.' Oh, you'd better put 'Will phone from Brussels' on it. Have it go out immediately. And I guess I'll be seeing you at O'Hare." With this last comment, his sense of grievance returned. He nodded curtly and strode back to his office.

Lorraine VanDyck watched him leave. She darted a glance down the hall at J.K.'s secretary. Amelia wasn't looking her way, but she must have heard Casperson's outburst, and sooner or later J.K. would hear about it too. A few more like that and Stuart might discover he wasn't quite as indispensable as he thought.

She wasn't going along on this trip because of her facility with languages, though it might come in handy. J.K. wanted

10

her to keep an eye on Stuart Casperson. Though he hadn't told her anything other than that he wanted daily reports on what was happening, it was obvious J.K. was concerned about her boss.

Lorraine reached into the desk's top drawer and touched the fax containing the information about her flight. So she was going to be a snitch, spend a week in Brussels, maybe more if the negotiations proved difficult. Why hadn't she told J.K. to do his own snooping? Why hadn't she said that she no longer did any traveling, that life was hard enough without giving up the sanctuary of her little apartment?

She'd learned to ignore the stares she met each day on the bus or during the three-block walk to and from work, though it was always a relief to step inside the huge glass doors of the Kaufman Building. The people here didn't notice any more. At least not unless they happened to be looking at her head on. And then there was usually only that familiar flicker in their eyes. No one let themselves reveal more than that. She was used to it. The stares she would meet on this trip would be no different, but she'd have no place to retreat, only a hotel room at the end of the day. Why hadn't she said no?

Because she liked her job, at least its security, because she didn't relish having to leave a place where people had grown to accept her face. And then the old man had made it difficult to refuse. He hadn't actually asked her to do anything. The inference was that she'd keep her eyes open and report anything untoward. After the initial circumvented harrumphings, J.K. had simply told Lorraine she was to get her ticket and go along. He'd gone back to the papers on his desk then, closing the conversation.

So that was it. How long had it been since she'd been to Europe? Thirty years? How she'd loved Paris, Rome. She'd loved the very idea of traveling, anywhere and everywhere.

But that was before, of course. Now she was a person who learned languages with no intention of using them. Lorraine closed the drawer with a snap. No—she'd go. And not just because it might mean her job if she didn't. She was going to enjoy seeing Europe again, even if part of the deal was having to ride herd on a sulky boss.

2

The Reverend Frederick Hampton put his briefcase on the slow-moving belt and watched it slide beneath the scanner. He'd finished the sermon in it this morning; plenty of time to re-read it on the plane and maybe do a rewrite. Would the carefully formulated arguments of a God-driven-versus-a-man-centered universe seem any more profound, any less trivial at twenty thousand feet than they had at sea level?

Or was Chicago at sea level? He looked at his tall, ungainly image reflected in the glass of an advertising poster and smoothed a hand over his thinning hair. The spot on top wasn't bald, but it was getting perilously close to it. Comb his hair over it? No.

Hampton picked up his briefcase and forced himself to smile at the uniformed attendant who met his eyes with an unseeing gaze as she watched the next case emerge from the scanner.

Did he really believe the reasoned arguments he'd worked so hard to articulate? Just what did he really believe? The doctrines and canons he preached seemed ephemeral these days, changing contour and configuration like a melting candle. The timely examples he'd researched so assiduously seemed sterile and contrived. Hampton hunched his shoulders, lowered his head. Was this waffling belief even worthy of being called faith?

"You there! You've got my case."

Hampton started. "Excuse me?"

The woman who strode up to him pointed to the case in Hampton's hand. "The briefcase. It's mine."

Fred Hampton stared at it. A soft, beige leather case. Not even the right color. "I'm terribly sorry." He held it out. "You have mine?"

The woman splayed empty, upturned palms, her irritation plain. "I don't go around picking up other people's briefcases." She grabbed the case and peered at it as though inspecting for damage. Then she relented and nodded to the security checkpoint. "Yours is probably back there."

"Yes, of course. Again, sorry. It was careless of me."

The woman looked at Hampton as though she were sorely tempted to debate whether "careless" was enough to describe his deed. Then she waved an impatient hand at the plump teenager standing behind her. "Come on, Christine. I want to see if they've arranged for our upgrades." And with that, she stalked off, the girl in tow.

She obviously suspected him of taking her briefcase on purpose. Would it have helped if he hadn't been in mufti? Probably not. The woman didn't seem the type to be impressed by a clerical collar. Fred Hampton returned to security. "I seem to have taken the wrong briefcase," he explained as he picked up his worn, brown case. For an instant, the agent's eyes narrowed, but then, taking in Hampton's unprepossessing appearance, she shrugged and turned away.

14

Hampton tamped down a spark of resentment. One hoped this wasn't an indication of things to come. No, that wasn't the right attitude; he might as well try to enjoy the trip, do some sightseeing, maybe some shopping. No. There was no one to shop for. Not any longer. Frederick Hampton lengthened his stride and made his way down the concourse.

❧

His lean face thoughtful, Jeff Edwards tapped his capped front tooth with a fingernail. He shifted, trying for a more comfortable position in the hard plastic airport chair. Yeah, that was better.

Jefferson Edwards bowed to the audience, then took his leading lady's hand. Who was she? Barbara Sherman? Too old. Deanna Hammond? Yes. The right age and a terrific stage actress as well as a movie star. Applause came at him in pulsing waves. No, he didn't take Deanna's hand. He simply held out his own and let Deanna put hers into it. Jeff lightly kissed the slim fingers, felt them tremble. Then he bowed, releasing her. The audience went wild, the applause reaching a crescendo that echoed in the packed theater like a breaking wave of noise.

"Jeff, you twit, I thought we were going to share a taxi."

Jeff Edwards brushed a curling lock of dark hair from his eyes. "Hey, Talia. I tried to call, but you were out. Larry, you know, that guy I told you about? He had a six o'clock flight to New York and offered me a ride. Figured I might as well save a buck and wait here."

Talia Innes rolled her eyes. "You mean you jumped at the chance to talk to a New York playwright and didn't give me a second thought. I bet you didn't even try to call."

Jeff grinned but admitted nothing.

"Look, Dirk should be here any minute. Flag him down if you see him, will you? I have to go to the ladies room. And could you keep an eye on my carry-on?"

"Your high-powered trader is leavin' the commodities floor to come kiss you goodbye? How's he gonna get past security?"

"He has a ticket; he has a flight for Dallas in an hour." Talia shouldered her large purse. "Tell him I'll be right back." She strode toward the rest rooms.

Jeff slumped in his chair, lacing his fingers over his stomach. It was flat, his stomach, satisfyingly flat.

He stood on the stage in the glare of a single spotlight, sucked in his gut and turned slightly sideways so that his lean figure showed in stark relief against the shadowed backdrop. "That's it, Larry. That's the scene played the way we talked about on the drive to the airport. Think it's effective?"

A cough came from the darkness of the seats, then a rough voice rasped, "Hell yes, Jeff. You had Mollie here in tears. You know, I didn't understand your interpretation until I actually saw it. I gotta admit you really nailed the scene; it's better than the way I wrote it."

"Couldn't have done it without your material, Lar. An actor has to have something really good to start with if he's going to be able to develop 'good' into 'great.'"

"Dirk hasn't shown up?" Talia plunked on the seat next to him.

Jeff sat up and blinked. "Haven't seen him."

Talia rummaged in her purse and offered him a banana. "How can you be so laid back? I can't believe I'm actually going to England. Y'know, life's so good it's scary sometimes. One more semester and I get my master's, the thesis is just about finished except for some tidying up, and now a couple of months in London compliments of a Wicker scholarship."

"Then what? Wait for the White House to call, or is it the World Bank that'll be asking for advice?"

Talia laughed and punched his shoulder. "Then the wedding, and starting the job I'll have decided on by then."

"Must be a bummer to have to choose between all those companies begging for your bod. Don't forget to buy your lakefront condo and hire a nanny for the two-point-two children you and the Dirk will fit into your busy schedule."

"Sweetheart!" The tall, balding young man strode up to them. "I've been up and down the hall at least three times looking for you."

"Dirk!" Talia gave Jeff a disgusted look before she leapt from her seat and threw her arms around the tall man. "Sorry, sweetie. Jeff was supposed to be watching for you."

Dirk didn't seem to mind Talia's assault on his person. His thin mouth relaxed and he kissed her. "Hey, Jeff," he said, acknowledging Edwards. "Should have noticed you, but I was looking for Talia. You headed overseas too?" He leaned over to scoop up the peel of Talia's banana from the carpet.

"We're on the same plane, but Jeff's going on to Brussels. Something to do with the NFA." Talia waited while Dirk tossed her peel into a trash container. "We saw each other at Bennigan's and found we were both headed out tonight. I was so busy telling him about winning the Wicker I didn't give Jeff much of a chance to explain about his trip."

Jeff waved a hand. "I'm used to it. Ever since grade school most of my conversations with Talia have been about awards she has been given or prizes she has won."

"Oh right. Like I haven't had to hear about every audition you've ever had." Talia wrinkled her nose. "I was just being polite about me monopolizing our lunch with the Wicker," she said to Dirk. "Actually most of the time we were lamenting the fact that the play Jeff's been in closed after two weeks."

"Three. See, you weren't even listening."

Dirk looked at his watch. "Much as I enjoy this, I make it not much more than twenty minutes before you'll be boarding." He put his arm about Talia. "And I'd like to use those twenty minutes to best advantage."

"Any broom closets handy?" Jeff peered about. "I see a door over there that says 'Employees Only.' You could try that."

But Dirk's attention didn't waver from the young woman he held. "There's an Admiral's Club down the hall. Let's go have a cup of coffee."

Talia nuzzled him. "Coffee, schmoffee." She flashed Jeff a dazzling smile. "See you on board."

"Right." Jeff raised a lazy finger in response.

He shifted, slouching until his spine rested near the front of the curved, plastic chair.

Someone had turned on the lights in the theater. "You've got to look at it this way, Larry," *he said looking out at the man sitting with a woman a few rows from the front.* "Either I have artistic freedom to make changes, or you do the production without me. Sorry to be hard-nosed, but that's how it is."

"That's really holding my hand to the fire, Jeff. You know there's no one around who understands my play the way you do, no one who could handle its dramatic intensity as well as the comic moments."

Jeff shrugged. "Take it or leave it." *He gave an easy smile.* "Look, I'm not asking for all that much, just the chance to give a performance that will do justice to your play, one that will make Broadway—"

"Flight 785 will now board," the voice from the loud speaker intoned.

Digger placed his suitcase carefully at his feet and opened his comic book. You shouldn't take your eyes off your luggage. Not even for a second. But even if he was reading, he'd feel it if someone tried to do anything with the big bag—like take it and put explosives or something inside and then sneak it back.

Digger darted a glance at the bag and casually toed it closer to his leg.

The kid opposite—had to be about his age, eight, maybe nine—was looking at him. Digger stared back. The kid stopped looking and turned and poked the little kid next to him. His sister, probably. The girl yelled, and the mother told the kid to stop it, and the kid started to argue that he didn't do anything, and the dad said, "Cut it out, Sam," quiet but real firm, and the kid quit. Must be nice to take a trip with your dad—even if he sounded like he really meant it when he told you to cut it out.

The kid looked over at Digger again, and Digger pulled at the square of plastic-enclosed cardboard that hung from a string about his neck. He wished he didn't have to wear the darned thing. You might think he was a baby or something. Soon as he got on the plane it was going in the seat pocket. He was used to flying alone, for Pete's sake. Maybe he hadn't been to Europe before, but he'd flown from Chicago to Phoenix plenty of times. Of course, Grandpa and Grandma were always there to meet him. What if Mom wasn't at the gate in London? Digger squared his shoulders. Of course she'd be there.

Digger saw the flight attendant approaching, clipboard in hand. Yup, she was heading for him.

"David Allen Diggert III?" she said, smiling.

"Yes, ma'am."

"If you'll come with me, we're ready to board you now."

Digger stood and walked after the woman, stiff legged. He hoped the kid opposite wasn't watching.

❦

"Look at those people rushin' to get on ahead of everyone else," Michael O'Meara flicked a gnarled finger at the passengers trooping to the attendant taking boarding passes, at the smartly dressed woman, an overweight teen in tow, who had plowed to the head of the line. The gray-haired man at the front stood aside for them, his harried expression unchanging, as though he barely registered their presence.

"She must have done something powerful great in her life, pushin' herself forward like that," Michael O'Meara continued. "Or d'you suppose it's just because that kind of folks paid more money than we did, because they'll land in London a split-second before the rest of us?"

"Hush now, Michael, she'll hear you," his wife shushed him.

"Just asking," he responded unrepentantly. "And speakin' of London, I don't know why you had to get us this flight that makes it so we have to give our money to the English while we traipse through their country on the way to Dublin."

"You know good and well this was the cheapest flight they had," said his wife, "and it was you who decided we should stay in England a bit and see some sights along the way."

"Ah, well, I've always wanted to see Stonehenge," Michael O'Meara acknowledged, "but I'll tell you this, Blossom, I'll not go around paying to see old mansions and towers or givin' over me money to gawk at crown jewels that were got by wresting away the wealth of conquered nations."

20

Blossom gave his thin knee a tap. "You don't need to be forever giving the surrounding world the benefit of your political opinions, Michael." Then she smiled, her pale blue eyes glinting with mischief. "And maybe you'll want to reconsider the Irish accent before we get to Dublin."

"Ah Blossom," he regarded her sorrowfully. "You're a hard woman, a hard woman indeed. Takin' me to task when I'm just gettin' in the mood for our holiday."

Blossom snorted, but she tucked her hand in his and gave it a squeeze. "This is a wonder, isn't it? So good of the children to give us the money."

"They can afford it, thanks to all the education we shelled out for 'em. Besides, it's not everyone who has parents who've been together as long as us. When I think of me putting up with fifty years of nagging and being ordered about, I'm surprised I didn't get a round-the-world cruise."

"Oh, you've had a terrible time of it." Blossom gave him a cuff. "Being cosseted and taken care of, your every want supplied by a dutiful wife. And anyway fifty was last Christmas; it's just shy of fifty-one now."

"—but who's counting?" Michael finished for her. "We'd best get going. They've begun announcing the rows for steerage." He hoisted a canvas overnight bag to his shoulder, then reached out to help his wife to her feet.

The old couple made their way to the covered passageway linking plane and terminal. Blossom winced as she stepped over the plane's threshold. Michael put out a hand to steady her. "Careful, old girl," he said, "careful."

"Anything wrong, Brad?" Cynthia Polanski looked up from the checklist.

Brad Nelson frowned at his first officer. He hadn't said anything. How had she known? "Nothing aside from a lousy head cold that's probably going to give me grief when we go aloft."

Cynthia lowered the clipboard. "It's just that I asked you twice about the stabilizer inspection."

"Gotta get the ears checked." He grinned. "Blame the cold."

Cynthia gave him a quizzical look but did not press further. "The stabilizer?"

"Passed inspection." Brad unbuttoned his jacket. "Man, I gotta start taking in a few less calories, or I'm the one who's not going to pass inspection."

Cynthia eyed the shirt bulging above his belt. "You said it; I didn't."

Brad did not respond. He had already slipped back into his absorption.

"Yo, Brad," Cynthia said quietly, "There *is* something the matter, not just your cold. Is it something I should know? I mean, is it job-related or personal?"

He gave a brief shake of his head. "Just the usual. Both twins have suddenly decided they're going to college instead of taking a year off the way they were planning, and I've been scrambling to get all the paperwork and applications done. Other than that, it's the same old stuff." He sighed and flicked three switches in rapid succession. "Same old, same old."

But not really. Brad Nelson jammed his finger against the next switch. Unless he could get Lydia to agree to less money, late paperwork wasn't the only thing that might keep the twins from entering college this fall. Never should have agreed to give her so much alimony all those years ago, but Lydia had had a smart lawyer, and he would have signed anything rather than leave the kids with her. His salary, even with alimony, should have been plenty for them to live on, but there never seemed to be enough money. Let's face it, he was a rotten money manager. Brad searched for the packet of aspirin he'd stowed in his jacket. Still and all, he'd managed to bring up the twins pretty well. If only he could figure out this college thing.

❧

Marion Draper was preparing to shut the door when the young couple came running down the corridor to the plane. Marion drew in a sharp breath when she saw the baby in the woman's arms.

"Don't run," she cautioned. "It's all right, you're in time." She reached for their stubs. "Row 16, E and F." she said. "If you'll just take your seats...."

A smothered wail came from the bundled baby. For a moment, the woman looked startled; then she hastily pushed aside the blanket and pressed the pacifier attached to the child's clothing into the little mouth. The man caught his companion's arm and propelled her down the aisle.

Cynthia Polanski looked around through the opened cockpit door at the baby's cry. It was all she could do to resist pressing her hands to her smarting breasts. How long would it be before she would be able to hear a baby's cry without feeling the let-down of imaginary milk to her nipples? It wasn't as though she missed nursing Tabitha, pleasant as it had been. Matter of fact, toward the end of the maternity leave, she'd begun to feel restive; certainly she'd been happy to give up the night feedings, the inconvenience of nursing every four hours. She'd loved getting back on the job.

But leaving Tabitha hadn't been easy, and it wasn't getting any easier. Leaving a screaming nine-month-old who stretched out her arms to her Mommy while Nanny held on tight wasn't something she'd ever get used to.

Nanny. Such a comforting name. But the sharp-faced, watchful-eyed woman who cared for Tabitha didn't look like a "Nanny." At least not the one Cynthia had imagined. The woman had had great references, of course. But should Tabitha still be crying like that every time Cynthia left?

She'd call Rob from Brussels tomorrow, tell him to try to get home early, pop in unannounced, and check things out. Maybe he'd find Tabitha playing happily with Nanny. Lord, let her be playing happily.

"Ready?" Brad Nelson asked as Marion Draper closed the cabin door.

Cynthia straightened her shoulders and nodded. "Sure. Let's get the show on the road."

3

Talia Innes looked at her watch rather than at the woman beside her. "We were half an hour late taking off," she said. "Think there's a chance we'll arrive on time?"

Lorraine VanDyck unbuckled her seatbelt and pulled a lap top from beneath the seat in front of her. "I make it just a bit more than twenty minutes late; the pilot should easily be able to make it up between here and London."

Talia nodded and opened her paperback. If you were looking at something else, it made it easier to talk. "You're going to London too?"

"Brussels."

"Vacation?"

"I'm accompanying my boss on business." As Talia scanned the nearby passengers, Lorraine added, "He's in first class." The lap top's blue screen blinked on.

"I'll let you work in peace." Talia creased the spine of her paperback, then closed it. "I don't usually chatter like this; guess I'm more excited about this trip than I realized."

25

Lorraine VanDyck's thin shoulders relaxed. "First time abroad?" she asked.

"Uh huh. I feel like a kid on the first day of vacation."

"I envy you," Lorraine said. She darted a sidelong glance at Talia through the curtain of her hair. "I was about your age when I first went to Europe. Going to be in London long?"

"Three months. I'm lucky enough to have been given a Wicker to attend school there."

"The Wicker! Congratulations. That takes more than luck." Lorraine returned her attention to the computer in her lap, murmuring politely. "I hope you have time to do more than study."

"Oh, I plan to see the countryside, maybe take the Chunnel to Paris for a weekend," said Talia. When her seatmate did not reply, Talia glanced at the screen in the woman's lap that showed a letter, or perhaps a report. Too bad about the woman's face. What must it be like to have to live with scars like that? Talia resisted the impulse to touch her own smooth-skinned face and reopened her book.

The "fasten seatbeat" sign blinked off as Sherwood Prescott put the phone back in its carrier. He rose, feeling the need to move about, to leave the curtained cocoon of first class. Prescott made his way down the aisle toward the rear of the plane. It hadn't been a successful call. Karen, guarded and uncommunicative, clearly unwilling to even mention the doctor's prognosis, let alone talk about it, and Phillipa's disappointment that he hadn't made it home obvious.

If there had been any way he could have stopped off in Washington and seen Karen, he'd have done it. Surely Phillipa knew that. After all these years of taking any scut work offered, of being available for mediations no one else wanted to touch, he'd been given this plum—no, damn it, he hadn't been given it, he'd earned it—and he wasn't about to jeopardize the whole thing by turning up late.

A baby wailed, and Prescott glanced at the dark-haired young woman trying ineffectually to quiet the child. The woman's frustration showed in the flush that darkened her cheeks. The man beside her ran nervous fingers through his thickly curled black hair and moved as far from mother and baby as the seat would allow. The father? No. An unwilling relative pressed into service? Sherwood Prescott moved aside to let an elderly woman pass, his hand ready to steady her. But as the old woman made her lurching way past him, she grasped the back of the seat beside the couple with the crying child and steadied herself.

"There, there, little one," she crooned at the infant. "There, there."

The baby stopped crying. He looked up at the wrinkled face, at the large-toothed smile, the chin from which a few wiry, gray hairs protruded, and then screwed up his little face and began wailing again. Sherwood Prescott escaped down the aisle. Near the rear of the plane, his eyes rested on a knock-out blond next to a gray-haired woman bowed over a laptop. Prescott's heart contracted. It was so damn unfair! His Karen given a death sentence while this girl, even sitting there reading, fairly glowed with vitality. Not that he begrudged this girl her good health. Still.

Prescott turned to head back to his seat. As he passed the young woman, he was struck once again by her blond beauty. She looked up, met his appreciative gaze with calm confidence, then lowered her head to read her paperback. He hoped the girl realized how lucky she was.

"Can't you keep it quiet?"

The young woman glanced at the man, then bent her head over the baby, her eyes lowered. "Something is wrong," she said quietly. "The medication should be working by now."

The man swore and turned away.

The old woman, weaving her way back from the lavatory grasping alternate seatbacks, stopped by them again. "He's still fussing?"

The flash of resentment that crossed the younger woman's face could have been aimed at the old woman's intrusion or at the world in general. "I'm trying, but nothing helps," she said.

"I'd love to hold him and see what I could do, but I'm afraid I'm not steady enough." The old woman smiled at the younger one. "Two of our five children yelled so much their first months that if they'd been the first ones, I'd have seriously reconsidered motherhood. I'm Blossom O'Meara, by the way."

"I'm Malvena Blatska," the young woman said, relenting. With an awkward movement, she tucked the blanket about the baby. "The doctor gave me something for him to take during the flight, but it is not working."

Blossom's smile disappeared. "A sedative?"

The man beside Malvena stirred restively. "Kid's got a cold, that's all." He leaned over the whimpering child. "How's it going?" he said, turning his back to the old woman.

Dismissed, Blossom went back to her seat. She struggled past Michael's bony knees and plopped down on the cushioned seat. "There's something wrong with that baby," she said.

"Now what's wrong with a baby cryin' a bit? Probably its ears are hurting."

"I don't think it's just that."

"The kid's crying, not yelling and screaming its head off, for pity's sake. You'd think you never heard a child cry before."

Blossom shifted to a more comfortable position. "It's not only the crying; it's the mother," she said at last. "It's as though she hasn't the slightest idea what babies are all about."

"And did you, when you had your first or Lara or Franny? It takes time to learn about babies." Her husband patted her hand. "Leave it be."

Blossom subsided, but her frown lingered.

Digger shoved the placard and string further down into the seat pouch in front of him. Maybe they'd forget about making him put it on when they landed. Maybe he wouldn't have to get up and parade around wearing the darned thing while the kid and his sister watched. Digger craned his head and took a surreptitious look behind him. Yeah, there they were, three rows back. The boy with his dad in two of the center seats, the girl and her mom across the aisle in the row's two left seats.

At that moment, the kid looked up and saw Digger looking at him. Digger whipped around and slouched low in his seat.

"The posse after you, bud?" The man beside Digger grinned and cocked a finger at Digger like it was a pistol.

Digger shrugged and looked away. Who was this weirdo anyway?

"Digger," Digger mumbled.

"Digger, huh? Great name. I'm Jeff," the guy said, "short for Jefferson, which is really a great name."

Digger risked a look at him. "What's so great about it?"

"You heard about the Oscar or the Tony?"

"Yeah. At least the Oscar I have. It's a movie award."

"The Jefferson is the name of an award too. They give it to you for work in Chicago theater. I figured anything would be better than my real name, and since I was choosing a new one, it might as well be something to remind me of what I'm shooting for. So I named myself after it."

Digger looked at him, interested. "What's your real name?"

Jeff considered the question. "If I tell, can you keep it to yourself?"

"Sure."

Jeff's rubbery face screwed in a scowl. "Harmony. How 'bout that for helping a conversation along at recess?"

"Geez. Harmony? How come?"

"My parents were probably the only people in America still into pony tails and pipes when they had me. Guess I'm lucky they didn't call me something like Sunshine or Joyful."

Digger's eyes widened. "They wouldn't have done that."

"Don't bet on it." Jeff settled back in his seat and closed his eyes.

Digger wanted to ask how you went about changing your name, but Jeff had settled back in his chair; and while his seatmate wasn't asleep, he wasn't exactly awake either. Jeff's eyes were glazed, and he seemed completely unaware of Digger's scrutiny. It was like he was listening to something Digger couldn't hear.

Digger pulled his comic book from the seat pocket and slouched down into the seat.

The plane jiggled once, then dipped and regained its smooth line of flight. Several passengers raised their heads and looked out the windows. At the steady hum of jet engines, however, most returned to their book, magazine, computer, or nap.

Beatrice Jorgenson in first class was one who did not. She closed the report she'd been studying and, restless, took a sip of orange juice. "They'll be serving dinner soon. The salmon they have on the menu is usually good."

"—and definitely less caloric than anything else," said her daughter.

"You know I didn't mean that. Really, Christy, if you're going to twist everything I say into something you can pout about, it isn't going to be a very happy trip—for either of us."

Christy gave a gusty sigh that seemed to come from her toes. Beatrice knew the drawn-out breath was meant to indicate that this trip hadn't been Christy's idea and she didn't much care whether her mother considered it happy or not. But since Christy stopped short of voicing the thought—this time—Beatrice couldn't very well call her daughter on it. Beatrice's lips pursed in an unwilling smile. Her obdurate daughter's sigh made the point and was at the same time completely unanswerable. How did teenagers become so adroit at mind control? And more to the point, how did one fourteen-year-old so easily manage to drive her mother to clenched fists and raging frustration, something a board room full of executives was rarely able to do?

The plane dipped again, just slightly this time. The seat belt light flashed on.

Fred Hampton tossed his sermon on the tray and buckled his seat belt. What a waste of someone's Sunday morning. Couldn't he come up with something better than these shopworn platitudes? Surely in three mornings of hard work, he could have formulated a real lesson in living, some vital insight he could give his listeners. Hampton shuffled the papers. There was nothing here even remotely inspiring. He knew he should pray for guidance, for enlightenment. But praying didn't come easily these days; and when he did pray, it didn't seem to help much.

His prayers had always embarrassed Sheila, so except for a few disastrous attempts early in their marriage, he didn't pray aloud. But somehow Sheila always knew when he was praying, even when they lay in bed with the lights out, their bodies not touching. She didn't comment on it and never interrupted him; but when she knew he was finished (a slight relaxing of his body? some involuntary motion of which he was unaware?), she would ask him a question or tell him something about her day. Sometimes Fred thought she was trying to reclaim his attention, attempting to bring his mind back to her.

There had been one time during their brief engagement that he had asked her to pray with him. The startled astonishment in Sheila's eyes made Fred feel as though he'd committed some grievous social error, and he had never asked again. Had it been moral cowardice to have retreated? He supposed so. But he'd been so afraid of losing the joy that she brought to his life that he hadn't dared risk it. And he'd lost her anyway.

Fred took a pipe from its felt pouch and tamped it down. He wouldn't smoke, of course, but the repetitive motion, the comforting feel of the bowl cupped in his hand eased him. One good thing about the conference was that at least for two weeks he wouldn't be coming home to an empty house. Coming back to an empty hotel room after meetings would be quite different from having to face those silent rooms, a closet bereft of her clothes, the bare wire arrangement that had held row upon row of her absurdly high-heeled shoes.

The man beside him made a sudden movement. Fred saw the man staring at his pipe with a disapproving frown. Should he say he wasn't intending to smoke? Or perhaps it was the slight odor of tobacco that was bothering him? The boy next to the man edged forward, pulling at his seat belt so that he could peek round and observe them. Must be his son. Perhaps the father simply objected to his son being exposed to any display of smoking.

"Sorry," Fred said, putting his pipe back in the pouch.

The man grunted and turned to the boy. "Stop wiggling, Sammy."

"I wasn't," the boy said, aggrieved. "How long 'til I get to switch with Becky?"

"Plenty of time for that. Right now you couldn't see anything but clouds anyway."

"Where are we?"

His father opened the airline magazine and studied it. "I'd say we're over Lake Huron," he said.

At that moment, a wide-eyed Marion Draper emerged from the cockpit.

The plane didn't split apart on impact. That happened ninety seconds later. It floated briefly before the left wing sheared off and the sides of the plane imploded, caving in as

33

though punched by a giant sledgehammer. There was time enough before the lake water rushed in for those still conscious to rip at their seat belts, to scream cries of terror.

Frederick Hampton found himself treading water. He grabbed at a piece of debris floating past. His legs didn't seem to work very well, but he managed to haul himself onto the metal section. Moans and cries and noises from the sinking plane came to him through the misty air, but his glasses were gone and he could see little in the choppy water. Then the piece of metal to which he clung rose to the top of a swell, and he glimpsed a circle of devastation: people, objects that might once have been people, parts of the plane. Hampton was thankful to be swept down into the next trough.

A head surfaced a few feet away; Hampton maneuvered his bit of debris toward it. It was the boy who'd been sitting with his father in Hampton's row. He looked at Fred, his eyes enormous, and opened his mouth. No sound emerged. A wave washed over the child, and he disappeared beneath the water. Hampton grabbed at the boy's shirt, caught it, and with the last of his strength dragged him onto the metal wreckage. Sammy. His name was Sammy.

"Hold on, Sammy," Hampton heard himself say.

The boy gagged, coughing out water. "He pushed me," he sobbed, "he pushed me away."

"Who?"

"A guy. Had a piece of the plane. Like this." The boy coughed. "I got hold of it, but he pushed me off."

"You can stay here, son." Hampton tried to think of something else to say, but his brain didn't seem to be working properly. Shock? Had he hit his head? "Help . . . help will come. We'll be rescued," he said. But would they?

"When? The water's c-c-cold." The boy's teeth chattered.

Funny, Fred thought dully, he felt no sensation of cold. He raised a hand above the water's chop, held it near his myopic eyes and saw that it was blue veined. "Soon. They'll come soon." Fred Hampton tried to think where they might have crashed. Lake Michigan? No, had to be one of the other Great Lakes. Which lake had Sammy's father said they were flying over? Name the Great Lakes. Michigan, Superior, Erie . . . ridiculous, but he couldn't think of the rest. Hampton roused himself from his drowsing, aware that the boy beside him was whimpering with fright.

"Going to be all right, son," he managed. "They'll pick us up."

"They won't see us. We're floating away."

Hampton lifted his head. So they were. "I see something. Try to swim . . . go toward it." Not that he'd be able to help much, not with his lower body refusing to respond. "Can you kick? Push and kick?"

Sammy gave a tentative flutter. The metal section dipped into a wave under their combined weight, and Sammy sputtered, spitting out water as the metal rose to the surface again. "Yes," he gasped.

"Good. Push us over." Pray God the child hadn't noticed their metal sanctuary was losing its buoyancy. Fred Hampton edged his body further off it and into the water. By the time they reached the bobbing object, the metal was inches beneath the surface.

"It's a seat cushion," shouted Sammy, disappointed.

"Flotation device . . . keep you afloat." Hampton made an enormous effort and reached for it. "Put your arms through . . . straps . . . hurry."

Sammy thrust his hands into the straps and clutched the cushion to him. "Like this?"

"Yes." Hampton was quiet, husbanding his strength. After a few minutes he said, "There's something that, that might...help us."

Sammy peered at Hampton from over the cushion. "What?"

"Prayer. Ask God for help." A flickering memory flashed in Hampton's consciousness—voices crying out to God, from the plane, from the water. Had He heard them? Hampton pushed away the thought.

"You m-mean the Our Father?" Sammy said.

"Sure." The piece of metal he was holding sank inches deeper, and Fred coughed, spitting out the lake water that filled his mouth. "Sammy—it . . . it'll be dark soon. If I . . . if we are separated—don't be scared. And don't, don't let go of your cushion." Hampton flexed a stiff hand and reached out to rest it for a moment on the boy's wet hair. "They'll come, Sammy. They'll come." He took a deep breath. "Close your eyes." And when Sammy obediently closed his eyes, Hampton began, "Our Father who art in heaven—"

Fred Hampton managed, just barely, to finish the prayer before the metal he was holding sank into the water, and the waves closed over his head.

4

In this late breaking news, we have information there may be survivors in the crash of TransAtlantic Air Flight 785 that went down in Lake Huron this evening. Low-flying emergency craft have spotted several people amid the debris, and rescue attempts are proceeding despite the fading light. Boats and medivac helicopters are reported headed for the area.

At first, Lorraine VanDyck was aware only of calm water and a sense of serenity. Then a buzzing roused her to push against the gentle swells, and she looked up to see what looked like a herd of dragonflies in the distant sky. The buzzing became a roar; the giant helicopters approached and hovered overhead. Lorraine raised her arm to shield her head from the heavy prop wash as she watched a khaki-colored figure separate itself from the copter's belly and descend to the water. Rescue!

Lorraine swam toward the figure; but as she neared the spot and raised her head, she saw two bodies dangling above the water. Someone else was being rescued. It looked like—yes!—the girl who'd been Lorraine's seatmate. Lorraine felt pleased, though she wasn't sure why. After all, she'd barely spoken to the girl. But as she watched them reach the yawning opening in the belly of the copter, Lorraine's throat constricted. What if the helicopter flew away? What if the rescuer didn't come back? But fast on the heels of this anguished thought came the calming realization that the water was no longer achingly cold, that she'd caught her second wind and was swimming strongly. Of course, the pilot would return. She could hold out until he did.

And indeed, after handing the woman into the waiting arms of a crewmember and making an adjustment to his lines, the paratrooper rappelled back down to the lake's surface.

"Over here!" Lorraine yelled. "Over here!"

For a moment, she thought he might not have heard, but then he swung in Lorraine's direction, dangled above her for a moment and jumped down, entering the water so deftly that there was hardly a splash. Lorraine had time only to be aware of a flash of white teeth beneath the blue-and-white helmet before she was turned and maneuvered into a sling attached to the overhead cable. The next instant she and her rescuer were airborne. Lorraine looked out over the sunset-streaked sky, at the lake on which danced a myriad diamond paths of light. Though she clung to her rescuer like a limpet, Lorraine realized she was quite unafraid. "Thank you!" she yelled into the helicopter's noise. "Thank you, thank you!"

Her rescuer smiled but did not attempt a reply. Then outstretched arms pulled her into the maw of the copter, and the paratrooper was on his way to the water again.

Lorraine accepted a cup of hot tea, nodding without

paying much attention to the whispered words of the attendant. Her hand moved to the gauze covering the right side of her face as she took a sip of the sweet, steaming liquid. The bandage must have some sort of analgesic on it, for she felt no pain, only a comfortable warmth. Ironic that the only damage she'd sustained had been to the old injury. No, she wouldn't think of that now. Anyway, the bandage meant she wouldn't have to worry about being certain her hair covered the scar.

She looked around. The huge copter was filled with people. Yes, there was the girl who'd been her seatmate, wrapped in a blanket and sitting with a young man further down the cushioned bench.

"Were they able to rescue everyone?" Lorraine asked the woman who'd given her the tea.

"Quite a few." The woman offered Lorraine a zippered, clear-plastic pouch. "If you'd like to get out of those wet clothes, here's a jump suit that should fit. Head's over there." She nodded to a gray metal door.

A helicopter with a toilet? Lorraine glanced at the bag's neatly folded contents but did not open it or get up. It felt so good to rest against the comfortable cushions, to feel warm and cared for. At the moment, she didn't think she had the energy to move, let alone change clothes.

"No hurry. Take your time," the woman said. She smiled and moved on to attend the next arrival.

Sherwood Prescott ran a hand over his damp hair and pulled the blue blanket about him. These blankets must have some sort of heating element in them—maybe wired; though down-soft, they were curiously flexible, curving to fit shoulders, waist, knees, feet. Prescott looked down the row of his fellow passengers seated along the bench like a row of cocoons. Did he look like that? Prescott watched the crew at the opening haul yet another rescued passenger into the helicopter. The crew moved with quiet efficiency, seldom speaking but perfectly synchronized. He must have been brought up to the copter like that, but he couldn't remember it. Didn't remember much of anything after that plate or whatever it was caught him on the head. He had only the vague recollection of an incredibly loud cracking, a great shudder, and the rush of cold, cold water.

Prescott took a sip of tea. He'd refused it when it was first offered, explained that he didn't like tea, never had. But then, not wanting to be impolite, he'd succumbed to the fatigue-clad attendant's whispered words and gentle insistence. Actually he'd found the hot brew surprisingly soothing and tasty.

Two of the crew approached down the center aisle, half walking, half carrying the newest arrival. They stopped, deftly wrapped a pale blue blanket about their charge and sat him beside Prescott. Then they moved aside to let the attendant offer the obligatory cup of tea and murmured counsel.

After taking an obedient sip, the man roused himself. "Did you pick up a boy?" he asked anxiously. "About nine or ten?"

"Matter of fact, we did." The attendant pointed to the front of the cabin where a young boy in a navy blue jump suit peered over the shoulder of the officer maneuvering the cables. "If Jack doesn't watch out, Digger's going to take over the controls for him."

"No, no. There's another boy. Sammy. He must still be down there somewhere." The man set down his cup and tried to rise to his feet.

Without letting go of her chrome canister of tea, the attendant expertly caught him as he stumbled. She eased him back onto the bench. "Oh, that one. Don't worry," she said gently, "he has been picked up. Sit down and drink your tea." She held the cup for him while he drank, then tucked the blanket about him and went to minister to a woman on the opposite bench.

"Your son?" Prescott asked.

The man looked at Prescott blankly.

"You were asking about your son?"

"No. I didn't know him. But we . . . we were together down there in the water."

"If he was all right when you last saw him, I'd say there's a good chance he's all right now. These people are really good. It's amazing how many they've rescued already." Prescott held out a hand from beneath his blanket. "Sherwood Prescott."

"Fred Hampton." The man touched Prescott's hand briefly. "I guess you're right. She seemed pretty certain he was picked up, didn't she?"

They sat in companionable silence, each safe, enveloped in warmth, sipping the hot, ambrosial tea. For the moment, it was enough.

❧

"Where is my daughter? Where's Christy?"

Blossom O'Meara patted Beatrice Jorgenson's hand. "Perhaps she's in one of the other helicopters."

Beatrice withdrew her hand and tucked it inside the blanket. "That's not good enough. I want to know exactly where she is, and I refuse to let them leave until I do."

"How are you going to arrange that?" Michael O'Meara asked her. "Run up to the cockpit and threaten to jump up and

41

down on the pilot's foot?"

Beatrice gave him an outraged stare, but before she could reply, the helicopter banked over the crash site, then leveled off and headed away from the rescue area.

"Go back! You can't leave—" Beatrice leapt up, letting her blanket fall. Rather than falling, however, the blanket subsided into a conical pile in front of her, effectively preventing her passage through the copter.

A crewmember hurried up. "Please, sit down. There's no one in the water back there." He spoke with such quiet certainty Beatrice looked half convinced.

"How . . . how can you be sure?" she said.

"Scanners," he said promptly. "State-of-the-art scanners."

"Even so, I can't leave, not without knowing where she is. Can you find out about Christy for me?" From anyone else it would have been pleading; Beatrice Jorgenson made it sound like a royal command.

"We're just about ready to land. You'll be given any information we have then. Now, why don't you just take your seat and buckle up?" He put a hand beneath Beatrice's elbow and steered her back to the bench.

"I'm sure your Christy will be all right," Blossom said. "Praise be to God, it looks like they've been able to rescue just about everybody I remember seeing on the plane. It's just plain amazing how many of us they dredged out and so quickly too."

"You're right. For a while there, they were fishing us out like mackerels," Michael said. "Seems strange that—" he paused, frowning.

"That what?" Blossom nudged him.

"That so many of us survived," he finished, speaking so only Blossom could hear him. "A crash like that—why weren't they picking up bodies as well as the living?"

Blossom's eyes sharpened. "Michael, what is it?"

His bony old hand covered hers. "I'm not sure, Blossom, m'love. But I've got a lot of questions, and when this thing lands, I'm sure gonna go try to find someone who has some answers."

❧

"Hey son, how 'bout you go sit with this lady for a while? I'd like to talk to the commander here." Without waiting for Digger's consent, Brad Nelson moved the boy to one side and steered him toward the attendant in the passageway. Then Nelson edged into the cockpit himself and stood with his back against the compartment wall. He cleared his throat. "I want to thank you guys," he said to the pilot. "It's incredible that you managed to save as many of my people as you have."

The man at the controls glanced at Brad. "Glad to be of help. You've had a rough time, haven't you?"

"I still can't believe it. I don't know what I'm going to tell them about what happened. Moments before we crashed the instrument panel went crazy, and then everything seemed affected at once. I think there was some sort of explosion." He stopped and gave an embarrassed cough. "Guess I should save all this for the debriefing." Brad had rejected the blanket offered him; now he surreptitiously smoothed his wet pants and shirt, hoping he wasn't dripping too much. Though it too would have been waterlogged, he couldn't help wishing he hadn't lost his uniform jacket. Wearing it would have made him feel more in control, less like a civilian.

"It's all right. Natural that you want to get to the bottom of it."

"Well, I do," Brad said gratefully. "Like I say, we were fine until whatever it was caused the instruments to malfunction."

43

He pulled his wet shirt away from his chest. "Wouldn't be surprised if they find some bastard got something aboard or in one of the cargo holds."

"You can let the Board worry about that," the pilot said smoothly. "They're already looking into it."

And curiously, this seemed to satisfy Brad. Perhaps it was the absolute conviction of the pilot's answer, the suggestion that it wasn't his problem to worry about. In any case, Brad's thoughts veered in another direction as he saw his copilot in the door of the cockpit. He moved aside to let her in. Cynthia must have toweled herself off, he noted. Though damp, her uniform wasn't as sopping wet as his, and she'd had time to comb her hair, make herself presentable. "You must have been hauled up a while before me," he said to her. "Have you checked out how bad the injuries are out there? Are there many who look like they won't make it?"

Cynthia shook her head, her eyes wide. "There aren't any."

"Say what?"

"There aren't any real injuries. Oh, some look a little dazed, and one or two seem to be in shock, but they're being tended to." She paused and said, "Brad, all I've seen are a few cuts and bruises. And how about us? How did we get out without a scratch?"

Brad looked at her and then at his hands. There had been something about one of his hands back there in the water. What was it? He half remembered a sound, a primal howl of despair. His mind recoiled. Had it been his voice? Had he cried out in disbelief at the sight of . . . of . . . . The memory closed. Like a door gently swinging shut, the dark vision dissolved to the earnest face of his copilot.

"I'm going to have to ask you two to go back and buckle in," the copter's pilot was saying. "And, captain, after you get through with the official business, I'd like to invite you and

44

your copilot to the base post for lunch and a beer. I know the rest of the crew would like to meet you; that was some mighty fine flying you did there."

Feeling more cheerful at the pilot's praise, Brad followed Cynthia back into the body of the helicopter. Why get upset about the absence of injuries? It was a crazy thing to worry about.

Cynthia surveyed the blanket-wrapped figures lining the benches as she buckled her seatbelt. "Where's Marion? I see two of our flight attendants here with us, and I saw a couple of the others picked up by one of the other copters, but I haven't seen Marion Draper."

"Don't worry about it." Brad leaned back. "Y'know, I wouldn't be surprised to find out they've managed to rescue every blamed one of us?"

Cynthia looked out the small window where a golden glow suffused the robin's-egg-blue sky. "I would," she said quietly. "I'd be very surprised."

But Brad Nelson, wrapped in his new-found serenity, wasn't listening.

❧

"Michael, look there!" Blossom O'Meara pointed to the line of passengers disembarking from the helicopter next to theirs.

"Wait," Michael reached out a hand to stop her, but Blossom was already darting across the tarmac, headed for a bedraggled young woman at the end of the straggling column. "Woman, you'll fall!" he shouted.

But she didn't. "The baby!" Blossom cried. "Where's your baby, Malvena?"

Malvena Blatska looked frightened. "I . . . I don't know."

Blossom grasped the girl, her scrawny fingers imprinting the flesh of Malvena's upper arm. "What do you mean, you don't know?"

"Here he is." A smiling woman approached them and offered Blossom a look at the pale blue bundle she cradled.

Blossom leaned over the blanket, her wrinkled face alight. "Ah, the sweet love." She darted a frowning glance from the baby to Malvena, concern in her pale-washed eyes.

But before she could speak, the woman tucked the knit covering closer about the child and reached out to touch Blossom's arm. "It's all right," she said quietly. "Daniel will be with me."

Blossom gave a satisfied sigh. "Daniel, is it?" A coo came from the blanket, and she laughed aloud. "Listen to that! The lad knows his name!"

"It seems so," the woman said, smiling.

Malvena made a sound. "Daniel? I don't—" she paused, then closed her lips on whatever she'd been about to say.

Blossom turned to the girl. "You won't mind, will you, dear? You won't mind if this nice lady takes care of Daniel for a while?"

Malvena gave a quick shrug but did not protest. Then her eyes narrowed, her attention caught by something she saw over Blossom's shoulder. Blossom turned, expecting to see the man who had been sitting next to Malvena on the plane, but the girl's companion was nowhere in sight. There was only a uniformed official, clipboard in hand.

"Who is he?" Malvena whispered.

"I don't know, but what does it matter?" said Blossom. "He's probably trying to get a head count against the manifest."

"Of course." Malvena gave her shoulders a slight shake. "It is just that, in the part of Europe I come from, we don't like

46

people who go around making notes. There has been for many generations good reason to mistrust such people."

Blossom nodded with interest to this, the longest speech the girl had volunteered so far, but before she could encourage more, Michael hurried up to them.

"Are you deaf, woman?" he said. "I've been callin' you for this age; they want us over there."

"I was just talking to Malvena here," Blossom soothed him. "She found a lovely woman who is going to take care of the babe while she's—" Blossom broke off. "Where are they?" she asked sharply. She turned to Malvena. "Where's the woman with your baby?"

Malvena looked about and then met Blossom's eyes. "They left."

"I can see that," Blossom snapped. "But where? Just now she was right here beside us."

Malvena's hands fluttered to her throat. "I don't know."

"She and the kid are here one minute and gone the next?" Michael asked, interested in spite of himself. "How'd she do that?"

But before Malvena could reply, a woman in khaki fatigues approached and gestured them to follow her. "They're waiting for you at the receiving center," she said. "Why don't you finish talking inside?"

They followed her obediently, Michael's hand on Blossom's arm. Michael paused to look back at the huge helicopters. The man with a clipboard stood on the tarmac beside the nearest copter watching them. He lowered his head and penciled a notation on the top page.

5

The woman on the raised dais at the front of the hanger/hall raised a hand until the buzz of conversation gradually ceased.

"Welcome. We're happy to have you with us. You were all given a bag containing clothes and necessary items when you entered, but I know that of far more importance to some of you are the questions you have about what has happened. Those who wish to ask questions now and change into new clothes later will find advisors to brief you in any one of the offices on the right side of the hall." She took a step back and clasped her hands in front of her. "I'll wait a few moments to let those who wish to leave us do so; then the rest of you can use the changing rooms at the other side of the hall, and we'll meet back here for breakfast."

At first no one moved. Then Cynthia Polanski rose and walked quickly to the right side of the hall. She hesitated, then entered the nearest office. Michael and Blossom O'Meara exchanged glances, then got up, and made their way down the row. They were followed by others; a man and woman with a little girl in tow went into an office together.

Beatrice Jorgenson stood. "I certainly do have questions," she said to the woman on the dias. "I want to know the whereabouts of my daughter. But I don't see why I have to meet with an official to get some answers. Why can't you tell us what we want to know?"

"The people to whom I directed you have access to whatever information you want," the woman said pleasantly. "But if you wish, you can stay here, and I'll see what I can do for you after we start serving breakfast."

Beatrice's eyes narrowed. "I don't want breakfast. I want some answers—now!"

"Then I suggest you ask one of our information officers," she said. She gestured to a man walking up the main aisle, clipboard in hand. "Or, if you prefer, you can talk to our chief coordinator."

"Two-hundred-forty-three and counting," he murmured to the woman as he stepped onto the platform. "I'm your chief coordinator," he said. "Beatha has already welcomed you, but I'd like to extend my welcome too. It's not every day we have so many visitors." He looked around. Several people in the hall found his penetrating gaze disturbing. He did not smile as easily as Beatha, but his expression, though sober, was not forbidding. "We hope that, while you're with us, we will be able to accommodate the needs and wants of every one of you," he continued. "At any rate, we'll try to make you comfortable and, as Beatha said, answer any questions you may have. If there's anything you'd like that you don't find in your parcels, come tell Beatha or me. That's what we're here for." He nodded to them all, stepped from the platform, and strolled to where Beatrice Jorgenson was sitting.

Cynthia Polanski fingered the table in front of her, smoothing the grain. "Thanks for confirming it. I think I knew as soon as I got on board the copter. Before, really."

"I could see the news wouldn't come as any big surprise," said the woman on the other side of the table. She reached a hand across the table to Cynthia. "My name's Janet, by the way."

"Why wasn't I more surprised? Why do I find it so easy to accept all this as . . . as normal?"

"Because it is. And then I see that, while you were on earth, you believed there was a life after what you call 'death.' Makes our job a whole lot easier."

"You're right; I always assumed I'd wake up in heaven," Cynthia said. "Right after my dad died, I sometimes felt his presence, and I just knew he was somewhere wonderful, but I couldn't imagine what it was like. I never thought it would be so . . . so real. Take this desk," she tapped it, "and these chairs. It almost seems I could pick up the phone over there and call home to tell Rob all about—" Cynthia stopped, her hands balled into fists. "Rob," she whispered, "my baby, my Tabitha."

Janet placed her square, blunt-fingered hand over Cynthia's fist. "They'll be all right," she said. "They are guarded—now especially."

"Can I see them? Can I be with my husband and my baby?" Cynthia barely got the words out.

She didn't hear her counselor's calm reply, for suddenly, instead of the polished wood table before her, there was Tabitha, asleep in her crib.

Cynthia's breath caught. "Darling Tabitha," she whispered. "My sweet T." As she leaned over the sleeping child, Tabitha's long, dark eyelashes fluttered. The baby's curled fingers spread and then curled again as she relaxed into deeper sleep. Cynthia felt her yearning for Tabitha as though it were a palpable thing, felt her love go out and envelop her child. And as she stood watching, a sense of peace flowed into and over Cynthia, covering her like a mantle.

Then another presence impinged on her senses, and she looked up to see Rob in the doorway. Cynthia's hand pressed hard against her stomach as she saw Rob's bloated face, his swollen eyes. Rob walked to the crib and reached out to touch the baby's damp curls, brushed at his face with the back of his other hand. Tears spilled from his eyes, followed the furrowed canyons of his cheeks, ran in rivulets that dropped from his chin onto his plaid shirt.

"Oh Rob," Cynthia said softly. "Rob, my love."

Rob pressed his eyes with the heels of his hands and took an already soaked bandanna from a rear pocket, wiped his face. He shoved the red rag back into his jeans, then leaned forward, grasping the crib sides. "Cin," he breathed. "Cindy-lou."

"I'm here, Rob." Cynthia raised her clasped hands. "I'm here."

Rob gazed up at the stars painted on the ceiling, stars Cynthia had carefully stenciled in the weeks before Tabitha was born. Gradually calm replaced the anguish in his face. "I don't know if I can do this, Cin. Don't know if Tabitha and I can manage without you."

"I am with you," Cynthia whispered. "I will be with you."

"I feel you," Rob said, still looking at the stars. "I feel you here, Cin. So strong, so strong." He bowed his head, and when he raised it again, there was a wan smile about his cracked lips. "But, Cin, having you around me somewhere in the ether isn't going to help much with feeding T or changing diapers."

Cynthia reached out involuntarily, but something told her not to try to touch him. "I'm not floating around, Rob; it's wonderful here, and real, not weird like some people think." She pressed her hands to her breast. "You'll manage with T, you'll manage just fine," she said. "I love you, Rob. I love you so much."

"I love you, Cindy-lou." Rob closed his eyes. His hand reached for the soaked bandanna in his jeans pocket.

Then it was gone. Before Cynthia was a polished wood table and across the table was a blond woman who watched her with quiet compassion. "They are cared for," Janet said. "Both of them."

Cynthia struggled to hold on to the peace she'd felt moments before. "Who's going to pick up my baby when she cries? Who's going to hug her?"

"My dear, your child has angels about her every minute of every day, and your husband will be able to find the help he needs to care for her physical needs. And if he opens himself to it, he'll be able to tap into the spiritual help that surrounds him." Janet opened the notebook lying in front of her. "His sorrow will heal," she said.

"You mean you saw him too? You saw my Tabitha?"

"I wasn't with you, but I can see your love for your husband and through that I see his for you. You are blessed to have such love."

Cynthia wondered that she felt no sense of irony in the statement. For despite seeing Rob's ravaged face, despite the tears that coursed down his cheeks, Cynthia found herself agreeing with this pleasant woman. It was blessed to love and be loved like this.

"I'm sure you have other questions," said Janet. "Why don't we get to them?"

"Michael, let the man speak!" Blossom gently smacked her husband's arm. "If you'll just listen, Howard here is trying to explain."

"I'm supposed to just sit here and listen to this guy tell us we've arrived in some spiritual-type world and not make any comments?"

"You know we both suspected something like this had happened. You said yourself it was funny that old codgers like us not only survived the crash but were able to paddle about in the middle of the lake for who knows how long and come out of the whole experience healthier than they were before."

"Ah, woman, you always take the opposite side no matter what." But his grumbling had the sound of an obligatory response. Michael O'Meara looked worried. "You're tellin' me this is heaven?" he asked the man opposite them. He gestured to the crowded hall beyond the small office. "You're tellin' me they're gettin' ready to give out the harps and halos?"

"No, this isn't heaven, though heaven is not far away."

"Well, I can't picture it bein' hell, not with all of you people bein' so polite and bent on givin' us anything our little hearts desire."

Howard's lips twitched. "You're quite right, Mr. O'Meara. This isn't hell."

"But that's nearby too?" Blossom moved uneasily in her chair.

"Yes, it is."

Michael pursed his lips. "Is this place some sort of way station between them?"

Their advisor nodded approvingly. "Very good, Mr. O'Meara. It is indeed—a whole world in between. Some call where we are now the world of spirits."

"We're spirits?" Michael cast a surreptitious look at his old hands and slid them under the table out of sight. He rubbed his palms together.

"Feels like real skin and with real muscles, right?" Howard asked.

Michael's veined face flushed. "Just testin'." He looked at Howard, puzzled. "Everything feels just like it did before. How come there isn't anything different about this place?"

"Actually it's totally different. You'll find quite a few things unlike what you experienced on earth, but you may not be aware of those differences. At least not at first."

"Like what, for instance?"

"I can give you an overview, but, y'know, I rather think you might be the type who'd like to find out for yourself, Mr. O'Meara."

"Maybe he would," Blossom cut in, "but I'm not taking one step from this office without learning everything there is to know about the place."

"That's a tall order, Blossom," Howard said gently. "You'll learn as much as you want to and need to; that's why you're here. But you'll learn at your own pace. I could sit here and rattle off all sorts of details and particulars, and when you left here, you'd find you remembered not a one."

Blossom's chin went up. "Do I detect a smidgin of sexism here?"

Howard regarded Blossom; again, his lips twitched. "How so?"

"For one thing, my memory's just fine, thank you, and for another, why is my husband 'Mr. O'Meara' and I'm 'Blossom'?"

"Because I sensed that's how you'd like to be addressed," Howard said, a trifle flustered. "Was I wrong?"

Blossom gave an impudent grin. "No, but you could have asked. And I guess Michael is 'Mr. O'Meara' 'cause he's the formal type?"

"I thought he'd feel more comfortable having someone who looks like his grandson address him more formally, yes. I could hear, or perhaps I should say I could *sense* the words 'whippersnapper' and 'know-it-all' when he first came in."

Michael guffawed. "I did think just that. And you could be my grandson at that—if you were maybe a bit more handsome."

Blossom shushed her husband, but Howard simply laughed. "Patrick is a good-looking boy," he agreed, "though I think he takes after your son-in-law, not you."

Michael sobered instantly. "How do you know that?"

"You were thinking about him."

It was an inadequate response, but Michael found himself unwilling to continue the conversation. He looked at Blossom and saw that she too was restive. "Maybe you're right," he said, tapping a bony finger on the table. "Maybe we should find out about this place for ourselves."

"It's your call." Howard rose and went to the filing cabinet behind the table. He took a folder from the top drawer and held it out to Michael. "Here's an information packet. It should help. And here's my card," he said, handing it to Blossom. "Call me if you have any questions that aren't answered in the packet."

"Just pick up a phone?" Blossom asked. She looked at the card. "There's no number here."

"My name's on it. That's all you need."

Blossom examined the card and then raised her eyes to regard him. "We just think of you when we need you? You'll come?"

Howard nodded. "Well done, Mrs. O'Meara. Good going."

Blossom grinned, her aplomb recovered. "It's Blossom," she said. She took her husband's arm and gave a little tug. "Come on, Michael, we can go through that packet out in the hall. I'm sure Howard has other people to see."

"I don't want to hurry you," Howard said. "If you have any specific questions, I'd be happy to answer them." But he did not attempt to detain them; and as Blossom and Michael went out, they saw a tall, white-haired man in a wrinkled suit waiting outside.

"Come in, Mr. Prescott," they heard Howard say. "Please take a seat."

Frederick Hampton hurried up to the young woman ushering Digger out of one of the cubicles. "May I ask, ah, may I ask if you've heard anything about another boy about this age being rescued?" he asked her.

The woman looked over Digger's head at Fred Hampton, then exchanged a glance with the enlisted man who came up beside them. "Why don't you take Digger outside, Tim?" she said to the uniformed young man. "Show him the jets; maybe let him sit in one?" She watched them leave, then held out her hand to Hampton. "My name's Kate; glad to meet you."

"Fred Hampton." Hampton shook her hand. "About the boy?"

"What about him?" Kate said encouragingly.

"I thought perhaps you'd be able to help me find out what happened to him. You see this boy I'm talking about, I saw his father and mother get off one of the other helicopters, but before I could get to them, I lost them in the crowd. And just a moment ago, I saw them go into one of the offices with their little girl, but the boy wasn't with them. I thought I'd ask about Sammy, but the windows are frosted or have some coating on them, and I couldn't see in. I waited a while, but they didn't come out; and when the instructor or whoever it was opened the door for the next, ah, inquirers, the office was empty."

"Your interest in this boy is . . . ?"

"Sammy was with me, you see—in the water."

Kate looked at him. "I do see," she said gently. "Sammy's a brave child. He held on to that cushion, Mr. Hampton; he didn't let go. He held on until he was rescued."

"So he was picked up." Hampton's stiffly held shoulders relaxed. "Thank God."

"Yes," Kate agreed. "Yes, indeed."

"He's here then?"

"No, not here."

Disappointment clouded Fred Hampton's angular face. "I . . . I'd like to see him—if you could arrange it."

Kate gave an odd little smile, put her hand on Hampton's arm and led him to a computer on one of the desks nearby.

Fred saw that the screen was not a computer, but a small television. It showed a hospital room in the middle of which was a bed and the still figure of a sleeping boy.

He leaned over, examining the picture. "Yes, that's Sammy. But what's he doing in a hospital?"

"He's being treated for exposure and shock, just a precautionary measure."

Hampton raised his head to look at the orderly lines of people serving themselves at the breakfast buffet in the rear of the hall, at the chatting groups seated at the round tables to the side. He frowned. "Nobody here seems in need of treatment for exposure or shock," he said. "Matter of fact, no one seems to need much more than breakfast and dry clothes."

Kate looked at him with interest. "What's your take on that?"

Hampton gave an uneasy shrug. "What do you mean?"

"You're fighting it. Look, do you remember those last minutes before you lost consciousness?"

The muscle in Fred Hampton's cheek twitched. "The cushion wasn't enough to keep both of us afloat," he said at last. "And the piece of metal I was holding onto had lost its buoyancy. I couldn't use my legs, couldn't swim." Hampton cleared his throat, closed his eyes. "I remember . . . warmth, light. I was aware of shining people about me, of kindness." He opened his eyes. "I guess the helicopter must have picked me up then, just as I went under."

Kate shook her head, the trace of a smile on her lips. She reached out to touch the television, and its screen went blank. Hampton raised a hand in protest, but at Kate's level glance, he stifled his objection.

"You're a clergyman, right, Mr. Hampton?"

"Fred, please," he said. "Yes, I am."

"How many times have you conducted funeral services and spoken of the person being 'in a better place'?"

"Of course, I've used that expression."

"And just what did you visualize about that 'better place'?"

"I didn't visualize anything, really. After all, none of us knows what lies beyond. How can we? One has hopes, of course, but one can't expect to understand what must remain a mystery until we too are claimed by death."

"Sounds like a set speech."

Fred had the grace to grin. "I guess we of the clergy are apt to pull out the old chestnuts when pressed."

"Don't tell me you haven't given serious thought to what happens when the body dies?"

"I think it's something everyone wonders about, clergyman and layman alike." He eyed Kate soberly. "But to tell the truth, it's been a while since I've spent much time thinking about it. There have been too many other aspects of my religion that have," he turned his head, "ah, claimed my attention."

Kate considered this. "Uh huh. Well, maybe you ought to give this particular aspect some thought now. Come on, Fred, hasn't it crossed your mind that you, along with all these people here this morning, may have left the natural world?"

"My dear woman, you're not trying to suggest—" Hampton looked at her, concerned. "You seem like a rational, clear-thinking young woman—" he stopped. "You really do believe what you were about to imply, don't you?"

Kate nodded, smiling.

"You're saying we're dead?"

"Obviously not."

"Obviously not," Fred repeated, relieved. Then suspicion crept back into his eyes. "You're playing with words, aren't you?"

"The words 'dead' and 'death' mean something very different to us than they do to you," she said.

Hampton took a handkerchief from his breast pocket and wiped his forehead. "And that would be?"

Kate touched his arm. "I can see you aren't ready to hear this. Later, maybe. You've seen Sammy and know he's okay, so that should help you feel less worried. Relax, Fred. Take things one at a time. Why don't you get some breakfast?"

Fred took the suggestion eagerly. "I haven't had anything to eat in quite a while." He made her an awkward little bow. "You know, I think I will get a little something. And take your suggestion . . . to think about this later."

Kate watched him go to the rear of the hall. "Wouldn't you know it," she murmured to the uniformed woman who had been waiting patiently to speak with her. "There goes someone who spent his life telling people about God and heaven and how to lead the kind of life that will bring them to both, and he knows zip."

"Clergymen," the other young woman said, "some of them crack me up. They really do."

Lorraine VanDyck speared a piece of pineapple and crunched it between her teeth. Sweetest she'd ever tasted. She looked across the table at Stuart Casperson who was plowing through a platter of pancakes and syrup. Funny. He'd sought her out after they'd been rescued, been solicitous about her injury, even tagged after her at the breakfast buffet. Lorraine watched him, feeling almost protective. So what if she'd always considered him a nuisance to be put up with in the intervals between his constant traveling; he was the one person here she knew. Probably he felt the same. Lorraine's solicitous feelings evaporated as she noted the covert glance Casperson was giving the girl next to him. Same old Stuart; he might evince concern for his secretary, but he'd made sure to take the seat beside Talia Innes. Of course, the girl was gorgeous, she'd give him that. But did he have to be so obvious?

Lorraine shrugged and took another piece of pineapple. It was no concern of hers if Stuart Casperson chose to sit by a pretty girl. And she really didn't envy Talia's looks. She was past that. It was the girl's cool assurance, the way Talia looked about the room, as though she knew she was young and smart as well as beautiful but was too polite to mention it. And wouldn't you know, there'd been a frosted green blouse and lime green skirt and jacket in the tote bag Talia had been given. Lorraine smoothed her light gray skirt. Not that she wasn't pleased with the summer-weight wool suit she'd found in her bag. No, she wouldn't have cared for lime green. She watched Talia cut a slice of melon. Talia's large hands with their big-jointed fingers and wide, square nails were businesslike, oddly unmatched to the rest of her. Lorraine glanced at her own slim, well-manicured hands. At least the girl wasn't perfect.

Talia looked up, as though drawn by Lorraine's scrutiny. "Think they'll get a plane for us soon?"

"Your guess is as good as mine," Lorraine said. Then she added more graciously, "Since this is a military base, I think that, rather than have a commercial plane fly in here to pick us up, they'll probably want to take us to the nearest airport that has transatlantic carriers."

Talia turned to the young man on her left. "Where do you think that would be, Jeff? Are we anywhere near Detroit?"

Lorraine felt a tiny surge of pleasure that Talia had asked her friend's opinion rather than Stuart's, but Jeff, absorbed in his thoughts, did not answer her, and Stuart leapt into the breach. "We can't be near Detroit; I figure they'll ship us back to Chicago," he said. "No question O'Hare's the place to handle a crowd like this."

"But they'll take us today, won't they? I mean I hope we won't have to wait around all day to fill out forms and answer questions."

"Not if they know what's good for them," he said. He leaned closer to Talia. "You have to get there for something specific?"

"Yes, I do. I'm going to London to—" Talia's lovely eyes widened, her words slowed. "That is, I have to be there in order to—" She stopped.

"You're starting a semester at the School of Economics," Lorraine prompted.

"Yes, of course." Talia's face cleared. "For a minute there, I couldn't remember. I can't imagine why."

"Shock," said Stuart.

"Sensory overload," said Jeff, coming to life.

"General ditzyness?" Lorraine put in. At Talia's surprised look, Lorraine gave a little laugh. "Just kidding." She touched the bandage on her face. "I have a couple of questions myself. Maybe I should have gone to one of the advisors in those little offices."

Talia looked around. A man in a crumpled suit was coming from one of the advisors' rooms. "I wonder what sort of things that man asked about?" she said. "I wonder what he was told."

"I don't have a clue, but the old couple over there at the buffet table had a conference just before him." Stuart half rose in his chair. "Hey, folks. Yes, you," he beckoned impatiently as Blossom and Michael looked his way. "Come on over, will you? We have some things we want to ask you about."

6

"Do we know you good people, or did you just look over and figure we were so darn charmin' you had to have our company?" Michael set his tray on the table.

Unruffled, Stuart Casperson met Michael's inquiring gaze. "We're interested in what you found out at your interview—thought you could give us the lowdown on what's going on." Stuart made it sound as though Michael and Blossom should be flattered to have been invited to join them.

Blossom gave an annoyed sniff. "If you're so all-fired anxious to discover what's going on, you could consider going to find out for yourself." But then she looked at her husband and said, "Do you think we're supposed to tell them, Michael? Did Howard intend us to spread the news?"

Michael shrugged. "Your guess is as good as mine, darlin'. I'm Michael O'Meara and she's Blossom," he said to the assembled group.

"What news is she talking about?" Stuart's voice was sharp.

"There were very few survivors when plane crashed," Blossom said quietly. "Not more than four or five."

Confusion replaced Stuart's annoyance, and Lorraine jerked to astonished attention. Talia stared blankly, while Jeff, roused from his thoughts, looked around and asked, "What'd she say?"

Stuart ignored him. "There has got to be a couple hundred people here," he said. "Do you mean to tell me—?"

Blossom nodded. "We're those who didn't make it, every one of us. We're no longer on earth, young man; this is another world, a spiritual one." She exchanged a glance with her husband. "And y'know, I think perhaps we were told this before. I have this vague recollection of hearing it when I was first in the helicopter. I think maybe each of us was told, but we've forgotten, or we maybe just didn't want to hear."

"I don't believe it." Talia cut in, lifting her chin. "I'm on my way to London. I'm going to go to—" she looked at Lorraine, "to the London School of Economics for a semester of, of—" She shrank back into the chair, but then leaned forward, tension in the angled planes of her lovely face. "We're not in some spiritual world; we're somewhere in Michigan. I survived the plane crash and no matter what, I'm going to London."

"I'm afraid I can't begin to tell you how to go about doing that," Blossom said into the short silence. She looked around the table. "You have a question?" she asked Lorraine.

Lorraine's fingers touched the bandage covering the right side of her face, but when she spoke it was not of her injury. "You said a few were rescued. Did they tell you who?"

"Howard mentioned a child, a boy, being picked up, and one of the flight attendants—and a teenager." Blossom glanced at the next table where Beatrice Jorgenson was sitting by herself.

"You don't know it was her daughter," Michael said quickly. He speared a sausage. "Best be careful not to assume anything—not 'til we find out more."

Talia pushed aside her plate and tossed her napkin beside it. "I don't know what you people are talking about. What I do know is that I'm not going to sit and wait for someone to decide when I leave and where I'll go. If there's anything I've learned in this life, it's to be proactive." She got up. "Coming with me, Jeff?"

He blinked. "Sure."

"Let's go shake some trees and see what falls down." Talia gave those seated at the table her flashing smile. "Maybe we'll see you all at Heathrow."

"Good luck," Blossom said as she watched Talia stride off, Jeff trailing behind her. Then she turned to the two who remained. "Apparently neither of you finds the concept that we're no longer on earth as difficult to accept as your friends?"

Stuart moved uncomfortably. "I'm not sure what I think, but when you said we'd been told where we are before, it rang a bell." He rubbed the back of his neck. "Anyway, I'm open to suggestions, at least until they're proved otherwise." He held out a hand to Blossom. "By the way, it's about time we finished the introductions. I'm Stuart Casperson." He reached across the table to Michael. "The girl who just left is Talia, and that was Jeff with her. Apparently, they're old friends, but we've just met them," he nodded at Lorraine, "'we' being me and my administrative assistant Lorraine here."

"How do." Michael shook Stuart's extended hand and gave a courtly half-bow to Lorraine.

"I'm not all that sure I'm still Stuart's administrative assistant," Lorraine said crisply. "If what you just told us is true, it's a whole new ball game. Who knows what we are," she paused, "or will be?"

Stuart looked startled, but then he gave a shrug and turned to Blossom. "Look, say you're correct and we're in some . . . some other world, why don't I feel more, well, anguish about the whole thing? Why do I find it so easy to accept the idea of leaving my life and all of its, ah, loose ends? I mean, I know my wife must be a basket case and, and—" He stopped and cleared his throat.

"I'm sure she is." Blossom's seamed face sobered. "I've wondered about that, about my children and grandchildren. Perhaps I'm not worrying about them because I have this strong feeling that everything is going to be all right."

"Y'know, it's true," said Michael, looking around. "Everyone here seems pretty much calm and stress free. But maybe it's 'cause they're like Talia?"

"I haven't talked to a counselor," Lorraine said, "but the more I think about what you said, the more I have a feeling it's true. I'm sure of it." She carefully folded her napkin and pressed it. "It's not as though I'm religious. I never went to church much. But as I grew older, I began to wonder, to feel that there had to be something beyond this life, there must be—" Her hand moved slightly, but she tucked it beneath the tablecloth rather than reaching up to touch her bandage.

"We've always gone to church," Blossom said softly. "At least I have. When we were young, it was mostly because of the children, but now that we're older, well, Sunday wouldn't seem right without going to church."

"Speak for yourself, woman," Michael grumped.

"But does that make us religious?" Blossom continued, paying him no mind. She kneaded her bony hands together. "I have to admit, when I think of all the times I've sat and thought about what I'd cook for dinner instead of the sermon, well, I'm a bit worried."

"Oh, cease and desist, you silly old woman," Michael covered his wife's hand with his own. "If you start wailing about how wicked you've been I'm going to get up and leave."

"Leave then, leave. Don't let me stop you." Blossom snatched away her hand and waved it at him as though swatting a mosquito.

He caught it back and gave it a squeeze. "Oh, I'm harder to get rid of than that, old woman. Come on, we'd better go see what's in these new bags they gave us. Some of the folks here are wearing some pretty spiffy clothes, and I'm hopin' they got somethin' special for me. A Nehru jacket would make 'em sit up and take notice, don't you think?" He rose and helped Blossom to her feet.

"What's a Nehru Jacket?" Stuart asked as they left the table.

"They were way before your time," Lorraine said absently. She watched the old couple make their way across the room, her face thoughtful.

"It's all right." Tim's hands gripped Digger's shoulders tight. "It's okay."

Digger twisted away. "I heard her. I heard my mom. She was crying and calling me."

"Of course. She loves you. She misses you."

"Can I tell her I'm okay? Can I tell her what it's like here?"

Tim regarded the boy. "You can try," he said.

Digger squeezed his eyes shut and held his breath. Tim relaxed and smiled as a shimmering haze enveloped the boy, and his body faded from view. He stood patiently waiting until Digger stood clearly before him again, eyes open.

"You saw her."

69

"She was on the phone talking to Grandma. She started to cry after she hung up, and I told her I was okay, but I don't know if she heard me." Digger paused. "But I think maybe she did."

"Because she seemed to feel better?"

"Yeah."

Tim nodded. "Good enough. If I were you, I'd be sure to say thanks."

"For what?"

"For being allowed to help your mom." Tim ruffled Digger's hair. "Now how about we put your things in the jeep outside so I can take you home."

"You mean you don't live on the base?" Digger said, interested.

"I don't even work on the base. I'm only here because you are. Came to pick you up."

Digger digested this. "You mean, like, you've been assigned to me?"

"Sort of. You could say we've been assigned to each other."

Digger decided it was pretty neat, whichever way it worked. "You said you had my things. The helicopter picked them up too?"

Tim indicated a duffle bag in the corner next to two boxes, one small, the other large and flat, that leaned against the wall. "We have everything you need. And some things that are just for fun."

"Like what?" said Digger, immediately alert.

"Scuba equipment, the big one's a dirt bike, and then there's riding gear, of course."

"No kidding!"

"You always wanted to ride a horse, right?"

"Yeah," Digger breathed.

"Well, I'm the one in charge of your riding lessons. My

70

brother's the scuba expert, and you already know enough about dirt bikes to give the other boys in the family lessons." He picked up one end of the large box. "Give me a hand with this, will you, Digger? They should have lunch on the table about now, and I don't want to miss Sarah's pizza."

Digger darted to pick up his end of the carton, grunting as he tried to lift it off the floor. "Who's Sarah?"

"My wife."

Digger almost dropped the box. Tim was married? He hadn't known you could be married in heaven. Digger considered asking Tim about it but decided not to risk sounding rude. Besides, he had an idea Tim would tell him all about it sometime soon. He could wait. He'd already learned a lot. Sort of made your head spin—in a nice way. Digger held the carton tight against his thin chest and managed not to let it drop as he staggered outside and helped settle the large box into the jeep's back seat. Then he trotted back with Tim to collect the duffle bag and smaller box. Pizza for lunch sounded good.

Jeff watched Talia stalk off. He settled against the cushions with a sigh. Maybe she'd get some action on securing seats on a plane for Europe, maybe not. He was just happy she'd decided to leave him here while she charged off to shake up the troops. Talia was a great girl, but exhausting to be around.

Not that he wasn't as anxious as anyone to get the show on the road, but how much difference would it make if he arrived in Brussels a day or two late? Who was going to argue with a plane crash? The papers must have been, must still be full of it. His name would be listed. Had they mentioned his theater credits? Had his friends told the papers anything about the play he'd been working on? It would look good to be described as "actor and playwright" rather than just "actor."

"How did you manage to survive the crash, Mr. Edwards?" The redhead with the note pad gave Jeff an admiring glance over her horn-rimmed glasses.

"I'm a pretty good swimmer, but I think what helped most is that I conserved my energy—didn't panic. I found a piece of the plane and managed to get on it. In a situation like this, the important thing is to keep your head." Jeff checked his watch. "Look, it's been a long day; my friend and I have to get to our hotel." He looked at Talia over the heads of the crowd, talking to a smaller, but just as importuning group of reporters. She saw Jeff watching and made a supplicating gesture.

"Speaking of my friend, I have to go rescue her," Jeff said, attempting to brush through the crowd of reporters.

"Is Ms. Innes . . . is she your fiancée, Mr. Edwards?" the red-haired reporter said as he passed her.

Jeff paused, meeting the redhead's eyes. There was no question about the message he read in the woman's green gaze, no question at all.

"Like I said, she's a friend," Jeff told her. "Just an old friend."

The redhead scribbled something on her note pad, tore off the top sheet, and pressed it into his hand so quickly none of the others noticed the exchange. Jeff smiled at her and put the paper in his pocket without looking at it. He didn't have to.

"Jefferson Edwards, will you answer me!"

Jeff sat up. "You don't have to shout," he said, annoyed.

Talia stood before him, hands on her hips. "I've been trying to get your attention for ages and all you do, you dimwit, is sit here with your eyes half closed, lost in your little dream world."

"So what's the big deal?"

She picked up his tote bag. "I have a ride for us. We're going to London."

"I don't have to go to London," Jeff objected, "I'm supposed to be in Brussels."

"London's a heck of a lot closer to Brussels than wherever it is we are now. Come on, Jeff, I don't know how long they'll hold our seats."

Jeff took the bag from her and swung it over his shoulder. He noticed the pudgy man who preceded them onto the plane, but aside from his usual cataloging of idiosyncratic passersby for possible use on stage—in this case, the man's slumped shoulders and shambling walk—Jeff didn't think anything more about him. Certainly he didn't recognize their former pilot. But then Brad Nelson looked quite different from the braided, uniformed captain who had flown the plane on its brief flight from O'Hare.

Brad fingered the zippers on his khaki jump suit. They'd all been so nice to him. Somehow that made it worse. He could have worn his uniform; he'd been assured his pants would be cleaned and pressed and a jacket found for him before breakfast was over. But they had understood when he said he'd just as soon wear the work clothes in his tote bag. He'd been surprised but not displeased to find the neatly folded jump suit. The anonymous clothes felt comfortable and somehow right. In London, he'd have to change into a uniform, of course. Couldn't meet with the review board looking like a maintenance worker.

"You were one of the pilots, weren't you?"

Brad's head jerked up. He met the inquiring gaze of the white-haired man standing in the aisle. "Yes."

The white-haired man put his briefcase in the overhead bin and took the seat next to Brad, carefully hitching his creased trouser legs as he crossed his legs. "Haven't ever seen this much leg room in a plane, other than in first class." He extended a hand. "Sherwood Prescott," he said.

He'd said it as though Brad should have recognized the name. "You in politics?"

"No," Prescott gave a wintry smile. "I deal with international arbitration."

It was the careful sort of answer that did not invite further questioning. Brad took a magazine from the pocket in the seatback in front of him and flipped through it. Mostly pictures with captions, probably vacation spots. Excellent photography.

"Curious the reactions people have to all this," Prescott said, almost to himself. "Far different than I'd have thought."

Brad pushed the magazine back into the pocket and glanced around him. "Shock," he said. "I was thinking myself that everyone was acting pretty laid back, but then I realized it must be shock. Not surprised. We've been in a plane crash, for God's sake."

Prescott sat silent a moment. "Apparently you haven't talked to an advisor?"

"Been talking to someone or other ever since I got here. Pilots, ground personnel, even a couple of the head honchos." Brad hunched in his seat. "Everybody tried to make me feel better, couldn't have been nicer, but they can't change what happened. I had to ditch my plane and some of the passengers—apparently only a few, thank God—didn't make it."

Prescott began to speak, cleared his throat, stopped.

Brad Nelson looked expectantly at the white-haired man, but Prescott was concentrating on his shirtsleeves, pulling at them so they showed an exact half-inch from his suit cuffs.

"What is it?" the pilot said. "What are you trying to tell me?"

Sherwood Prescott closed his eyes briefly. "I don't know if I'm supposed to tell you, but somehow I feel I must. Lord knows I can't begin to do it with the gentleness and tact with which it was explained to me." He adjusted his cuffs again. "The advisor I met with back there told me that we, that is, all of those gathered up by the helicopters, have left the world in which we lived. We are in another, a spiritual world."

Brad moved an instinctive few inches away. He checked the aisle for an attendant, but they all were busy boarding passengers. "Now let me get this; you're telling me we're not on a 747 scheduled for London? We're in some sort of twilight zone?"

Prescott gave a short bark of laughter. "I'm really making a hash of this. No, this isn't something out of science fiction; it's real. We're real." He looked across the aisle at Blossom and Michael. "See those two over there? They were in Howard's office just before I saw him." He caught Blossom's eye and raised his voice, "Maybe you can you help us. I'm having some trouble explaining to Captain Nelson just what's happened to us."

"You're not the only one who has been having that particular trouble, dearie," Blossom leaned forward. "When I told the people at our breakfast table that we hadn't survived the crash, half of them got up and left." Blossom's pale blue eyes lit with mischief as she took in Brad Nelson's consternation. "I'd say this young man would like to do the same thing, that is, if the plane wasn't just about ready to take off."

"Captain Nelson was the pilot of our original plane," Prescott said repressively.

"Oh." The breathed syllable was filled with apology and regret. "I didn't recognize you in that get up. And I'll bet you're feeling terrible about this whole thing, aren't you? Forgive a stupid old woman, Captain."

"I'll thank you to remember this the next time you tell me to mind my tongue, Blossom O'Meara." The old man beside her gave Blossom a poke. Then he peered at Brad. "But she's right, young man. You're dead as a door nail. We all are."

The look Blossom gave Michael should have made him cringe; instead the old man's eyebrows went up in injured innocence. "Well, what do you want me to say? That we're flying back to home and hearth? We're not. He's not. I don't know exactly where we're headed, but so far everything's been pretty good, better than good, matter of fact. I can't wait to see what comes next."

Brad Nelson seemed to have trouble breathing. "You're crazy," he said, "all three of you." The words were defiant, but Brad's expression didn't match them.

"I'm sorry I haven't been more of a help," Prescott said stiffly. "You've been under a lot of stress, and—"

"That's it," Brad said quickly. "It's the stress. I suppose it isn't surprising we all have some, ah, mental disturbances." He unbuckled his seatbelt. "I see my copilot up there a couple of rows, and I ought to go talk to her. You'll excuse me?" He stood and edged past Sherwood Prescott's knees, nodded briskly to Blossom and Michael, and hurried up the aisle.

"Cynthia, we need to talk," he said as he slumped into the empty seat beside her.

"Brad, are you okay?"

"Sure. Fine. Wonderful."

Cynthia put a hand on the sleeve of Brad's jump suit. "You're shaking!"

"Those people back there. They just told me, they said we were, that we'd—I can't say it. I don't believe it."

She examined his ashen face and said quietly, "What do you think happened?"

"We were in a plane crash. We ditched and were picked up by rescue copters. That's what happened." His tone dared her to contradict him, but he did not meet Cynthia's eyes.

"Doesn't it strike you as strange that there are no injuries?"

"Lucky maybe, but strange—not really. We set that baby down pretty gently considering the circumstances."

"We hit the water like a bomb." Cynthia winced, remembering. "When I asked, I was told boats in the area picked up a few survivors. But not us, Brad, not us. We came here. Just about everyone who was aboard that plane is here with us."

"No!" It was an explosion. "Look, I know what happens when we die. We decay, we rot, we turn into compost. That's what's in store for everyone on this green earth. I've never tried to fool myself about that, and I'm not about to start now." His voice cracked, but he hid it behind a manufactured cough. "Besides, I don't feel any different."

"Don't you? What about that lousy cold you had?"

Brad's eyes widened. "It's go—; it's better." He swallowed. "So what?"

"Why is it so hard to believe we've passed into a spiritual world?" Cynthia gave his arm a quick pat. "It all seems so . . . sensible to me. I've always known there must be something like this, afterward. I felt it when Dad died."

Brad put his elbows on his knees and rested his forehead on his hands. He looked up as the plane doors closed, listened as the jet engines roared to life. "I don't believe it," he said, his jaw jutting stubbornly. "I believe what I see and what I feel. I'm alive. We all are."

"Man, oh man." Cynthia settled back in her seat and sighed. "You know that scene in the old Betty Davis movie where she says, 'Fasten your seatbelts folks; it's going to be a bumpy ride'?"

Brad wouldn't look at her or acknowledge Cynthia's bantering, but her teasing smile was affectionate as she added, "It's always been one of my favorite lines. And y'know, I have a feeling it applies here—in spades."

7

"What do you think? Will they decide it's London when they land, or will it be someplace else?" Kate asked the man sitting in the contour chair behind the desk that faced hers.

Howard closed his book a shade regretfully. "I don't know. I was surprised that they needed the accommodation of appearing to travel by plane, but then some of this group are having quite a bit of trouble accepting the transition. More so than usual."

Kate smiled. "Not like you."

"Not like me. I woke up and saw you, and that was it."

"You had no doubt about it, did you?"

"No doubts, no concerns." He grinned. "Only the sure, sudden knowledge that you'd been waiting for me, that what I'd hardly dared hope for had happened and we were together again."

"But you had questions. Plenty of them. Not that I didn't expect it. You wouldn't have been Howard if you hadn't."

"And so does this group, of course." Howard made a notation on the open pad on his desk and closed it. "But they don't seem to want to ask the right ones." He picked up the top three pages from the pile of papers on his desk. "Take this one. The Reverend Frederick Hampton."

"Yes, I know. Fred's questions were all about Sammy, the child he was with in the water."

Howard nodded. "He showed up very well there. But the rest of it—" He gestured to the pages before him. "He has got some really troublesome baggage he's going to have to unpack before long—and as far as that sermon he was working on, I've never seen such a collection of half-baked stuff. It's enough to make me wonder whether the man is simply an imbecile or if he's—" He stopped, silenced by his wife's startled look. Rueful chagrin replaced his annoyance and he said, "Sorry, I thought that part was gone, or at least in abeyance."

"You do very well—most of the time," Kate said quickly.

"I forget how quick I was to judge, how blind, how blind I'd still be if—"

Without saying a word, Kate got up, came round her desk to stand behind his chair, her hands on his shoulders. She leaned over and kissed the top of his head. "We're so alike," she murmured. "It took a whole raft of experiences here to make me realize that all my life I'd masked my intolerance of other people's mistakes as justified impatience. Sometimes I thought I'd never manage to get a handle on it."

Howard swiveled around and reached to smooth back a strand of chestnut brown hair from Kate's temple. "I can't begin to think what life would have been like if you hadn't walked into that faculty meeting."

Kate's fingertips brushed his lips. "We would have met. Somehow, somewhere."

Howard caught her fingers before they left his face. "Yes,"

he said. "Yes, we would." Then he swiveled about to face his desk again. "All right, back to work. Since the bunch we've been given doesn't seem to want us with them, and of course, we can't join them until they do, how do you think we should handle them, at least in the initial stages?"

"I've been thinking about that." Kate riffled through the papers on her desk. "What they'll see at the airport should help some of them make the connection—again. Why don't we have a meeting there, and see where they're at?" She began to separate the papers. "I've made some notes here."

❧

"This is Heathrow?" Talia said, waiting for the crowded aisle to become navigable. "It looks different than I expected."

"How?" Jeff ducked his head to peer out the window.

"I don't know. Doesn't it look sort of misty to you? As though you're seeing it through gauze?"

Brad Nelson, who stood just ahead of them looked back and said shortly, "That's because it's raining. Looks exactly like it did when I was here last month."

Talia cocked her head, taking in Brad's coveralls. "You look familiar. Were you part of our original flight crew?"

"The captain." Brad turned away.

But Talia didn't miss a beat. "Traveling incognito?"

Brad Nelson turned back. "Don't you think I should—considering?"

Talia gave a cheerful laugh and held out her hand. "I'm Talia Innes, one of your luckier passengers."

Brad looked at her from beneath beetled brows. "One who made it out alive," he said, his tone daring her to dispute it.

"Of course."

His face relaxed. He nudged the woman ahead of him.

81

"See?"

Cynthia Polanski gave a tiny shake of her head and shouldered her tote bag. "Let's go," she said.

It was chaos, but an orderly chaos. Crowds surged through hallways and into the great rooms of the terminal, passing, momentarily mingling with or making their way through the group that had been on the plane that had just arrived from the air base. There were all nationalities. A cluster of African families followed white-robed leaders who herded them along like guides leading a tour; attentive Asian businessmen crowded about a bearded older man who appeared to be giving them directions; women in festive Native American dress carrying blanket-wrapped bundles filed past, heading for the opposite side of the room where each was ushered through a turquoise door to an inner room whose smoked glass walls reflected the outer lobby's swirling crowds but gave no indication of what lay beyond. A company of Pakistanis in military garb stared at, then shouldered their way past a crowd of turbaned Sikhs without incident. A group in black leather, rings dangling from ears and every visible orifice, the men dreadlocked, both men and women tattooed, milled in front of a ticket counter where a smiling, smartly uniformed agent handed out tickets. Next to the gaping arrivals, several couples of balding men and white-haired women clamored like unruly teenagers for the attention of a young woman at the center of their group.

Even Jeff had forsaken his daydreams and was taking in all the teeming activity about them. "Wow, is it always like this?" he asked.

"It's always busy," said Brad Nelson, "but this is pretty

incredible, even for Heathrow." The pilot leaned toward Cynthia Polanski and muttered, "Where the heck's the media? Haven't seen a reporter since we got off the plane." Then without waiting for an answer, he shrugged and said, "Probably there has been something they didn't count on, like a whole bunch of conventions and celebrations falling on the same week. Must have been a reservations nightmare."

Sherwood Prescott exchanged a look with Cynthia, who shrugged in reply but did not comment.

"You motherfuckers keep your hands off me!" The man crouched into a fighting stance and raised his fists.

There was a quick intake of breath among those watching the scene.

The three uniformed guards seemed unmoved by the snarling man's anger. They moved no closer nor attempted to touch him, but neither did they retreat. The crouching man feinted first left, then right in an obvious attempt to break away into the crowd that surrounded them, but the guards, moving in unison, effectively cut off any avenue of escape.

"That's the man who was with Malvena and the baby," Blossom said in a loud whisper.

The man made a lightning fast move toward the center guard, dodged back, then gave a snap kick that should have landed on the guard's chest. It didn't. What happened next was so quickly over none of those watching was certain what had taken place; but suddenly the man was on his back on the floor, staring up at the guards. The man scrambled to his feet, shaking his head like a dazed boxer.

He examined his captors from between slitted lids and rubbed his stubbled chin. "Hey, what you guys doin'?" he said, his tone conciliatory. He folded his arms over his chest and rocked back on his heels. "I wasn't doing nothin'," he said, lifting his chin. "Got a little agitated here 'cause you guys get in my face. Hey, you got questions? I'll answer any you got."

"We haven't any questions for you," said the guard in the center. "We stopped you because you were hurting the lady. That's not allowed here."

Attention shifted to the young woman who hesitantly stepped forward.

The man flicked a finger at her. "Come on over," he said, his voice easy. "You tell them Jackson Delion wasn't doing nothing. Tell 'em I was just askin' where's the baby is all." He turned to the guards. "I'm takin' care of this lady here, and when I don't see the kid with her, I get concerned, 'cause I'm responsible for them, y'know?"

"You shook her," one of the guards said quietly.

"Well yeah, 'cause I was gettin' kind of annoyed. Here she is with no kid and no explanations."

"I think she'll do quite well without your help," the guard said. "I suggest you move along. Now."

At first it seemed that Jackson Delion would protest, but then he shrugged and raising a finger to his eyebrow, flipped the guards a defiant salute. "Okay, okay." He turned to the young woman. "See you later, girl." The words could have been a pleasantry or a threat. He sauntered off.

Blossom went to the girl and put an arm about her. "Come, Malvena dear," she said. "We arrived on the same plane as this young lady and the . . . the person you were talking to," she said to the guards. "She's welcome to come with us."

"Certainly," said the one who seemed to be in charge. "Matter of fact, there's a meeting set up for you folks in Conference Room H-3."

Those in the little group looked at each other with a trace of unease.

"Will everyone on the plane be there?" asked Sherwood Prescott.

The guard took a notepad from his shirt pocket and riffled through the pages. "Just you folks and one or two more. Looks like there're about ten of you." He tucked the pad back in his pocket and indicated a large arch. "See that arch? Follow the hallway beneath it to the end and turn left. There will be signs." He tipped his cap. "Enjoy your stay."

"Why just us?" said Stuart Casperson. "How about everyone else?"

Blossom looked around. "Where are all the other passengers on our plane anyway?"

"Perhaps they have meetings of their own." Sherwood Prescott picked up his bag. "Since it seems logical to do what the gentleman suggested, I'm off to find this conference room."

Lorraine VanDyck moved to follow him. "Let's hope it's quieter than it is here."

An easel with a large, white sign announcing Conference Room H-3 stood outside a smallish room with a long, polished table in the center and comfortable-looking, blue padded armchairs about it.

Led by Sherwood Prescott, the little band straggled into the empty room. Blossom, her arm protectively about Malvena, paid no attention to the grumbling Michael close behind her; Jeff ambled in beside a distracted Talia Innes; and finally Brad Nelson and Cynthia entered, followed by the clergyman, Fred Hampton, who stood aside to let the others enter before him.

"There're chairs for more," said Prescott, taking a seat at the table, "I wonder who—"

"Oh, oh," Blossom interrupted him, "Look there." She nodded at the man and woman standing at the head of the table. The man was in a muted plaid sports coat and dark blue slacks, while the woman wore a red business suit and crisp white blouse.

"How'd they get in here?" Stuart Casperson's startled question rasped into the sudden silence. "And who invited them?" he added under his breath.

If the woman heard the addendum, she gave no indication. She merely looked around the table and smiled. "For those of you who need to be reminded, I'm Kate. We met at the base when you first arrived."

"And I'm Howard," said the man beside her. "I met a few of you too. Kate and I are your coordinators." He paused, and both he and Kate looked at the closed door. "Come in," Howard said, raising his voice slightly.

The door opened, and Beatrice Jorgenson swept in, coming to an abrupt stop as she saw the rest. "Can someone tell me what's going on?" she said, glaring at the assembly indiscriminately. "Can anyone here tell me where I can find someone who has the slightest interest in giving a paying customer some assistance?"

"Won't you have a seat, Beatrice?" Kate said politely.

"It's Ms. Jorgenson, and no, I will not have a seat. I will not attend some phony information session where I'll be given more excuses and told more lies. I haven't any intention of moving from this spot until I find out what happened to my daughter."

Kate came around the table and put a hand on Beatrice Jorgenson's shoulder. "My dear," her words were soft, infinitely tender, "you mustn't be afraid."

It was as though she had thrown cold water on the raging woman. Beatrice Jorgenson's face crumpled, her eyes filled with tears. She bowed her head and hid her face in her hands as her body shuddered with racking sobs.

Kate put her arms about the weeping woman and held her while the rest at the table sat, embarrassed but spellbound.

Finally Beatrice Jorgenson's sobs quieted, and she raised her tear-stained face. "What's happening? I can't get in touch with anyone at the office, I've lost all my important papers, and on top of everything I still can't find Christy." Her face crumpled again. "Where is my daughter?"

"She'll be all right, Beatrice. She has been given the opportunity to continue to learn in the natural world, to find her way and make her choices." Kate guided Beatrice to the far end of the table and pulled out a chair.

"Now, if I can have your attention," Howard said, "we'll get started with your orientation."

"More orientation meetings?" Michael O'Meara muttered. "How many do we need? Blossom and I already met with you at the airbase."

"Hush, Michael," Blossom scolded.

But Howard was unfazed. "Were all your questions answered?" he asked Michael, "or are there some you hadn't thought to ask?"

Michael O'Meara frowned. "I can't remember exactly all the stuff you covered. I mean, of course, I remember the big one, the fact we're no longer on earth, but the rest of it ...." His voice trailed off. "As for other questions, I guess I'd like to know where we're goin' from here." Michael scratched an ear. "I'll admit I've been wondering about that."

"And I want to know about Tabitha," Cynthia put in anxiously. "Can I, will I see her again, the way I did at the base?"

"Yes," Howard said quietly, "I'm sure it will be permitted."

Blossom was the only one who noticed that without anyone getting up, six of them—she and Michael, Cynthia, Sherwood Prescott, Stuart, and Lorraine—were now sitting close together on either side of Howard, who had taken the chair at the end of the table and that Kate was sitting with the others at the further end of the long table. Blossom also realized that, although Kate appeared to be animatedly speaking, she could not hear not a word Kate was saying.

"Why are we here with you and the rest down there with Kate?" she asked Howard. "Is it because they still think they're on earth and we know we're not?"

"Very good, Blossom. You do pay attention, don't you? Yes, we often put people together who are in differing stages of acceptance. Right now Kate is telling your fellow passengers, far more gently than I could, what has happened. They'll probably retain the information she's giving them—at least for a while—unless their former beliefs make it just too difficult a concept for them to handle."

"If it is too difficult, then what?" said Prescott.

"In that case, they'll forget it as soon as they look away from Kate," Howard said. He looked around as though welcoming comment, but no one seemed willing to investigate this further.

"Our being met at the base and then coming here to be with you and Kate, is this what happens to everyone?" Lorraine asked.

"No, your arrival was somewhat unusual. But there are almost as many different ways of arriving here as there are newcomers. Most awaken in a place very like wherever they were when their natural body ceased to function."

"Y'mean, if I was on an operating table, I'd wake up there?" asked Michael, fascinated.

"You'd probably be in what seemed like a hospital room."

"Then everyone out there," Stuart's gesture indicated the airport beyond the room, " was traveling when they, when they—" he stopped, his face working. "Why can't I say it?"

"Perhaps because here the word 'death,' the very concept of it, has a totally different meaning. To us, a person who has

died is one who has chosen evil as a way of life while on earth."
Howard's expression lost its momentary severity. "As to your
other question, yes, some of the people here were traveling
when they made the transition, but for others this is simply a
secondary stop, as it was for you."

"Who are you?" Asked by anyone else the question would
have been a challenge; Sherwood Prescott made it a polite
inquiry.

"Someone who came here a while ago." Then, seeing
Prescott's dissatisfaction, Howard nodded and said, "Yes,
you're right. I'm an angel. Kate and I are both angels."

"No wings?" It was Michael.

"Sorry." Howard smiled briefly.

"Why are we sitting here talking about wings?" Cynthia
twisted her clasped hands. "I want to know how Rob and
Tabitha are. Please," she said to Howard, "please, can you help
me be with them?"

Howard studied her. "I'm not the one you need to ask," he
said. Then he looked about the table. "Any further questions?"

"If we knew the questions to ask, we might be closer to
figuring out the answers by ourselves," Sherwood Prescott
said.

"There is that," Howard acknowledged. "It's beginning to
look as though this group may be one that has to experience
things rather than have them explained."

Prescott did not look satisfied with this but did not press
further. Perhaps it was because Cynthia had been sitting
beside her that Blossom was the only one who noticed that
Cynthia was no longer at the table. "Where's—" then she
stopped, wondering if she perhaps she should have pretended
she hadn't noticed.

"We're not big on pretense here," said Howard. "We can
talk about Cynthia, if you'd like." A glimmer of amusement lit

his eyes as he surveyed Blossom. "Oh, come on, it doesn't take an angel to tell what you're thinking when you look at Cynthia's chair and then look at me with your eyes as wide as saucers."

"Is she . . . did she go back to earth?" Blossom asked, oblivious of the others' stares.

"No. She's not visible to us because her thoughts and her love are with her husband and child, but it's their spirits she's with, not their physical bodies. She'll come back when she's ready."

And as if called by their conversation, Cynthia appeared in the chair beside Blossom. She looked about her absently, her eyes dreamy and unfocused. Then her glance drifted to Howard and a beatific smile lit her face. "Thank you," she said.

"No, Cynthia. Not me."

"Oh," she said, comprehending. "Oh. Right." She closed her eyes briefly, then opened them.

"What happened?" said Stuart. "What was it like?"

Cynthia clasped her hands together tightly and took a breath. "I don't know if I can explain—"

"She doesn't have to tell us," said Blossom. "It's none of our business."

Cynthia flashed Blossom a look of gratitude.

"I think Kate's bunch is ready to join us anyway," said Howard. And suddenly the other group was sitting with them as before, Kate beside Howard at the head of the table.

Howard turned to her. "It seems our arrivals may be happier discovering this world by themselves rather than listening to explanations," he said.

"My group too," Kate said matter of factly.

But no one at the table was listening to this exchange. Several gasped, Lorraine let out a little cry, Stuart threw up his hands to protect his eyes.

"Did you see that light that flashed between those two?" Michael whispered to Blossom.

"You know what I've just realized?" she whispered back, "That's the first time they've turned completely to face each other. D'you suppose it happens whenever they do that?"

Sherwood Prescott cleared his throat. "Does that, ah, brilliance happen whenever you look at each other?"

Howard smiled. "The light? Yes. We know others see it, but we're not aware of it. I see only the face of my beloved wife, and she sees—"

"Her husband," Kate finished.

"You're married?" Lorraine's eyes widened.

"Uh huh," said Kate, waiting for the rest of her question.

"But I thought angels—"

"You thought wrong."

"When you say 'married,' do you mean really married?" Stuart Casperson said, his disbelief obvious.

"Yes, I do." Howard gave a faint smile as he took in the dumbfounded expressions before him. The light about the couple had lessened now that they were not facing one another. "It's interesting that you find it so hard to believe." He looked at Blossom and Michael. "Do you two feel any less married here than you did in your natural life?"

"How does the man know I felt married?" Michael twirled an imaginary mustache, but with something less than his usual panache. "Not that I didn't," he added hastily, catching Blossom's look. "Most of the time. So you're saying Blossom and I will be married here?"

Howard and Kate exchanged glances, and even this brief connection caused a glow to appear around them. "That's something that remains to be seen," said Howard.

Blossom shivered as though she felt a chill. "We've been married more than fifty years," she snapped, her faded eyes flashing. "I'm not about to go anywhere without Michael, and he's certainly not going without me."

"You'll be together for now," said Kate. "But we don't know what will happen as you and Michael find your way in your new life." She stopped Blossom's impatient gesture, holding up her own hand. "Be patient. Learn to listen with your heart." She looked around the table. "And that's advice for all of you. You've been placed together for a reason, though that reason may not be clear yet. Be alert to the opportunities that will present themselves, opportunities to learn and to help each other."

"Sounds as though you're about to cut us loose," Stuart Casperson said uneasily. "Don't we get any say about that?"

"You may not be ready for formal teaching yet, but you're well able to learn all the same." Kate looked about at each in turn. "Find out all you can about this world and about yourselves." Then she added with sober emphasis, "And please know that Howard and I are available to help you if there's trouble or if you simply wish us with you."

And with that, she and Howard were gone.

Those left at the table looked at each other.

"If there's trouble—what does she mean, trouble?" Lorraine said, her voice trailing off uncertainly.

"And what are we supposed to do, pick up a phone and ask for information?" asked Michael.

Blossom fingered something in her pocket. She drew out a card and looked at it.

The Reverend Frederick Hampton cleared his throat. "We really are in another world, aren't we?"

"Yes," said Blossom, "we are."

"Well then, I suppose I should ask," Fred Hampton said, his tone diffident, "does anyone know where heaven is?"

8

Everyone looked at Fred. Fred Hampton looked back at them, a sheepish smile playing about his lips. "From what Kate said, I gather this isn't heaven."

"Hey, aren't you a minister, a padre, a man of the cloth?" asked Michael.

"I was. I . . . I'm not sure if I am now. I'm not sure of anything."

Michael shook his head. "You'd think someone like you would take to all this like a hog to mud." Cynthia noticed that, though O'Meara had recovered his aplomb, he'd studiously avoided looking Blossom's way since Kate's pronouncement. Even now his glance skipped over his wife to take in Beatrice Jorgenson. "What's the matter with her?" he growled.

Beatrice didn't hear him. She sat, lids half closed, the fingers of one hand lightly touching the wrist of the other. Her eyes snapped open. "I have a pulse!" she announced. "A steady, rhythmic pulse! That couple obviously has psychiatric problems."

"Kate and Howard?"

"All that talk about waking up in another world. How could I have arteries with blood pulsing through them if I'm dead?" She looked at them triumphantly.

"But you were crying in Kate's arms just now," said Cynthia. "You accepted what she told you about your daughter."

"I was hysterical. The crash, the trauma afterward—it's not surprising I'm not thinking clearly. Christy has been taken to some hospital, I know it; and of course, I intend to find out where she is." Beatrice rose and brushed a speck of lint from her charcoal gray pinstripe suit with an authoritative hand. "But meanwhile I'm due in Brussels for a very important meeting, and I'm going to demand that the officials in charge here get me to it. If they know what's good for them, they'll have me on the next flight out. I intend to make a formal complaint of course, but that can wait until later."

"My oh my," Blossom murmured.

"And since nobody else seems to want to take the obvious steps, I'd like all of you to give me your names and addresses." Beatrice opened her briefcase and took out a paper and pen. "I'll need to contact you about the lawsuit." She scribbled on the paper and then reached up and touched her cheek in surprise. "Where are my glasses?"

"My glasses are gone too." Fred Hampton touched his face. "I don't think we need them any more."

"But, but, I can't read without my glasses."

"Can't you? Seems like you were doing okay just now." It was Michael O'Meara, a sardonic gleam in his eyes. "Try it again."

But Beatrice gave her head a fierce little shake. "No, no. I'll have to get a pair of reading glasses. They'll surely have some in one of the airport shops." She handed the paper to Brad

Nelson. "Just print out your information."

"Never needed glasses, hope I never will." The captain took the paper and pen and began writing. And then stopped. "Captain Bradley Nelson," Brad stared at the paper. "Address—" he looked up. "Funny, I can't quite remember."

Cynthia Polanski got up and came around the table. "Come on, Brad, relax," she said, kneading his tense shoulders. "Don't worry about it. Just go with the flow and see what happens." She looked at Beatrice who stood tapping an expensively shod foot. "I don't know whether you'll get your flight, Ms. Jorgenson, but if it will make you feel better, why don't you give us a phone number where we can reach you?" She turned to Sherwood Prescott and said, "What about you, Mr. Prescott? Are you going to try to go on to Brussels too?"

Sherwood Prescott ran his fingers along his silver head, lightly touching the place on his forehead where, in another life, a plate had smacked it. "I don't think there's a need for that," he said slowly. "From what Howard and Kate said, I think we're meant to stay together."

Blossom nodded. "We're supposed to help each other."

"You may find reasons to stay here, but I'm supposed to be at a business conference," Beatrice said, drawing a calling card from her briefcase. "If you want to join me in contacting an attorney, my offer stands." She handed the card to Cynthia. "I doubt if I'll need to contact you," she said to her, "but if you wish to reach me, here's my email and phone numbers."

Michael O'Meara popped up from his seat to come peer over Cynthia's shoulder. "What, no water stains? Just found these all nice and clean in that fancy leather case of yours?"

Beatrice Jorgenson looked from her briefcase to Michael. For a moment she seemed confused; then she tossed her head and snapped the case shut. "This is a very good briefcase; obviously it's watertight." And with that she strode out of the room, slamming the door after her.

"Well, well, well." Sherwood Prescott's expression was almost admiring. "There seems no end to the equivocations a stubborn mindset can find."

Lorraine VanDyck spoke for the first time since they'd been left alone. "I guess we all react in our own way. A part of me wants to go outside and explore, to see if it's raining still, if it's like the London I once knew; but there's a part that wants to stay right here in this room and have Kate and Howard tell me everything I need to know."

"You know London? I didn't know you went anywhere," said Stuart, surprised.

"Yes, Stuart, I used to travel—a lot. I went all sorts of places, and if people stared at me then, it was because I was young and reasonably pretty. It's true I'm not that person anymore, but I'm still a human being, you know. I think, I feel, I do all sorts of things other than write your reports and send out your letters."

Stuart flushed. "You're saying I regard you as an object?"

"I've worked for you for over five years. Do I have a family? Brothers? Sisters? Do I live in an apartment, a condo, a house? What did I do on my last vacation? On any vacation?"

"I know you're not married," Stuart said, "and that you never have been." He hesitated, the flush deepening against his fair skin. "You have a sister." But his tone made it a question.

"You're thinking of Janine. She's a friend. I have no relatives aside from two cousins in California." For once forgetful of her bandaged face, Lorraine lifted her chin and crossed her arms in front of her. "Any more guesses?"

"Perhaps you two could finish this some other time? I think there are other, fairly important matters before us." Prescott adjusted his cuffs and looked round the table.

"Perhaps we should reach a consensus as to what we should do." He waited as the people before him shifted uncomfortably.

"I suspect things 'outside' pretty much resemble the world we left," he went on when no one spoke. "There's a hotel I usually stay at when I'm in London that's comfortable, if a bit old-fashioned." He gestured to the phone by the door. "If the rest of you agree, I'll try to phone them and ask if they can take the lot of us."

A murmur of assent traveled around the table; several changed positions as though eager to rise. Even Jeff looked animated. Prescott went to the phone, punched in a number, and made his request.

"You do? You can? Ah, yes, I'd appreciate that. Thank you." He hung up. "Shall we go see if this is the London some of us have known before, or perhaps I should say, shall we see just how it differs?"

9

"I ASKED THE BARMAN," JEFF SAID TO TALIA, "AND Y'KNOW the little park this hotel looks out on?" His eyes half closed, Jeff took in the room's dark wooden panels, the sofas and chairs about the fireplace. "I saw an old World War II movie once, and there was this song about a nightingale singing in a square. The barman says it's a different square—anyway, this place could be right out of that movie." He took his glass of ale from the low table and took a long, appreciative drink.

Talia leaned back and smoothed the leather of her overstuffed armchair. "Isn't it fabulous? The whole thing I mean, London, the double-decker buses, the misty rain. I've always wanted to come here."

"But is it really London? Remember what Kate told us?" At Talia's look of distress, Jeff leaned forward and rubbed her wrist. "Come on, Tal, I know you're going to try to say everything's the same as before the crash, but you know it isn't."

"Of course, it isn't," Talia snapped. "I'm not supposed to be in some hotel, I was supposed to—" She stopped, her attention caught by Sherwood Prescott who had entered the lounge and was heading in their direction.

"You're the last ones I have to notify," he said, taking a seat on the loveseat beside Talia's and Jeff's chairs. "I thought the group should meet here for a conference as soon as everyone can gather. Discuss the situation, decide where we want to go from here. Pleasant as it is, this is clearly an interim arrangement." He nodded at Talia. "Your room's all right?"

"It's okay, I guess. But who decided Malvena should room with me? It's not that I mind; it's just I think I should have had a say about it."

"Whom would you have chosen?" Prescott asked her.

Talia thought. "Cynthia, I guess. I wouldn't have minded getting to know someone like her, a pilot for a major airline at her age. Not that I have anything against Malvena, but she's afraid of her own shadow," she said with a toss of her blond head. "I bet right now she's up there cowering in our room."

"Give the kid a break, Tal," Jeff said easily. "Didn't I hear that someone took her baby, just went off somewhere with it?"

"It's more than that. She's scared of something—jumps every time she hears a sound."

"Wouldn't you, if you had that kick-boxing character on your tail? I'd be jumpy if I thought he was going to turn up anytime soon." Jeff raised an eyebrow at Prescott. "Think there's any likelihood he will?"

But Sherwood Prescott wasn't listening. "If you'll excuse me," he murmured as he got to his feet and headed for the hallway and the front desk where a man and woman stood speaking to the clerk.

Jeff watched him. "That guy would try to organize a one-car funeral," he said, reaching for his ale. "Who are those people anyway?" He frowned, peering at the couple. He gave an involuntary jerk and a splash of golden liquid splattered the Oriental rug at his feet.

"You recognize them?" asked Talia.

"They were on the plane. Had a couple of kids with them. Matter of fact, right after the crash I think I saw one of the kids, a boy, in the water."

Sherwood Prescott strode back to the lounge, the couple in tow. The man had his arm protectively about the slight, pretty woman's shoulders. "Nick and Amanda Sianas were on the flight with us," Prescott said. "Kate and Howard told them they could take a look at our group and see if they'd like to join us."

Nick Sianas, a stocky man with a large mustache, didn't look as though he particularly cared to have been summarily waylaid in the midst of their check-in. He grunted a monosyllabic greeting to Talia and Jeff and steered his wife to the leather loveseat Prescott had vacated.

"I asked Nick and Amanda if they'd mind joining us for our conference and going to their rooms later," Prescott rubbed his hands together. "Ah, here come the O'Mearas." He waved Blossom and Michael over and introduced them to the Sianases.

"I remember you at the air base," Blossom said to Amanda. "Wasn't your little girl with you?"

Amanda brightened. "Yes, Becky was there. That's where we met Mother and Dad. Becky's with Mother right now, thank goodness. If only Sammy—" she stopped. "But no, I shouldn't want that, should I?" she said, looking at her husband uncertainly.

Nick took her hand and laced his fingers with hers. "He'll be fine, remember?" he said gently. "Look, I think we'll give your meeting a pass," he said to Prescott. "It looks like it's going to be some time before the rest of your people get here, and my wife could do with some rest. Besides, we're not exactly sure yet whether we'd like to hook up with your group. We'll go wash up, put away our stuff. Maybe we'll see you later." He got up, giving his wife's hand a small tug. "Come on, Mandy."

Amanda rose with a grateful smile. She nodded to the rest and followed her husband to the rose-carpeted stairs.

Blossom's face was thoughtful as she watched them leave. "The children are all gone, have you noticed? All the children on the plane—the baby, the boy, Digger, and now this couple's daughter."

"What do you mean, they're 'gone'?" said Talia.

"It's nothing bad, I'm sure of that," Blossom assured her. "I just meant they're being cared for elsewhere. You notice Mrs. Sianas isn't at all distressed about it. She seems perfectly happy to have the girl with her grandmother."

"I don't know why they couldn't have stayed," Prescott growled, taking his seat, "but I suppose we can tell them whatever we decide."

"Just what is it we're deciding?" Michael arched his wispy eyebrows.

"I have an agenda," Prescott said. He brought a folded paper from his pocket. Then he looked at the paper and turned it over, puzzled. "At least I had one."

Blossom looked at Prescott, a half smile on her lips. "You know, Mr. Prescott, I think perhaps we should wait on the meeting idea. I have a feeling soon enough there will be some indication of where we should go and what we should do." She glanced about the room. "Meanwhile this looks like a nice place to sit and chat and get to know each other. Michael, would you have the man over there bring me a glass of wine?" Gingerly she took a seat on the low leather sofa. No one noticed Blossom's surprised look as she leaned back against the cushions. She sat bolt upright and gave her back an experimental twist, then sank back again into the deep, soft leather cushions with a blissful smile. "A nice Merlot, if you please, Michael."

Lorraine VanDyke sat on the straight-backed chair, her legs neatly crossed at the ankles, hands resting in her lap. She watched Cynthia put on a hasty dash of lipstick, then survey herself in the mirror and brush a speck of lint from her flight uniform.

"I didn't think you were one of those women who can't go anywhere without having all the bells and ribbons in place," Lorraine observed.

"You ought to see me off duty—it's jeans or chinos and maybe a comb through the hair." Cynthia's brown eyes shadowed a moment; then she took a breath and said, "But I always try to look good when I'm in uniform; looking good is important professionally, don't you think?" She bit her lip and darted an apologetic look in Lorraine's direction.

But Lorraine wasn't paying attention. She was looking passed Cynthia at her own image in the mirror. She saw a neatly dressed woman in a gray suit with a white swath of gauze covering one side of her face. Was the bandage smaller than it had been? And the eye! Her left eye was uncovered! Lorraine's hand moved to touch the gauze. She was too far from the mirror to see clearly, but it seemed as though the sunken socket had filled out and something—a fold or crease of skin—now protected the lidless, clouded left eye. Was she seeing out of that eye? No, no, of course, she couldn't. Lorraine got up abruptly.

"What is it?" Cynthia, make-up case in hand, met Lorraine's gaze in the mirror. "And don't say 'nothing.' You're white as a sheet."

"What an original turn of phrase! You ought to consider a writing career."

Cynthia faced her roommate. "Stuff it, Lorraine," she said, but her tone was gentle.

Lorraine turned away, but not before Cynthia saw her hand once again seek the bandage on her face. "Maybe something has happened. I don't know yet. I don't want to talk about it."

"Right." Cynthia shrugged into her jacket and buttoned it. "We'd better get down to the meeting. You ready?"

"You go. I'll stay here." At Cynthia's questioning look, Lorraine said impatiently, "Just because this Sherwood Prescott says 'jump,' we don't all have to say 'how high.'"

"It's perfectly reasonable to get the group together to discuss what we want to do," Cynthia said mildly. "Why are you so angry, Lorraine? You've been angry ever since we came."

Lorraine's lips curved in a sardonic smile. "Gosh, I don't know, Cynthia. Why am I angry? It couldn't be because I haven't been able to feel 'normal' for most of my adult life, could it? Nah, that'd be too simple. And as for going to your stupid meeting," she said, "did you stop to consider that I might not relish the idea of sitting next to you or the beautiful Talia, or even mousy little Malvena when I look like something from a horror movie?"

"Get real, Lorraine. I don't know how you looked before, but right now no one can see anything but a bandage," Cynthia looked more closely, "and not a very big one. There's something else bugging you. What?"

Lorraine's lips pressed together in an uncompromising line, but then her shoulders slumped. "You know what Howard told us back there? That all the choices we made while we lived on earth, all the decisions, big and little, have made us into the people we are now and that we're here to discover just who that person is?"

"Yeah." Cynthia waited.

"Frankly, it scared the heck out of me."

"Why?" Cynthia sounded honestly puzzled.

"Is that how it is? We're going to be held accountable for every single decision we made?" Lorraine burst out. She caught her lip between her teeth. "It's not fair. How can anyone be expected to make all the right decisions in every instance? Anyway, if I have to worry about every single decision I made during my life, I just wish someone had told me about it before now."

"I'm not sure he said that exactly," Cynthia said, considering. "From what he did say, I don't think we have to sweat the little things so much. Let's face it, often we hadn't a clue about what was the right thing to do. But we knew the basics. Just about everyone knows that hurting someone is bad, trying to help them is good. I think that's the kind of choosing Howard was talking about. Not what brand of toothpaste you decided to buy."

Lorraine stooped to pick up her purse. "Well, thank you, Mother Teresa." But she said it under her breath. "Okay, let's go find out what prissy old Prescott has on his mind."

Malvena Blatska crept down the staircase. She reached the lobby and stood for a moment watching the group gathered about the lady airline pilot and the older, peevish-looking woman with the bandaged face. Everyone seemed to be talking at once; no one looked in her direction. Malvena took a gliding step toward the hotel's entrance, then another and another. And she was outside on the busy street.

Malvena surveyed the steady stream of men and women, avoided two scruffy-looking teens dodging among them, moved aside for a couple sauntering arm in arm. No one here she had to be concerned about. She turned left and coming to the corner, walked toward the underground station sign. Where was he? Would she have to go down the steep steps into the underground to look for him?

"Hey!" The word was soft.

Malvena whirled. He was behind her, his head dipped forward.

He looked at her over small, oval, dark glasses. "Took you long enough," said Jackson Delion.

"I had to wait until the girl I am with went downstairs and I could be sure no one would see me leave." Malvena adjusted her scarf.

"Okay, where is it? Everything safe?"

"I was telling you at the airport—they took the baby." She saw the muscles in his cheek tense and hurried on. "What I had no chance to tell you is that the baby wasn't with me when they pulled me from the water. They took him into the helicopter first, and when we get off the plane at the base a woman already had him." Her eyes sought the ground. She made a little gesture with her hand. "So you see I didn't have a chance to do anything."

"You mean it's still with the kid?" Delion cracked his knuckles. "Shit, girl, you just let them take the kid off somewhere and don't do anything?"

He was working himself from anger to fury, Malvena thought. Just like Daron used to. "There was no chance."

Malvena ducked her head and folded her hands before her in a subservient gesture, one she'd often used to placate her brother. "No one will know what to look for."

Jackson Delion gave an impatient snort, but her assertion diverted his anger. "You'd better be sure about that." Delion caught Malvena's elbow and pulled her out of the way of a passing bicycle. "The way I see it is we keep on like it's business as usual. And that means getting to that stuff and getting it back before anyone knows we lost it."

"How?" Malvena said uncertainly.

"Listen, you say you got to go to the kid. See if they'll tell you where it is. Say somethin' like you just want to see him, be sure he's okay. Then it's up to you. You're the one who knows the technical stuff."

"I don't think this is good idea," Malvena began unhappily, then stopped as Delion swiveled his head and directed the opaque dark glasses at her. "All right, I'll try," she said hastily.

"You go on now—tell 'em you gotta go visit the kid; then when you get it, you put it somewhere safe."

Malvena looked up, her eyes opaque. "How will I contact you?"

"Don't worry 'bout that. I'll be around." Jackson Delion glanced up and down the street one more time and then made his unhurried way down the stairs to the underground.

10

LORRAINE STIRRED, AWAKENED BY THE ODOR OF THICK, yellow pus. Time for the bandages to be changed? She cringed at the inescapable pain she knew would accompany a dressing change. Lorraine's eyes snapped open. No, no. She wasn't in a hospital. That was long ago, those times long past.

Lorraine moved her head gingerly. In the next bed, Cynthia slept, an arm thrown over the embroidered coverlet, a bouquet of lilies and roses on the table beside her bed. Lorraine took a cautious breath, then breathed deeply, inhaling the heady fragrance of the flowers, the scent of fresh linen, and underlying all, the aroma of coffee from somewhere nearby. Not a trace of the foul odor that had awakened her.

Lorraine's hand reached up to touch the bandage on her face, her fingers light as butterflies. No gauzy bandage! The only thing she felt was skin—soft, smooth skin. Lorraine raised herself on an elbow and swung her legs onto the carpet. Bunching her cotton nightgown about her, she crept to the dressing table where she stood looking down at the polished wood. There was Cynthia's lipstick and comb, her own gold wrist watch lying beside Cynthia's business-like chronometer. Lorraine's peripheral vision encoded a reflection in the mirror, the image of the lightly clad figure standing before it, but she could not make herself look up. For several shuddering heartbeats, she could not look above the scooped, buttoned neckline of her patterned nightgown.

But then she did.

And saw a face with smooth, high-colored apple-cheeks, a face whose small, straight nose had a little dent at the end, a dent someone long ago had told her was charming. Instead of one well-shaped eyebrow, there were two and in place of the left eye's staring, clouded lens, a perfectly formed eyelid with gently curving lashes protected a clear hazel eye that matched the other. Lorraine took a shuddering breath. She arched her neck and pulled back her silky fall of hair, checking for any remnant of her sunken, gouged left cheek with its thick, transplanted skin, and saw only the smooth, high-colored contour of softly curving cheek. Lorraine pressed shaking hands to her face, felt tears wet her cheeks. Whole. She was whole again.

Her hands fell to her sides as she avidly studied her reflection in the mirror. Not only was her face restored; instead of a fifty-two-year old woman, the fresh and supple-skinned face that looked out at her was one she hadn't seen since that day in the African desert. She was pretty! Perhaps this face did not have the classical beauty of Talia Innes, but it was sparkling, attractive, alive. Lorraine cocked her head. She'd forgotten how attractive she'd been.

She darted a flickering glance at the sleeping figure of her roommate, feeling suddenly shy. Part of her wanted to share her transformation yet part wanted to keep it to herself, to hug it to her. For a while, at least.

Lorraine frowned, her hazel eyes darkened at the remembered pain, the countless surgeries that had attempted to correct the initial, bungled patch-up. Was this new face supposed to make up for all that she'd had to live through afterward, a life spent avoiding people, trying not to react to the horror and distaste in their eyes? Not likely. Nothing could compensate for what she'd endured.

Lorraine's lips thinned to a tense line that turned down at the corners, the nostrils of the straight little nose flared. The face that looked at her from the mirror wasn't quite as attractive as it had been.

Her eyes widened. "No, please," she whispered. "I didn't mean that. I'm grateful, truly grateful. Please."

Lorraine couldn't see through the blur of tears that suddenly brimmed and threatened to spill; she couldn't tell whether the image's prettiness had been restored. She turned from the mirror, not daring to look.

"Lorraine! My God, what happened?" Cynthia sat up in bed.

Lorraine brushed away her tears. "Nothing."

"You are Lorraine, aren't you?" Cynthia said uncertainly.

Lorraine let out a breath. "Am I . . . am I . . . pretty?"

Cynthia pulled back the covers and extended her long legs from the bed. She bounced up and came to examine Lorraine's face. "Yes," she said with a slow smile. "You are. Very." She took a closer look. "You also look about twenty years younger than you did yesterday." She went to the wardrobe and grabbed khaki slacks and a plaid shirt. "How about we go down to breakfast and give the others a look at the new you?"

Lorraine followed behind Cynthia, her arms still clutching the cotton nightgown about her. "Do you think this will last?" she said anxiously. "Are you sure it isn't just some illusion?"

"Illusion?" Cynthia put on the shirt. Her hands slowed as she began to button it. "Is that the way you feel?" she said. "As though this change isn't quite real?"

Lorraine's hands sought her cheeks. "No, it feels real. I know it's me, or at least the way I used to think of myself." Her voice sank to a whisper. "Do you suppose that's why the accident happened? Because I was vain? Too concerned with my looks?"

"What a load of crap—of course not!" It exploded from Cynthia. She took Lorraine's hands in hers and looked into her roommate's troubled face. "I don't know a whole lot, but one thing I've always been sure of is that God doesn't want awful things like what happened to you to occur. Sure, terrible things do happen, but that's not how God deals out his messages."

"How can you be so sure? How do you know?"

"I just do." She paused. "Well, I guess it's something I was taught as a little kid. Mom and Dad didn't actually say it in so many words, but I was brought up with the idea of an all-loving Heavenly Father, and I've always had the absolute certainty that nothing bad ever came from him." Her breath caught as she saw something behind Lorraine. "Oh," she breathed, her eyes alight with joy. "Dad!"

Lorraine knew before she turned around that she would see no one behind her. And turning back, she was unsurprised to find herself alone in the hotel room. Bemused, Lorraine went to the wardrobe and pulling a linen pants suit from it, began to dress. Apparently if you thought of someone who had come to live in this world that person was likely to appear. Seemed to be the way it worked around here. And Cynthia would appear at breakfast, or perhaps they'd meet on the way downstairs. Probably full of more little gems of wisdom she'd learned from her dad. Lorraine picked up a brush and smoothed the hair from her forehead. Not that she wasn't pleased that Cynthia was with her father, but who was there she wanted to see? No one that she could think of. Maybe Jane Austen?

Lorraine looked around half expectantly and then placed the brush back on the dresser, feeling foolish. Maybe not. You probably had to have a real connection with the person to have them appear. Lorraine went to the door, then paused, her hand on the knob. But if that was the case, what about . . . what was her name . . . Malvena? The girl had burst into their meeting yesterday, hysterical about going to see her baby. If she wanted to see the kid so much, why hadn't it appeared the way Cynthia's dad obviously had? What was going on? Besides, if Malvena cared so much about her baby, why had this outburst been the first time she'd even mentioned the kid? Don't go there. No business of hers whether or not Malvena loved her child. But Lorraine could not repress the shudder that swept her at the thought of an unloved, unwanted child. Another thing from a long time ago.

No, she wouldn't think about that.

"Lorraine, wait up."

Cynthia trotted down the hallway, her tennis shoes noiseless on the carpet as she padded up to Lorraine.

"You saw your dad?"

Cynthia beamed. "He's an angel! He showed me the community where he lives."

"So did he tell you anything more about what to expect?"

"I did ask some things, but he said that, considering where I am now, it's probably better to discover things for myself." Cynthia's fingers skimmed the polished bannister. "Actually, we didn't really talk all that much. He hugged me and told me how proud he was I'd become a pilot." Her smile widened. "I always wondered if he knew."

"He did?"

"Yup. He knew about Tabitha too." Cynthia sobered. "I asked him if he'd watch out for T, and he said he'd already been with her. Then he said something about my needing to pay attention to what's going on, something about me letting T and Rob go on with their lives. I don't know, it was like I couldn't hear him so well anymore."

"Then what?"

"He said I had lots of terrific things I was going to see and hear, and then we hugged again and, and here I am." They had reached the arched doorway of the breakfast room. "Or here we are," Cynthia amended. "Okay, Lorraine, ready to make an entrance and wow the troops?"

Stuart Casperson speared a bite of omelet. "How about that?" he said to Sherwood Prescott, pointing his fork at the other side of the large, round table where Lorraine was talking with a fascinated Talia on one side and Blossom O'Meara on the other. "Did you get a load of the new, improved Lorraine?"

"Marvelous about her face, isn't it?"

"Oh yeah." Stuart shrugged, eyeing the chattering women. "But if we have to hear any more accounts of how it happened and how great she feels, I'm going to find myself wishing for the old Lorraine. Matter of fact, I think maybe I prefer the before version."

Sherwood Prescott gave him an intent look, but said nothing. Instead he rose to his feet and tapped his spoon against the water glass before him. He cleared his throat. "Ladies and gentlemen," he said, "I'd like to propose that we reconvene yesterday's meeting. Since the Sianases are with us now, perhaps we can come to some decisions."

Michael O'Meara stopped him with a wave of his hand. "If we're going to sit here talkin', I could do with more coffee. You there," he called to a passing waiter. "Any chance of getting another pot of coffee?"

The waiter paused and came to the table, looking annoyed. "Dunno if there's more," he said.

"Well, you'll have to go check then, won't you?" Michael raised an eyebrow.

The waiter stared at him glumly and went away muttering under his breath. The man's rudeness was a small thing, but had a sobering effect on at those sitting at the table.

"Now that's strange," Blossom said, "I haven't seen a sulky employee since we've come here."

"Neither have I," Frederick Hampton echoed. "That is, until this morning."

"What happened?" Blossom asked him.

The minister looked down at his plate. "When I came down earlier to ask whether I might have a pen and some paper, the young woman at the front desk said no." Fred looked up with a sheepish smile, "Actually, what she said was that I could get my own bloody writing things. And when I asked if she knew where I might buy some, she said, um, rather more along the same lines."

The diners eyed each other uneasily.

"Now let's not make too much of a couple of discontented hotel workers." Sherwood Prescott, still on his feet, looked as though the impoliteness of the hotel's employees bothered him a great deal less than having his meeting disrupted. "We have quite a few things to decide."

"Like what?" Nick Sianis looked up from his cornflakes. "Is there any reason we have to decide anything? We've been pretty well taken care of so far, and you can always call on Kate and Howard if you don't know what to do."

115

"Some of us feel the need to be proactive, rather than ask others to make decisions for us," Prescott told him stiffly. "And surely it makes sense to discuss possibilities rather than sit here and wait for something to happen."

"What possibilities?"

"Where we might like to go and who would choose to go with us."

"Well, you can count us out," Nick Sianas said politely. "Amanda and I have already talked about it, and we've decided we'll ask to meet with Howard and Kate to see what we should do next." He smiled at his wife. "Matter of fact, that's what we're about to do now that we've finished breakfast."

"Yes," Amanda Sianas said happily, "we've been told we can visit Becky today."

"Fair enough." Prescott looked around the table. "Anyone else feel they want to go off on their own?"

When no one volunteered an opinion, Prescott rubbed his hands together approvingly. "Good, good. I suppose the first thing to do is to discuss options." He gestured to the pad of paper in front of Fred Hampton. "I see you did get your writing materials, Fred. Could I ask you to take notes?"

Jeff Edwards rolled his eyes and looked at Talia. She, however, was looking disconsolately at Sherwood Prescott and did not respond. Poor kid, she looked as though she hoped but didn't really expect that Prescott was about to announce this was all a mistake, that they were in London after all and the School of Economics was just a few streets down and over. Jeff felt a flicker of compassion that disappeared as his glance slid from Talia to the animated, revamped Lorraine whose face job's psychic effects were already evident, and on to the Sianases beside her. Jeff jerked his gaze away from the whispering couple. What had happened to the kid? No, don't think about it. Anyway, at a time like that it was everyone for himself.

Jeff slouched in his chair, letting the drone of Prescott's voice wash over him. Who elected this guy Prescott boss anyway? And what did it matter what decisions they came to? Ever since they'd come here things seemed to just happen, mostly things you didn't expect. Like that Kate telling them at the airport meeting that they were supposed to find out what they loved and who they were, like it was some kind of school assignment or something. Who was he? Good question.

First off, he was an actor, a good one—make that better than good. But he could be a lot of things if he wanted. A leader, for one thing. A much better one than the guy standing up there acting like he was conducting a board meeting.

Jeff stood motionless before the roaring crowd. His security guards shifted nervously behind him, and Jeff knew they were uncertain where this overwrought adulation might lead. Though all of the guards were battle-hardened veterans, their unease was palpable. The roar increased, filling the night air until it seemed ready to split, as though a plane were about to crash the sound barrier. But as the cheering reached an unbearable pitch Jeff lifted a hand, palm out, and at once the assembly fell silent. They knew he was about to tell them—tell them—what?

"My friends," Jeff's dark, rich voice reached every corner of the packed room without effort. No, outside was better; they were outside. His dark, rich voice reached every part of the packed stadium, the people in the upper sections as clearly as those in the first rows. "My friends, I stand before you not to persuade you, not to move you by words, but to simply inform you of your choices. Now I know you've been told you must look into yourselves and discover who you are. They've told you that what you are is what you love more than anything else. Well, I have something to say about that. Baloney! What you are is what you dream! And what you dream is the highest ideal of what you can be." Jeff gathered his

thoughts as the audience cheered. What had he meant by that? Still, it made sense, didn't it? Wasn't a person really, deep down inside, what he dreamed of being?

"One choice," he resumed, "one choice you have is to—"

"One choice we have is to contact someone in authority." Sherwood Prescott's words mingled with Jeff's, and the cheering crowds vanished. Jeff sat upright, annoyed.

"—ask for input as to how we go about following the instructions we've been given," Prescott droned on. "Another choice would be to head for our original destinations and see what happens. I, for instance, could go on to Brussels for my meetings, our pilot and copilot could try to locate their airlines, Blossom and Michael would head for Ireland," Prescott made a circular motion with one of his hands, "and so on and so on."

"Why would you want to attend your Brussels meetings if we're not in the natural world any longer?" Fred Hampton asked. "What possible use could that be?" The thought of having to give the paper that had been in his briefcase made his stomach lurch. Fred risked a wild hope that it lay, waterlogged, at the bottom of Lake Huron, its contents lost and forgotten.

"I think trying to carry on as we did in the natural world isn't going to get us anywhere—" Whatever else Cynthia was going to say remained unspoken as the waiter who was supposed to have brought Michael's coffee approached the table.

He carried no coffee pot, however. With elaborate formality, he went around the table and carefully placed a piece of paper before each diner.

Stuart Casperson snatched up his and read it. "It's a bill!" he said. "And it's a hell of a big one!"

The others looked at theirs with cries of dismay or angry expletives.

"Just a minute, now. If yours are like mine, they're outrageous, but let's not lose our heads." Sherwood Prescott reached for his wallet. "You take Visa, I trust," he said with a grim smile.

"Sorry. No credit cards accepted." The waiter answered Prescott's smile with a smug one of his own.

"You want £2,000 cash?"

"Yes, sir. If you please, sir."

Sherwood Prescott's eyes narrowed. "And if we can't pay?"

"You'll have to take that up with management," the man said smoothly.

Prescott sat down. "Let's do that," he said slowly. "Yes, I think we'd like to meet with the management."

The waiter inclined his head and went from the room, his step so sprightly he almost pranced.

Michael O'Meara held up his bill and tore it in two, then put the pieces together and tore them again. "I see they gave you one too," he said to Blossom. "I suggest you do the same to yours, m'love."

Blossom did not, however. "Doesn't it seem strange that they don't give a single bill to couples?" she said, examining her paper thoughtfully. "And look at the name of the hotel at the top of this bill; mine says 'First Lodging.'"

"So does mine," said Lorraine.

"And mine. Why doesn't it have our hotel's name on it? What's this place called, anyway? Does anyone remember?"

"You asked to speak to the management?" No one had noticed the dark-suited man arrive; he was simply there, standing beside Sherwood Prescott's chair.

To Prescott's credit, he didn't turn a hair. He leaned back to get a better look at the manager and tapped the bill with a fingernail. "Two thousand pounds for a couple of nights and a few meals. It seems a bit much, don't you think?"

The manager bowed his head as though Prescott had paid him a compliment. "We try to have the very best of service and accommodations," he said.

"You'll have to try a lot harder," Michael snapped. "The service, at least this morning's, doesn't even come close."

The manager's hooded eyes flicked to Michael and quickly dismissed him. "Should there be any trouble with payment, we can make arrangements."

"What arrangements?" Stuart Casperson said quickly.

"You'll find us most accommodating," the manager said, his tone soothing. "I'm sure a place can be found for each of you until your debt is paid. The kitchen needs help, and our wait staff is woefully undermanned."

They gaped at him. Jeff was first to find his voice. "No way, no how. Not on your life, buddy. I've waited enough tables; I'm not going to get into that gig again."

"How unfortunate you feel that way. But perhaps we can find some other assignment. Please feel free to come to my office and speak with me about it." The manager's dark eyes glinted with pleasure. Or perhaps it had been merely a trick of the light for a moment later, they were blank, impassive. "If there's nothing else . . . ." He bowed again, turned, and glided from the room.

"What a jerk," Stuart snarled. "I think I'll take him up on that offer to see him in his office—if only to tell him what he can do with his job."

"I don't like him," Cynthia said, shivering. Then she looked around the table. "Where are Nick and Amanda?" she said abruptly.

The others looked blank. "Anyone see the Sianases leave?" Sherwood Prescott asked.

Apparently no one had.

"Since they didn't want to come with us, they're probably back at the hotel," Cynthia whispered.

"What's that supposed to mean?" Brad asked her irritably.

When Cynthia spoke, it was not so much to her fellow pilot as to herself. "I don't think we're at the hotel anymore. We're somewhere else."

11

"THEY DON'T HAVE A CLUE, DO THEY? DESPITE EVERYTHING they've been told." Howard leaned the weight of his foot into the pitchfork and turned over a clod of rich earth.

"Cynthia does." Kate reached over the great dog lolling at her feet and handed her husband a slender green shoot. "She's quite perceptive. And then she has been doing a lot of thinking."

"That helps, of course." Howard's tone was dry.

Kate gave him a playful swat. "You know what I mean. She's paying attention—unlike some of the others." She handed him another seedling to plant. "Too bad she decided to go with them to the hotel when they weren't ready to hear any more of our lecture. Ah well, she won't come to any harm, and she's a good example for Lorraine." Kate cocked her head. "Do you ever miss your graduate classes?" she said.

Howard looked up. "Sometimes. It was exciting to explore a subject with my students, look into a topic in some real depth. But I enjoy helping our newcomers. I realize I'm learning to guide them without being didactic, to help them find out about themselves without actually telling them how to do it. I figure when I've learned how to handle this job well, maybe I'll be given a graduate class to teach." He gave her a half smile. "Whatever happens, right now I'm perfectly happy doing the job we've been given. How about you?"

"I don't miss my classes, not at all. And I love helping our arrivals too." Kate leaned over to breathe in the fragrance of the pink lily-like flower that bloomed from what was now a hardy plant in the freshly dug ground. "I would like to get back to writing though."

"Why don't you?"

"I've thought about it, but somehow it hasn't seemed quite right. I have this feeling I should wait—perhaps until I'm more certain about what I want to say?"

"It'd be good to have a general idea." Howard's grin sobered. "Of course, you must trust your feelings, Kate. The Lord will direct you." He rose from his knees and brushed his hands on his work pants.

"You don't think it's wrong of me to want to do something other than what we've been assigned?" Kate persisted.

Howard nudged aside the dog and put his arms around Kate. "Why do you suppose you want to write, darling?" he said, nuzzling her neck. "Because you developed the gift you were given and became a writer, a good one. You'll have the chance to use that talent here." He stood back and regarded the bank of crimson delphinium that rose from the fresh earth before them, crowding the pink lily clusters. "How do you like the combination?"

Kate regarded the flowering plot. "It's a picture of our love for each other, right? And the pink lilies are the affection we feel for our friends?"

"She got it right. Give the lady a cotton candy."

124

"Listen to him, Buster," she addressed the dog. "He can't resist giving a quiz." The big tail thumped on the grass. "Buster agrees; it's much too early for guessing games. Besides, it's time we got to work. Or are you having too much fun gardening?"

"Listen to her, Buster; sounds to me as though she's sidestepping the issue." But Howard followed her to the amber-colored stone house, the dog lumbering behind them. "It is fun, isn't it? The whole thing. This learn-as-you-go business."

"It is." Kate flashed a smile at him. "But now that we're together again, everything is fun. It's absolutely wonderful—and I mean that in all senses of the word."

Howard set his garden tools beside the carved wooden door. "That's one thing Nick and Amanda have. They came together."

"Yes." Kate paused.

Howard saw her hesitation. "What is it? I thought they seemed very compatible."

"Oh yes, but Nick seems a little, well, domineering, a little too ready to make all the decisions. They're both good people, and they love each other," she paused again, "but is it a lasting love or something they had during their life on earth but that won't be with them here?" Kate gave herself a little shake and strode into the stone house. "But, of course, we don't have to concern ourselves with that. If they're not meant to be together, the Lord will provide each with a partner they will love to eternity. Right now, the one I'm worried about is Jeff."

"The actor." Howard nodded thoughtfully. "His dream world seems to be gaining strength, doesn't it? What a shame. Well darling, we can only wait and see what happens there. In the meantime, what else do we have scheduled?"

Kate entered the comfortably furnished study and picked up a packet of papers from one of the two rosewood desks that faced each other. "These evaluations. Let's get them done before Birgitta and Hans come for lunch, shall we?"

Sherwood Prescott regarded the work schedule for a long moment, then strode purposefully past the uniformed porter, heading toward the hotel doors. Just yesterday the man at the entrance had leapt to attention as Prescott approached him; now the ferret-faced porter remained lounging on his high stool, not bothering to raise his eyes from his newspaper. Or was this the same man? Prescott realized he wasn't sure, that he hadn't really looked at any of the hotel's employees.

Prescott hesitated. Would the door open if he pushed it? Would an alarm sound if he attempted to leave? Would he be hauled back to take his place as—Prescott glanced down at the schedule—as barman at the Queen's Oak Lounge. A barman! Not bloody likely. Prescott's hand slammed against the door.

It opened with a sucking sound that made the hair on the back of Prescott's neck rise. Was that echoing noise someone calling him? He took the steps two at a time without looking back, reached the sidewalk and stood looking out at—what was this? Prescott studied the terraced landscape of woods and gardens that stretched out to distant blue-wreathed hills. Cynthia was right. They certainly weren't in London anymore.

Prescott turned to look at the hotel behind him, substantial and solid. If it wasn't the hotel at which they'd been staying, it was a building exceedingly like it. There was the porter peering over his newspaper at Prescott, a sly smile on his narrow face.

Prescott took a deep breath and forced himself to think. He should have been more on guard. Everything had been so pleasant since they'd come that he'd allowed himself to be lulled into complacency. What were the others doing back at the hotel? Obediently performing the duties they'd been given? Should he have left them to fend for themselves? After all, the little group depended upon him—had ever since they'd arrived. Prescott glanced back at the vestibule. Even if he decided to go back and help them, would the weasel-faced doorman let him in?

Prescott looked out over the sunny lawns. He wasn't going to be much help to anyone unless and until he figured out what was going on. Right. So figure it out. Somehow they'd been transported out of the city. That in itself might be considered a step forward, but the attitude of the hotel workers, the changed ambiance of the place argued a definite minus. Was it some kind of test? Prescott breathed in the soft, fresh aroma of damp earth, of rain-cleansed air. When had it rained? The sun shone now, and the only clouds, a bank of them near the horizon of the October blue sky, were fluffy white. Prescott took another breath of the deliciously fresh odor of rain-cleansed air. He saw a stone bench a few feet away, walked across the damp grass, and sat down. Think. According to Kate and Howard, everyone was supposed to discover who he or she was. Whether good or evil, he supposed. What was the story of the sheep and the goats? But no one was wholly one or the other, good or evil. Was the purpose of all this to separate those who'd lived a mostly good life from those who hadn't?

Well, he'd lived a decent life. Achieved his modicum of success in an honest, straightforward way and with a minimum of guile. Prescott shifted uncomfortably. Well, he had, hadn't he? And as for his private life, he'd been a faithful husband and a good father, perhaps impatient at times, but he'd tried, honestly tried. Prescott's jaw tightened at the thought of those abortive attempts to talk with Karen, of Phillipa's annoying habit of barging in when she considered things were escalating out of hand. His lips trembled. Oh Phillipa! He was in a hospital room. Phillipa stood watching the labored breathing of the pale, wasted figure in the bed. Karen. Prescott could feel his daughter's exhaustion, sense her all-pervasive weariness.

"Fight it, Karen. Don't give up." Phillipa didn't say the words, but Prescott heard her thought as clearly as if his wife had spoken. His heart contracted as Phillipa closed her eyes and a tear squeezed past her tightly closed lids.

"Don't cry, Phil," Prescott reached out. "You know I can't stand it when you cry." Somehow he must try to relieve the pain emanating from his wife. He looked at his daughter, saw her eyes flutter, saw color come to her cheeks. "It's going to be all right, Phil," he murmured thankfully. "Look at her; she heard you. Look—she's breathing more easily."

Phillipa gave no indication she'd heard him speak, but after a moment, she opened her eyes and went to the bed. She stared at the sleeping girl. "Karen!" she cried. Prescott felt the joy exploding from her. It reached him in a rush of warmth that filled his chest and reached his fingertips.

Phillipa wiped her eyes. "Oh God, God, thank you! I don't have to let her go, do I? Not this time."

Hearing her silent prayer of thanks, Prescott realized he'd never heard his wife pray aloud. Of course, he hadn't prayed aloud either. Was it something she'd always done silently, separately, because of his own reserve? Sherwood Prescott's hand caressed the air near Phillipa's shoulder. "Don't worry, Phil," he said. "It will be all right. Even when you do have to let her go, she'll be all right. I'll be here for her; I'll take care of her." But with that thought came the crushing realization that he, Sherwood Prescott, arbitrator and negotiator, might very well not be there for Karen. How could he? He hadn't the power to take care of himself, let alone anyone else. Only the God Phillipa had thanked just now, the God Prescott had prayed to without understanding and all too often perfunctorily, had that power. Sherwood Prescott lowered his head. Please, help Phillipa, he prayed. And Karen. And please, if it is your will, help me be with our child when you bring her here.

The stone bench felt cool beneath Sherwood Prescott's spread fingers. Prescott shook his head, trying to clear it. He got up and brushed his thick hair back from his forehead with a practiced hand. He'd been so pleased when his hair had turned from a nondescript brown to distinguished gray. Was it still gray? Did he care? Why had he wasted even a moment's thought on such a nonsensical thing? Prescott gave a wry grin and walked toward the hotel. Maybe he'd be able to keep the gray hair so that, when Karen came, she'd recognize him—if he was given the opportunity to be with her, care for her.

He paused to watch several tiny butterflies alight on a honeysuckle bush, their bright blue wings glinting in the sun. He looked more closely and saw that others were struggling to emerge from their small chrysalises. After waving damp wings, they too flew among the flowered branches, sipping at the flowerlets. Okay, he got it. When Karen arrived new-made, like a butterfly emerging from its chrysalis, she would be provided for and cared for. Probably by others far better equipped for the job than he. Angels, he supposed. Prescott took the steps up to the hotel. "But please," he murmured as he reached the hotel door, "I know she'll be cared for, but when Karen comes, please may I be there to greet her too?"

Brad Nelson looked in the mirror and buttoned the uniform's jacket. How long had it been since he'd been able to button his jacket and not feel the uncomfortable pinch of over-stressed material? Didn't even have to suck in his gut. Not that he'd been easing off on the calories. Just the opposite, he thought feeling just a twinge of guilt—he'd been chowing down pretty much everything in sight.

Brad turned to admire the rear view. Not bad. Sure he'd rather be wearing his flight uniform, but the tailoring of this one was excellent, the lightweight wool an attractive steel blue and the gold braid not too obvious. Until he received his flight orders, he might as well humor these people and play doorman for a few shifts. How bad could it be? They'd said he could order meals from the menu any time he wanted. Brad patted his flat stomach, gave his reflection a final approving look, and headed downstairs.

Talia gritted her teeth and plunged her hands into the soapy water. How dare they assign her to the dishwashing detail? Why not Lorraine or Cynthia or the old woman? Yes, why not Blossom? Blossom wasn't too old to wash dishes; heck, she'd probably enjoy it. Anyway, Blossom didn't seem all that old anymore, not nearly as old as before. Talia wiped a wisp of soapsuds from her cheek. Before what? What did "before" mean? She frowned and held a thin china dish beneath the stream of hot water. Lately it seemed she couldn't keep her mind on anything, couldn't follow a thought to its logical conclusion. No! She wouldn't allow this. She was a magna cum laude graduate and just a few months from an

MBA; she was not going to let her brain turn to mush.

She'd do math. Talia plunged her hands into the water again. That was it—math. Something that required pure, reasoned analysis. She washed a glass, rinsed it, and held it up to the light. Sparkling clean. Nice. She reached for another glass and washed it. And another. And another.

"Goodness, my dear, aren't you industrious?" Blossom's head with its cap of feathery red-blond hair peeked around the arch separating the kitchen from the pantry.

Talia blinked. She looked at the racks of clean dishes, the shelves of shining crystal and wiped her hands on the towel at her waist. "I guess I didn't mind doing them once I got started," she said. "It was sort of soothing." Then her grip on the towel tightened. "But that's it. I don't care what the rest of you do, or how much this place says I owe—I'm not washing another dish. I can't believe we let them trick us into doing their scut work."

"Oh, I don't mind making beds," Blossom came all the way into the pantry and hitched her apron around to the front, smoothing it over her navy-blue uniform. "But I draw the line at picking up after those people on the fourth floor. You ought to see their rooms." Blossom rolled her eyes. "Goodness knows what they've been at."

Talia shuddered. "How can you go into strangers' rooms and make their beds?"

"It's not so different from what I've done all my life," Blossom said mildly. "Anyway, the people in this place are really interesting. If I could make Michael behave, I'd be perfectly content to just stick around and see what happens next."

"Oh yes, I saw your husband run through here and up the back stairs a while ago," said Talia.

Blossom shook her head in exasperation. "He thinks if he moves fast enough, they won't be able to find him and make him carry suitcases or wait on tables."

"I don't blame him," said Talia. "Why should any of us wait on other people and lug their things around?"

"Michael wouldn't mind doin' the work; it's just that he'll have no one tell him what to do. Never has, never will." Blossom looked anxious. "I hope that stubbornness of his won't get him into trouble." She started, staring over Talia's shoulder.

Sherwood Prescott entered the pantry carrying a tray of dishes. "Yes, it's me."

Talia put her hands on her hips. "You can put those anywhere you want, but I'm not doing them," she snapped.

"They have you waiting tables?" Blossom asked, shocked.

Prescott put the laden tray on the counter. "I was supposed to be a barman in the Queen's Oak Room, but I went for an unauthorized walk outside, and it seems I've been demoted." He didn't sound as though he minded. "I'm glad to see you ladies. We don't seem to have had much luck with our meetings, but I think we should try to gather after dinner. I have a feeling we should press on and decide when and how we're getting out of this place before it's too late."

Talia raised a beautifully shaped eyebrow. "What do you mean, 'too late'?"

Prescott gave a slight shrug instead of answering her. "Let's see: the Sianases are gone, and I've talked to you two, so who else do we have to contact?" He ticked them off on his fingers. "There's your young friend Jeff, Talia, and Blossom's husband, and Stuart Casperson and Lorraine and the pilots."

"Has the minister left?" asked Blossom.

"Oh, and Hampton. One tends to forget Fred."

"So we all get together after dinner and natter about leaving," Blossom said. "What makes you think the folks around here will stand for it? If they punished you just for going out and taking a walk, it's not likely they'll let us gather for a meeting, let alone decide to take off entirely."

"We won't know what we can do until we try, will we?" Prescott didn't seem to enjoy being challenged, but he made a show of considering her point. "Of course, we'll keep it private, meet in one of our rooms—let's say my room—and we won't troop upstairs together. We'll arrive separately." He leaned back, his hands against the pantry counter behind him. "As to my so-called 'punishment,' I've been thinking about the consequences of my little excursion, and when you consider it, you can hardly call it onerous. So I have to wait tables instead of tend bar." He gave a half smile. "I think that, though the people here are allowed to issue orders and directives, there are definite limits to what they can do about making us obey them. If we choose go our own way, I'd bet nothing much will happen. Of course, it would be stupid to take chances; we'll have to be circumspect." He regarded them. "Would one of you open the back door and look outside? Perhaps you, Ms. O'Meara?"

"Why?" Talia said, frowning.

But Blossom had already gone to the door and opened it wide enough to look out. "For pity's sake, we're in the country. There's a whole great forest out there!"

Prescott gave a relieved nod. "It's more open land than forest in the front. At least it was when I was outside."

"But how can we be in the country?" Talia said.

"Remember what Cynthia said this morning? We're no longer at the London hotel."

"Never were," murmured Blossom.

Prescott ignored this. "We've moved, or rather been moved, and I'm not sure why. But I wonder if it has something to do with how we react to events, as a group or individually." He shifted and stood upright. "That's one of the subjects I want to address at our meeting this evening." He went up the stairs to the archway. "I have to get back to the dining room, but if you ladies see any of the others, will you pass the word that we'll meet in my room right after dinner? And tell them to try to be inconspicuous." He nodded and left.

Blossom looked after him, her bright eyes considering. Talia's attention, however, was on the tray of dishes Prescott had put on the counter. She took the towel she'd tucked in her belt and tossed it beside the dishes. "Let's see what happens when they come in and find the whole room filled with dirty dishes." She looked up as a moving shadow flitted across the unlit archway. As though someone had flicked a switch, light filled the space, and Malvena Blatska stood blinking uncertainly.

"I . . . I was told to come wash the dishes," she said.

"Do you think they heard me?" Talia whispered to Blossom.

Blossom ignored the question. "Did you get to see your baby, Malvena?" she asked. "Did you see Daniel?"

"Yes. I saw him." But Malvena didn't sound certain. She pushed a heavy plume of dark hair from her face. "The woman wouldn't let me come near though." Malvena made a quick movement with her long-fingered hands. "She didn't actually say I could not, but somehow I didn't feel so well when I come close. So I'm there just a little while and then I say maybe I should go, and she says yes, if that's what I want."

"The baby's all right?" said Blossom. "He's doing well?"

"Of course, he's doing well," said Talia. "She would have said if he wasn't." She frowned. "Y'know, I've been wondering—who told you where your baby was, Malvena? And how did you get to him? Did you walk or take a taxi or what?"

Malvena shot Talia a keen look, then quickly lowered her gaze, heavy lids covering her dark eyes. "I asked the man at the desk who I must ask to see the baby," she said quietly. "At first, he would not call the manager, but then I insisted, and he did." She hesitated.

"And?" Talia prodded, intrigued by the thought of this shy young woman insisting on anything.

Again Malvena's eyes flicked to Talia's face. The look could have been annoyance or something more. She gave an acquiescing shrug and went on. "The manager said he will go see if it is allowed. After a while, he returns and says yes I can go. A car is waiting for me in front of the hotel, and we drive, how long I don't know, only that we go out of the city and into the country. There are farms and fields and over us is a sky I cannot describe, a sky bright with many colors."

"Yes, but what about the baby?" Blossom said impatiently. "Tell us about Daniel."

"He is with other children."

Blossom's face fell. "You mean he's in an orphanage?"

Malvena considered. "No, I don't think so. It is a house. Three other children are there with the woman, and a man, her husband, I think." A frown crossed her face, disappeared.

"What?" Blossom asked.

"Nothing," said Malvena.

"What happened?" Blossom insisted. "Was something the matter?"

"It isn't right, how they look at me," Malvena muttered. Then she gave a quick shake of her shoulders. "Nothing is the matter. It is just as I say—all of a sudden I don't feel so good, so I ask if I can go back and right away I'm here."

"The car brought you back to the hotel?" said Talia.

Malvena looked puzzled. "I . . . I don't remember. All I know is that suddenly I am back in front of the hotel."

"But when the car took you to see the baby you did drive through the city, through London, right?" Talia persisted.

"Of course."

"There, you see, we're in London," Talia said to Blossom. "I knew you all must be mistaken. You know, I don't see any particular reason why I have to wait for this meeting tonight to leave. I've half a mind to just take off on my own and go find the school and register."

"For a smart girl, you're willing to overlook a lot of things that don't add up," Blossom murmured. Then she reached up and patted Talia's shoulder. "Going there means a lot to you, doesn't it, dear? Well, if it's that important, I'm sure you'll find a way to get to your school."

"Of course, it's important! And if Malvena can get her way and go see her kid by 'insisting,' I'll show them what a real uproar's like. No one's going to keep me from going where I want." Talia stopped, confusion clouding her face. "Where is it I'm trying to go?" she said. "I can't remember."

"Never mind, dear. It will come to you." Blossom untied her apron.

Malvena had been standing a bit apart from the two women, but at this pause, she moved nearer. "Has anyone come here to ask for me?" she said hesitantly.

"Who would be asking for you?" said Talia.

"It's that Delion person, isn't it?" Blossom said quietly. "What is it about that man? Why are you afraid of him? Obviously, he's not your husband or boyfriend."

"I am not afraid of him. But he is sometimes . . . difficult, and I . . . I have to travel with him." Malvena stroked her skirt with her long-fingered hands. "You have not seen him?"

she repeated.

"Not a whisker. Look, Malvena, the meeting Talia was talking about is to be in Mr. Prescott's room after dinner, and I'd advise you to be there. We're going to discuss leaving here." Blossom tossed her apron on the counter beside Talia's dish towel. "Now if you girls will excuse me, I've got to see if I can track down Michael before he decides to start a revolution."

"He is going to start a revolution?" Malvena said sharply.

"Michael's been a union shop steward for forty-five years," said Blossom. "Putting him with a bunch of workers who've been pressed into service is like inviting a fox into the chicken house. Not that that's necessarily his motivation. I wouldn't put it passed Michael to stir up trouble just for the devil of it." She went to the staircase by the rear door, her step light and sure. "Like I said, it's not wise to try to force Michael to do something he doesn't want to."

Malvena looked after her. "I thought she was old, but she doesn't walk like an old woman," she said, her tone disapproving.

"Maybe she's on some new medication or something," said Talia. "Look, I'm out of here." She headed for the archway.

"You are leaving? You are not going to help me?"

"I've been doing dishes all morning, and I'm not about to go for an all-day stint; my hands are like prunes." Talia paused on the top step. "I suppose I'll go to this stupid meeting. If I don't see you back in our room beforehand, I'll see you then."

Malvena looked after her blond roommate, her face unreadable. As she turned to the sink full of dishes, she made a guttural noise that came from deep in her throat. It was not a pleasant sound.

Stuart Casperson drummed his fingers on the polished wood of the registration desk. According to Stanley, a batch of new arrivals would be coming shortly. Nice to discover Stanley wasn't such a bad guy after all, that he appreciated a person's talents. Stuart adjusted the lapels on his suit. Had the manager asked anyone else to call him by his first name? Not likely. And as far as Stuart knew, none of the rest of their group had been given management-level employment. Look at what Sherwood Prescott had landed—a job waiting tables! And though he'd muffed it, Prescott's original assignment of tending bar hadn't been all that great for a big-shot negotiator. Even their pilot hadn't managed anything better than a job assisting the doorman, though to tell the truth Brad didn't seem to mind.

Of course, you tended to do what Stanley told you to. Stuart flinched as he remembered the manager's dark eyes. You wouldn't want to make Stanley angry. He caught sight of himself in the mirror and drew back his shoulders. Then he saw another image in the mirror and turned quickly. "Hello there, Cynthia." He inclined his head in an approximation of Stanley's gesture, taking in her apron and dark blue uniform. No management job here either. "I see they have you hard at work."

"Blossom and I are making beds," Cynthia said. She shifted the pile of linens she was carrying to her other hip. "Can't say that, after fighting my way into a copilot's seat, I relished the idea of being somebody's maid, but working with Blossom's a blast." She paused before continuing toward the elevators. "You heard about the meeting tonight?"

"What meeting?" Stuart's gut tightened. Why hadn't anyone told him about this meeting? Were they trying to keep him out of the loop?

"Mr. Prescott called a meeting to decide about when and how we're going to leave this place. We're to go to his room right after supper." Cynthia smiled. "Be there and bring any bright ideas you might have for the great escape."

Stuart stared at Cynthia's retreating back. They were planning to leave? They expected him to chuck his new job and go on some wild goose chase with them?

"Right," he called after her. "I'll be there."

Stuart smoothed the bound leather ledger on the counter before him and making an infinitesimal adjustment, aligned it with the edge of the registration desk. He'd tell Stanley. That was it. He'd tell Stanley about the meeting and offer to attend and report on it.

Stuart picked up the phone and dialed. Surely Stanley would be pleased.

12

SHERWOOD PRESCOTT LOOKED AT THE CIRCLE OF FACES. Blossom and Michael sat on the carpet, Blossom leaning comfortably against Michael's shoulder; Malvena was on the floor next to them. Lorraine sat on the king-sized bed, Cynthia next to her; and slightly apart from them, Fred Hampton perched awkwardly at the foot of the bed. Stuart Casperson and Brad Nelson, Brad in his new doorman's uniform, stood by the door. Only Jeff Edwards was in a chair. The first to arrive, Jeff had taken the only chair available, a deep-backed wing chair where he now sat, his eyes half closed.

"I appreciate your coming," Prescott said. "I know it's a bit crowded having all of you in here, but it's important to avoid arousing more suspicion than necessary."

"But we're not all here," Lorraine said, looking about. "Where's Talia?"

Jeff's eyes flicked open. "Yes, where is she?"

"She is in the room." Malvena's fingers picked at the material of her skirt. "She must stay there I think. I think it's because she said she would not work in the kitchen any more."

"You mean they've locked her in her room?" Prescott said, incredulous.

"I only know the door will not open." At the stares of the group, Malvena moved uneasily, tucking her legs beneath her and continued, "When I went upstairs before dinner, I could not open the door, and the doorknob was hot to my hand. When I called to Talia, she tells me she can't get out, the doorknob will not turn."

Blossom regarded her. "You didn't think this was worth mentioning to anyone else?"

Malvena flushed. "I was going to tell about it, but I was late for dinner. When I came into the dining room, there was no room for me at your tables, so I sat by myself, not near any of you." At Blossom's dumbfounded expression, she added defensively, "And when we come here, everyone was talking, so I waited for the meeting to begin to say anything."

Blossom's expression did not change, but Sherwood Prescott merely waved an impatient hand. "Maybe I was wrong," he said, frowning. "I was fairly certain the people here are unable to make us do anything we don't want to."

Cynthia nodded. "I think you're right; they can't."

"Then why is Talia being kept in her room?"

"Is she?" Blossom asked. She drew up her slacks-clad knees and folded her arms around them like a college coed making herself comfortable at a dormitory hen session. "Could it be the girl just needs some time to herself, even if she doesn't quite realize it? She talks a lot about going to that school of hers, but I think when it comes right down to it, she doesn't want to go off by herself. What she has been told about being in this world is rattling around in that pretty head of hers, whether she acknowledges it or not."

"Could be you're right." Prescott turned to Jeff, who for once was paying attention. "Why don't you go ask if she wants to join us?" he asked. At Jeff's blank look, Prescott said testily, "Go to your friend's room. See if she really wants to be with the rest of us. If Blossom is correct, she'll be able to open the door."

Jeff rose reluctantly. "Anyone want to come along?"

"Oh come on, lad." Michael O'Meara scrambled to his feet. "What are you scared of—being jumped in the corridor and abducted by pixies?"

"For God's sake, who's afraid?" Jeff snapped. But he seemed glad of the little man's company.

"As you all know, the purpose of this meeting is to figure out how we're going to get out of here," Sherwood Prescott said as the door closed behind them. "Perhaps we should start with an obvious question. Is there anyone who would rather stay here," he glanced at the paper in his hand, "at the 'First Lodging' as they call it?"

Fred Hampton spoke for the first time. "By virtue of the name, it rather sounds as though we're supposed to move on."

"But what about the charges we've run up?" said Cynthia. "If we're supposed to leave, why give us outrageous bills we've no way of paying?"

"Why indeed?"

"We *do* have the means of paying our bills," Brad Nelson patted his well-tailored jacket. "They obviously have a labor shortage here, and all we've been asked to do is put in a little time helping out. Let's face it, it's not like we're being asked to work in some sweatshop. I, for one, wouldn't mind staying a while. The food's good, and the beds are comfortable."

"Have you seen your most recent bill?" Fred Hampton asked him.

All looked at Fred. He blinked at the attention but continued, "They're still charging us for our rooms and meals," he said, "—and the rates have doubled."

There was a stir of outraged murmurs. "What about all the work we've been doing?" Cynthia scooted off the bed and scowled at him, arms akimbo, hands on her hips. "You mean we're not being paid for it?"

Fred Hampton flicked a glance at Stuart Casperson; but when he spoke, he addressed Cynthia. "All I know is when I asked to see my bill it was . . . pretty staggering."

Sherwood Prescott raised a hand. "Hold on, let's not panic. Stuart, are you aware of this?"

Stuart Casperson drew himself up. "Actually, yes, I am. Stanley explained it to me, and it's not as bad as it sounds. It's mainly a matter of fiscal management, you see. We are only one of many First Lodgings, and in an organization this large, there are things like debts and credits and ROI to be considered. You want to look good, you want the books to look good, and of course, having a large margin of profit does just that. Stanley knows we don't have the money to pay the hotel; all he really expects us to do is sign our bills, give him an IOU if you will. If you do, you'd be perfectly free to go wherever—"

"I know what an IOU is, and I don't like it," Blossom interrupted him. "But what's an ROI?"

"Return on investment," Prescott said without taking his eyes from Stuart. "Let me get this straight, Stuart. Am I right in assuming this 'Stanley' is cooking the books? He wants us to sign phony bills so he looks good?"

Stuart shifted uncomfortably. "I didn't say that. I'm simply letting you people know how you can—" He stopped as the door opened, and Talia stormed in, Jeff and Michael trailing behind her. Michael took his place beside Blossom who began whispering an abridged update of the meeting. Talia strode to the center of the room and surveyed the group. She tossed her tangled blond mane, her eyes sparkling with anger. "Okay, you people, who locked me in my room?"

"What makes you think one of us did it?" Prescott said mildly.

"The manager told her someone must have locked the door from the outside," Jeff explained. "Claimed he hadn't done it or told anyone else on the staff to."

"The manager? Where does he come into this?"

"By the time we got there, he'd come up and let her out." Michael's tone was laconic. "Seems she finally got the bright idea of phoning the desk to ask for help."

"Why didn't you do that before?" Lorraine asked her.

"I tried to, but the phone didn't work," Talia snapped. "Then I thought my roommate would get help," she glowered at Malvena, "but when none came, I tried the phone again, and it was working."

"You get the feeling somebody's yanking our chain?" Michael murmured with a grin. "More'n that, get the idea we're bein' given the old bait-and-switch routine?"

"What do you mean?" Cynthia asked.

"First it's, 'Here's the bill, and we know you can't pay, so's you're gonna have to work.' Some of us worked, and some of us told 'em to stuff it. Didn't seem to matter much to the folks here—just so we stayed. So now Blossom tells me it's, 'Well, if you don't want to work, you don't have to; but here's the bill, and you folks just sign it so's we can look good for the boss.'" The wiry little man paused. "Who do you suppose is the boss—God?"

"Michael!" Blossom's tone was sharp. "Merciful goodness, Michael, how can you say such a thing?" she said more temperately. "As though the Lord would have anything to do with the likes of what's going on here."

145

"So are we in hell?" Jeff sounded more interested than worried.

"How many times do you have to be told?" Blossom scolded him. "We're in a place between heaven and hell."

"From the looks of things, I'd say we're closer to hell than the other place," Michael said, arching an unrepentant eyebrow at his wife.

Blossom regarded him, her blue eyes troubled. "I agree," she said.

Sherwood Prescott gave another impatient gesture. "Let's stick to the business at hand, please. I don't know what happened to your door," he said to the still-seething Talia, "but I doubt that anyone in this room had anything to do with it." He indicated the wing chair Jeff had vacated. "Why don't you sit down, and we'll get on with the meeting? Stuart was telling us why our bills are going up like stocks in a bull market." He gave Stuart a quizzical glance. "Maybe he can explain what would happen if we refused to sign these promissory notes before we leave."

Lorraine gave a shake of her head that was reminiscent of Talia's patented gesture and flicked the hair from her face. "Yes, Stuart, how can we be expected to sign anything when we don't know if we'd ever be able to pay?"

"Is there even the concept of money in a spiritual world?" Fred Hampton's voice was hesitant. He gave them a shy smile. "No one's been more surprised, and I must say delighted, than I at what we've discovered since we've come here. I'm ashamed to say that on earth I hadn't entertained the slightest idea we'd be, well, men and women still." Fred flexed a hand, looked at it in wonder, "—or that we'd find ourselves in such familiar surroundings. But some things are very different here. Perhaps you haven't noticed. Most of you seem to have been able to accept our, ah, transition much more readily and unquestioningly than I; but though I've decided I can't argue with the reality of this world in which we've found ourselves, there are, ah, several things I've been puzzling over." He drew a breath.

"Well, don't keep us in suspense, padre," Michael O'Meara folded his hands over his lean little paunch. "If you preach your sermons at this rate, it's a wonder anyone in your congregation stays for the finish."

Fred bobbed his head in an odd little ducking motion. "I've been told I do tend to be verbose."

"If that means long-winded, I agree."

"Michael, hush up, and let the man talk!"

"We're not in some airy-fairy world of spirits. We're in London!" The wail erupted from Talia. Her full, red lips pouted like a frustrated two-year-old's. "I don't know why everyone insists that we're dead. Obviously, we're not."

"No, we're not," Blossom said gently. "Just sit there and hold that thought, dear, and let Reverend Hampton finish talking."

"If he ever does." But Michael's grumble went unheard, and Fred's remarks remained unuttered as a sharp rap sounded at the door.

At Prescott's nod, Stuart opened it.

Beatrice Jorgenson stood in the hallway. "Are you going to stand there staring or ask me in?" she demanded. Not waiting for Stuart to step aside, she swept past him into the room. "You people have stayed together, I see," she said as she glanced around the circle. Her eyes widened as she came to Lorraine, but she made no mention of Lorraine's transformation, saying only, "I've decided to join you. At least for the time being."

13

"WHAT CHANGED YOUR MIND ABOUT GOING TO BRUSSELS?"

Beatrice waved a gloved hand at Cynthia. "Brussels isn't part of the schedule, not anymore. Oh, you needn't worry; I'm fully aware we've entered another existence, now that I've talked to the people in charge and had them explain it properly."

"What did they say?" Cynthia asked, fascinated.

"Well, first I insisted that they use plain, logical terms," Beatrice said briskly, "none of your metaphysical gobbledygook." She frowned. "I can't say I remember exactly how they put it, but it was all quite . . . quite sensible." Her face cleared. "Anyway, in the course of my questioning, I asked about whether there were opportunities in the local hotel industry, and it seems there's a great demand for a person of my abilities. So when I heard you people were here, I thought I'd check this place out and see if it suits me."

"You're in the hotel business?" Lorraine asked her.

"Spent my life in it," said Beatrice.

Prescott had remained standing throughout Beatrice's speech, only slight shifts in his position conveying his annoyance. Now he cleared his throat and said, "I'm afraid we're gathered here to talk about leaving. I was on the point of asking whether anyone wanted to stay when we got waylaid into a discussion of our burgeoning hotel bills."

"You have a problem with the billing?" Beatrice stiffened like a birddog confronted with an unexpected grouse. Her eyebrows shot up. "What's wrong?"

"Look at this bill of Blossom's!" Michael drew a paper from his back pocket and waved it at Beatrice. "Highway robbery, that's what it is."

"We've been charged exorbitant prices for everything—rooms, meals—mine even had a charge for hot water." Lorraine scrabbled inside her large, leather purse.

"Not only that, they've been making us wait tables and work as maids and kitchen help," Cynthia added.

Beatrice took the bill from Michael and examined it, muttering exchange rates to herself. She said nothing until she'd inspected Lorraine's paper too. "Are the rest of them like this?" she asked.

"Yes." "Oh yeah." "Uh huh."

Three did not join the chorus of affirmation. Prescott merely pursed his lips at this further disruption of his meeting; Stuart remained silent at his place by the door; and Jeff, standing beside Talia's chair, seemed lost in some world of his own.

After a few moments' further perusal, Beatrice handed Michael and Lorraine their bills. "Highway robbery doesn't begin to describe it." She glanced around the room in brisk appraisal. "I can give you an approximation of what you should pay for these rooms—actually I could probably tell you within a few shillings what you should expect—and let me tell you, what you've been charged isn't even in the ballpark." She brushed invisible lint from her slim skirt and turned for the door. "I'll speak to the manager."

"Hold on! Who elected you speaker of the house?"

Beatrice flicked a look at Stuart. "What's got your shorts in a knot? You enjoy being overcharged?"

"I was just explaining before you came in that it's a simple matter of bookkeeping." Stuart ran a finger across his forehead and seemed surprised to find it beaded with sweat. "Nobody has to worry about paying his or her bill. All we need to do is sign for the charges. It's just a formality."

"Nonsense," said Beatrice. "Signing a paper is never just a formality. I'll just run downstairs and clear things up." She reached for the doorknob.

"Did you learn what happened to your daughter?" Stuart said quickly. "Christy, isn't it? You haven't mentioned her, and I know you were very concerned."

Beatrice's firm jaw slackened. Slowly she withdrew her hand from the doorknob. "Christy?" she said, her voice trembling. Her eyes searched Stuart's face. "Who?" she whispered.

"Never mind, Beatrice," Lorraine said quickly, "we all seem to be forgetting things." She turned to Stuart with a level stare. "Stuart, you really are a little shit, y'know?"

Beatrice Jorgenson seemed oblivious to both Lorraine's reassurance and Stuart's ensuing denial that he'd intended any harm. "Christy," she said, her voice husky. "Yes, of course, I remember. She's all right. Yes, I remember. They told me she'll be fine." She gave herself a little shake. "I . . . I think I'll go ask about your bills," she said. She walked into the hall; she held her shoulders straight, but she moved without her former certainty, and she seemed somehow diminished.

Stuart met the group's accusing eyes and raised his hands, palms up. "So sue me. I had no idea I'd get that kind of reaction."

"Let's finish this meeting before we have any more interruptions," Prescott said, ignoring him. "Whether or not Ms. Jorgensen is able to make any headway with the matter of our bills, I think we all agree it's time for us to leave. I take it Stuart has decided to stay. Are there any others?" He looked around the room. "Very good. We'll meet," he did not look at Stuart Casperson, "at, ah, a location and time to be disclosed later."

Sherwood Prescott stopped at the table where Fred Hampton sat alone and placed Fred's plate on an already overloaded tray. "As soon after dinner as everyone can manage it, we'll gather in the pantry behind the kitchen," he said in an undertone.

Fred nodded. "Lucky our group has just about taken over the kitchens." He gave a little cough and searched for something to say to extend the conversation. It was pleasant to have Sherwood Prescott stop to talk, even though thus far it had been only an exchange of information. "So everyone's going with us but Stuart and Brad? I must say I'm surprised Captain Nelson decided to stay."

"The man's a lightweight." Prescott dismissed him. "I don't think Beatrice is coming with us; when I talked to her, she was having too much fun raking the manager over the coals about our bills. And there may be some question about the foreign girl. If Blossom hadn't told me the girl was running from her boyfriend, I'd swear Malvena was stalling until she could find him and talk to him about leaving."

"Waiter. Over here!" bellowed a corpulent man at the next table.

"Look, I have to go," said Prescott, adding in an undertone, "Don't be late and don't call attention to yourself." He hurried off, a laden tray held high.

So they were leaving. Fred toyed with his beef. Rather pleasant to be one of a group, certainly better than exploring this new world alone. Though, of course, he was used to being alone. Fred tore off a piece of bread and dipped it in the gravy on his plate. The food was excellent here, he'd give them that. Would it be as good at the next place? He had never been particularly interested in food, but lately he'd found himself becoming something of a connoisseur. Perhaps because he'd been assigned to the concierge's desk and not involved with the serving and cleaning up as were so many of their group. Whatever the reason, he'd begun to look forward to the gong that announced meals with an eagerness he'd be embarrassed to have anyone know about. Matter of fact, it was a little embarrassing to acknowledge even to himself how much time he spent thinking about food. He'd have to watch it, ration himself. Fred pushed away his plate. Yes, he just wouldn't eat as much. If only it was this easy to stay away from some other things.

"Sure I'm leaving with the rest of you," Talia said, watching Jeff devour his apple strudel. "I'm not into washing dishes a minute more than I have to. But let me tell you, if we find ourselves anywhere near the School of Economics," she beamed as the name rolled off her tongue, "—there you go, I remembered—or if I hear anything about how to get there, I'm history."

Jeff reached over and speared a strawberry from Talia's plate. He looked at it moodily. "You don't suppose they have theater here? At this point, I wouldn't even ask for something professional; I'd settle for a community troop doing *The Man Who Came To Dinner*."

"Poor Jeff," Talia said absently as she applied herself to her remaining strawberries and cream.

Jeff knew she wasn't listening. It didn't matter. He was already ensconced in a chair in the seventh row of a darkened theater.

He leaned forward and clapped his hands, and the two actors on stage stopped the scene, peering uncertainly into the darkened auditorium.

"Was it wrong? Again?" asked the red-headed girl.

"Just relax; you'll get it." Jeff kept his tone light. Wouldn't do to destroy their confidence, let them know how woefully inadequate they were. "Let's do it over, and this time I'd like a little more emotion. Not over the top, of course, but I'd like to hear some real feeling."

"Once more with feeling," said the leggy young actor, and then blushed at his attempt at levity.

Jeff remained silent a couple of beats longer than necessary. He wasn't going to fall into the "all-pals-together" bit. A director had to keep a certain distance. "If you're ready then, we'll take it from the top of page five," he said crisply.

The chastened actors threw themselves into the scene, the redhead fairly spitting her lines at her partner. Jeff leaned forward, intent. Actually, the kid wasn't bad, not bad at all.

The scene ended. Both actors breathed out in released tension and looked in Jeff's direction. The girl smiled slightly as though she knew she'd aced it.

"Better," said Jeff. "Not good, but better." An amateur wasn't going to decide when a scene was done. "Let's have it again."

The girl's half smile vanished, but she took her position obediently. They began the scene again. When they finished, Jeff let them stand for a few uncertain moments before he left his seat and vaulted easily onto the stage.

"Okay, that'll do. You've brought it along. Now go home and practice. I want to hear the rest of your lines the way you've worked this scene. With passion."

The angular young actor bobbed his head. "Right, Mr. Edwards," he said, "I think I see what you want."

"I doubt it," Jeff murmured, but he smiled and waved them on their way. Released, the boy bolted from the stage. The girl, however, stood her ground, hesitant but determined.

Jeff arched an eyebrow. "Yes?"

"I . . . I wanted to thank you, Mr. Edwards, for . . . for getting that scene out of me. I didn't know I could do it."

"That's a director's job," Jeff said. Then relenting, he gestured the girl to join him as he went down the steps into the auditorium. "I'm terrible with names. Afraid I didn't get yours."

"Lacy," she said. "I hear you're an actor as well as a director, that you've been in lots of plays, in New York and Chicago."

"My work is pretty well known in Chicago," Jeff admitted. "Actually, Chicago is where theater is really happening these days; but, of course, I haven't ruled out New York. Just the other day a big producer was asking me about doing a play for him."

Lacy's eyes widened. "Really, Mr. Edwards? Wow!"

"Call me Jeff."

"Jeff?" she said, her voice pitched high in uncertain wonder.

"Jeff." He tucked her arm beneath his.

"Jeff!"

"Jeff!" Talia's nails gouged his arm like talons.

"Ouch!" He jerked his arm away and glared at Talia. "What the—what was that for?"

"It was either pinch you or shout," Talia said. "I've said your name three, count 'em, three times, and you just keep sitting there with that stupid expression on your face."

Jeff rubbed his arm. "You 'bout drew blood."

Talia paid no attention. "Everyone else has left, and Mr. Prescott's been giving us the signal that it's our turn."

Jeff, still smarting from the jolt of his unwilling return, gave her a sullen scowl. "Want to bet we all get caught trying to sneak out because Stuart has told his new pal what's up?"

"You heard Mr. Prescott tell Stuart what he'd do if Stuart did that. Besides he made Stuart and Brad leave before we discussed details and didn't even tell the rest of us the exact time we were going until just now." She got up. "Come on, Jeff, stop being a brat. Act normal and don't rush."

"I'm an actor, remember?" Jeff grumbled. But he got up and ambled after her without further complaint.

❧

"Quiet please. Now that we're all here, I think we should move quickly. Please form a single file as you go out. Michael, you're in front; if you see anyone, alert the rest." Prescott hovered at the end of the hastily formed line. "Expecting someone?" he said to Malvena.

"Oh no."

"Then why do you keep looking over your shoulder?"

"It is nothing. I am nervous only." But Malvena darted another look at the archway that led into the kitchens before she went out into the gathering dusk.

Prescott went out last, but before he could pull the door closed behind him, a voice called out, "Wait. Please. Don't leave me here."

Beatrice Jorgenson stood in the archway. She carefully negotiated the stairs in her high-heeled shoes, holding her briefcase out in front of her with both hands. "I decided, that is, I'd like to go with you," she said as she reached the bottom stair. "I don't want to stay here. This really isn't my type of place at all."

"What made you change your mind?" Prescott asked her. "You haven't racked up any bills yet, and it seemed to me you were doing such a good job of raking Stanley over the coals, he wouldn't dare try anything with you."

"I . . . I'd rather not be on my own." It seemed to cost her something to say it. Then Beatrice looked him in the eye. "Would having one more person along disrupt your plans?"

"We don't have any plans. Aside from getting out of this place and finding one where we won't be gouged."

At the mention of her area of expertise, Beatrice regained her self-possession. "Well, of course, you should have asked questions before you signed the register. You people could use someone who knows her way around, you know. There isn't much I don't know about the travel world."

"This isn't your ordinary, everyday travel experience, Ms. Jorgenson." Sherwood Prescott waved her to the door. "All right, let's not stand here discussing it. Come along if you like." He hustled Beatrice outside and followed her down the path toward the others.

Blossom adjusted her chair to a sitting position and watched the sun's promise of morning lighten the far horizon. When they'd come upon this secluded garden, drawn by the gentle light of unseen lanterns, she'd chosen one of the many large, wicker chaise lounges set about the lawn and, like the rest, gratefully stretched out on the comfortable, flowered cushions. But she hadn't slept. She didn't need much sleep, hadn't since those long ago nights with babies and small children.

A soft snore came from the chair beside her. Blossom looked at Michael's sleeping form, a small burst of warmth spreading through her chest. Thank you, Lord, for taking us together. Blossom resisted the urge to reach out and smooth back the short, silky hair that fell over her husband's forehead. She smiled. Well, well. It had been years since Michael had enough hair to warrant a comb. When Michael looked in the mirror and saw how handsome he was, how middle-aged, would he want more? Would he long to be the youthful Michael O'Meara she'd married? A chill dispelled the warmth in her chest. There had been far too many nights she'd spent waiting for that youthful Michael to come home from the tavern one block down and two streets over. Blossom fought back a dark shaft of anger. That was past. They'd come out of it. Not without scars. But they'd come out of it.

Someone whimpered. Blossom looked over the sleeping bodies, some covered with the light blankets they had discovered in a neatly folded pile on the low table, some with their coverlets thrown aside, unwanted in the spring-warm air. Was it Malvena who'd cried out? Blossom felt a flutter of distress at the thought. No matter how kind, how competent the people might be who cared for the child, Blossom couldn't imagine the pain of having to give up a baby. True, the girl didn't seem to grieve, but Malvena was a strange young woman; perhaps she was the type who kept her feelings in check by refusing to acknowledge them.

Like Dulcy.

Blossom's heart spasmed, a clenched fist in her chest. She closed her eyes. Oh, Dulcy. My sweet, wayward child. You may be a grown woman, but in many ways, you're more of a child than even the grandchildren. You and your "meaningful relationships." Each time so certain this one is the soul mate you've been searching for—and despite what you say, dear, I know that's what you're looking for—a forever love. That's what you called it when you were a little girl. You were dressed up in my old clothes. When I caught you primping in front of the long bedroom mirror, you said you were getting ready to meet your "forever love." I laughed, not knowing what lay ahead. Oh, my child.

Blossom started at the faint sound of quarreling voices. Before her a man and woman stood beneath the dull rays of a streetlight. They were on a bridge that overlooked a railway yard; the man held an umbrella against a misty rain that fell from the night sky. He gestured angrily with his free hand, demanding something, but the woman turned away, refusing to answer. He grasped her shoulder and yanked her about, forcing her to look at him, but the woman wrenched from his grip with a snarl. She drew back her arm like a boxer about to give a roundhouse blow and slapped him hard. Blossom heard the sharp, explosive sound, saw the man raise his own hand in instinctive response, but then let it drop. He said something short and sharp, then shrugged and turned and walked away, still holding the umbrella. The woman remained standing in the rain, her head up, proud and unyielding, her dark hair glistening in the wet. But when she turned to the light—yes, it was Dulcy—Blossom could see tears streaming down her daughter's cheeks, blending with the rain.

A train whistle sounded in the distance, then the chug and clank of an engine nearing the bridge. Dulcy took a step in the direction the man had gone, then gave a choking sob and ran to the bridge's metal railing.

"Dulcy, don't!" Blossom called out without thinking.

The woman gave no indication she had heard. She leaned far over the railing and stared at the tracks crisscrossing the yard below. Blossom saw two swirls of darkness darting about her head.

"No, don't!" Blossom cried again. "My dear, dear love, you can't do this—you mustn't."

Dulcy hesitated.

"You can't throw away the life you've been given," Blossom said, her voice breaking. "It's not your decision to make, darling. You have to stay and do the best you can. You have to stay, Dulcy, stay and fight."

The sound of the approaching train grew thunderous; the woman's hands tightened on the railing. A swirl of smoke obscured her from Blossom's view and for a heart-stopping moment, she thought Dulcy had flung herself to the tracks beneath.

But when the smoke cleared, Dulcy was standing motionless, watching the endless train roar past. In the stillness that followed, Dulcy unclasped her hands from the railing, took a careful step back, and peered behind her into the gloom. "Ma?" she said uncertainly. "Ma?"

Blossom let out a deep, wavering sigh. "Things will be better in the morning," she said gently. "Go home, child. Try to get some sleep."

"Ma?"

"Yes, darling. You can't hear me, but I'm with you. Now go home. Rest."

The woman looked about, then gave her shoulders a slight shake and began to walk away. After a few steps, however, she halted to look behind her again. She brushed the tears from her face with a quick gesture. "Ma?" she said.

"Go on," said Blossom. "Go home."

Dulcy waited a long moment, then turned and walked on.

And Blossom, watching as her daughter's figure disappeared into the quiet rain, saw that two soft, luminous lights darted about Dulcy's head, traveling with her.

"Time to rise and shine, friends." Sherwood Prescott walked between the chaise lounges, coming to stand between Fred Hampton's and the one he had occupied a short while before. "There's some sort of bathhouse over there with soap and towels and all the accoutrements," Prescott pointed to a low, white stucco building a few steps away from a swimming pool in one of the lower gardens. "I suggest you freshen up, so we can meet without further delay and decide what we want to do about continuing our travels."

Talia got to her feet, yawning. "I'm not deciding anything until I have breakfast."

"Well now, that might be a problem," said Prescott. "These grounds seem to go on for miles, but so far I haven't seen any sign of buildings other than the bathhouse."

That got the others up to look about. All but Blossom, who remained seated, and Jeff Edwards who lay on his chaise, hands folded over the coverlet drawn up to his chest like the stone statue of a knight on a sarcophagus.

"Hey there, old girl," Michael said, holding a hand out to Blossom, "aren't you coming to do yer morning ablutions?"

"Done them." His wife smiled at him briefly. "I've been up for a bit."

"Did some exploring of yer own, did you?" He looked at her. "What's wrong?" he said sharply.

Blossom gave a tiny shake of her head. "Later." Then she said to Prescott, "If we want to find out where we might get Talia's breakfast and, more importantly to my way of thinking, where we should be heading or whether it's a good idea to stay here, maybe we should just ask."

Both Michael and Prescott stood still.

"Ask who?" said Michael.

"Kate. Or Kate and Howard, I should say. It's silly of us not to take advantage of them when they said they'd be available if ever we needed help."

"I thought we decided we would rather do this on our own," Prescott said stiffly.

"Oh pish, tosh, and pididdle," Blossom brushed away her cover. "You decided that. I think it's high time we called on Kate and Howard."

"And how do we manage that?" Michael asked her. "You've come across a phone underneath one of the rose bushes?"

"I think they'll come if we want them to." She allowed Michael to help her from the chaise lounge, though she rose with the ease of a dancer. "How about it?" she asked Prescott. "Shall we call on Kate and Howard for advice, or are you all just set to keep on wandering around the country like a pack of gypsies?"

Sherwood Prescott's jaw tightened, but then he nodded grudgingly. "All right. When everyone gets back, let's give it a try."

14

"Now that you've had breakfast and everyone's comfortable, Howard and I would like to thank you for asking us to come join you." Kate's smile encompassed each of them. "We're so very happy you've decided you'd like our help."

Happy? Lorraine cocked an amused eyebrow. Happy didn't begin to describe Kate's ecstatic expression. And all because the group had given Kate and Howard the opportunity to come help them? Lorraine resisted the impulse to snort.

"Oh, come on, Lorraine; drop the fake cynicism." Kate came down the stone stairs and sat beside Lorraine. Lorraine did not notice that Howard had taken Kate's place at the top of the stairs. She did not hear him speaking; she was unaware of anything but the searching, hazel eyes that looked into hers.

"Don't try to pretend you haven't a clue how wonderful it feels to be given the chance to help someone," Kate said. "What about Africa? What about the child?"

Lorraine drew back with an infinitesimal movement. She stared at Kate. "How did you—?"

"It's a bit early to see beneath the surface of someone as newly arrived as you, but then you've never bothered hiding your thoughts from others, have you? The whole thing was right there on your face just now when you saw the breakfast table." They both looked at the table, its white linen cloth almost obscured by the dishes that contained the mouth-watering food, by pots of coffee and tea and glass pitchers of juices. "When you saw it, you immediately thought of Africa," said Kate.

Lorraine nodded reluctantly. Yes, she'd thought of Africa, had seen herself at a similar table, the girl traveling as a junior-grade appendage of the safari, dutifully catering to the whims of rich clients in exchange for the chance to soak up another month of incredible experiences. Had she really once been that girl, young and fearless, certain of life?

"And you remembered the child, Yussef," Kate continued.

Yes, she'd remembered the child. "The table did remind me of Yussef," Lorraine said quietly. "The way he looked the day he sneaked into camp and saw all the food the staff had set out—it just about broke your heart. He crept up to the table, stood there looking at the food as though afraid to move, scared it might vanish." She looked away. "You know, I never found out what happened to him . . . afterward. I've always wondered."

"You were in no position to do anything about him. You had all you could contend with just staying alive."

Lorraine put a hand to her face, felt the smooth skin beneath her long fingers. "I asked about him when I woke up in the hospital . . . when I was able to speak," she said. "No one seemed to know anything. Then after, when I saw my face—" She bit her lip.

"You stopped caring about much of anything," Kate finished for her.

"I suppose you think I should have forgotten how I looked and taken up good works," Lorraine snarled. "I'd like to see what you or the others would have done if they'd been—" Her eyes widened, she looked around. "Where are the others?"

"Talking with Howard," said Kate. "We thought you needed a little individual attention."

"But where are they?"

Kate reached over and turned Lorraine slightly so that she faced the right. And there they were, not far away at all, standing in an attentive cluster about Howard.

"I can't hear anything."

"Because you're not really concerned with what they're saying. You want to know about Yussef."

Lorraine looked as though she would like to deny it, but then she said, "Yes, I suppose I do."

The tall young man with curly black hair who appeared at the top of the stone steps leading to the upper garden looked about briefly and then strode toward them, his multicolored caftan swinging about his ankles. He held out a hand to Lorraine.

She glanced up at him uncertainly. "Yussef?"

His white teeth flashed. "That was once my name."

She looked at her hand that had all but disappeared in his large one. "You were such a skinny little boy. How . . . that is, have you been here long?"

"Since the accident," he said, his tone matter of fact.

"What happened?" Lorraine had difficulty speaking. "I . . . I never knew."

"It's no longer part of my active memory, but I think I can call it up," he said. "Let's see; the jeep rolled over, and I jumped out. There was an explosion, yes, then a fire. I ran and kept on running until I could run no more."

"And then?"

He shrugged. "I had no water, no food."

"You . . . you mean you died out there, all alone?"

His smile gleamed. "Ah, but I am alive, am I not? God is good. I have been given much joy."

Lorraine looked up at him. "I'm glad," she said simply.

"And I am glad I've been given the chance to thank you," said the man who had once been Yussef. "Three people gave me kindness when I was on earth. My mother, who held me and loved me for the few months I was with her before she was called here, the headman of our village who took me in and fed me until the starving time, when there was no longer food for anyone—and you."

"I didn't do that much," Lorraine mumbled. "Just gave you something to eat."

"Even before I could beg, you made a plate for me and gave me food. And you wouldn't let them drive me away. You shamed them into letting me stay, and when the camp moved on, you persuaded them to let me ride in the jeep with you."

"And got you killed," she said bitterly. "I should have been able to get the people at the hospital to understand, make them search for you."

Yussef merely shook his head, smiling. "I had a wonderful time growing up in heaven. All children who leave their natural lives are taken to heaven and raised by angels, you know. They don't have to go through the period of self-assessment adults do. Digger, the little boy who was with you on the plane, is having quite as wonderful a time as I did," Yussef's smile widened, "though possibly he creates a bit more trouble for his heavenly household than I did. Interesting ideas for adventures that boy comes up with."

"Ah." Yussef looked over Lorraine's shoulder at a tiny hummingbird that darted among the drift of yellow flowers in the bush behind her. He exchanged a glance with Kate. "I must go," he said to Lorraine. He raised his hand in a salute. "I welcome you to your new life and wish you well." And he was gone.

Lorraine stared at the space Yussef had occupied moments before. "He's an angel, isn't he?" There was wonder in her voice.

"Of course. All who come here as children become angels. Shall we join the others?" Kate put a hand on Lorraine's shoulder and guided her toward the group about Howard.

"There you are, Lorraine," said Sherwood Prescott. "We've decided to stay."

"We have?" Talia's tone challenged the statement. She stood, her arms crossed over her chest. "I don't remember a vote being taken."

"I thought we all agreed that it's the obvious thing to do," Prescott said stiffly. "I know Howard said we can be wanderers and travel around if we want; but since, if we stay here we'll be given food and shelter, and more importantly, Howard assures us we'll be safe, I'd think it's a given. As we have something of a scarcity of men in the group now, I'd think you ladies especially would want to stay."

"Perhaps Talia feels quite capable of taking care of herself," Beatrice Jorgenson said. "I know I do."

"Then feel free to trot off," Michael O'Meara told her. "Go wherever you please; leave the rest of us to enjoy the place. The grub here's as good as anything we got at the hotel and Howard says it's free. And I don't know about the rest of you," Michael looked about him, "but as far as a place to sleep, if it doesn't rain, I'll not complain if I have to make do with the deck chair. It suited me fine last night and will again."

"I didn't mean that I don't want to stay," said Talia, "I just think we should discuss it thoroughly. I was going to ask Howard if traveling would be dangerous." She looked at him.

"Danger is more likely to come from within," Howard replied enigmatically.

There was a small silence as the group absorbed this; and when Talia continued, it was with less certainty. "I still say we ought to talk about a decision that affects all of us."

"I thought we did that," Prescott said.

"You were doing most of the talking," she observed. "In any case, it's something everyone should vote on and Lorraine has just joined us."

Prescott gave an elaborate sigh. He looked around. "All right. Is everyone in agreement that we should stay? If not, I'd ask that person to share with us any ideas he or she has about what we should do."

"We still can't vote," said Beatrice.

Prescott raised an eyebrow.

"The minister—the man who took my briefcase at the airport." Beatrice frowned. "What's his name? Anyway, he has gone."

They looked around, Michael O'Meara going so far as to peer into the bushes as though he might discover Fred Hampton crouching beneath.

"Howard's not here either," Blossom announced.

Kate had been standing to one side watching with quiet amusement. Now she took a step forward. "Howard and Fred are having a talk," she said. "If you'd like, the rest of us can discuss some of the things you'll need to know if you do decide to stay here."

"It's embarrassing. More than that, it's humiliating." Fred Hampton moved uncomfortably in the rattan chair in which he was sitting. "When I think of the thirty-odd years of platitudes I've been preaching," he paused, looking at the pool's aqua water, "and especially when I think of the empty phrases I used when trying to comfort the bereaved—" His anxious gaze sought Howard's. "But you see, I hadn't the slightest idea of any of this, this—"

"Reality?" Howard supplied.

Fred considered. "Yes, I suppose you'd have to call it that. But what is reality? Is your reality mine? Is anyone's reality—"

Howard raised a hand. "Cut the philosophical cant, my friend." He gave a tiny smile. "Sorry, couldn't resist." He sobered. "You've just been talking about the empty phrases you used before and the first chance you get, here you are spouting them again. Look about you. Look into your heart."

Fred fidgeted. "Must I?" he murmured. His wispy eyebrows shot up in surprise. "Did I say that?"

Howard's eyes glinted. "One tends to say what one thinks, if not at first, then after being here a while."

"Ah," said Frederick Hampton, drawing out the syllable.

"Ah, indeed," replied Howard.

"Even . . . " Fred crossed his legs, then uncrossed them, "even inappropriate thoughts?"

"I'm afraid so."

"Is there some trick to . . . to not having that happen?"

Howard nodded. "Certainly. Not thinking them."

"Oh dear. But at times everyone thinks things that . . . but I suppose you don't."

"Not usually."

"But you do sometimes?" Fred said, astonished.

"I had a sharp tongue; I often said things that hurt." Howard looked thoughtful. "Far too often. I'm still learning about that." He gave Fred the glimmer of a smile. "Fortunately, it's an aspect of mine I have been allowed to put aside."

But Fred wasn't listening. "I've always tried not to think the kind of thoughts that I know I shouldn't have. But there are times—" He twisted his hands, then laced them together. "You probably know about the Internet business," he said.

"No," said Howard, "I don't. I haven't examined you."

Fred peered intently at his folded hands. "Chat rooms," he said at last. "Teen-aged girls. Despicable."

"You tried to contact these girls?"

Fred looked up, startled. "Oh no!"

"Someone discovered you were doing this?"

"No, thank heaven. I stopped before that happened. Cancelled my Internet. Inconvenient not having email, but it was the only thing I could think of. You see, since Sheila left, I've been so lonely. Everything seemed so barren. I tried to make do with my work, but that had its own difficulties." He darted a look at Howard. "In my profession, even a person as, well, as unprepossessing as I has to be alert to, ah, a good many things."

"Such as?" Howard said, interested.

Fred made a small, uneasy movement. "Staying clear of relationships that could lead to dangerous situations— dissatisfied wives, distraught widows. It would be absolutely unconscionable if one used one's calling to take advantage of them."

"I suppose this explains what you call the 'Internet business.'" Howard's voice was noncommittal.

Fred hung his head. "No," he said. "It doesn't."

170

"I'm glad to hear it." Howard stood. "Why don't we join the others?"

"Wait! Aren't you going to give me advice; tell me what to do?" Fred rose too, but he stayed by his chair clasping and unclasping the rattan back. "I never thought I'd say something like this, but . . . what should I do, that is, can you tell me how I can get to heaven?"

There was compassion in Howard's clear-eyed gaze. "You've done whatever will lead you to heaven—or not," he said.

Fred looked at him, his face ashen. "You mean I've already made—" He blinked. "But I can change, can't I? I can learn?"

"We never stop learning; that's one of the things that makes it so exciting here. And yes, change is part of spiritual life. What you can't change is what you grew to love above everything else, those things that make up the real Frederick Hampton."

Fred thought a moment. "You're talking about whether I loved good or evil, and that's all very well; I expected that," he said. He seemed more comfortable now that the conversation had taken a philosophical turn. "But when you talk about what I loved above everything else, you've lost me. 'Love?' While I grant you that, when a person is doing something, whether good or bad, you could say the person 'loves' that particular thing, it's temporary, transient. No one loves only good or only evil. We all love and do both."

"Of course," Howard said, "but the choices you made day by day throughout your life on earth became predominately one or the other; those choices formed you into someone who either is capable of loving what is good or someone who is not. When you came here into the spiritual plane, the essential you arrived, and that you cannot change." He looked at Fred intently to make sure Fred was following him. "What you loved most of all, those loves you acted upon in the natural plane remain, but that plane is no longer part of you. What is left is your internal self, the self that lives in the spiritual world."

"You're saying that, when one comes into the spiritual, ah, plane, one can no longer amend one's ways?"

"If those ways are what you really love, you're not going to want to amend them."

Fred nodded, but not happily. "I'm still not sure what you mean when you harp on this 'love' business. I reiterate—what a person loves changes from moment to moment. From what you say, it sounds as though whatever we may happen to love at the time we come here is what we're stuck with to eternity. How could a loving God countenance that?" He rubbed his lower lip. "Look here, say someone is engaged in, ah, in a disreputable act; say he's thoroughly enjoying it, and at that moment dies—would heaven be closed to him?"

Howard had been listening with his arms folded across his chest; now he said with a slight smile, "I don't know how many ways I can say this, but let's try it one more time. It's not what you're doing at the moment of transition, or in the moments just before, that decide who you are; it's what you've been doing all your life. If this hypothetical person of yours had made the evil of his 'disreputable act' part of his life, if he felt it perfectly acceptable, there'd be no question about where he was headed. But a thousand different people would have a thousand different reasons for doing the same act."

"Surely not a thousand."

"I merely used the word because you would understand it. I could have said a million, a myriad, countless. Every person and every spirit are unique; a person's loves are not and cannot be replicated."

Fred dabbed at the perspiration that dotted the hairline of his pale forehead. "How does one know—" He paused, began again. "How do I know what it is I've come to love more than anything else?"

"That's what you're here for," Howard said quietly. "This is where you will discover what you truly love."

Jeff Edwards slouched in his chair, his rear against the front edge of its frame, his long legs sticking out before him. It should have been an extremely awkward position, but Jeff seemed unaware of any discomfort. His lids half closed, he regarded Kate as she answered a question from Cynthia. Occasionally his lips twitched.

"Come on, Lacy, you can do better than that." Jeff found he had to fight to keep the irritation from his voice.

"Sorry, sweetie; guess I'm a little tired today." Lacy flashed him a smile that was an invitation to remember why she had reason to be tired.

Jeff moved uncomfortably. Last night had been a mistake. A director might bed a leading lady, no strings attached, but fooling around with a wide-eyed amateur like this was asking for trouble. The kid obviously thought having sex meant he'd agreed to be her Svengali. He should have known better. Have to put a stop to this. Pronto.

"Then we'd better try the scene again while you're still awake," he said in an even tone, "and if you can manage it, this time it would be nice if you remembered the words in their correct order."

Lacy stood absolutely still. She looked as though the breath had been knocked out of her. The rest of the cast watched in fascination as Lacy walked slowly to the edge of the stage and looked out into the darkened auditorium, her blue eyes filled with tears.

"Jeff, why are you talking to me like that?" Her voice shook. "Jeff, darling, don't you love me anymore?"

Jeff felt his face grow scarlet. What? Why was she doing this? Wait a minute. Why was he doing this? This was his fantasy. He wasn't supposed to sit here and be humiliated. This shouldn't happen.

"Okay, let's do this over," Jeff muttered. He cleared his throat. "Come on, Lacy, you can do better than that."

"Sorry, sweetie, guess I'm a little tired today." Lacy said the words he'd intended her to say, but there was a distinctly aggrieved tone to her voice and instead of giving Jeff a seductive smile, her luscious lips curved in a downward pout.

"No! Stop that!" Jeff struggled to stand up. He couldn't. "You're not supposed to do this," he whimpered. A spasm of fear twitched at the back of his neck. "You're supposed to say what I think—that is, what I want—" He drew a breath. "Lacy, please," he said, "let's . . . let's do this again."

Lacy stood in the center of the stage, her face sullen. "Okay, but this time don't give me that shit about not remembering my lines."

"Oh God! What's happening?" he whispered. "Help! Help me!" He tried to jerk himself upright again.

"Here, drink this." Howard spoke, but it was Kate who handed Jeff the tall, frosted glass. Jeff drank the water thirstily.

"Jeff, what happened?" Talia hovered above him. "We thought you were having a heart attack or something."

"Hah! What good would it do to have one of those?" Michael peered at Jeff from over her shoulder.

Jeff's eyes darted from Talia to Howard and Kate. "Guess I fell asleep," he mumbled. "And, and—"

"Couldn't wake up?" Howard supplied.

"Yeah. Something like that." The fear in Jeff's face lessened. "That's it. I was having a nightmare."

"Perhaps you should try staying awake for a while?" Howard said, his face grave.

Jeff gave his head a vigorous shake. "He means I should have been paying attention to your talk," he gave Kate a winning smile. "Sorry about that. Guess I didn't get enough sleep last night." He stopped at the sound of thudding feet on the upper garden's flagstone path and turned with the rest to see two men running down the stone stairs.

Brad Nelson staggered to the nearest chair and collapsed. "Thank God, we found you!"

"They're right behind us," Stuart Casperson gasped. He flung a terrified glance over his shoulder. "They'll be here any minute."

"Who?" Prescott whipped the question at him.

"The police. Stanley called the cops."

15

"Calm down," Howard ordered. "What's the trouble?"

"They're coming, I tell you!" Stuart said, still looking in the direction of the upper gardens. "They have guns."

Howard put a hand on Stuart's shoulder and guided him to a chair beside the shaking pilot. "Relax," he said, "I can assure you no one is going to come here after you, with or without guns."

"Easy for you to say. You didn't see them."

"He's right," Brad said earnestly. "They were hideous. And it wasn't only the guns. What really scared me were the whips."

Stuart looked at him, eyebrows raised. "What whips?"

"That's enough." Howard's quiet voice sliced through their babble. He went to the stairs that led to the upper gardens and climbed them, pausing on the top step. "Ah yes," he murmured as he surveyed the geometric expanse of lawns, trees, and shrubs. He looked back at Kate. "They're at the north garden entrance," he said to her. "Of course, they won't be able to come in unless someone here—" He paused, a question in his eyes. When Kate gave a tiny shake of her head, he nodded in agreement.

"That'll do." He said it quietly, seeming to address the empty air. Howard watched a moment, waiting, listening. "They're gone," he announced to the assembled group.

Brad looked at his clasped hands, gripping them more tightly as a tremor shook them. "Will they be back?"

"Only if you call them."

"Why would we do that?" It was Stuart Casperson.

"Good question."

Stuart frowned at the non-answer, but then, his confidence returning, asked another. "What'd you do just now? Don't tell me you can just say a few words from a mile away and the men who were chasing us run like scared puppies," he said. "The guys I saw wouldn't be afraid of someone like you."

Howard dismissed this with a shrug. "Could be you're right." He turned to the group, "I want to ask our two newcomers a couple of questions and then Kate and I will be available for the rest of the morning if any of you want to talk one-on-one with either of us. We would be more than happy to explain the many options available to you. Feel free to come talk to either or both of us . . . please." He gave a brisk nod to the two men, indicating that they should follow, and then held out a hand to Kate.

Once again those in the little band of onlookers had to shield their eyes at the blinding light that flashed between Kate and Howard, enveloping the two in a glorious radiance as they looked at each other.

Talia blinked. "I wish they wouldn't do that."

"I don't think they can help it." Blossom looked at the couple walking toward the pool. "I think we've just seen the shape and color of love." She caught her lower lip between her teeth, her eyes hooded as she glanced down at her clasped hands.

"I hope you're not sitting there expecting me to send out sparks, old woman," Michael said testily. "Don't think I could manage it." He smirked. "At least not right here with everyone looking."

Blossom laughed. "Oh, Michael," she said, "do be sensible—or just be quiet." But she seemed troubled, almost angry.

Cynthia glanced up sharply at an edge in the old woman's voice she hadn't heard before. Cynthia paused and looked at Blossom more closely. Blossom wasn't old! Not anymore. The woman who looked over at Michael as though she'd like to smack him, was middle-aged, if that. And pretty. Really pretty. Cynthia's eyes narrowed as she looked over at Michael O'Meara. Instead of the scrawny old man who had been with them since they'd arrived, she saw a slight but muscular man who might have been thirty-five talking with Sherwood Prescott, oblivious of both Cynthia's inspection and his wife's glare.

How long had they been this young? Was she the only one who had noticed? "Blossom, how long has this been going on?" she said. "Both you and Michael look great."

Blossom dismissed the compliment with a wave of her hand. "Since we got to the hotel, I think. At least that's when I realized Michael was beginning to remind me of . . . of when we were young." She looked away.

"What's so bad about the two of you looking so wonderful?" Cynthia said gently.

Blossom gave a wry smile. "Nothing, I guess." She got up. "Maybe I'm beginning to look pretty good on the outside, but inside I'm still a scared, foolish old woman worrying herself sick over something she can't do a blamed thing about." Her eyes were suspiciously bright as she looked at the couple by the pool. Howard sat talking to Stuart and Brad while Kate stood beside him, her hand on Howard's shoulder.

"I just had a thought, Blossom," Cynthia said. She touched her face. "How do I look? Am I any different?"

"Goodness child, why would you want to look different?" Blossom roused herself from her introspection and surveyed Cynthia. "No, you're the same good lookin' gal I saw boarding the plane in Chicago. Glad to see you've given up wearing that uniform. Not that it didn't suit you, but you look a whole lot more comfortable in jeans." She smiled. "I have to say, though, you could do without the handkerchief. That hair of yours is far too pretty to cover up."

A shiver swept Cynthia. Her hand went to her head and felt the folded cloth tied about her hair. She knew without looking that the fabric was red with a white design. Slowly she untied the cloth and held the red-and-white kerchief in her hands. Why? Why was she wearing a western bandanna she had last seen in her top dresser drawer? She gave her shoulders a slight shake. No, it couldn't be the same one. Still, it was exactly like the one she kept in her drawer. Why?

Because seeing this piece of cloth, holding it in her hands, made her happy. The thought came to her, unbidden. Rob had given her this bandana, or one like it, had laughed as he tied it about her neck and called her his cowgirl. She'd been eight months pregnant with Tabitha, huge and ungainly and certain she would never be slim again. But Rob had told her how beautiful she was and convinced her there would be a life after pregnancy, a life with a waistline and the ability to touch her toes. And had given her the silly bandanna. Not jewelry or flowers or even a book of poetry, the kind he loved and she pretended to. He'd given her a bandanna. Cynthia held it to her face and breathed in its fragrance, her own fresh, nonallergenic soap.

Rob was beside her. He stood in front of the dresser, its top drawer half opened, his face buried in a red-and-white bandanna. He breathed deep and Cynthia smelled the clean soap smell, and with it, the subtle, indefinable scent of her own body. Rob groaned.

Cynthia reached out to him. "Oh, my love," she whispered, "darling Rob; I'm here." Her outstretched arms half circled his lanky frame, but did not touch him.

Rob stood unmoving, his face buried in the bandanna. Cynthia stayed where she was, feeling the way she did when she found a last, missing puzzle part beneath the card table and put it in place. "Thank you, Lord," she breathed.

Rob raised his head. "Cyn," he said, his voice husky, "Cyn." His eyes glinted with unshed tears, but held a curious tranquility. "I needed you just now, needed you so much I thought I'd die if I had to go on alone. And all of a sudden I have . . . this feeling of peace. Is it from you?"

Cynthia reached out a hand, so close she felt the warmth of his body. "No, darling," she said, "This is God's gift to you— and to me." And in that instant, she knew that, though he could not hear her words, Rob too felt the love that surrounded them. She pressed her hands against her chest. "It's going to be all right, Rob. It's going to be okay."

Rob smoothed the red cloth, then folded it. His hands steady, he replaced it in the top drawer. "Maybe we can keep on going—T and I. I'll try, Cyn." He shut the drawer. "God knows I'll try."

"Are you all right?" Blossom's face mirrored her concern.

Cynthia brushed the hair from her eyes. "Was I gone?"

"Until this moment. You just sort of became misty." Blossom's shrewd gaze assessed her. "You were with your husband, weren't you?"

"How did you know? Has it happened to you?"

"I've been with one of my daughters."

"I wonder—" Cynthia looked at the little group where the two new arrivals, having finished their session with Howard, had joined Michael and Prescott. "Do you think we've all been given the chance to see someone we love who is still on earth?"

"I doubt it. I don't think it happens often, not unless there's a special reason." Blossom looked toward the pool. "But, of course, I may be wrong. There's so much I don't know."

"Why don't you go ask Kate and Howard?" Cynthia said. "I was going to talk to them now that they're free, but I can wait."

Blossom shook her head. "I have enough on my plate at the moment. I don't think I care to find out any more—not just yet."

Cynthia looked at her, troubled, but didn't press it. "Well, if you don't mind then, I have a whole bunch of questions I'd like to ask." She folded the red-and-white cloth and tied it loosely about her neck as she looked at the couple by the pool. "Do you suppose there's a chance I could learn to be like Kate?" she murmured.

Blossom caught her breath at the sudden glow that illuminated the young woman's face. "I think you may find you're more than half way there, my dear," she said gently.

But Cynthia, already bounding up the steps, didn't hear her.

"So that great and wonderful position at Stanley's hotel didn't turn out quite as you thought it would?"

Stuart's eyes narrowed at Michael's mocking tone. "It's your fault they gave us such a bad time. You people sneak off in the middle of the night and leave Brad and me to face the music. Of course everyone thought we were in on it."

Sherwood Prescott interrupted the wrangling. "I'm surprised to hear you say they gave you a bad time. What exactly did they do?"

Brad and Stuart exchanged a glance and for a moment neither spoke. Then Stuart said, "It's not easy to explain. No one beat up on us, if that's what you're asking."

"I think it would have been easier if they had," Brad Nelson put in. "Mostly it was just threats, but they were the kind that make you scared to go to sleep without double-locking the door." The pilot was still wearing his doorman's uniform. Now he loosened his tie and unbuttoned the top button of his shirt, easing the bulge of skin that sagged over his collar.

"Put on a little weight, haven't you?" Michael observed.

Brad ducked his head. "There was stuff like that too. It happened like overnight. One minute I'm looking pretty good and the next I've got an extra ten, fifteen pounds on me." He shifted uncomfortably. "I don't know how it happened, but from what that guy Howard just told us, I think maybe it's some sort of punishment thing."

"Shut up, Brad, nobody's interested in your weight gain," said Stuart. Then he continued more temperately, "You don't need to go into what Howard said. That was just for us." He yawned. "Y'know, I could use a nap. Haven't run that fast or that far since I tried out for the high-school track team. Are the rooms already assigned, or do we pick our own?"

Michael sniffed. "What rooms? You want some shut-eye you'll go find yerself a lounge chair over there like the rest of us."

"Then what's the building back there for?" Stuart pointed in the direction from which he'd come. "Brad and I didn't stick around to check it out, but when we passed by, it sure looked like some kind of hotel."

The men craned to look.

"There is something," Michael said to Prescott. "You see? Over there set back in the trees. Don't know why we didn't notice it before."

Lorraine had been quietly listening. Now she said, "Why don't we go see what it is? We don't have anything else to do."

"Why not?" Michael looked over to where Blossom was sitting. "Come on, woman," he called out, "we're going to check out a building these folks think might be a hotel."

Blossom roused herself and padded over to look where Michael was pointing. "I bet that's exactly what it is," she said.

Michael eyed her. "What makes you so sure? Got inside information?"

"I just think odds are it's some kind of housing," Blossom said mildly. "Now that we've decided to stay I doubt they mean us to keep on sleeping on lawn chairs, no matter how comfortable."

"The logic of the woman never fails to amaze me," Michael observed to the group. "It's positively frightening." He looked at Jeff who was slouched in a nearby chair. "Someone's gonna have to wake that young feller up if we're goin' anywhere. Looks like he nodded off again."

"You do that; I'll get the ladies." Sherwood Prescott started toward the small tables where Beatrice sat drinking coffee and Malvena and Talia were finishing off the last of the

Danish pastry.

"Rise and shine, Jeff," Michael prodded the actor, grinning unrepentantly as Jeff woke with a start and scowled at him. Michael looked about. "Where's the preacher?"

"Here." Fred Hampton hurried up to them, coming from the pebbled path that led toward a small grove of aspen and birch. "Sorry, I was taking a walk," he explained. "I wanted to see what was on the other side of the trees."

"We're going to take a look at that building over there," Michael told him. "Probably a good idea for us to stick together. Sherwood's getting the others."

They headed off. No one bothered to ask Fred Hampton what he'd found on the other side of the birch and aspen grove. And he did not volunteer any further information.

The low, freshly painted stucco building could have been a motel or an apartment house or even a dormitory. The arrow on the sign set in a bed of sunshine yellow and sunset orange-red flowers outside the large, plate glass window announced "Office" and the one on the counter inside said, "Welcome to Selveridge House," but there was no sign of any staff.

"Anyone here?" Prescott's voice rang out. He rapped sharply on the countertop. "Desk?"

The others crowded in behind him.

"Look, there's a sheet of paper under that glass fruit." Beatrice moved the blown-glass apple and picked up the printed note. "Please feel free to use the facilities at Selveridge House," she read. "You will find room assignments listed below. If you have any needs or requests, please use your room phone to call #333 and leave a voice-mail."

"Does anyone besides me recognize a distinct resemblance to *Beauty and the Beast*?" Jeff leaned against the door, his arms folded. He met the stares of the group with a grin. "Not the whole plot line, of course, but you know the part where Beauty wanders around this empty castle and gets whatever she wants? Anybody asked me, I'd say it's a clear case of plagiarism."

"Weren't there singing teacups or something?" Talia said.

"Please!" Sherwood Prescott said, unamused. He turned to Beatrice. "May I see the room assignments?" he asked her. "I'd like to know with whom I'm to room."

Beatrice studied the sheet. "You won't have a roommate," she said. "None of us does. Apparently everyone has his or her own room."

"We do?" Blossom asked, her eyes widening.

Beatrice looked at the paper again. "Oh, right. All except you two, but you're not in Selveridge House."

"Where are we?"

"Rose Cottage, wherever that may be."

"May I?" Prescott held out a hand.

For a moment Beatrice hesitated; then she handed the paper to him. "You need to be the one to tell people which rooms they have?" she said. "Okay, I don't care. I know mine and that's all I care about." She paused, glancing at the numbers on the wall behind the counter. "Humph, no keys, I see. Well, whatever their security system is, I hope it proves adequate." She marched past the counter and disappeared down the far hallway.

Prescott colored. "I certainly don't particularly care about being the one to—" he began, then started again. "It's simply that there are things to be decided—whether we should meet once we've seen our rooms, how we can get in touch with each other, that sort of thing. I've found it's easier if one person chairs the gathering rather than having everyone fend for himself."

"And you'd be that person, naturally," Michael observed.

Prescott's thin nostrils flared; he held out the paper to Michael.

The little man took it and glanced down the sheet. "Ah, here it is. Don't know why that woman couldn't see these directions. Says right here Rose Cottage is in the east garden." Michael gave the paper back to Sherwood Prescott. "You're right—someone's got to organize things. So go ahead; be my guest. If you folks decide on having a meeting, you can call us on that telephone they mentioned." He waved to his wife. "Come on, Blossom. All we have to do is figure out which way's east."

"Thank you," Prescott said, his voice heavy with irony. "I'll post this on the bulletin board," he said to the rest. "I suggest you each write down who is in what room in case you'd like to visit; I also propose we gather back here as soon as we've seen our rooms so that we can talk about what we'd like to do next."

16

BEATRICE JORGENSON STOOD IN THE MIDDLE OF THE WALK-
in closet and examined its contents. What looked like a
beautifully tailored red suit with navy piping hung beside two
skirts, one a forest green, the other a slightly flared blue in a
lighter material, and next to them, three blouses, one white
and two in solid colors. A pair of sensible-looking shoes and a
pair of dress shoes rested side by side on the carpeted floor
below the clothes.

Beatrice reached for the green skirt and held it up. Yes, it
looked exactly right. What a pleasure to have just the sort of
clothes she liked without the bother of shopping for them.
Beatrice looked around for the advertising material she knew
must be left for her to find. Surprising that it wasn't
prominently displayed somewhere in the room. Talk about an
imaginative approach to merchandising! Had to hand it to the
staff that ran this place; except for the fact that the brochures
or catalogues ought to be more readily available, these people
knew a thing or two about marketing.

She went to the dresser and opened a drawer, fingering the neat piles of white underwear. Excellent quality. She would certainly have to congratulate whoever was in charge. Beatrice smiled at herself in the mirror. Might not be a bad place to work. She walked back into the comfortably furnished bedroom and gazing around, saw a door that must lead to the bathroom. Entering the bathroom, she surveyed the white-tiled walls and floor, the shining clean fixtures, the marble counter. Beatrice picked up a vial of ruby-colored oil from the assortment of bottles and lotions on the marble ledge, removed the stopper and sniffed the heavy, fruity smell of her favorite perfume. Yes, she'd definitely consider a position in an organization like this.

She wandered back into the bedroom and saw a blinking message light on the bedside phone. Probably Prescott calling about another of his silly meetings. It could wait. Right now, she was going to take a nice long bath. Beatrice returned to the bathroom where she turned on the faucet in the bathtub and poured a stream of ruby oil into the warm, rushing water.

Lorraine stood in the middle of the sunlit room. She turned in a slow circle, taking in the soft blue carpet, the matching blue coverlet on the queen-sized bed. It was the little touches she liked so much; the pastel tapestry pillows, the hem-stitched white sheets, the flowers—oh, the flowers! Lorraine picked up the little bouquet of violets and lily of the valley on her night table and breathed in its fragrance, then put it down and admired the large vase of pink and blue delphinium on a table before the window. And the view! Lorraine went to the open window and leaned over the windowsill to look out over the rolling hillside to the fields in the distance. No screens. Maybe they didn't need them here.

What else was there? Lorraine crossed to the carved antique wardrobe and opened it, pleased but not surprised to find a soft-gray skirt hanging beside a matching silk blouse and next to them two pair of slacks and two shirts. A comfortable-looking pair of shoes and sandals peeked from a shoe bag hanging from the back of the wardrobe door. She knew without trying them on that they would all fit perfectly. The pleasure she felt at finding the clothes surprised her. How long had it been since she'd been interested in new clothes? How long had it been since she'd been interested in anything?

Thank you, she said. Her hand went to her smooth cheek. Thank you. Not just for the room and the clothes, but for all the excitement of this new life. She thought of the years of gray days, one succeeding another, that had made up so much of her other life. Such a waste. A shiver caught her, eclipsing her pleasure. Where had that thought come from? Had she really wasted her life?

Please. I did what I had to do to survive. I had to protect myself. But fragments of memories came flooding. The crumpled face of a young secretary in response to an acid witticism, the flash of resentment of a colleague whose kindness had been angrily rejected, the shocked hurt of a friend—a former friend—at Lorraine's brusque dismissal of her engagement announcement.

Lorraine was on her knees without knowing how she came there. Please, Lord, forgive my blindness to anything outside myself, my self-pity, and—yes, her breath caught at the acknowledgement—the times I derided or lashed out at the happiness of others because I was so unhappy myself. Lorraine pressed her hands to her face, for the first time since its healing, unmindful of her smooth, unmarked skin. She squeezed her eyes tight shut. Please, don't make me remember. Please.

She bowed her head. The movement caused a ray of the morning sun to touch her shoulder; she felt its warmth spread through her, and with it felt a measure of comfort. Lorraine raised her head. The remembering was over, done—for now. She pressed her eyelids. Would she have to return to these thoughts another time? How could she stand it? Lorraine's breathing slowed. What would be, would be.

She got to her feet, went to the wardrobe, and took the pearl-gray skirt and blouse from their hangers. In spite of her anxiety Lorraine felt a frisson of satisfaction as she touched the supple fabric of the blouse, the light wool texture of the skirt. She'd never owned clothes like these. Lorraine moved to the bathroom with sudden energy. She'd have to step on it if she wanted a quick shower before the meeting.

❦

Fred Hampton rubbed his chin. Dress slacks, a camel blazer, jeans—Fred's expression lightened at the sight of the blue jeans—he'd always relished the informality of jeans but didn't feel comfortable enough wearing them to try it often. A couple of dress shirts, one discreetly muted plaid shirt, and on the tile floor below, a pair of dark-brown loafers and running shoes. How long since he'd gone running? Fred moved the hangers of the slim assortment of clothes, searching, but that was it.

He stepped back, trying not to be disappointed. It was plenty, certainly all he needed for the time being. He should be grateful. Still. He couldn't help wishing for what wasn't there. Maybe they didn't wear that kind of clothing here. After all, not many of his denomination still wore black suits with clerical collars; it was old-fashioned. And yet. He'd hoped to find a black suit included since so much else he'd wanted seemed to turn up. He'd expected it really. When he hadn't discovered a clerical collar with its dickey in the chest of drawers, he'd thought maybe it would be on the hanger with a clerical suit. But there wasn't any suit, only these clothes.

Fred shook himself like a dog coming out of water. Appreciate what you've been given. The slacks were perfectly suitable. Surely he didn't have to advertise the fact he was a clergyman. But was he one? Fred shrank from exploring the thought.

Yes, slacks would be fine. Urbane yet informal. But Fred's hand, as though acting of its own accord, reached for the jeans instead. Well, well. Fred looked at them, a half smile easing the deep lines at the corners of his mouth. He tossed the jeans onto the narrow, neatly made bed and went to look for something in the chest of drawers to wear with them.

Malvena peered around the door at the back of Selveridge House. No one around. She darted outside and ran down the path toward the grove of tall pines at the foot of the hill, not stopping until she had reached their shelter. Malvena smoothed the skirt of her gray-blue cotton dress and shivered. The shadowed air beneath the pines was cool after the sunlit gardens. She walked further into the woods, her steps soundless on the soft, fragrant bed of needles, and craned to see past the tree trunks into the gloom ahead. Where was the stupid man?

"Over here, girl."

Malvena gasped. "You frightened me."

"Yeah? You didn't look scared a minute ago. You looked mad."

"I didn't mean frightened, I meant—" Malvena paused, "I meant surprised." She shrugged as though the discussion was not worth continuing. "You are no longer needed. Why did you call me?"

Delion's eyes narrowed. "Where you get off talking like I'm some piece of dirt? I called you 'cause I called you, that's why." He caught her wrist. "Maybe you should go back to being scared."

Malvena looked at him a long moment. She removed her arm from his grasp and rubbed her wrist. "We should not fight with each other," she said calmly. She made a quick movement with her long-fingered hands. "You were to escort me, but it is no longer necessary, I think. It was a good idea of yours to go see the baby, but now I have what I wanted, and we are here there is no need for you to accompany me."

"Yeah, we're 'here,' but where's here?" Delion eyed her. "You know what they're sayin'? About it being, like, a different world?"

"That is what they say." Malvena smiled, her lips thin.

Delion shook his head. "Never thought Grandma had it right about that heaven stuff. Seems like all the church goin' she did wasn't a waste of time after all." He shoved his hands deep in the pockets of his leather jacket. "Thought I'd like to see her, but then all of a sudden I had this feeling that she might not like some of the things I've done, so . . . so I decided I didn't want to see her just yet."

"What has your grandmother got to do with anything?" Malvena made no attempt to hide her growing impatience. "If you do not tell me what you want, I must leave."

He scowled at the confidence in her tone. "I told you, girl, don't get smart with me." He took a step toward her.

"All right," she said hastily. "But what is this about? I can't stay much longer. They will miss me if I don't get back soon."

194

"Some dudes are after me." It was grudgingly said. "They're not like the ones we were supposed to look for when we boarded the plane. These guys are big trouble, like the guys I hang with in the 'hood. I gotta find someplace to stay, someplace where they can't come find me."

"How many are there?" said Malvena, immediately alert.

"Dunno. More'n two." Delion looked aggrieved. "I didn't expect I'd have to keep on running here, y'know? That there'd be guys from the 'hood. Where are those cops who jumped me in the airport? If they have cops here, how come they don't come take care of the dudes chasin' me?"

"What did happen at the airport?" Malvena said, interested. "What did they do to you when they took you away?"

Delion attempted a nonchalant shrug. "They hauled my ass off to some office and told me I couldn't do any rough stuff here. Acted like I was some grade-school kid." He looked over his shoulder. "Listen, girl, I gotta find a place to stay. You just bring me up to that house you're at, okay?"

"I can't." Malvena took a step away. "It is safe here, and I think I will stay. These people have allowed me to be part of the group, but some of them don't trust me. I see it in their eyes, especially the old woman; she looks at me different than she did before. So I cannot ask them to take you in. It would not be good to remind these people we were together. Besides, they saw how you acted at the airport; I don't think they would let you join them."

"You got all kinds of reasons I shouldn't be here, don't you, girl?" Delion's hands balled into fists, but he shoved them into the pockets of his leather jacket. His tone turned cajoling. "Nobody knows about what we were doing—not if you didn't tell them. I'm just a friend, okay? You take me up there, tell them you found me out here tired and hungry. You just couldn't help yourself and invited me back with you." Delion's tone lost its last trace of belligerence. "Look, the tired and hungry part is for real. I can't remember last time I ate."

She looked at him, surprised. "You mean you're hungry? You haven't been able to find any food? There is food here whenever we need it. It just appears."

"Ain't had nothing since I been on the run."

Malvena frowned, then shrugged. "I still don't understand why these people are chasing you. No one here could have any idea what we were doing."

"I don't know either," Jackson confessed. "Only met one of them. He said he'd been waiting for me, that I should come to a meeting that's been set up with 'the boss.' I get this feeling I'm not going to like gettin' with the boss, and Jackson Delion pays attention to what his gut tells him. So I don't show, just take off. Next thing I know the guy and his friends are on my tail. Haven't been able to shake them." He glanced over his shoulder again. "Hey, girl, let's go."

Malvena didn't look happy at the prospect of having to introduce Delion to the group; but after a moment, she shrugged and headed up the hill. She didn't bother to check whether Jackson Delion was following.

At the sight of Brad Nelson sitting in one of the sunroom's cushioned chairs, Talia paused on the threshold, hesitating as though half inclined to retreat. But at that moment, Brad looked up. "I was just looking for a magazine," she said.

The pilot didn't seem as haggard as when he and Stuart Casperson had come rushing into their midst, but his smile was strained, and his tone when he spoke, tentative. "Don't go. Come in. Please."

Talia stepped into the pleasant room and made her way across the brick floor, maneuvered around a group of flaming geraniums in ceramic containers and a huge, potted ficus tree, and took a seat on the chintz couch near the pilot. Brad relaxed, his smile genuinely pleased.

Talia arranged herself on the cushions. She was used to people wanting her company, used to the fact that men liked being seen with her. She accepted it, usually enjoyed it. And it was always a kick to see the man's reaction when he became aware of her intelligence. It either intrigued a man or scared him silly. Talia smiled. It had been her mind as much as her beauty that had persuaded—her thoughts skidded to a stop. Talia looked at the ring on her left hand. Who had given her this? She could remember her pleasure when she'd slipped it on her finger; remembered thinking its emerald-cut was just the shape she'd have chosen herself. But who was the man who held out the small, velvet-covered box?

"Don't you think they will?"

Talia started, aware that Brad Nelson had asked his question twice. "Sorry. Who will what?"

"I said it looks like this guy Howard and his, ah, companion Kate know pretty well what's going on here," Brad repeated patiently. "Don't you think they'd let us know if someone managed to get through the gates?"

"What gates? There weren't any gates where we came in."

"Over in that direction," Brad pointed at the gardens beyond the floor-to-ceiling windows. "There's a brick wall around this place with a couple of humongous iron gates that opened just long enough for Stuart and me to run through." His face reflected the relief he'd felt then, but the worried look returned. "The wall wasn't very high. You suppose there're wires or something on top that will keep them from climbing over?"

"I haven't the faintest idea." Talia stretched her long legs in front of her and crossed her ankles. What a bore. After begging her to come join him, the least Brad Nelson could have done was initiate a reasonably intelligent conversation. Instead he was whining about whether their security was everything it should be. Where was the confident pilot she'd seen board their plane in Chicago? Who would have guessed that beneath that calm, assured facade lived a fat, scared little man? Good thing she didn't have that problem. How nice that her intelligence was as much a part of her as her beauty.

Talia sat up abruptly. Where had that thought come from? Thank goodness it had been just a thought; wouldn't do to say something like that. She picked up a magazine, but another thought came like an unwelcome knock at the door. Was she really as self-absorbed and pretentious as that thought would have sounded?

Surely not. Maybe she was a little conceited. She'd always known she was smart—let's face it, in some areas brilliant. But she'd worked hard to hone that brilliance; could she be faulted for acknowledging it? And after all, she wasn't really vain. Sure she knew she was beautiful—how could she not? But she'd never dwelt on her looks. Not a lot, at least. What else? Some people thought her cold, she knew that, but she wasn't really. What people perceived as coolness was simply the result of a natural reserve and her preoccupation with a crowded, busy life. No, all in all, she didn't have a lot to worry about or apologize for. Maybe there hadn't been a lot of time for anything or anyone not on her agenda, but honestly how could she have behaved differently? She couldn't. Not without giving up what she'd worked so hard to accomplish.

Talia tossed aside her magazine and picked up another from the neat pile on the low glass table. She opened it and riffled the pages, not hearing Brad's continued nervous chatter. Though her head bent low over the magazine, Talia did not read; the black words on the glossy pages might as well have been hieroglyphics. As she sat hunched on the chintz sofa, Talia was filled with a growing certainty that perhaps her quick perusal and excuse of her faults hadn't been quite enough, that more might be required of her.

Nonsense. Talia sat up straight, the magazine slipping to her lap. What good was it to agonize over mistakes she might have made in her life on earth? The memory of that life had already dimmed. It had taken a while, but now she accepted the fact that she was beginning a new life. Surely that was enough. Talia gave herself a little shake and reopened her magazine. But she found, despite her determination, she couldn't give it her full attention, couldn't push aside the nagging feeling that sometime soon she would be expected to face things she'd rather not, to delve into places she didn't particularly want to go. She felt the way she did when an important exam was in the offing. But with a sickening difference. This wasn't something she could study for.

"All right woman, tell me what's on that devious mind of yours." Michael O'Meara crossed his arms and leaned against the wall. He watched his wife dust her face with a large, peach-colored powder puff. How long had it been since he'd seen her sit at a dressing table? When they'd first married, he'd enjoyed witnessing Blossom's beauty regimen, enjoyed watching her fuss with creams and unguents and perfumes. Then the children came, and it had been a dab of lipstick or nothing. He'd forgotten how enthralling he'd found Blossom's mysterious machinations.

"Y'know, that looks mighty like the dressing table you had when we got married," he said.

Blossom gave the table's floor-length swiss-eyelet skirt a tweak and reached for a jar. "It is. At least it's a twin of the one I had then. There are several things in Rose Cottage that are like the ones we had in the old times, haven't you noticed? The books in the sitting room are the ones we read when we were first married, and the little inlaid table is exactly like the one we had in the walk-up apartment." She unscrewed the jar's cap and dabbed a finger at the cream inside. "What makes you think I have something on my mind?" she said casually. Blossom looked up and met Michael's bright blue eyes in the mirror, then lowered hers and became busy with the little jar.

"It was seeing Dulcy," she said. "She's desperately unhappy."

"Isn't she always? Desperately unhappy or else walking on air. The girl doesn't know the meaning of moderation. Not that I wouldn't like to talk about Dulcy's problems, but that's not what I meant when I asked what was on your mind." Michael did not shift his gaze. "What else is worrying you, love?" he said quietly.

Blossom bit her lip. "I'm scared," she said finally. "Scared about what's coming. I'm terrified we didn't live the life we should have, didn't make the right decisions."

Michael shook his head, his eyes for once without a hint of ironic humor. "Maybe you're worried some about the things you've done, but that's not why you've got yourself in a swivet. It's me you're scared about, isn't it?"

Blossom's face crumpled. She turned away and hid her face in her hands. She cried silently at first; then small, keening sounds emerged and grew until her breath came in gasping sobs that shook her whole body. Michael stayed propped against the wall. His jaw clenched and his muscles in his folded arms twitched with the effort it took to resist comforting his wife, but he remained where he was.

The shuddering sobs diminished, then stopped. Blossom grabbed a tissue from the box on the dressing table, wiped her streaming eyes and blew her nose. "I didn't think people would blow their noses here," she said without looking at Michael.

"Maybe it's different in heaven."

"Or not."

"Or not," he agreed.

"I couldn't bear it if we weren't together," Blossom said, her voice low. "I can't even stand to even think about it." Her lips pressed together thin and fierce. "Anything, anything would be better than not being together."

"We may not have a choice."

"God wouldn't let it happen," said Blossom, but she didn't sound certain.

"Was I so bad?" Michael said helplessly. He went to the wing-backed chair by the bed and flung himself into it. Then he slid to the front edge of the chair and, elbow propped on a knee and chin resting in his hand, he regarded the patterned carpet. "I know I've got a tongue I should have learned to mind by now," he said. "And I know I'm a grouch. If it wasn't for you, none of your lady friends would give me the time of day." Michael's gaze flicked to her, then back to the carpet. "But I did the best I could. For you and the kids. Tried to shoot straight, on the job and off. I think anyone at the shop would tell you I'm a man of my word."

"I know that," Blossom protested. Her face softened in a smile. "I've always known it. Why do you think I've stood your nonsense all these years, you old rogue?"

But Michael did not look at her or answer her smile. "You're worried I haven't been good enough, and maybe you're right," he said, his voice heavy. A frown creased his forehead.

"But y'know since we've come here, when I'm talkin' to God and tellin' him about my day, it seems easier, more uncomplicated. I thought maybe it meant I hadn't been so far off on the things I was supposed to be learning when I was livin' my life on earth."

Blossom's eyes widened. "You're talking about praying? You, Michael?"

"Sure. I've always talked to him, woman," he looked at her, his surprise as apparent as hers. "I know it's not something we discussed; we never did talk about things like that. But I've always prayed."

"When?"

"Shavin' was a good time for me." Michael didn't seem bothered by Blossom's obvious skepticism. "Lookin' at myself in the mirror brought a lot of things to mind, some I'd just as soon have left alone, but figured I'd best think about 'em. And then most times I sort of reviewed the day with him before I fell asleep. 'Cept after we made love," he added with a grin. "I never could stay awake long enough after that."

"I never knew," Blossom said, a catch in her voice.

"Don't know why you're so surprised. I figured you were doing the same thing." He looked at her closely. "Weren't you?"

Blossom moved uncomfortably. She realigned a perfume bottle so that it matched the row of little jars. "Of course I prayed. I always prayed when we went to church. And most times I said the Our Father at bedtime and then when something awful happened ... like Danny's accident."

"Come on, you were always thankin' God for this and that," Michael told her. "What are you so worried about?"

"Hearing you say you talked with him, like you were discussing things—" Blossom paused. "Michael, I didn't really talk to God when I prayed. Even in church, so many times when I was saying the words I was thinking about, oh, other things. I'd find myself wondering whether I set the oven temperature too high for the roast, or I'd catch sight of Mary's skirt and be wondering whether I'd ever be able to get the grass stains out." She gave an impatient wave of her hand. "Sure, I said 'thank God'; everybody does. But it was more of an expression than anything else." The fear rising within her shone in Blossom's eyes. "Oh, Michael," she whispered, "Oh, Michael, maybe I'm the one in trouble."

17

"WHO *is* THAT MAN? AND HOW DID HE GET IN HERE?" Beatrice Jorgenson, at the far end of the table, made no effort to lower her voice.

"That's right, you missed the little episode at the London airport, didn't you?" said Stuart Casperson. "Name's Delion; he was with Malvena on the plane. Ambled in with her just now and says he wants to stay here. The guy's got balls, you have to give him that."

Jackson Delion, who was stuffing a gargantuan wedge of pizza into his mouth, gave no indication he'd heard the exchange. He reached for the beer mug before him with an easy grace, took a slurp to wash down the pizza and wiped his mouth with the back of his hand.

"Disgusting." Beatrice got up. "If you'll excuse me, I find I'm not particularly hungry." She did not flounce from the dining room, for Beatrice Jorgenson did not flounce; but she left with a studied decision that gave the general impression of flouncing.

"What's with her?" Delion set down his mug.

"Careful, you'll crack the glass," Malvena hissed. She looked around anxiously at the five diners who remained. "My friend is very hungry," she said. "You see he has not had anything to eat since, since—"

"Since some dudes started chasing me," Delion finished for her.

"And exactly why are these 'dudes' chasing you?" Stuart asked him. "Or is it something we really don't want to know?" He looked around and raised an eyebrow at Fred on his right and Lorraine on his other side. He tried to catch Talia's eye across the table, but she sat, toying with her salad, seemingly as oblivious of her surroundings as Jeff Edwards who sat beside her examining his eggroll with half-closed eyes.

"Dunno." Jackson Delion dismissed him, taking another piece of pizza. "Hey, who's in charge here?" he asked the table in general. "Who do I ask about signing in and getting a room? That place of Malvena's is just about big enough for her and that's if she don't turn around too fast."

"I don't know who is in charge," Lorraine said thoughtfully. "There doesn't seem to be anyone at Selveridge House but us. I guess you could say Mr. Prescott is the group's leader—sort of. You could ask him."

"Prescott?" said Stuart. "Now that's interesting. Did the rest of you elect him el supremo while I wasn't looking?"

"By the way, where is Mr. Prescott?" Lorraine continued, ignoring Stuart. "Has anyone seen him lately?"

"I haven't." It was Fred Hampton.

Talia roused herself. "Me neither. Come to think of it, I haven't seen him since the meeting last night."

Lorraine frowned. "And what about the others? Where is Brad Nelson?"

"He was on the sun porch with me a while ago," said Talia, "and just before lunch I saw Blossom and Michael walking near the woods, but what about Cynthia? She didn't come with us to Selveridge House, did she? Funny none of us noticed until now that she hasn't been around since she went to talk to Kate and Howard."

This was met with blank looks.

"How about that? Our little group has dwindled." Stuart Casperson did not sound displeased.

"Someone wants me?" Sherwood Prescott stood in the doorway of the dining room. Cheeks unshaven, hair tousled, Prescott was as unkempt as anyone of the group had ever seen him.

Fred Hampton half rose from his chair. "Are you all right, Sherwood?"

Sherwood Prescott brushed aside Hampton's concern. "Of course. Well, what is it? Who needs me?"

"Says he's all right, but it sure looks to me like he has been pulled through a knot-hole backwards," Stuart commented.

Prescott stared at Stuart Casperson. His eyes contained something more than puzzled consternation. Fred Hampton, who was watching him, wondered briefly whether it might be fear, but then dismissed the thought as ridiculous.

Prescott pressed his lips together. His gaze flicked over the rest and stopped when he got to Delion.

"Jackson Delion," Delion supplied, waving a nonchalant finger in Prescott's direction.

Prescott gave him a short nod, then grasped the back of the nearest chair and eased himself into it.

"You are hurt," Lorraine said quickly.

"I had a … an accident last night," Prescott acknowledged. But that was all he seemed willing to say about it. "Now that I'm here I might as well have something to eat." He helped

207

himself from the salad bowl in the center of the table. "Anyone going to tell me why I was called?"

"Who said anything about calling?" Delion leaned back in his chair. "I was asking these people about a room here and this lady," he nodded to Lorraine, "she said you were in charge and I should ask you."

Prescott nodded again. "That's how it seems to work here. If a person wants to speak to you, either he's right there with you or else you get a kind of mental bulletin."

"Yes," Malvena said. "When I got the message from my friend here, I could hear him talking, but there was no phone."

"Why don't you check the foyer," Sherwood Prescott said to Delion, "There are spindles behind the desk that designate the available rooms. Unless I miss my guess, you'll find your name on one of them." He gave a tired sigh. "But I'm not in charge here; far from it. I only wish I knew who was." He pushed some salad on his fork with a piece of bread and began to eat.

"Come on, Prescott, what's the big mystery?" Stuart took a piece of pie from the dessert tray. "Why are you sitting there looking like Brad would if someone told him there weren't going to be any more free lunches?"

Sherwood Prescott simply looked at Stuart Casperson. "You really don't remember?" he said finally.

A brief moment of recollection seemed to lurk behind Stuart Casperson's eyes; then he shook his head and laughed. "I don't know what you're talking about. Right now all I'm remembering is how I used to love my Aunt Maggie's pecan pie." He took another bite and smacked his lips. "And y'know, this is just as good. Matter of fact, if I didn't know better, I'd swear it is Aunt Maggie's."

Sherwood Prescott turned his attention to the others. "I'm beginning to feel we made a mistake when we took off by ourselves."

There was a brief silence, and then Lorraine said, "What do you mean 'mistake'?"

"During our meeting with them at the airport, Kate and Howard were pretty clear about the fact that they were there to help us, but we elected to take off on our own. Then when we were camped out and wanted to see them, they came and offered again. It was as though they'd been waiting in the wings for us to ask them, that they were anxious to—I don't know—tell us things, take us somewhere. Anyway, they gave us every chance to take advantage of what they had to offer. But Cynthia was the only one to take them up on it. After Howard told us we'd find food and shelter if we stayed in the area, that's all we were interested in. I know I for one didn't give them another thought; I even forgot that they were up by the pool talking to Cynthia."

"And now they've gone," Fred Hampton said quietly, "and Cynthia with them."

"They didn't go; we're the ones who left," Prescott reminded him.

"We could ask them back," said Talia. "Remember how we did it? We just thought about wanting to talk to them." Her lovely forehead creased with concentration. She looked at the door expectantly. "I guess not."

"What's so bad about this place?" Jackson Delion took the last piece of pizza from the platter. "I don't know where you think these Kate and Howard people were going to take you, but I don't see it gettin' much better than this."

"Nobody asked your opinion," Stuart snapped. He turned to Prescott. "So what if we didn't take them up on their basket-weaving classes? They're going to give us a bad report card?"

"The man's got an attitude," Jackson Delion said as though to himself. His silky tones belied the sparks that ignited his black eyes as he stared at Stuart. He put his hands on the edge of the table. "Y'know, I don't like guys with attitudes. Especially guys who dis me."

Stuart's glance was cool. "You're here only because we let Malvena bring you in. The jury's out on whether you stay, so if I were you I'd keep my mouth shut."

"Yeah, but I'm not you, right?" Delion pushed himself from the table and rose to his feet. He was not a tall man, but as he leaned toward Stuart, lightly balanced on the balls of his feet, his shoulders slightly hunched forward, Delion projected a panther-like menace that made him seem larger than he was. "Looks like I'm going to have to teach you a lesson, you goddamn moth—" Jackson Delion stopped, his eyes bulging. He clenched his jaws, his lips widening in a rictus of pain that showed a bite of half-eaten pizza between his teeth. Slowly the spasm lessened, then passed. Delion took an unsteady step back and slumped into his chair. He gave a tentative chew, his eyes closed, then another and swallowed. He opened his eyes. "Who did that?" It was a whisper. Delion's glance darted around the table. "One of you guys do that?"

For a moment nobody answered.

"I don't think that particular kind of talk is allowed," Prescott said with the ghost of a smile. "Not here. This is a protected place; I think if you elect to stay at Selveridge House, a certain level of behavior is expected while you're here."

"Somebody shoulda told me." Delion took another experimental swallow.

"We didn't know," Lorraine said, her eyes still wide.

Talia giggled. She coughed and covered her mouth, but another giggle escaped. "I'm sorry," she said, "but he looked so surprised, and then the rest of you—it was like watching the Three Stooges. You were all thinking about things you've done and wondering if you'd be zapped the way he was." She regarded them. "Malvena looked sort of pleased when it happened, but then she thought of something that made her look as though she wanted to jump out of the window and keep on going. And Stuart, I thought you were going to get there ahead of her." Talia's burble erupted in a cascade of helpless laughter.

"Nice we're providing you with so much amusement, little Ms. Perfection," Stuart snarled.

"How could she know what we were thinking?" asked Lorraine.

"I didn't exactly," Talia said defensively. "I mean I didn't know the actual words or anything, just ideas, emotions. It was right there on your faces."

Lorraine's hand rose to her new, swept-back hairdo, relief replacing her momentary discomposure. "Of course. It's no big deal. It's pretty obvious how a person feels."

"Look! Out there!" Fred Hampton half rose from his chair and pointed out the window. Those at the table followed his gaze, except for Stuart, who nudged Lorraine and whispered, "Get a load of the reverend's jeans; think he's making a fashion statement?"

But Lorraine wasn't paying attention. Like the rest, she was staring at the man running across the smooth lawn. Hampton had reached the french doors and opened them as Brad Nelson staggered across the patio. The pilot stumbled passed Hampton into the dining room, dripping water on the tile floor and the carpet beyond it. He ran a shaking hand over his wet hair. "Michael and Blossom took a boat out on the lake; I saw it go down," he gasped. "I went out on the dock but I fell in—"

"Where?" Sherwood Prescott was at the pilot's side, grasping his arm. "Show us where."

The pilot cowered, seemed unwilling to leave the safety of Selveridge House. "Out there," he flicked a thumb over his shoulder, "past the trees."

Prescott turned him around firmly. "Take us there."

"But they're in the middle of the pond," Brad objected, "and the only other boat at the dock had . . ." he shuddered, "awful stuff in the bottom."

Jackson Delion took Brad's other arm. "Let's go," he growled.

Between them, Prescott and Delion half dragged, half carried the protesting pilot onto the patio and down the sloping lawn. They were followed by Fred, Stuart, and the women. Only Jeff Edwards remained seated at the table, his vacant eyes registering no interest or emotion as he watched the others leave. He reached for another eggroll, nibbled, then settled back in his chair, a secret, dreamy smile on his face.

Willows leaned over the edge of the pond, dripping leafy bows over the still water. A wooden dock jutted out into it, the upward-tilted, broken board at the end testifying to Brad's recent immersion. A rowboat rested in the shallows beside the dock, the weedy spikes that grew from the boat's rotten decking almost obscuring the wooden paddles.

"Where were they when they went down?" Prescott asked the pilot.

But Brad was staring at the boat beside the dock. "That didn't have weeds in it before," he said uncertainly. He took a few tentative steps and peered into the boat. "It is different. It had . . ." he gulped, ". . . snakes in it before. Big ones."

"Shit," said Delion, "means there're more snakes around." He moved back from the water's edge. "Maybe in there."

212

"Sure, the boat had snakes in it, Brad," Stuart gave the pilot a sardonic grin. "And by the time you ran up to the house, they'd turned into four-foot weeds."

Prescott had his shirt off and was unbelting his trousers. "There is no time here, remember?" he grunted. "Not as we knew it." He kicked off his shoes and slipped off his neatly pressed slacks.

"What is the man doing?" The acerbic tones came from behind them.

The little group whipped about. Michael O'Meara stood on the sloping bank, uncharacteristically neat in khaki pants and a navy check golf shirt. Michael surveyed them, arms crossed, hands tucked beneath his armpits. "This place has enough clothes to stock a bloody department store. If the man must go for a swim, couldn't he could find a bathing suit?" he asked.

Sherwood Prescott hastily turned his back on those present, scrambled into the slacks he'd kicked aside and pulled on his golf shirt. "All right, Michael," he said, looking over his shoulder as he tucked the shirt in his pants. "Apparently the boat didn't sink. Was there ever a boat in the first place?"

"Oh, yes, we went for a boat ride. Saw Brad hollering at us from the shore, but we couldn't figure out what he was yelling. Thought we were sinking, did he?"

They all turned to Brad, who rubbed his nose and looked at the ground. "I swear it sank," he mumbled. "Everything was covered with mist, but I could see clearly enough that the bow dipped down and the boat just . . . sank."

"So you went to get help and everyone came running. Appreciate the thought, lad, even if we didn't need it."

"Where's Blossom?" Lorraine asked him.

A shadow crossed Michael's face. "Ah, that's a question, isn't it?" He uncrossed his arms, but seemed not to know what

213

to do with his hands and tucked them beneath his armpits again. "But wherever she is and what she's doing are Blossom's business, aren't they? And maybe a bit of mine." Distress flickered in his eyes, but then his chin came up and he said, "In any case, it's certainly not yours." He gave one of his cocky grins. "Hope it's not past lunchtime, folks; I could use a sandwich." And he turned on his heel and marched toward Selveridge House.

There was nothing for the little group to do but follow. After another searching glance over the serene pond, Sherwood Prescott strode up the hill, quickly passing the lagging stragglers. Last to come was Brad Nelson, who had taken a detour to peer into the weed-clogged boat before hurrying to fall into step with Talia.

"I saw their boat go down," he whispered to her. "I really did."

"A lot of things that happen here aren't exactly as they seem," Talia said. "Matter of fact, some are pretty weird when you think of them, though they seem perfectly reasonable at the time. Remember when we checked into the hotel in the city and then found ourselves in the country? Looking back, the whole situation at the hotel was bizarre, but I can't recall that it seemed out of the ordinary to any of us."

"Yeah," Brad sounded wistful. "That place wasn't so bad, except for that bastard Stanley. The food was really good, and I haven't been that thin in years."

Talia eyed his bulging jacket. "Why do you suppose it has all come back?"

"The fat?" Brad sighed. "I think maybe I'm being punished." He gave an embarrassed grin. "I mean it. I've wondered if I'm headed for hell. I never gave it a lot of thought, but lately I've been wondering what hell is like ... if maybe it's a place where you have to join some dieters' club where they keep an eye on everything you eat."

Talia gave a snort of laughter but quickly suppressed it. "Poor Brad," she said, her tone affectionate, "I bet you haven't done such a lot of terrible things in your life. And surely a person has to do more than gain a few extra pounds to end up in hell. If there is any such place."

"Oh, I don't think being fat has anything to do with it," Brad said seriously. "Sure, I've been overweight most of the time, but it's not like food was on my mind all the time like it is here. And you're right—I haven't done anything so terrible, that is, if you don't count falling behind on my ex-wife's alimony a few times or loaning my crazy brother Jerry money I'd set aside for the twins' college." He blew out a long breath, puffing out his plump cheeks. "I'm so sorry about that. If only I could set it right." He shook his head and then continued, regret softening his already quiet voice, "but you see, that's the thing. When Howard talked to me and Stuart, he told us you can't change what you've done during your natural life. And anyway, what you've done isn't the only thing that counts; it's what you've wanted to do, what you would have done if you'd had the chance. All those things have become a part of you . . . they're still with you here." They had reached Selveridge House, but Brad hung back and somehow Talia could not bring herself to leave the pilot as he struggled to finish his halting explanation.

"Howard told us we were going to have to obey certain rules as long as we were on the grounds here, that breaking them carried certain consequences."

"So that's what happened to Malvena's friend," said Talia. "I wondered." She told him about the painful aftermath of Jackson Delion's profanity.

"I'm not surprised," Brad's voice was glum. "He'd better watch it. We all should. I'm not about to do anything that

215

would make them toss me out of here. There are guys with guns and whips outside the gates just waiting to have at us."

"What guys?"

"Oh," Brad looked stricken. "Stuart doesn't want me to say anything about them."

"Never mind Stuart. Tell me."

But he wouldn't. Not even to keep the beautiful Talia on the terrace with him. Brad made a half-hearted attempt to take her arm; but when Talia shrugged him off and brushed past, the pilot sighed and tagged along behind her, looking like a puppy who had been deprived of a particularly appealing bone.

Beatrice opened her door and stepped onto the small flagstone patio outside her room. She eyed the low-slung canvas chair beside the knee-high rattan table. The chair looked as though it would be difficult to get out of, but then Beatrice remembered that she didn't have any trouble getting in and out of chairs and couches these days. She moved to the edge of the patio and looked out over the manicured lawn, the gardens and reflecting pool in the distance. Very nice. Though she'd seen none in evidence, there must be an army of gardeners somewhere around. Beatrice turned and saw in place of the canvas chair one with invitingly soft, flowered cushions; the table was different too, higher and with a laminated wood top. On the table sat a lap top computer, a pen, and a pad of paper. Well! You had to like the way they did things here.

Beatrice arranged herself in the chair. Yes, it was as comfortable as it looked. She turned on the computer and suddenly felt a vague unease. Strange, she wasn't quite sure what she wanted to do. Read her messages; that's what she always did first. But there were no messages. Beatrice stared at the blank, blue screen. Then, ignoring the wave of panic that swept her, she placed her fingers lightly on the keys and typed.

"Who am I? What have I loved?"

Why had she typed that? What possible reason—

The screen before her shimmered; a picture took shape, a picture of a girl and a boy on a hot summer day.

The girl watched the boy swing out over a muddy river, clinging tight to an oversized inner tube.

Beatrice sucked in her breath. It was she and Tommy Cravits. It was ten-year-old Beatrice.

"Get out of the way, Shortstuff," Tommy called out.

"Don't call me that, you booger" the girl yelled at Tommy. "And give me a turn. It's my turn now."

Beatrice sat, unable to move, her fingers curved above the computer. She didn't want to look, didn't want to remember.

"Come on, jump off," Beatrice's ten-year-old self shouted. She swung an ineffective slap at Tommy, but he ducked away.

"Make me, Shortstuff," the boy said, grinning. He took one hand off the tire and waved at her.

The girl reached out to grab his hand, but missed. "Booger, booger, booger," she yelled, her face red.

"No," Beatrice screamed at the computer screen. "Don't! Don't let it happen!"

But it did. The tire swung out over the water and back again, and this time the girl was ready. As the tire swooped low over the grass, she caught at the boy's open hand and tugged hard. He yanked his hand free, but in doing so his legs jerked from the tire. The tire bobbled away, spinning. Tommy hung on with one hand, but as the tire reached its apex out over the water, his grip loosened, and he slipped and fell like a great, crooked-legged crab. Tommy splashed into the muddy water, submerged, broke the surface, and submerged again.

Though Beatrice shut her eyes, she saw it all. The picture on the screen continued in miniature on the back of her eyelids, and Beatrice saw the girl's frightened face, the round O of her gasping mouth. Saw the girl run to the steep bank and peer into the rushing water, saw her clamber to her feet and back away, go back to take one more frightened look at the empty river. Saw the girl turn and run.

"You didn't go call for help, did you? You never told anyone you were there. You pretended it never happened." At first Beatrice thought it was Kate standing at the edge of the little patio. But Kate was taller, slimmer, and rather than Kate's customary expression of kindly concern, this woman looked, well, she looked pissed.

18

"IT WOULDN'T HAVE DONE ANY GOOD. THEY FOUND Tommy—his body—a mile down the river. They'd never have gotten to him in time." Beatrice tried to steady her voice. "I didn't mean to leave—I was only ten—"

"I know," said the woman. "You were a child; you didn't fully realize what you were doing. But you chose not to go look for your friend, and you chose not to look at the consequences of your momentary spite and anger. Did the pattern begin there?"

"I don't know what you're talking about."

"Oh, come on, Beatrice; you're not stupid. It was natural that you were terrified you'd be blamed, but afterward your relief at not being found out changed to something else, didn't it? You came to believe that if no one found out about the things you'd done, they didn't matter. You began to think that if you toughed it out and played it close to the vest, you could get away with just about anything." The woman crossed her arms and regarded Beatrice. "And it worked. That ability to compartmentalize made you extremely successful, but it caused all sorts of problems in your personal relationships, didn't it? You never learned to own up to what you'd done, not even to yourself, certainly not to God."

Beatrice made an effort to regain her composure. "What is this? An adaptation of Dickens with you as the ghost of Christmas Past?" The words were derisive, but she couldn't quite conceal her apprehension.

"I'm probably giving you too much, too soon. Why don't we let you go back and try something else." The woman sat down in the chair opposite Beatrice, a chair that had not been there a moment before and took up almost every available inch of the deck on the other side of the small table. "I'm Lexia, by the way. You've been assigned to me," she said, adding with a slightly rueful grin, "and I have a disconcerting feeling I know the reason why."

"I don't want to see anything more," Beatrice said quickly. "You can't make me."

"True. *I* can't make you do a thing; I'm just along for the ride. Nevertheless, you'll see what you must. It's time you took a look at the things you've spent a lifetime hiding from."

"You can't mean I'm going to have to review every last thing I did in my life?" Beatrice asked, aghast.

"I told you that you weren't stupid," Lexia said, approving. "But no, not everything, only those you allowed to become a part of the adult you, the things you welcomed into both your business and personal life."

"Oh, business! Well, certainly I made some mistakes there, but who doesn't? There were times when I had to make decisions that hurt people, but you know the old saying, you've got to break some eggs to make an omelet."

Lexia rolled her eyes but said only, "We're not talking about making tough, necessary business decisions. We're

220

talking about how you felt when you made them, or rather your lack of feeling. Did you ever think of anyone but yourself? Matter of fact, Beatrice, did you think of anything in any context other than how it would affect you?"

"I didn't agonize over my decisions, if that's what you're looking for." Beatrice sat straighter. "It's not my style, and besides a good businessperson can't, not and still function."

"I'm talking about how you enjoyed your power to hurt." Lexia pointed to the screen. "Here—take a look."

"No!" Beatrice protested, but a picture had already appeared on the blue screen, and despite her reluctance Beatrice found herself leaning forward.

A small woman in a neatly pressed tan uniform pushed a cleaning cart down a long, carpeted hall. She tapped on the hotel room door, listened, and on hearing no reply, unlocked the door and entered.

"What do you think you're doing?"

The question was an explosion in the quiet room, rocking the dark woman back with the force of a physical blow. "Oh, I am so sorry," she gasped, "I did not hear—"

"Of course, you're sorry," Beatrice Jorgenson snapped, "but not as sorry as you're going to be. This was just what I talked about at the employee seminar this morning. You're supposed to wait for a reply a full twenty seconds before coming in; I was counting, and I'd just gotten to ten." She glared at the woman, arms akimbo.

"I did wait after I knocked . . . I did." Near tears, the woman twisted the neat white apron about her waist. "I listen. I hear nothing."

Beatrice motioned her away with the flick of a hand. "Go tell the office I said you were to pick up your check. You're fired."

"Oh, please," the woman's dark eyes beseeched her, "I need this job. My daughter is sick."

"Spare me; that one went out with twirling mustaches. If your job was so important, you'd have done it the way you were supposed to." Beatrice turned away, and the picture on the screen faded.

"Yes, I remember that one," Beatrice said. She lifted her chin defiantly. "Matter of fact, I did that particular firing on purpose. It sent a message that by the end of the day had reached everyone on staff. And let me tell you, it worked. In the next few weeks, the number of guest complaints at that hotel dropped like a rock."

"Nice try. You fired that woman because you were in a filthy mood. You'd just received a message from your daughter's school asking for a meeting about her grades, and you were ticked. You wanted to lash out and make someone else as miserable as you were, more miserable if you could manage it."

Beatrice opened her mouth, then closed it.

"What's more, you enjoyed the whole thing. You get a real gut-level rush from having that much power over someone, don't you?" Lexia raised an eyebrow. "This wasn't an isolated incident. You practically raised the firing of low-level workers to an art form. You enjoy seeing them quake, just love that look of fear when they realize who you are."

"Oh, for pity's sake, you're making me sound like Dracula just because I won't stand for sloppy work. After all, my responsibility is to the hotels, not to incompetent employees."

Lexia shrugged. "All right, you can see for yourself. But if we have to watch every time you got a charge out of firing people for inconsequential reasons I'm going to miss my dinner."

"Who are you?" Beatrice eyed her distrustfully. "You're too cranky to be an angel."

An odd expression crossed Lexia's face. "Never mind who I am; you have other things to worry about."

Beatrice closed the computer's lid. "You said you can't make me do anything I don't want to. Well, I don't choose to watch any more."

"You are a caution, Ms. Beatrice." Lexia sounded amused. "You just don't bend at all, do you? Poor Christy. I'm a pretty tough bird, but the thought of having you for a mother gives me the shivers." Her expression softened. "Christy's a good kid, you know. She has been having a rough time lately."

"Well, of course, she's a good kid. I never said she wasn't. Scatter-brained, thoughtless, but if she put her mind to it and listened to advice once in a while, if she dropped a few pounds—" Beatrice shrank back into her chair at Lexia's look. "What? What did I say?"

The fire left the other woman's eyes. "It's what you didn't say—or ask." She considered Beatrice a moment. "Didn't you ever realize how much Christy needed your approval? Didn't you ever consider what a few words of praise might have done for her?"

"Why should I praise laziness and petulance? I gave the girl everything she could want; she had chances I never did, but she has blown them all. I've already spent a fortune on three schools in four years and heaven knows when she'll get her high-school diploma. And while we're talking about praise, what about me? Do I get any consideration for what I accomplished while being saddled with a kid all the time I was working fourteen-hour days? It's like running a race while carrying a dead weight." She looked aggrieved. "Besides, my childhood wasn't all that great either."

"Yes, you had reason to be a nasty little girl. But the things you did as that child weren't imputed to you; the things you did as a nasty adult were."

Beatrice struggled to control her breathing. "I don't see why you're trying to make such a thing of a few times when perhaps I let my temper get the better of me."

"The more you grew to enjoy those episodes, the more they became a part of you. How essential a part of you remains to be seen." Lexia reached over and opened the computer again. "You're right; I can't make you look at your past, Beatrice; but it's there waiting for you and will remain at the edge of your consciousness until you face it. If you take my advice, you'll sit here and get it over with."

Sherwood Prescott looked out over the lush, green valley to the aquamarine sea in the distance. Two macaws swooped low over the treetops, their scarlet brilliance flashing against the green jungle; the melodious trill of an unseen bird echoed against the steep, leafy slopes. Did the others have rooms that looked out over this magnificent scene? Prescott tried to peer beyond the white stucco walls that angled out the sides of his deck, but its clever design prevented him from seeing anything but what looked like a bush of purple and crimson bougainvillea beneath the next deck and the lush tangle of green ferns immediately below his.

He let out a long sigh and uttered a silent thanks for this respite, however brief it might be. What a contrast between this scene and last night's. A chill shook Prescott's large frame. Please, God, not another night like the last.

Why had he found himself out there in the darkness anyway? What possible connection could there be between him and what he'd witnessed? Surely he wasn't anything like the creatures in the caves. Prescott felt the palms of his hands sweat. If he were like them, would he be here looking at this beauty right now? The thought made him feel better. Yes, this is where he belonged, here in the sunlit warmth.

He resolutely pushed aside a nagging suspicion that perhaps he wasn't done with the things he'd witnessed last night. No. He would not allow himself to entertain such thoughts. All it took was the will power to concentrate on something else.

He'd think about the others. Apparently this Delion character had joined the group, at least for the time being. There could be a problem there, but nothing he couldn't handle. Actually Delion had been a real help when Brad Nelson had fallen apart and refused to take them to the pond. The weed-enclosed pond. Lucky the pilot had been mistaken about the boat going down. Strange that Blossom hadn't returned with Michael, even stranger that Michael didn't appear to know exactly where Blossom was. Though Michael had seemed to slough it off, it was apparent he was worried. Where was she? Could Blossom be somewhere out where Prescott had been last night? Sherwood Prescott gripped the rough bark of the railing. No woman should be out there on her own. What should he do? Try to find her?

"Just who appointed you guide and guardian of the human race in general, Sherwood?"

Prescott jumped.

The man beside Prescott rested a hand on his shoulder and gave him a friendly smile. "You do tend to leap right in and provide solutions, don't you—whether or not you're asked?"

"I tend to be aware of difficulties that may crop up, if that's what you mean," Prescott said stiffly. "If I foresee problems, I try to avert them; should they happen, I attempt to solve them. It's my job; it's what I do."

"And you do it very well indeed. I was commenting on how that attitude seems to extend to your personal life; I might say to the lives of everyone around you."

Prescott's lips compressed, but he held out a hand and said courteously, "I'm afraid you have the advantage of me. You are—?"

"Don't you know me, Sherwood?" There was a wealth of love, of gentle warmth in the words.

Sherwood Prescott's tense jaw grew slack. He gaped. "Grandfather?"

The man's smile broadened. "I'm glad to see I don't have to have white hair and a cane for you to know me."

"Grandfather, I, I . . . Grandfather." Prescott reached out.

His grandfather took Prescott into his arms and held him a long moment before releasing him. "I was so pleased to hear you'd come," he said quietly.

Dazed, Prescott regarded this man who looked half Prescott's age, who had been, who was his grandfather. Never could he recall his grandfather touching, let alone embracing him as he'd just done.

"Yes, I had to learn how to do that. Astonishing how much I had to learn when I came here. Luckily your grandmother was able to help me."

Prescott swallowed. "Is Grandmother with you?"

"Of course." Prescott's grandfather sounded appalled that Prescott could consider anything else.

"Don't harass the boy, Kenneth. He has had to adjust to all sorts of things; I'm sure he's learning as fast as he can."

The woman who stood beside Prescott's grandfather looked about twenty-eight. And she was gorgeous, beautiful beyond anyone Prescott had ever seen.

She touched Prescott's face. "Thank you, dear," she said. "But then even as a small child, you appreciated pretty women. You were always trotting over to Elizabeth or Thelma and holding out your arms."

"I remember you," Prescott said slowly. "You read me bedtime stories. You were the only one who ever did. How old was I? I couldn't have been more than four or five when you were—"

"When I was reborn," she finished for him. "I was so happy Kenneth had you after I left. Your spending the summers with him helped a great deal to lessen his grief."

Prescott hadn't thought of those summers that way. Therapy for Grandfather. He'd only known summer vacations posed a problem for his parents, that they'd eagerly grasped the opportunity to have him off their hands. And he'd gone willingly because it was either visiting Grandfather or going to summer camp, which he hated. At first he'd been afraid of the stern, aloof old man; but before that first summer was over, he'd grown to feel affection as well as respect for his grandfather. And he'd reveled in his freedom at the seashore estate, the chance to explore the woodland trails, to investigate the tide pools and rocky beaches. Only as an adult had he realized what a solitary little boy he'd been, only then had he felt a profound gratitude for his grandfather's acceptance of that lonely child.

"What a nuisance I must have been," Prescott said to him.

"Your grandmother is right; it helped." Kenneth smiled at his wife, and Prescott saw the flash of brilliance he'd seen envelop Kate and Howard, though the radiance that surrounded these two seemed even brighter.

"I hoped against hope that I would be with her again, someday, somewhere," said Kenneth. "Sometimes I felt sure we'd be together, and sometimes, the bad times, I thought perhaps I was being a fool, deceiving myself because I wanted it so much."

"You were given that heart-knowledge," his wife said.

"I know; I wish I'd paid more attention to it."

Prescott blinked. Here he was entertaining two angels, two angels who happened to be his grandparents. Incredible. But then again, not. "Is it always this difficult to look at you?"

They laughed at that, and immediately the light about them lessened. "We don't notice it."

"Does everyone, I mean . . . do all angels—"

"Light up like a Christmas tree when they look at the one they love?" Prescott's grandmother chuckled. "Oh yes. But the light is not ours, of course; it comes from the source of light."

"You wouldn't notice it if you were in our community," said his grandfather. "The light there is very bright, another type entirely. Perhaps—" He exchanged a glance with his wife. She shook her head slightly and put her hand in his.

"We came to you because Howard and Kate thought perhaps we might be able to explain things so that you'd understand," she said to Prescott.

"You mean in words of one syllable."

"Don't be sarcastic, dear," his grandmother said, unruffled. "Of course, these night travels of yours are disturbing, but your reaction so far is simply to put them out of your mind. Don't you see you're missing the point, dear? You must reflect on what you've seen and experienced."

Prescott closed his eyes briefly. She'd said "these nights." That meant there would be more of them.

"Only until you understand what they mean," his grandfather said, his gaze compassionate. "Think. Why did you find yourself with the creatures of the caves?"

"I'm not like them," Prescott said, stung. "As soon as I saw them, I tried to leave. And if it hadn't been for Stuart Casperson, I'd have made it. As it was, Stuart caught sight of me and alerted them, and I was grabbed and beaten nearly senseless."

"But you got away. Did you wonder about that? Did you ask yourself how you got back here?"

"When I woke up in my room, I thought it had been a dream, a nightmare. Then I saw the bruises." He said it grudgingly, then looked directly at his grandfather. "Why did it happen? I've never knowingly done anything to harm anyone. What have I done in my life that was so terrible I was beaten silly?"

"Nothing. Nothing terrible. You tried very hard to live the kind of life you thought you should. That's why we're able to be here with you. You have, however, certain flaws in your basic concepts and, if I may say so, some rather spectacular blind spots."

Prescott turned away at that. He grasped the wooden railing and looked out over green treetops that moved gently in an unfelt breeze. "I suppose I should appreciate your pointing out my shortcomings," he said. "And now I suppose you'll be happy to explain those basic concepts and enlighten me about my 'blind spots.'"

On receiving no answer, Prescott glanced over his shoulder.

He was alone on the little deck. His hand went to his mouth, covering it. His breath quickened. Stupid of him to have turned away; they'd been trying to help.

The thought struck him that when you turned away from someone here you were no longer in his or her company. Was that how he'd gotten away from the people of the caves? No, it had to be something more than that. He had turned away, tried to run when Stuart had pointed him out, but his feet might as well have been encased in lead, and he was easily outpaced. They had swarmed about him, jeering at his efforts to flee. How had he gotten back here? Prescott's knuckles showed white against the bark railing. Don't think about it.

Don't replay last night's humiliation. No matter what Grandmother said. Anyway, he had always found it best not to dwell on things you couldn't change. What was past was past, and it didn't do to spend time on it or encourage others to do so. It was an attitude, he might have pointed out to his grandparents had they had the courtesy to stay, that had enabled him to function pretty well all his adult life.

Sherwood Prescott looked over the valley and frowned. Funny, he'd thought it must be a lowland rain forest down there, but now it seemed dry and dusty. His eye drifted to the ground immediately beneath his portion of deck. He stiffened. In place of the feathered stems of lush, tall ferns, a few sere, bent stalks rose from the parched ground.

A blistering heat seared through Prescott followed by cold, cold fear that froze his gut. His joints seemed to liquify. He clasped his hands and sank to the smooth wood deck, his knees barely holding him upright. "Oh God," he groaned, "what an ass I am. What a complete and total ass." He buried his face in his hands. "Don't let me destroy this beauty. Show me what I have to know. I'll pay attention, I swear I will. I'll try to learn."

"Jeff! Jeff, wake up!" Talia looked at Lorraine in panic. "Lorraine, I can't wake him."

Lorraine put aside the notebook in which she'd been writing and rose to come look at the man who lay curled, fetus-like against the soft, flowered cushions of the sun-porch couch. "I think he's trying to wake up," she said, "but he can't open his eyes. See how his mouth is moving?" Lorraine leaned over to poke Jeff's shoulder, but quickly withdrew her hand. "Ugh! He feels ... squishy."

"It's gone now, but a minute ago it looked as though some sort of mist was coming from him," said Talia, worried. "What do you suppose it means?"

"I wouldn't even try to guess." Lorraine cautiously prodded him again. "Jeff. Wake up."

And he did. His eyes flickered open, and Jeff looked from Lorraine to Talia and licked his lips. "Oh. Hi there. How's it going?"

"You tell us." Talia took a seat beside him, but Lorraine noticed she was careful not to sit close enough to touch him. "We thought you weren't going to make it back just now."

"Back from where?" Jeff stretched, raising his arms above his head.

"Jeff, don't try to con me. This is Talia, remember? You nearly stayed in that catatonic state or whatever it is you're in when you sit there drowsing."

"Guess I'm a growing boy and need my rest."

Talia's eyes narrowed. "You were scared out of your mind when it happened before; now you're acting as though not being able to wake up isn't a big deal."

"It's a different scene, babe, a totally different scene." A secretive smile played about Jeff's lips. "I'll tell you something; I think I've got it knocked."

"Got what knocked?"

"How to direct traffic." He grinned sleepily. "Yeah, that's what it is, I've learned how to direct the traffic in my mind." He seemed pleased with the phrase and repeated it again.

Talia glanced at Lorraine who had pointedly returned to her lounge chair at the other side of the porch. Talia leaned toward Jeff and said softly, "Listen, bud, I don't know what's so attractive about that dream world of yours, but it's getting dangerous. You've got to get a grip. You're always asleep these days, and it's getting harder and harder to wake you up."

231

"Give it a rest, will you? It's my life. If I'm happy, why should you get your shorts in a knot?" Jeff reached for an apple from the bowl on the low table before the couch. "Did I miss lunch?"

"You were there, but I didn't notice if you ate anything. That's another thing, Jeff; when you do wake yourself enough to come to meals, you just sit there and daydream and hardly eat a thing."

"The food doesn't taste all that great anymore." Jeff took a bite of his apple and grimaced. "Like this. Looks great but tastes like cardboard."

A puzzled look crossed Talia's beautiful face. She took an apple from the bowl and bit into it. "Mine's delicious," she said through her mouthful. "Cool, crisp," she chewed some more, "with a hint of something else—pear maybe?"

"So you got a good one. You always were able to pick the good stuff, while I always seem to choose the duds." But Jeff seemed to have lost interest in the conversation. He made a hook shot into a nearby wicker basket with his unfinished apple. "Look, do me a favor and drop it, okay? I won't tell you how to live your life, and you don't tell me what to do with mine." He leaned back and closed his eyes.

Talia regarded his relaxed body, the dreamy smile that crept over his face. "Oh Jeff," she sighed. She looked up and saw Lorraine watching.

"You can't do anything about it," Lorraine said slowly. "He'd rather be there than here."

"Yeah, but where's 'there'? And what happens if one time he finds he can't come back from it?"

Lorraine shrugged. "I've been wondering what he is to you. Former boyfriend?"

"Boyfriend? Uh uh. Jeff and I have been friends since I was in fourth grade, and he flunked back to my class, but

232

boyfriend, no. Jeff is probably the only male I've ever had as a friend who never tried to date me."

"He's gay?"

Talia laughed. "Obviously you don't know Jeff. He's not one to stay with a girl for long, but he sure enjoys using them before he shows them the door. It's different with Jeff and me. He's bright, you know; it's just that he never bothers doing anything he doesn't want to. We've always enjoyed each other's company; we just like talking things over with each other. After high school, we even decided to go to the same college, but Jeff dropped out after six months when he got an offer to act professionally. He's that good."

She gave a last look at Jeff and stood. His smile had disappeared, leaving his open mouth moist and slack. His unseeing eyes were half opened too, the lower irises showing pale against his dark lashes. "He *was* that good," Talia murmured. She came to sit in the chair next to Lorraine. "What are you doing?" She nodded at Lorraine's notebook.

"Homework." Lorraine closed the book, capping her pen.

"'Scuse me? There's a school here? I haven't seen any sign of one. Matter of fact, I haven't seen a soul around except our people—if you can count Malvena's boyfriend as one of the group now," she added.

"I've had a visitor," Lorraine said noncommittally.

Talia assessed Lorraine's closed look. "When?"

"I was doing some thinking—about my life, about the things I've done—and a woman appeared in my room. Well, not in my room, exactly, in the wildflower garden outside my room."

"You have a wildflower garden?" said Talia, momentarily diverted. "There's just grass outside mine. It's beautiful— looks like a putting green—and there's a nicely trimmed boxwood around it, but there aren't any flowers." She recollected herself. "What was the woman doing in your garden?"

"She said she'd come to see me and to, to talk with me."

Lorraine gave Talia a curious look. "Haven't you talked to anyone since you came, even with Kate?"

"About what?"

"About reviewing your life, the things you did on earth."

"You mean a 'why-did-you-do-that-you-bad-person-you?' sort of thing? No, I haven't, but it's funny you should mention it. On my way here, I saw Beatrice come out of her room looking like a bomb about to go off. When I asked what was the matter, she wouldn't say anything except to growl about some woman who appeared out of nowhere to poke her nose into things that were none of her business."

Lorraine gave a half smile. "It's not easy to feel sorry for a person like Beatrice, but if she just came from a session like mine, I almost can."

"What's so bad about reviewing your life? Might be kind of fun. There's a lot of my life I'd love to relive. And I really don't think I've done anything much I'd be ashamed of. After all, I haven't had much of a chance; I'm only twenty-one." Talia hesitated. "Oh, there might be a few things," she said slowly, "like the time I found Carla Suarez's science notes and didn't return them until after the exam." She bit her lip. "But you have to understand I was under a lot of pressure. We were competing for the same scholarship and I—" Talia stopped, startled. Why had that last bit come out? It wasn't like her to be running off at the mouth like this. Carla Suarez. She hadn't thought about Carla in a long time. She'd felt bad about it at the time, but the whole thing had just happened, an opportunity had presented itself and though she'd certainly had qualms, she'd taken advantage of it. And when Carla had won a different—if less prestigious—scholarship, Talia had been able to convince herself that there had been no real harm done.

"You don't just go over what you did; you remember exactly what you intended when you did it," Lorraine was saying. "They're big on intentions here. They want you to realize what things you feel are allowable, or what you feel would be allowable if no one knew you did it."

"Things you'd do if there were no consequences, you mean." Talia moistened her underlip. "So how could a person know for sure what he'd do if he had the chance?"

Lorraine studied her hands. "The woman in my garden told me there are different ways. Some people find themselves in situations that, though they're staged, seem so real they're sure it's happening. Their reaction is right there for them to see; they can't deny it. Other people review their life, sort of like seeing a video, only you can see your thoughts as well as what you did." She looked up. "She told me that's what we were going to do—review my life and then talk about it. I begged her not to make me. The idea of having to talk about some of the things in my life, let alone see them happen, was more than I could bear." Lorraine pressed her hands to her cheeks. "I asked if there was some other way, something else I could do."

"Is that the homework you're doing?"

Lorraine nodded. "It seemed like she was having a conversation with someone, but I couldn't see her lips move or hear anything. Then she said if I wanted I could go over my life by myself, do some thinking and then talk about it with her."

"I'd have told the woman if she wanted to talk so much she could go to a chat room. Who does she think she is anyway?"

"She said her name was Kwan."

"She's Chinese? Korean?"

"She told me she'd lived on a farm in China, and when I told her she spoke perfect English, she grinned and said that when she first came here, she thought everyone was speaking her Cantonese dialect. She said what we're actually speaking is a spiritual language that has no similarity to the languages we spoke in the natural world." Now that the discussion was no longer about her, Lorraine seemed more relaxed. "I asked her if she was an angel like Kate, but she said she wasn't. She didn't say so, but I think she's what they call a good spirit."

Talia eyed her. "What's a good spirit?"

"People who are being prepared for heaven," Lorraine said promptly. She picked up a pillow and twisted its fringe around her finger. "I wish I'd stayed and let Kate and Howard teach us. I didn't realize it was a one-time offer." She gave Talia a wry smile. "Like everyone else, I wanted to get away, to take off and explore this place for myself. Even then I think subconsciously I was scared of being judged."

"Why should they judge you?" Talia tossed her golden mane. "Who gave Kate or Howard or anyone else the right to judge us?"

Lorraine's smile thinned. "They don't judge us."

Talia looked at her sharply. "What do you mean?" Then her tone became uncertain. "Oh, you mean God does?" She fingered the gold chain about her neck and said with assumed nonchalance, "Well, that should be okay. If I remember correctly from the few times I went to Sunday School, God loves us, right? He's loving and merciful," she ticked off on her fingers, "and compassionate and—"

"He doesn't judge us either," Lorraine said softly.

"Then who?"

"I think we judge ourselves."

19

FRED HAMPTON TOOK HIS FOLDED JEANS FROM THE PACKAGE of clean laundry that had been left outside his door and with a twinge of regret, put them in the drawer. He looked in the dresser mirror. The gray slacks were better, more in keeping with his persona, but wearing jeans for the past few days had made him feel, well, they'd given him a certain panache. He eyed his image again. The navy jacket was good, the hint of white handkerchief in the breast pocket added a nice graceful note. Fred tweaked the handkerchief a half-inch higher. Now, where to go? What to do? The gong wouldn't announce dinner for a while. Fred didn't know how he knew this, but he did. He'd enjoyed several books from Selveridge House's well-stocked library, but he didn't feel like reading just now. Didn't feel like joining the women for afternoon tea on the sun porch either, though he'd seen Brad Nelson there yesterday and even Stuart had stopped by for a while.

Fred looked about, feeling something less than his usual pleasure at the sight of the comfortable, cluttered room. He had the fleeting thought that it would be nice to have a window or two. The safe harbor of this room was marvelous, of course, but lately he'd found its enclosed stillness unnerving. And lonely.

Fred heard a sharp, business-like rap at the door and ran a hasty hand over his hair. "Come in?"

"You'd like company?" The large, well-dressed man at the door gave Fred's jacket and slacks an approving nod as he strode into the room. "Much better than the jeans. More your style."

"Who the hell are you?" It slipped out before Fred could stop himself. "Sorry. I don't usually say things like that—can't imagine what's gotten into me."

"Ha!" The single syllable erupted from the big man and seemed to bounce off the walls of the small room. Fred wasn't quite sure whether it had been a laugh or a snort. "Can't imagine what's gotten into you; that's a good one," the man said jovially. He edged by the low coffee table, taking in the day bed with its tailored coverlet, the night table and dresser next to it, the leather armchair with its reading lamp and matching leather couch on the opposite side of the room. "You don't think it's a little cramped, having so much furniture in a room this size?"

Fred began to say something apologetic, but caught himself. "I find it quite satisfactory," he said. Then he added without knowing why, "Except I'd have liked a couple of windows."

"Oh no." His visitor shook his head. "No, no. You don't want to look out there. Not if you can help it." He took a seat on the leather couch and crossed one leg over the other. "Aren't you going to offer me a drink?"

Fred wished he didn't feel so off-balance. He made a vague gesture toward the door. "I suppose we could go downstairs to the lounge if you want."

"No need. You can get me something from that." His guest pointed to a small refrigerator beside the dresser.

Fred stared at it. "Where did that come from?"

"You have so much stuff crammed in here you might as well have a bar too," the other man said.

"Look here, who are you?"

"Sorry, you asked that before, didn't you? Dalrymple," the big man got up and extended his hand to Fred. "George Dalrymple. I hear you're a preacher."

"I'm a clergyman, yes." Fred shook Dalrymple's hand.

Dalrymple waited expectantly and then gave an impatient shrug and went to the refrigerator. "You don't mind if I help myself, do you?" he said, taking a glass from the shelf above. Dalrymple poured himself a generous drink from what looked like a bottle of Scotch and took a large swallow. "Ah, that's more like it. And how about you?"

"No, thank you," Fred said it politely before he could stop himself. His jaw tightened. "May I ask what you're doing here?"

"You may, you may. We've met before, actually. On your walk? When you wandered away from the others to explore the birch and aspen grove?"

"The birch grove—?" Fred paled.

"Yes, back when the rest of your group was listening to that couple, the teachers, by the swimming pool."

"Oh." It was an indrawn breath.

"Yes. Never thought much of that satyr-and-nymph business myself, but to each his own."

"I didn't have anything to do with that—I only happened upon them—" Fred stopped. "I came straight away," he muttered. "I went right back to the group at the pool."

"Not before you'd enjoyed a small session with yourself."

Dalrymple winked. "Come on, man, who's to blame you? Certainly not I."

Fred Hampton could only hope his flaming blush wasn't as visible as it felt. "I didn't ask to be exposed to that scene; one can't help what one's—" Fred gave up. "I don't remember seeing you."

"You didn't. Not likely you'd have missed this bulk of mine if I was one of the, ah, dancers. I was in the bushes behind you. Remember? I asked if you'd like to join the party. Wasn't polite to dash away without answering."

"I'm not a bad man." The words barely escaped Fred's tightened throat. He gave a strangled cough. "Sinful, yes. Full of sin, as are we all, but I have asked forgiveness." His voice partially regained its plummy, ministerial tones, "I've prayed. During my life in the world, I made my peace with God; I have been saved."

"Really?" Dalrymple said, interested. "How can you be so sure?"

"I, I thought. . . . Aren't we promised if we acknowledge Jesus as our personal savior, if we repent of our sins—?"

"Ah yes, repentance. That's what you call those vague acknowledgements you made every now and then, isn't it? Good going, Fred. There were times I was concerned, times you actually admitted to a specific—ah well, let's go ahead and call it 'sin.' But I needn't have worried because, as far as I can tell, you seldom actually did anything about it."

"I don't know what you mean."

"Yes, you do. You know, the 'go-and-sin-no-more' stuff."

"But I did! I tried—"

"Not very hard. You're not the soul of persistence, Fred. That's another thing. You're lazy, my friend—have been from the get-go. Aside from a week's worth of committee meetings and those sermons that even you aren't very proud of, you didn't do much of anything."

"Perhaps I'm not what you might call, ah, energetic, but it's hard to be a self-starter when one is alone," Fred's voice lowered, " . . . when there's no reason to go on."

"You mean since Sheila left you? Come on, good buddy, you've been living on that for so long it's growing whiskers. One of the reasons your little bird took off was because living with you was so frigging boring. I'd get tired too—all you did was whine about how much you had to do and how you couldn't seem to get started."

"I procrastinate; I admit it. Readily." Fred made himself look at Dalrymple. "It's not something I'm proud of; it's simply a part of my make-up."

"It's something you excuse with a lot of self-justification and very little thought," Dalrymple said amiably.

"Surely something as insignificant as procrastination isn't going to have, well, eternal repercussions."

"'Eternal repercussions.' I like that. You can tell you've been in the religion business, Fred."

"I *am* in the religion business," Fred said firmly. "Look here, I'm not sure who you are or what exactly is going on, but one thing I do know: I don't fear hell. I don't believe in it. I do believe in a God of love, a merciful God who would not countenance such a thing as hell."

Dalrymple applauded, his hands clapping silently. "Good. Very good."

Fred's confidence evaporated. "You mean there is a hell?"

"No, no. You're quite right. There isn't a hell." Dalrymple chuckled and then said, "Glad to see you've become so certain about your beliefs. As I recall, you weren't quite as definite just before the plane went down."

Fred frowned. What had he been thinking then? He'd been pretty discouraged, he remembered, his prayers fruitless, without life. "But I did pray," he said aloud. For the first time since Dalrymple had come into the room, Fred gave a genuine smile. "I just remembered. At the end—when I was there in the water with the boy, I prayed. Just before—at the moment of death you might say—I prayed."

"Sure you did; you were scared out of your wits," Dalrymple said, amused.

Fred colored. "Are you telling me it didn't count, that it wasn't heard?"

"How would I know? You weren't praying to me."

"Who are you?" Fred whispered it. "You can't be the Devil. If there is no hell, there are no devils."

"Didn't say there's no hell."

"You did!" Why was he arguing with this maddening man who looked like a gone-to-seed basketball coach? Fred gave the big man a sharp, reassessing look. His first impression had been of well-dressed sangfroid, but now Fred noticed that Dalrymple's suit was stained, that it didn't fit quite as well as it should have. "You said there wasn't any hell."

Dalrymple's single guffaw ricocheted off the walls. "I said there isn't a hell; quite right, I did. And there isn't, strictly speaking." He erupted in a spasm of laughter at the look on Fred Hampton's face. "There are," he choked and wheezed and caught his breath, "there are lots of them."

"No." It was an agonized whisper.

"Yes." Dalrymple grinned happily. "Innumerable hells, countless hells, myriads of hells—"

"Stop it! Stop!" Fred put his hands over his ears. "God help me," he moaned.

"Oh Fred, you can't make me stop. I'm having too much fun."

"You've outstayed your welcome, Dalrymple." The quiet words smoothed the pulsing currents in the room like balm.

Dalrymple's large frame seemed to shrink against the couch cushions. His glee evaporated, and he wiped a sudden sheen of perspiration from his ruddy face. "The guy was bored; he wanted company—"

Howard strode to the door and opened it. "Your coming here was permitted, but you've abused your parameters. You know the consequences."

"Oh, come on, fella, gimme a break. Maybe I did overstep the bounds, but it was hard not to," Dalrymple gave a sheepish grin. "This guy is so darn easy to spook."

"Out." Howard nodded to the hallway.

Dalrymple rose to his feet. Fred Hampton held his breath as the big man paused in front of Howard, towering over the slightly built man holding the door. But Dalrymple only ducked his head and shambled out into the hall.

Howard shut the door. "It took you a while, didn't it?" he said with a faint smile.

Fred felt for the arm of the chair behind him. He sat down. "To do what?"

"Ask for help."

Fred held his pounding head. "I beg your pardon, but . . . look, you're really an angel, aren't you?"

"Yes." Howard's smile broadened. "Frankly, I'm still getting used to the idea."

"Is Dalrymple . . . is he the Devil?"

"There isn't a devil. He's one of many."

"You mean there really are, as he said, innumerable—" Fred stopped.

"There are innumerable heavens too," said Howard. "Though Dalrymple doesn't like to mention them."

"Some of the things he told me—" Fred decided to stay away from that. "Look, if you're an angel and he's not, why is he so much bigger than you? I'd have thought—"

"He thinks of himself as large, larger than he appeared just now, in fact. Sometimes he appears quite differently. I don't think of myself as large. Of course, I never was. And then I've always been quite comfortable being of medium stature," he regarded Fred, "while you, for some reason, seem to have had a problem with your height."

"I'm uncoordinated. I've always thought being tall made it more obvious. You don't know how it felt, standing in the pulpit—" Fred paused, "Or do you? Were you a clergyman?"

"No." It seemed to Fred that Howard had to think. "I was a professor," he said. "Medieval history." He took a seat on the couch opposite Fred. "Dalrymple went further than he should, but he had some valid points. You sought out those dancers, you know."

"No, no. I was . . . simply exploring my surroundings." Fred swallowed. "How could I know I'd find nymphs and satyrs?"

"You don't want to admit you were looking for something like that when you left the group? Think, Fred—haven't you considered that there might be a relationship between your seeking out what was happening in the birch grove and your Internet activities?" Howard looked as though he smelled something not quite right; he moved an inch further from Fred.

Fred hung his head. "You don't believe my walking into that scene was an accident," he said.

"You don't believe it yourself." Howard's severe expression relaxed. "Interesting that you can still say things you don't believe. It won't last, you know."

Fred felt a chill that settled in his stomach. "What won't?"

"Your ability to dissimulate. Not being able to lie comes as quite a shock to some people."

Fred swallowed. "I always try not to lie. Outright."

"True."

"Does that count?"

Howard raised an inquiring eyebrow.

"Will it help? I mean will it help me get into heaven?"

"Fred, you've got to stop thinking in terms of keeping a score card. You're not toting up points for a boy-scout badge."

Fred Hampton flushed. "I hope I'm not that unsophisticated. But if, as Dalrymple says, my prayer at the moment of my death didn't save me and if, as you admit yourself, I don't lie, and that doesn't get me into heaven, what does?"

"I didn't say you don't lie; I said you're not comfortable with it." Howard gave an exasperated snort. "Haven't you begun to see? What will decide whether you could be happy in heaven is who you are. And who you are is what you've come to love." He scratched his head. "How else can I put it? Good loves, loving others, plus doing good equals happiness. Self-love makes those good deeds equal zero. The same prayer can be one person's 'talking with God' but merely vain repetition with another? Tell me I don't have to put it any more simply, Fred. I don't think I can."

"When I was praying in the water—it wasn't vain repetition."

"No, you couldn't have been more sincere; you reached out to God because you were afraid and, believe me, he heard you. But a moment of fearful prayer is not a ticket to heaven." Howard stopped and listened intently. "Kate needs me; I must leave." But when he got up, Fred put out a tentative hand in a gesture that begged him to stay.

"I'm a weak man. I know that. But I've tried to fight against my weaknesses and I do believe in God. Is, is that enough?"

Howard took Fred's extended hand. Fred felt an electric-like jolt but held on tight, as though Howard's strong grip would pull him from whatever might engulf him.

But Howard gently disengaged himself. "I know some of what is within you, but at this stage, not everything is clear. And it appears you, my friend, know even less. Despite all your equivocating and agonizing, you haven't the habit of looking deeply into your motives. I can help you learn about yourself however, or if you wish, you can learn from others."

Fred suppressed a shudder. "Not like Dalrymple, I hope."

"Dalrymple has his uses. As I said, you can call me whenever you're ready to learn more." Howard raised a hand. "May the Lord bless you," he said and was gone.

Fred looked at the empty space where Howard had stood, slightly surprised at the relief he felt. Not that Howard had been anything but cordial—the angel's parting blessing had brought tears to Fred's eyes—but there'd been some extraordinarily uncomfortable moments during his visit.

It was the scent of jasmine, the waft of a breeze on the back of his neck that made Fred turn around. He stared. Instead of the bare wall above the narrow bed, a window stood open, gauzy curtains blowing. Fred stumbled forward to kneel on the bed. He grasped the window sill and leaned out to see a pasture far below. Horses grazed near a rushing, sun-silvered stream; one of the mares lifted her head to watch as two colts kicked out their spindly legs and raced after a third. Fred's head spun. Was this heaven? It must be!

Whatever Howard may have said about prayers (that "vain repetition" bit had stung) if the pastoral scene before him was any indication, it was obvious heaven might not be far away. Perhaps the last prayer had done the trick. In any case, it looked like he'd made it.

The memory of the scene at the birch grove flashed through Fred's mind and with it Howard's suggestion that there was a connection between it and the Internet problem.

Fred pushed away the thought. What good did it do to dwell on things like that? Surely it was better to attend to the here-and-now.

Fred leaned out further, inspecting the flowering vines that climbed the stucco walls. Could he get down? It was too far to jump, and though the vines looked sturdy, he doubted they would hold his weight.

"What are you waiting for?"

At the same instant he recognized Dalrymple's jovial voice, Fred felt a sharp shove at his back. He fell, screaming an unheard shriek, his long legs spread-eagled, his arms flailing against the soft spring air.

Blossom O'Meara straightened the pleats of her powder-blue cotton dress. Did Michael miss her as much as she missed him? She blinked hard, willing the tears not to fall. Surely they'd be together soon. For certain they would. Blossom brushed back a stray curl and firmly tucked it behind her ear. Right now she had work to do; probably Michael did too. To think all the time she'd thought she was the one who prayed; and Michael had not only been praying, he'd been thinking about what was right and trying to live it. She'd been so sure she knew him through and through, right side up and upside down.

Blossom picked up the breakfast tray, elbowed open the louvered swinging door and entered the dim, quiet room. She set the tray on the bedside table without bothering about the clatter it made and then opened the heavy draperies to streaming sunlight. When even this didn't wake the sleeping girl, Blossom came to sit in the chair beside the bed.

The dark-skinned girl smiled as a ray of sun touched her

hand, then her arm; still she did not waken.

"Wake up, dear," Blossom said. "I've brought your breakfast."

The girl's brown eyes opened. She frowned. "You're not an angel, are you?"

Blossom laughed. "Not by a long shot."

The girl flushed. "I didn't mean to be rude. There have been angels with me every time I woke up, but when I looked at you . . . I sort of thought—" She stopped.

"It's all right." Blossom smiled. "I know exactly what you mean." She glanced at the card on the tray. "Your name's Jessie? Mine's Blossom. Do you want help washing up, or can you get yourself to the bathroom while I get on with making the bed?"

The girl sat up and swung her feet from beneath the covers. She stood, took an experimental step, then another. Her eyes widened. "It isn't a dream, is it? I'm well?"

"Were you ill a long time?"

"Forever."

"'Forever.' I think you'll find the word means something entirely different than it used to." Blossom smiled again and handed Jessie the cream-colored robe lying on the bed. "I have to say you seem mighty perky now."

"This last time I thought I'd taken up permanent residence at the hospital." Jessie smoothed the heavy satin of the robe and slipped her arms into it. "Where did this come from? It's not mine."

"Yes, it is. If you need something around here, it has a habit of appearing. That color is perfect with your dark hair."

"I love it." Jessie disappeared into the adjoining bathroom and continued to talk over the sound of splashing water, "It sure seems like heaven here, but they told me it isn't, that we're somewhere outside it." Jessie's head popped around the door frame. "Why am I outside? I didn't think to ask." Then she chattered on without waiting for a reply, "Hey, I'll take this even if it isn't heaven. I mean, all those months in and out of the hospital I had a lot of time to think about what would happen . . . after. I was sure there is a heaven, y'know? But I wondered what it was like, whether I'd wake up and find myself on some cloud?" She disappeared again into the bathroom. "But it's not like that at all. It's like, like normal, except everything's okay. More than okay; it's great."

Blossom was only half-listening. She pulled up the white embroidered coverlet and smoothed it over the pillow. She straightened with a start as the lacy embroidery beneath her fingers disappeared. In its place she saw a packed auditorium, filled except for five empty front rows that awaited a double line of robed graduates standing at the rear of the room. Blossom heard the rich strains of Handel's "Water Music," smelled the fragrance of roses and lilac banked on the stage. She looked intently at the robed students. Most were young, but not all. One, older than the rest, gave the tassel of her mortar board an impatient twist, then closed her eyes, her lips moving.

Blossom's breath caught in a bubble of joy. Dulcy! Instant understanding illuminated Blossom's joy. Her wayward daughter had gone back to school. She was this moment praying that Blossom knew it and could share the moment's happiness.

"Yes, baby, I know. I'm here," Blossom breathed. "And I am happy, so very happy for you."

"Doug is in the third row, there with Franny and Tom," Dulcy's thought rose to Blossom. "He's the one, Mom. This time I'm sure."

Blossom saw the sandy-haired man in the third row, saw with a lift of her heart Franny and Tom sitting beside him. "I pray you'll be blessed," Blossom whispered as the music swelled and the line began to move down the center aisle. Blossom could feel her daughter's thoughts drift from her, and the auditorium faded, Dulcy's image along with the rest.

Blossom blinked at the white embroidered coverlet in her hands. She patted it in place absently, then lowered her head. "Thank you," she said silently. "I don't have the words to say it right, but, thank you."

"Is your name really Blossom?" Jessie entered from the bathroom, drying her hair with a fluffy, white towel. She gestured to her beige-and-white checked shirt, her khaki chinos. "Guess this is more of the stuff that appears when you need it. I swear these clothes weren't in there before, but the moment I wondered what I'd wear, I saw them hanging on the door."

Did the girl never wait for an answer? No, don't be annoyed; go with it, Blossom told herself. The girl was chattering nonstop simply because she was so happy to be alive and well. Blossom handed Jessie a brush and watched her slick back her short, curly hair. "Why don't you sit down and have some breakfast?"

Jessie inspected the tray on the bedside table. "Coffee! And are those blueberry muffins?" She stretched her arms above her head. "Yes! Real food!"

"I guess the hospital food wasn't all that great?"

Jessie shot her a look. "Food? The only thing I've had for the past few months is Jevity through a tube; and let me tell you, Jevity isn't food."

"You weren't able to eat?" Blossom said gently.

"After the second operation, I had no mouth."

Blossom caught her breath. She looked at the vibrant young woman before her. "How wonderful it must be to wake up whole."

"You can't imagine." Jessie stared out the window, viewing something only she could see. "You just cannot imagine."

Blossom moved a chair to the table. "Sit."

Jessie sat. "Hey, you were going to tell me your real name," she said, brightening. "And how come you're here taking care of me? Are you in charge of this place?"

"Stop with the questions and eat and maybe I'll have a chance to tell you." Blossom took a cup of coffee for herself from a shelf above the table and drew up another chair. "Blossom is my real name. The story is that, during labor, my mother was watching blossoms float from the apple tree outside her window." She took a sip of coffee. "To tell you the truth, I've always wondered about that; I've had five kids, and I can't see watching anything much during labor."

"I think it's kinda cute."

Blossom snorted. "As for the rest, first off, I'm here for the same reason you are, to learn. Second, I'm not in charge, kiddo, not by a long shot. And lastly, I'm taking care of you because I like being busy and asked if they'd let me help wherever I could."

"So you're new too?"

Blossom frowned. "I'm not sure. In a way it feels as though we've just come, but such a lot has happened that I just don't know. Some of it seems, well, far off," her voice slowed, "almost as though it happened to someone else, someone who knew so little—"

"You say 'we' came? Who's with you?"

"No one." There was pain in Blossom's eyes as they met Jessie's. She swallowed. "I was with my husband, but I guess it's best that we're not together—at least for now."

"You said you're here to learn. What are you learning?"

Blossom sighed. "About myself. About a lot of things I never gave much thought to before." She put down her cup.

"But let's talk about you. I've learned enough of how things work around here to know that when you first get here you can do just about whatever you'd like. Is there anything you'd especially like to do, anyone you'd like to see?"

Jessie smoothed a curl above her ear and thought. "I think I'd like to see my roommate," she said at last. "I'm pretty sure she's here by now." She finished her muffin and licked her fingers. "We shared a room before I had to go on the surgical floor and got put in solitary."

"You were put in solitary?" said Blossom, diverted.

"Up on six-east there was a bunch of us who didn't have roommates," Jessie said airily. "Not that we were locked away or anything. Matter of fact, they encouraged us to go out into the halls, but we sort of knew we weren't supposed to wander around the rest of the hospital."

Blossom decided she wouldn't go into this. She busied herself with gathering plates and mugs and putting them on the tray. "This friend of yours was quite ill?"

"Yes, she—" Jessie jumped from her chair with a squeal of surprise. "Karen!"

"The very same." The lanky girl in the doorway opened her arms and rushed into Jessie's.

They hugged, chattering through each other's sentences. "Can you believe it!" ". . . you look great!" "Isn't it super?" ". . . haven't felt this good since—"

The tall girl took a step back. "Oh wait! I forgot." She looked at the door and called out, "Dad, come meet Jessie."

Blossom wondered why she wasn't more surprised to see the handsome man who appeared beside Karen.

"Glad to meet you, Jessie," said Sherwood Prescott. When he turned to Blossom, she saw that hies face had regained its customary dignified composure, that his eyes were clear and unclouded. "Hello, Blossom," he said, "so this is where you got to."

20

STUART CASPERSON TOOK A TALL, BULBOUS GLASS OF PINK froth and leered at the bikini-clad waitress. "Flowering Passionaide? What kind of prissy drink is that?"

The girl pursed bee-stung lips; her long, cherry-colored nails stroked her glistening thigh. "I guess you could say it's kinda like lemonade with a kick," she said. She offered a glass to Brad Nelson who declined with a shake of his head.

Brad leaned across the arm of his chair. "Stu, don't you think we ought to get back?" he whispered.

Stuart, who hadn't taken his eyes from the girl, ignored him. "I was hoping it was called passionaide for another reason," he said.

"Because it's an aid to passion?" The girl's white teeth gleamed. "Could be. If you think you need it."

"Don't need a pink lemonade for that, baby." Stuart's gaze traveled her smooth, rounded curves. "Don't need anything more than a couple of minutes alone with you."

"Hey, that's what we're here for." She set her tray on the table, perched on the edge of the caned chair between Stuart and Brad, and crossed her long legs. "You just gotta ask, honey. Why do you think they call this Hedonism Bay?"

Stuart cleared his throat. "You mean you'd come with me—just like that?" He took in the scantily clad male and female servers about them, the patio crowded with dazed, happy customers lounging around the torch-lit pool. "You mean all of you—?"

"You want all of us?" She laughed. "Were you thinking one at a time maybe, or in bunches?" Her laugh became a burble that threatened to convulse her.

Stuart's unbelieving grin widened. "Maybe another time. Right now I have a feeling you're all I could handle." He drew a curled finger along her bare arm, reached the end of her long fingernail and pushed gently against it. "Am I right?"

"More than you could imagine."

The metallic strains of an unseen band grew suddenly louder, more insistent; several couples moved onto the dance floor and began to writhe to the pulsing beat.

"Stuart, I think we should talk," Brad Nelson said. "There's something wrong here. We shouldn't have come."

"What's with your friend?" the girl pouted. "The invitations said this was for people who know how to have a fun time. So far it doesn't look like he qualifies."

Stuart flicked a dismissive hand in Brad's direction. "Don't bother with him. If you were serious about what you just said, how's about we, ah, go for a walk? Check out the cabanas over there?" He stood up and grinned again. "I'll take my Flowering Passionaide with me. Just in case."

The girl uncoiled herself from the chair and stood too. She moved close to Stuart, so close her upturned face was mere inches from his chin. Her erect nipples brushed his ribs.

"Trust me, lover, you won't need it." She turned, sashayed to the dance floor, and crossed it without bothering to look back.

Stuart followed the girl through the crowd as though attached to her by an invisible cord. Brad watched them go. He wiped a trickle of sweat from his forehead. Had the others at Selveridge House found invitations like his slipped under their door? No one else from the house was here. Why had he listened to Stuart?

"Has anyone offered you a Flowering Passionaide?" The girl who sidled up with a tray of drinks looked little more than a child. "They tell me they're very good." She gave Brad a shy, uncertain smile.

Brad stared at her in horror. "I don't want—Why are you here? You're much too young to—" He stopped, his cheeks aflame.

"Oh, oh, you don't like 'em young? My mistake." The girl put down her tray of drinks and gave a quick toss of her head that caused her long hair to flounce over her face; when she brushed it back, Brad found himself looking at a beautiful, assured woman of about thirty.

"Better?" she asked. She sat down in the chair Stuart had vacated. "I apologize, but it's so hard to keep track of everyone's likes and dislikes, y'know? I must have been thinking of the guys who were at this table before you two came."

Brad felt as though his stomach was being sucked through a strainer, leaving only bile that rose to his throat. He licked his lips. "I don't want to be here."

"Funny, that's what one of the men said who came here just before you did. But he didn't leave," she added with a grin.

"Where, where is he?"

The woman shrugged. "Around. You wouldn't recognize him."

Brad took a quivering breath. "I think maybe I should go," he said.

"If you want," the woman said, unconcerned. "You can pay your bill at the bar."

Brad felt for his wallet automatically, then realized it wouldn't be in his pants pocket. He hadn't had a wallet since, since—when? "I, I didn't drink anything," he said.

"That's right, you didn't, did you? O.K., you can just pay the cover charge."

"But I don't have any—No one's ever asked for money." Yes they had, back at the hotel where they'd first stayed. "What's the cover charge?" Brad said weakly.

"You don't have any money?" The woman's eyebrows rose. Then she smiled. "Don't worry about it, honey; go talk to Steve. Arrangements can be made."

Brad didn't want to make any arrangements. He didn't want to go see Steve. He wanted to go back to his room at Selveridge House. He wanted to shut the door and find the cup of hot chocolate that usually appeared about this time of the evening. He wanted to sit on his comfortable couch and watch T.V.

Brad saw the expectant look of the woman before him and realized she'd asked him a question. "Beg pardon?" he said.

"I said, how are you at taxidermy? Know anything about it?"

A wave of sickness washed Brad. He didn't know why she'd asked the question, but he was fairly certain she was going to tell him. "God, help me," he blurted aloud. He didn't notice the woman flinch. He clasped his hands and shut his eyes. "Please, God, please. I don't want to be here, I don't—"

He got no further. A rush of wind roared in his ears, tearing at his clothes, abrading his exposed skin. He felt himself lifted up, up. He tried to cover his ears against the shrieking wind, but couldn't lift his arms. He whirled round and round, the hurricane winds engulfing him.

Then it stopped and there was silence.

Brad smelled the delicious aroma of hot chocolate. He knew without opening his eyes that he was in his room at Selveridge House. He lay back, exhausted, sprawled on his comfortable plaid couch. Brad blinked away the tears that blurred his vision. "Thank you," he murmured. He sat up. "Thank you," he said again. He thought of Stuart Casperson. Oh God. No, he didn't even want to think about what might be happening there. He looked longingly at the hot chocolate but knew his hands weren't steady enough to handle the cup yet.

Brad gave a shuddering sigh, then wiped his eyes, and reached for the T.V.'s remote control.

Fred Hampton shifted to a more comfortable position on the sun-warmed rock, easing his tender bottom onto a scooped-out section of the stone. Fortunately, the huge willow's branches had broken his fall, and even more fortunately he'd landed on a great pile of grass clippings. Aside from hindquarters that felt as though he'd endured a spanking, he'd apparently suffered only minor bruises and abrasions. Fred took an offended sniff. If only the grass hadn't covered a pile of manure. He rubbed at the brown stains on the elbows of his shirt-sleeves and gingerly brushed the seat of his still-damp slacks. Why had George Dalrymple pushed him out the window? More to the point, why had Dalrymple been allowed to return? Had Fred brought him back? No, how could that be? As he remembered it, he'd been looking out his new window and thinking the scene below must be heaven.

Fred inspected the meadow; mares still grazed by the stream, their foals still cavorted about the pasture. He sniffed again. Was there manure in heaven? He knew some people liked the smell of barns and horses and manure. He wasn't one of them.

And where was everyone? Shouldn't there be angels? Fred looked up to see a couple emerge from the woods at the far end of the field. The woman stumbled once, and there was something familiar about the way the man impatiently grabbed her arm to help her. Fred leaned forward, straining to see, and the man, as though drawn by Fred's gaze, looked in his direction.

"Hey Preacher, that you?" Jackson Delion called out. "What you doin' here?"

Fred scrambled to his feet. Wherever he was, it wasn't heaven.

By the time Malvena and Delion reached Fred, Malvena was panting slightly and a sheen of sweat coated her forehead. She jerked her arm from Delion's grasp and took a seat on Fred's rock. "I'm thirsty," she said. She pointed to the stream. "Is the water safe?"

"Wouldn't think so, the way it stinks around here," Delion said.

Fred flushed. "It's the horses."

"What horses?" Malvena looked about.

Fred winced as he turned to look. "There were horses—over there."

"What happened?" Delion looked him over. "You hurt?"

"I fell," Fred said shortly. He nodded up at the white-walled building on the cliff high above them.

Delion's mocking smile vanished. "That's where we came from? Selveridge House is all the way up there?"

"How did you get down?"

Malvena and Delion looked at each other. "Makes no difference how we got down," Delion replied. "We're here. Question is, how do we get back up?"

Fred shrugged off a chill. "Why do you want to go back?"

"Safer up there," Delion said briefly.

Fred thought of George Dalrymple. "Not necessarily." Then he shot Delion a questioning look. "Why are you implying it's not safe down here?"

Delion gave Malvena a mirthless grin. "Hey girl, are we 'implying'? We even know what the fu— what the word means?"

Malvena waved him away. "Don't make jokes," she snapped. "You want to go outside the grounds to talk and what happens? We end up here. You've been nothing but trouble since the beginning."

"Don't give me that shit," Delion's black eyes glinted. "You were the one who was in charge, the one who knew how it all was s'posed to work; only thing I had to do was make sure you got on and off the plane without no one hassling you."

Malvena ignored this. "It was stupid to go away from Selveridge House," she said. Though her slim shoulders drooped with fatigue, her voice was sharp. "We were safe there."

"How we gonna talk? I can't be in your room, and there ain't no place in that house we can be without somebody coming in on us."

Fred looked from one to the other, intrigued by the apparent change in the couple. Until this moment he'd thought of Malvena as subservient, definitely the junior partner of the duo. Now, though Delion might still attempt to call the shots, the young woman wasn't having any of it. And if she was afraid of something or someone, it certainly wasn't her companion.

"It was crazy to wander off like this," Malvena was saying.

"I thought we had a better chance of getting into the . . . the really safe place if we maybe talked to someone here about what we were doing, explained how we were only doing business stuff, not anything that would get anyone hurt."

Malvena gave a sharp laugh. "Why don't you go ahead and say it? When you talk about this safe place, you mean heaven, no?" Her tone was contemptuous. "But you do not even know what heaven is. None of you does."

"But you do know?" Fred asked her.

"Yes, but that does not concern you," she flicked the reply at Fred. She looked worried. "I must find my way," she muttered. "Things did not turn out as they should have. I have to find my people and explain." Contempt swept her face again as she looked at Delion. "You—you listen to everything they've been telling us and believe it. You think we have died. Me, I think we are in some kind of fancy prison." She leaned toward Delion. "Think about it. The people here try to make us think we are in another world so we will tell them what they want to know. Me, I will never tell them anything." She gave a short laugh. "You can do as you like, tell them everything if you want to. They have you so frightened you act like a little boy, not a man."

"What is she talking about?" Fred asked Delion.

"Had a visit from a dude back up at the house," Delion mumbled. "Brother told me I better do some thinking about the stuff I done." He did not meet Fred's eyes.

Fred shifted uncomfortably. He folded his long arms across his chest and said, "I know what you mean."

Delion flicked him a surprised glance. "You too?" He shook his head. "Man," he breathed, "if a preacher's scared about what he done what chance do I have?"

A stab of shame pierced Fred at the hopelessness in the man's voice. If only Delion knew. Fred's hands clenched. He'd dismissed both Dalrymple's accusations and Howard's intimations with defensiveness and excuses. Back up there when he'd stood in front of his new window he'd been given the opportunity to examine himself, but he'd shrunk from it, refusing even to allow the thoughts to surface. "I wouldn't be surprised if your chances were better than the preacher's," he said quietly.

Delion wasn't listening, he was staring at Malvena. "Girl, what you doin'?" he said.

A panicked gasp came from Malvena's throat. She pointed to a plump, wet, black line on her ankle. The line moved. "Off—get it off," she moaned.

"Hold still." Delion squatted to examine the slug. He flicked at it with a fingernail, but it would not be dislodged.

"Get it off!" Malvena whispered through clenched teeth.

Delion picked up a shard of bark and scraped it against her leg. The slug gave up its hold reluctantly, one sucker at a time until it fell with a plop on the grass. "Looka' that," Delion breathed, "that's one ugly mother."

Malvena jumped to her feet and rubbed at the pink line on her leg. Her face worked. "I'm going," she said. "I must find my people." She raised a hand to stop Delion, though he hadn't moved. "Do not come with me. I'm going alone."

"Hey, fine with me."

Malvena edged away, giving the slug a wide berth, and took off in the direction from which they'd come. Half way across the field she staggered, her shoe sucked off her foot into the soft earth. She quickly recovered and, balancing on one foot, wedged her toes into the shoe and hurried on.

Delion watched her disappear into the forest. "Crazy woman. Can't make up her mind if we're here or not. First she thinks yes, then no."

"You said you couldn't talk in Malvena's room," said Fred. "Why not? You must have gone there when you first came; I remember you saying it was hardly big enough for one person."

Delion scratched his head and examined the toes of his basketball shoes. "I didn't say it, but that first time wasn't no fun. It's like when I forget and say . . . the stuff I'm not supposed to. When I went passed the door to her room, it was like *wham*, like an electric shock." He looked up, aggrieved. "Wasn't like her and me was planning on doing anything." He paused and gave Fred an intent look. "But I could have, y'know? Can't hardly believe it, but everything still works here. And I mean everything."

Fred coughed. "Yes, I'm aware of, ah, of that conundrum."

Delion's eyes widened. "How's a preacher know about that stuff?"

"I saw, that is, I happened to—" Fred stopped. "Look here, let's drop the subject. You want to go back to Selveridge House? So do I. Let's see if we can find a trail." He inspected the scree of tumbled rocks. "There's no way anyone could get up this cliff without equipment." He gingerly stepped from one of the larger rocks to another, grimacing as his foot slipped into a crack. "The cliff goes on as far as I can see in either direction, and there seem to be flatlands everywhere else," he called back to Delion. "I can't see any way up."

"Seems like you got some kind of conundrum there."

Fred's head snapped around. He stared at the smaller man a long moment and then carefully climbed to the ground.

Delion grinned at him. "I talk the way I do 'cause that's how I talk, but I understand all those big words, y'know? Ever since I got here, I know what everybody's saying no matter what kind of words they use. Know when you said 'implying' a while back? I knew what you meant."

Fred's mouth twitched. "I rather thought you did."

"So how we goin' to get back up there?" Delion surveyed the endless cliff.

"Do you mind telling me how you and Malvena got down here?"

At first Fred thought Delion was going to ignore the question, but when the younger man had finished his inspection, his gaze returned to Hampton. "Don't know. One minute we're outside of Selveridge House, next we're someplace else. Not someplace like here," he gestured to the bright meadow before them, "it was a forest, an' so dark, could have been day or night." A stab of fear flickered in Delion's eyes. "We heard a lot of soft, slithery noises, and there were these shadows you see out of the corner of your eye, the kind that aren't there when you turn around to look. Man, I was like to piss my pants, but Malvena, she wasn't scared, at least not 'til we come out here and she found that worm on her." There was grudging respect in his voice.

"I'm surprised she was so willing to go back into the forest alone," said Fred.

"I told you, half the time she still thinks she's headin' for the place she comes from. Maybe that's why she didn't mind bein' in the forest—reminded her of her country."

Fred nodded. "I've noticed it's much brighter here than on earth. That is, most places."

"All that woman thinks about is gettin' back to her people and explainin' about the mission," Delion continued, "She may not mind the forest, but she's sure scared of explainin' how she come to louse up the mission."

"Ah, yes, just what is this mission of yours?"

Delion shot him a startled look. "Ain't none of your business, is it?" He shook his head and mumbled, "Don't know how I come to be doing all this talkin'." He turned his attention again to the tumbled rocks and squatted on the dusty ground to peer into a space between two of the larger boulders. "Hey, I see somethin' in there. Take a look. Think we should see where it goes?"

Fred craned to look over Delion's shoulder. There appeared to be an opening in the base of the cliff, a dusky hole that showed dark against the cliff's pale sandstone striations. Delion scrambled over the boulders and let himself down into the narrow space between the rocks and the bottom of the cliff. After a moment's hesitation, Fred followed. When he got there, Delion was on his knees peering into the waist high slit.

"Sure looks like it goes somewhere."

Fred stooped to look. He shivered, wrapping his arms about his chest. "It does. It slants down."

"You sayin' you don't think that passageway is going anywhere near Selveridge House?" Delion nodded. "You know, I think you're right." He backed away, eyeing the dark hole warily. They had both begun to clamber back over the rocks when they heard noise coming from the cave. It was a sighing sound that vibrated through the quiet air as though calling, coaxing them to return. Jackson Delion increased his speed, scrambling over the boulders, not stopping until he reached the grassy meadow. When he finally looked back, he saw Fred sprawled, frozen, on one of the huge stones.

"Man, you crazy?" Delion yelled. "Get out of there."

Fred slowly turned his head to look at Delion. "I . . . I don't think I can."

"'Course you can, you asshole!" Delion's eyes widened as he realized what he'd said. His hand went to his stomach in anticipation, but dropped away as nothing happened. The obscenity, however, seemed to break whatever spell held Fred paralyzed. He moved one leg experimentally, then the other, then slid from the boulder, his long arms flailing.

Delion didn't wait for Hampton. He ran along the trampled grass until it gave onto a path that ran parallel to the towering cliffs, putting a good distance between him and the cave before he stopped and waited for Fred to catch up.

"Looks like someone's been using this," Delion said shortly. "I say we see where it goes." He trotted off, moving easily along the path but careful to leave a broad space between himself and the rocks that lined the cliff's base.

"Wait for me," Fred called as he panted behind.

Delion gave an annoyed grimace. "Better get your ass in gear, you want to come along," he called back. But he slowed down until Hampton caught up again.

"Thanks," Fred said, out of breath. "It would be better if we stayed together, don't you think?"

Delion gave him an exasperated look, but then shrugged. "Sure," he said, "sure."

21

LORRAINE'S STEPS QUICKENED AS SHE REACHED THE ARCHWAY leading to the sitting room. Where was everyone? She strode through the sitting room and into the dining room where, instead of the usual dozen woven placemats on the glass table, there were two set with silver knives and forks and turquoise ceramic plates.

Why only two place settings? Had the others left Selveridge House? Left her here without saying anything? Why? And who was the other person still here? Lorraine's heart sank. Please, not Stuart Casperson. Sure they'd been together on earth, but they had nothing in common now. She hadn't spoken to him more than a couple of times since they'd come to Selveridge House. Matter of fact, Stuart seemed as anxious as she to forget that they'd ever known each other, probably because she knew more than she should about a lot of things Stuart would rather not remember.

Lorraine's breath caught at the sound of someone coming down the stairs. She let it out in a small breath of relief; the light steps couldn't be Stuart's.

"Hi, Lorraine!" Talia swept into the dining room, her knee-length crisply ironed skirts swishing over layers of petticoats. "Where is everybody?"

"Good question. I can't find anyone." Lorraine eyed Talia's low-cut blouse, the flaring petticoats. "Going to a square dance?"

Talia glanced down at her billowing skirts with a touch of embarrassment. "Corny, isn't it?" Then she smoothed her pinched-in waist, pleased despite her demur. "I've always wanted to wear this kind of get-up. When I was little, Mom and Dad used to go square dancing every week. I'd watch Mom get ready and dream about when I'd be able to wear clothes like hers."

"You've seen her?" Lorraine said, her voice suddenly gentle. "She's here?"

Talia tossed her blond mane. "Oh no, both my parents are still on earth. Mom's probably messing up her life as usual. She took off for Los Angeles when I was fourteen. She'd intended to set Hollywood on fire but ended up married to a producer, or if not married, something close to it. Anyway, I haven't seen much of her since then; no room in her life for a daughter who looks the way she used to when she was twenty. And Dad remarried a couple of years after Mom left; Donna was his secretary and all of about four years older than I." Talia shrugged. "For all intents and purposes, I've been on my own since Dad and Donna shipped me off to college."

"Must have been tough." But Lorraine didn't seem impressed.

Talia eyed her. "I suppose you think with your face you had things a lot harder than I did."

Lorraine touched her cheek with the tips of her fingers in a gesture that had become familiar. "Actually, I was thinking of what I'd have given to have someone help me go to college," she said evenly. "Look, we might as well sit down to lunch; it looks as though everyone but us has gone somewhere."

"Oh, we're not the only ones here," Talia said as she slid into a chair, arranging her ballooning skirts beneath the table. "I don't know why there are only two places set, but I saw Brad Nelson upstairs just now." She lifted the cover of the soup tureen in front of her and sniffed appreciatively.

"I must say I'm surprised Jeff roused himself enough to take off," Lorraine said. "Unless he's in his room?"

"No, I checked. When he wasn't in his usual place on the porch this morning, I was worried he might not have been able to wake up, so I went to his room. But he wasn't there, thank goodness. That's when I saw Brad. He had his head poked outside his door; but when he saw me, he darted back into the room as if he were scared I was going to put a hex on him. I was sort of surprised since he has been trying to hit on me ever since we came here." Talia paused. "Well, maybe not exactly hit on me, but the guy's always trying to corner me."

"Poor Brad. I bet he's in the middle of some kind of examination." Lorraine spooned a helping of seafood salad onto her plate.

"You mean someone's been tutoring him the way the woman who appeared in your garden taught you?"

"Wouldn't be surprised."

"Why hasn't anyone come to see *me*?" Talia said, a slight frown creasing her lovely forehead. "You don't suppose there's something wrong with me?"

"Oh, I don't think so." Lorraine had only meant to be polite, but to her surprise, she found she hoped this was true. "You've been doing some hard thinking about your life; could be that's your way of learning what you're supposed to know."

Talia shook her head. "I don't think so," she said slowly. "I don't think I'm able to look at myself the way you do. Maybe I'll never be able to." For a moment, Talia looked frightened. "Maybe I'm just not ready." She crumbled a cracker into her soup and said glumly, "If I ever am, it'll be just my luck to find myself in a remedial class. Phi Beta Kappa, summa cum laude, and I end up taking the dummy course."

Lorraine suppressed a laugh. "Does it matter so much?"

"Sure it does. You guys get your own personal tutor to take you through your life," Talia fingered her flaring skirts, "and so far all I have is a bunch of childhood memories and this tacky costume."

"Oh please. You wouldn't be wearing that get-up if you didn't like it. Anyway, you know very well you look gorgeous." Lorraine studied her. "Y'know, used to be I couldn't bear to look at someone like you; now I actually enjoy it."

Talia gave her a level look. "Don't tell me—let me guess. You've graduated from Heavenly Postulates 101 to Elementary Love and Kindness and want to share what you've learned?"

Lorraine gave her an annoyed look; then she became thoughtful. "You want to hear what I've learned?"

"I was kidding."

"I'm not. I may not have been Phi Beta Kappa or summa cum whatever, but I don't have to be hit on the head with a two-by-four. We've been left here together; obviously we're meant to do something about it. Maybe I'm supposed to share what I've learned. So go ahead. If there's anything you want to know, shoot. I'll do the best I can."

Talia eyed her. "I am so not ready to hear this. You're going to be my teacher?"

"Oh, for Pete's sake, girl, grow up. So what if you have to make do with a lowly administrative assistant for a while?"

Lorraine bit her lip and said more moderately, "Anyway, it's not as though I'm your teacher; I'd just be passing along what I've learned."

Talia carefully aligned her knife and spoon, then looked up and sighed. "Okay. So what have you found out that you think I should know?"

Michael O'Meara picked up a pillow and placed it on the couch, then took his empty cereal dish and spoon to the kitchen and put them in the sink. Michael snorted. When had he last straightened up a room? Here he was, Michael O'Meara, reduced to doing women's work.

Women. Blossom. Michael clutched his chest at the stab of pain that accompanied the thought of his wife. Ah, but it was a sweet pain. He closed his eyes. "Blossom, my lovely girl," he murmured, "when are you comin' back?" There was no answer, but then he didn't expect one. He returned to the little sitting room and inspected it approvingly. Wouldn't do to have Jorash come in and find a clutter. Michael felt an uneasy flicker of disquiet. Would Jorash find his work adequate? Had he put enough thought into the self-evaluation? Then a surge of anticipation swept away any anxiety. What new things would Jorash tell him? What wonders would he present for Michael's inspection?

Michael looked out the window. No one coming down the path to the cottage. Who'd have thought he'd look forward to the daily lessons like this? Might think he was some bloody intellectual. Michael hitched up his trousers and patted his flat stomach. These weren't an intellectual's muscles. Those workouts at the gym were showing results. Maybe he'd ask Jorash to join him when they finished. He looked at the door.

Where was the man?

"Jorash asked me to give you his greetings, Michael."

Michael blinked at the brown-skinned man before him, then took his outstretched hand. "What happened to Jorash?"

"I'm taking his place."

"And here I was just getting used to the fella." Michael gave a shrug, attempting to hide his disappointment. "Any reason he decided to hand me off to someone else?"

"Jorash and I are of the same community," said his visitor. "I sometimes take his pupils when he thinks they would benefit from the routes I travel. You have passed his stage of teaching," he added as his light-gray eyes searched Michael's. "Do you wish to come with me?"

Michael hesitated. Why did he feel as though that brief glance had seen to the depths of his soul? "Why sure, laddie. What d'ye say you're called?"

"My name is Yannish."

"You're the solemn one, aren't ya?"

Yannish gave a fleeting smile. "Just processing. Don't feel you have to needle everyone you meet, Michael. You've enjoyed your sessions of becoming acquainted with early memories?"

Michael's eyes softened. "'Twas the memory of ridin' on Pa's shoulders I liked best. The feel of Pa's hands on my knees, keepin' me safe while high above the pavement, me breathing the cool air and feelin' his love." He paused. "I must have been less than a year old, for I had this feeling I was high above the earth, and I know full well he was a small man like me."

"But you're not small."

"Ah, that's so." Michael gave an abashed grin. "Was it wrong of me to want to be taller?"

"It could have been. But it wasn't."

272

Michael looked at his shoes. "Y'see, it's just that I've always wondered what it would be like to have a couple of extra inches."

"And what was it like?"

"To tell the truth, after the first look in the mirror, I've hardly even noticed."

"Isn't that the way of it?" The lilt of Yannish's commiserating words could have been Michael's own.

Michael bristled, but only for an instant. "Are you mockin' me, man?" he said lightly. "And you an angel. For shame."

Yannish smiled at that. "You're a good man, Michael O'Meara. We'll be pleased to have you with us."

Michael stared at Yannish with delighted wonder. Then delight changed to alarm. "What about Blossom?" He backed away. "I'm not goin' without Blossom, hear?"

"So you decide where you'll go, what you'll do?" The question was gentle, but Yannish's meaning unmistakable.

Michael flushed, his jaw thrust out, his hands clenched into fists at his sides. "I'll not go anywhere without Blossom," he said. He caught his lower lip. "God wouldn't part us. He wouldn't take her from me." His eyes pleaded with the young man before him, and he whispered, "He wouldn't, would he?"

"Have trust in him." Yannish's gray eyes held complete understanding. "There are things you must do, states through which you must travel." He held out his hand to Michael.

"Where are we going?"

"Have trust."

Michael took a breath so deep it hurt. Then he reached out and took the proffered hand.

Jackson Delion tightened the rope about his waist and gave the knot a tug. "If this thing don't hold, be ready to grab something—fast," he said to Fred.

Fred Hampton checked a handhold on the boulder around which Delion had looped the rope. "I still don't understand why we have to go down the rock face in order to get up to Selveridge House," he said.

Delion glanced up from where he knelt by the ledge. "How else you gonna get across that plain there?" he said, pointing below. "You see another way, you tell me. Anyways, we didn't find this rope by accident. The thing was lying here like it was waiting for us."

"I haven't done any rock climbing," Hampton objected, "not ever."

"You think I have? But we gotta try, man. If I make it down, you tie the rope round the bottom of that rock there and let yourself down, understand?" Delion put a leg over the ledge and then eased his body over. "You're lettin' it get too tight," he called up a moment later, "Give me some slack."

Fred let out more of the rope, leaning against it to let the boulder take the strain. "Is that all right?" he called out. He nervously fingered the double loop around his waist, making sure the end hung free.

"Shit, this is harder than I thought," the panted comment came from below. "You holdin' it tight? I gotta try to reach—" Words changed to indistinguishable grunts that concluded with the triumphant cry, "Made it! I made it!"

"You're down already?" Fred called out, incredulous.

"Hell no," came the faint, disgusted reply. "Who you think I am? I meant I made it to the next shelf down. Gimme more rope."

Fred awkwardly eased the rope over, then held it tight with one hand as he flexed the other. "How much longer is this going to take?" he called out. "My hands can't stand much more of this."

For longer than Fred liked, there was no answer. Then came the faint call, "I'm more'n half way down. Hold on, okay, man? This next one's gonna be hard."

There were grunts, then silence. Fred leaned back, the weight of the rope taut against the rock. He listened anxiously but heard nothing but the roaring of his own blood in his ears. He wiped the sweat from his face with a forearm. "Delion?" he called, "what's happening?" Was there a sound, or was it his imagination? Fred loosened the loops about his waist. "Delion? Are you all right?" Nothing. Still holding tight, Fred let the rope slide from his hips to his knees and stepped free. He had just begun to edge toward the cliff when a strangled cry came from below and the rope against the rock spun from Fred Hampton's hands, burning the tender flesh of his right hand as it pulled his fingers between rope and rock. Fred yanked his hand free, snatching the lacerated fingers to his mouth. He watched in horror as the last of the rope flew over the edge of the cliff, its end rising in the air like a disappearing snake's tail.

"Well done, Fred. Well done."

Fred Hampton whirled around. George Dalrymple was standing a few feet away, a grin on his red-veined face. "Way to go."

Fred's mouth worked. "I didn't mean to—I tried but I couldn't keep hold—"

"No need to explain. Smart of you to think to loosen the rope before he fell. I'd have done the same. Be prepared's my motto. Why go over the edge just because the young fella down there had a yen to be a mountain climber?"

"I was trying to see what had happened," Fred protested. "You can't think I just let him fall."

"If that's your story, you go ahead and stick to it." Dalrymple strolled to the rim and looked down. "Dear, dear." He shook his head. "Looks like your friend made it to the bottom a bit faster than he intended."

"Is he . . . will he be all right?"

"How would I know? I'd say as right as anyone would be after falling sixty feet or so. Anyway, why do you care? You and him buddies?"

"The man's a casual acquaintance; I assume he's with our group because he was on the plane. Look here, shouldn't we do something—get help?"

"No need. S'already done."

"What?" Fred edged to the cliff's rim and peered down to see tiny figures far below easing Delion's limp form onto a stretcher. They lifted the stretcher and slid it into the rear of a red, all-terrain vehicle. "Where did they come from? How did they know?"

"Don't it beat all? I swear those guys are always popping up when you people need 'em," said Dalrymple. "Sort of like the cavalry coming to the rescue. You look up, and there they are."

"How far is the nearest hospital?" Fred asked anxiously.

"Near? Far? Interesting you still use those words. They're at the hospital now. If you look, you'll notice you can't see the truck any more." Dalrymple hoisted himself up on top of the large flat rock and sat down, cross-legged. He looked like a Buddha in a wrinkled suit. "Tell me: how did you get hooked up with someone like Delion?"

"I told you I barely know the man," Fred snapped. "Since we were both trying to get back to Selveridge House, it seemed logical that we join forces."

"No need to get huffy. I'm just interested 'cause last time I knew he was with Malvena. Any idea why he's not with her now?"

"I'm sure I don't know. When we were in the meadow just now, the young lady marched off in what I can only describe as a fit of pique. They were arguing; they don't seem to like each other very much." Fred scratched his head and continued, "There's definitely something shady going on there. Delion as much as admitted it."

"He did, did he?" said Dalrymple. "Such sly children, those two! Now, let's see, what is it Delion thinks? Ah yes, that he was supposed to guard Malvena and the industrial plans she was smuggling into Europe. A micro-dot taped to the adhesive on the baby's diaper, I believe she told him. But, of course, that was just window dressing. Matter of fact, if only Delion knew it, he was just window dressing." Dalrymple chuckled and shook his head admiringly. "A woman to be reckoned with, Malvena, unsuspected depths there."

Fred stared at him. "How do you know all this?"

Dalrymple pursed his lips, puffing out his cheeks. "Well now, I know lots of things, friend. More than you could imagine. But enough of this idle chitchat. Let's continue the interesting conversation we were having when Howard so rudely interrupted us."

The memory flooded back. Fred glared at him. "You pushed me out the window!"

"A momentary lapse!" Dalrymple snickered. "A boyish impulse. I simply couldn't resist the sight of your rump so close to that open window! And you weren't hurt, at least not much. If you will keep inviting me to pop in, stay away from windows."

"*I?* I invited you?"

"Let's say your thoughts are the sort that beg for my kind of companionable society."

Fred struggled to recall what he'd been thinking. "Heaven," he said at last. "The meadow, the horses, the sunshine—it looked like heaven."

"And you decided you'd made it, didn't you?"

"Well, perhaps I hoped—" Fred's jaw tightened. "After all, when you think of it, I have spent a good deal of my life dealing with matters of religion. And I didn't only teach it; I attempted to apply those teachings to myself."

"Oh Fred, Fred. You didn't try very hard."

"What gives you the right— How can you say that?"

"Hey, like I said, I'm not blaming you. Matter of fact, if you cut right through the baloney, we're a lot alike, you and me." He raised a hand at Fred's outraged expression. "Look, buddy, I was right with you on that Internet business, every step of the way. Remember how you felt when that little girl told you the things she dreamed about, the things she wanted to do?" Dalrymple's eyes gleamed. "She sounded like a pretty knowledgeable kid—old for her age."

Fred flinched. "I stopped contacting her. I dropped my Internet service."

"Yes, you did. Just when I was really enjoying myself."

"There. You admit it!" Fred said, wiping his forehead. "You've just admitted that I made myself stop."

"Yes, but why? You gonna tell me you stopped because you thought it was wrong?"

"Of course!"

"Come off it, Fred. You and I know you cancelled your service only because you were getting close to the point of not being able to control your desires. You wanted to meet this kid and act out some of those delicious daydreams. You knew it, and you were scared shitless you'd be found out if you did.

What you couldn't bear was the thought of what would happen to your reputation if the kid squealed on you."

Fred looked as though he was going to deny it. Then he said softly, "I guess that entered into it, but I did stop, and partly because I knew it was wrong. I swear it."

Dalrymple sighed. "You still don't get it, do you? This whimpering shame isn't enough to erase the fact that you got quite a kick out of the chat room business. You can't get out of that." His fat face creased in a grin. "When I saw how much you missed them, it almost made up for my not being able to listen to those chats of yours. Knew right then and there you and me were gettin' real close."

Fred felt a quiver of fear. "No! No, I don't want to be anywhere near you." He drew himself to his full height, looking for once rather impressive. "I don't want anything to do with you, Dalrymple."

"Don't be too sure."

"I wasn't going to mention this, but I did do one thing I'm proud of. In the water after the plane crash . . . I gave Sammy the seat cushion when I realized it could not support us both. I can only hope saving the boy's life might be enough to set me apart from your kind."

"Ah yes, the Sammy episode. Disheartened me, I can tell you. And just after we'd all enjoyed the sight of that young actor so spectacularly shoving the child off a piece of wreckage in an attempt to save himself—unsuccessfully, of course. I must confess you had me worried when you came along with that Boy-Scout merit-badge stuff. Thought for a while there we'd lost you. But it wasn't long before you invited me along with you on that nymph-and-satyr episode and I was back where I belong."

Fred's eyelids quivered. "Where . . . where you belong?"

Dalrymple unfolded his legs and slid from the boulder. "Oh, I've been with you pretty constantly during these past years. Anyone told you yet about the spirits who are with a person during his life on earth? The two so-called 'good' spirits and two they like to call 'evil'? They change from time to time, but gradually a person begins to feel more comfortable with a certain type and those are the ones who stay with him or her. Well, Freddie, my man, can you guess whom you've come to feel real comfortable with?" Dalrymple gave Fred a wink and nodded. Then he was gone.

Fred Hampton looked at the place Dalrymple had been. Then he clutched his stomach, tottered to the edge of the cliff that overlooked the vast plain, leaned over, and was sick.

22

DELION HEARD THE VOICES; BUT INSTEAD OF ALLOWING himself to waken, he burrowed deep beneath the covers. He felt the way he used to when he was six and his grandma called him down to breakfast on cold winter mornings. No way was he going to leave the comfort of a soft warm bed, not until he felt the sharp thump of her knuckle on his headbone.

"Hey!" Delion sat up, holding his head. He squinted and raised a hand to shield his eyes against the light flooding the room. "What the hell?"

"That's enough of that, mister."

Delion stared at the tiny woman beside his bed. "Grandma!"

His grandmother's snapping black eyes softened at the sight of his astonishment. "Didn't I teach you better than that, boy?" she said.

Delion leapt from his bed and scooped the little woman into his arms. "You're here, you're here with me!" Then he released her and smacked his forehead. "Of course, you're here—been here since I was ten. You're an angel, right?"

"Praise the Lord."

Delion frowned. "You're young! I don't know how I knew who you were just now. Why, you're real young!" He grinned. "And pretty!"

"Do tell?" His grandmother chuckled. "I wouldn't say that's anything to brag on; you won't find any ugly people where I live."

"How come I didn't notice it right away, I mean you being so pretty and young and all?"

"You saw the person you remembered, else you wouldn't have recognized me. It's only when you really looked that you saw me as I am. Even now you hear me talk as I did in the life I left behind." Her voice had changed. The thin, sharp quality was richer; it held the hint of a musical lilt. "Time for you to start learning, Jackson. Time for you to get up out of that bed." It seemed to Delion her flowing speech was now entering his mind as pictures rather than words.

"Yes," his grandmother said gently. "You're hearing the language of my community. We are very different from you and those you are with. You and I still share the love we had for each other, but other things, the things that now make up my life, can't be shared with you. At least not as you are now."

A tremor arced through Delion's body. He started to say something, but before he could speak, his grandmother leaned toward him and took his face between her tiny hands. She looked deep into his eyes, her own dark ones glowing, absorbed. Suddenly she drew back.

"Oh, Jackson, what have you done? What have you allowed to become part of you?"

Delion shrank from the pain in her eyes. "What? What is it, Grandma?" Then he remembered the baby in Malvena's arms. Was that it? "You don't understand—it wasn't my fault

282

we had the kid along. I didn't know anything about the baby bein' part of the plan until I saw him at the airport. Matter of fact, I never saw the girl, Malvena, before then. I was hired to keep an eye on her. All I was supposed to do was make sure she got on the plane and to where she was supposed to go without no hassle." He paused, uneasy. "It was just a job."

"You have no idea, do you?" his grandmother continued as though he had not spoken, ". . . no idea of what you've done." She shook her head.

Delion hugged his muscular arms about his chest and struggled to think of something to say. But he could not. Strangely, this seemed to please his grandmother. "You haven't thought it through yet, have you? You haven't understood the consequences of the lawlessness you allowed yourself to become a part of?" she said in her silvery voice. "You're going to have to find out what you've done and own up to it." She gave a whisper of a sigh. "There's a lot you have to learn." She paused, listening to something she alone could hear. "I have to go, child."

"Don't leave, Grandma!" Delion knew he sounded like a six-year-old, but he couldn't help himself. "I need you. Please. You gotta tell me what to do." His face worked. "Sure I did some bad things, but nothing real terrible. Like I never killed anybody—and that's the truth."

Her gentle gaze was sober. "I can't be with you, not the way you are now. Anyway, it's not me you need, Jackson. It's the Lord. And he's here. All you have to do is ask his help. I taught you how to do that, remember?"

Delion felt the brush of a kiss on his forehead before she turned away. A surge of fragrant air rushed through the room. He was alone.

"Grandma?" he said. But he didn't expect an answer, and there was none.

"So you're up and about?" Blossom O'Meara nudged open the door as she held the full tray before her. "I'd say it's about time." She put the tray on the small table by the window.

Delion adjusted his expression, hoping it did not reflect the turmoil his grandmother's warning had triggered. "You're the lady from the airplane, right?" he said to Blossom.

"Right, me bucko. The nosy one who didn't particularly care for the way you and Malvena were treating that baby," Blossom said tartly. Then she stopped. "What's the matter, boy?" she said, studying him. "Ah, someone's been telling you some home truths, I see."

Damn. What had happened to the poker face he'd perfected over the years? "So how come you're here?" Delion said, his tone as offhand as he could manage.

"Never mind that. It's what you're doing here that should concern you."

"Last thing I remember I was falling—man, I musta gone all the way down off that cliff! Should have been hurt bad, but I'm not, I'm fine. And where's Fred?" He looked around as though expecting Fred Hampton to appear. "He was at the top when I fell."

"I haven't seen Fred." Blossom said, frowning. "I heard there was someone with you when you fell, but the men who brought you in said it wasn't anyone they could bring here."

"This some kind of hospital?" Delion asked.

"You might call it that. Now listen, young man; let's stop with the questions. Are you hungry?" Blossom removed a large dish cover to disclose a stack of pancakes, sausages, two pieces of toast, and two eggs over easy.

Delion realized he was ravenous. "Got any syrup there?"

Blossom eyed him with amusement. "Blueberry,

boysenberry, cherry/raspberry, or plain old maple?"

"Plain old maple, I guess."

"I think you'll find it in the little china pitcher."

"What if I said I wanted some of that boysenberry syrup?"

"Then that's what would be in the pitcher."

Delion shook his head. "Guess I should be used to this kind of stuff by now." He took a seat at the little table and glanced up at Blossom. He found he didn't want her to leave just yet, didn't want to be left alone to think about what his grandmother had said. "You want some of this?" he asked her. "There's plenty."

"No, thanks; I've had breakfast." But Blossom drew the easy chair by the bed up to the table and sat down.

Delion took a large bite of pancake. "My grandma was just here, y'know?" he said.

"No. But I knew you had a visitor and that it must be an angel—there's always a bright light coming from a room when an angel is there. That's why I waited to bring in your tray."

"Seems like she thinks Malvena and I did something real bad," Delion said slowly. "Gotta find out about it," he murmured, then stopped. What had gotten into him? He hadn't meant to say anything about what his grandmother had told him. Jackson Delion didn't go around whining to strangers. But when Delion looked at Blossom, he saw she wasn't listening. "You're not paying me no mind, are you?," he said. "You're just sitting here because I asked you to." He waved a hand. "Listen, you got stuff you want to do, go do it."

Blossom flushed. "I'm sorry, lad. It's something I've been working on—this habit I have of thinking about things I should be doing instead of attending to the person I'm with." She folded her hands in her lap. "Go ahead. What about your grandmother?"

Delion shoveled a sausage into his mouth. "No, I'm more interested in hearing about you. How come you left that nice little place you had by Selveridge House?"

Blossom examined her folded hands. "I didn't want to," she said quietly. "I left because there are things I have to learn, things I must face, and I can best do it here. Michael . . . ." She stopped and pressed her lips firmly together. "Michael . . . ." She stopped again, took a tissue from her pocket, and blew her nose. "It seems Michael is able to learn what he must while staying in Rose Cottage, and I am not," she continued briskly. "I . . . I'm sure we'll be able to be together soon." The look in her eyes begged Delion to agree.

"Sure," Delion said gently. "Sure you will." He took a large bite of toast. "But I don't get it. If you want to be with him and he wants to be with you, what's stopping you?"

Blossom took Delion's empty plate and placed it on the tray. "I don't know. It's one of the things I'm trying to understand. I know I'm here because I love doing things for people, feeding them, just helping out." She took a quick breath. "But maybe another reason I'm here is because I'm beginning to discover there are other reasons why I enjoy doing things for people, motives that aren't so great. I've never been much for thinking, but there are thoughts that have come to me while I'm working here, some I'd just as soon not have around. Like realizing that part of the reason I enjoy helping people is because I want things done my way." Blossom gave a short laugh. "I like to 'set things straight,' you see, that is, I like to set them straight according to my lights. Matter of fact, I've been treated to a few memories—times I've barged right in and given my help when it wasn't wanted, times I've hurt more than helped." It seemed difficult for Blossom to say this, but once she'd begun, the words came faster. "I've never been one to consider much about the whys and wherefores of a thing; mostly I see something I think needs taking care of and just go do it. I pretty much feel I know what's best for people, especially for my family." She grimaced. "Looking back, seems like I've fairly made my life's work informing Michael and our grown children what to do whilst all the time practically breaking my arm patting myself on the back. It's a wonder Michael stuck with me all these years."

Delion looked at her. "You're puttin' me on! You get bent out of shape just because sometimes you helped people who didn't appreciate it? Holy shit, lady—" Delion doubled up as the pain hit his midsection. "Damn." His face contorted as another pain gripped him. "I don't see what's so bad about sayin' sh— that word," he gasped. "Anyways, I said worse before, and it didn't hurt," he finished lamely.

A smile quirked the corners of Blossom's mouth. "Perhaps it was your attaching 'holy' to it rather than simply saying 'shit' that caused your, ah, distress, or maybe when you did it before it was excusable."

Delion's black eyes snapped with frustration. "Then how come you can say both of them and nothing happens?"

"That's not my particular problem," she said. Then she sobered, murmuring, "Mine appears to be this control thing. I guess my habit of wanting to be the one to call the shots is what I have to watch out for."

"Like the way I talk," Delion said, rubbing his stomach.

"You could say so." Blossom said absently. She gave Delion a considering look. "Tell you what—why don't you come get me when you're dressed and in your right mind? There's someone who could use a little company that I want you to meet." Then she put a hand to her mouth. "Oh my . . . there I go doing it again."

"Yeah, but I don't see you getting a belt in the gut for your bad habit." But Delion said it wryly. "Hey, don't worry; you're not controllin' anybody. No one makes Jackson Delion do anything he don't want to." He leaned his chair back to a dangerous tilt. He was going to have to think about what his grandmother had said. Maybe he should ask for help as she'd suggested. But not now. Not right away. "Who's this person I'm supposed to go see?" he said.

Blossom's stricken look had eased at Delion's reassurance. Now she collected the rest of the dishes and picked up the laden tray. "It's someone who has just come. Her name's Jessie."

"Why can't Karen stay with me?" Sherwood Prescott looked as though he would rather be sitting behind Kate's desk than in his present seat, the comfortable chair to one side of it. "After all, I am her father."

Kate laced her fingers together and put her elbows on the desk, propping her chin on her hands. "Karen has a lot to learn, about herself, about this world. Do you think you're the best person to teach her?"

"I'm her father," Prescott repeated stubbornly.

"We have one Father here. Don't you think you can safely leave her in his care?"

"But she has just arrived, and we've seen each other so briefly," Prescott protested. "And I can tell her some of the things she needs to know, things I've already learned." He shifted uncomfortably. "Besides I . . . I would enjoy having her with me."

"Ah," said Kate, "so this is more about you than Karen."

"I don't see it like that at all," Prescott said stiffly. "I'd say it's more about my wanting to spend some old-fashioned family time with my daughter."

"You did a lot of that with your family while you were on earth?"

"As much as possible." Prescott's jaw twitched. "Though I admit it wasn't always possible." He met Kate's steady gaze and his own faltered. "Actually, I wasn't home nearly as much as I'd have liked, especially during Karen's younger years." His chin lifted. "But I had a demanding job, a good many responsibilities."

"You did." Kate's tone was mild. "Tell you what—shall we see what Karen wants?"

Prescott looked at her sharply, as though assessing the possibility of some ploy. Then he nodded. "Yes. Yes, go ahead and ask her."

Prescott felt the rush of a lilac-scented breeze from somewhere behind him, and there she was, standing beside his chair. "Karen!" He rose to his feet and awkwardly took her hand. "Kate and I were speaking of you." He gestured to the seat he had vacated. "Do sit down."

Kate smiled at the girl. "Nothing wrong with your father's manners, Karen; you'll have to give him that."

"I've always loved Dad's courtly shtick," Karen said, eyeing Prescott affectionately, "that is, I did when I got old enough to appreciate it." She took a seat in the chair her father had offered and casually placed one jean-clad leg over the other knee. "So what's up?"

"Your father wonders whether you'd like to be with him for a while."

Karen looked at Prescott, disconcerted. "But Dad, aren't you supposed to be learning stuff about yourself the way I am?"

"You're already doing that?" Her father's eyebrows rose in astonishment. "But you've just come; I thought this would be an introductory period, something I could help you with."

"You did quite a bit of wandering about when you first arrived, Sherwood, but Karen doesn't need to," Kate explained. "And then you didn't go into self-examination quite as easily as she did or accept things as quickly as she has been able to."

"You think that's because I was sick?" Karen asked her, interested.

"No, very little spiritual growth occurred during your illness; there wasn't much you could do other than endure." Compassion flashed across Kate's lovely face, "And may I say it was something you did quite beautifully. No, I was speaking of the fact that you made very few unfortunate choices during your young life—actually you didn't have the chance to do much adult-type choosing." Kate turned to Prescott. "While you, on the other hand, have had a long life of choosing both what was good and what was not, of settling into habits, some of which you seem to be finding remarkably difficult to shed."

"I'm afraid one or two of them are here to stay." Sherwood Prescott's shoulders slumped, but then he straightened. "Well now, I imagine all this is your rather convoluted way of telling me I've got work to do and it would be best that I do it alone."

"What do you think?"

"You sound like me trying to pry an admission of accountability at the negotiating table. All right. You've got it. I think I should try to work on my own tasks and let Karen get on with what she's apparently already doing so manifestly well with the aid of you and your cohorts."

"Oh, Daddy!" Karen went to Prescott and threw her arms about his neck. She took a step back. "You taught me everything I know about honor and decency and truthfulness," she said, her voice husky, "and not only telling the truth, but living it. You may have missed a lot of school plays and piano recitals, but you were always there for me when it counted."

Prescott swallowed. "I'm glad you feel that way, Karen," he said, clearing his throat. "I wish I could believe it were true."

"Believe it." Karen took a quick breath. "Look, would it help . . . would you like me to be with you for a while, Daddy?"

Sherwood Prescott exchanged a quick glance with Kate. "I don't think so, pet. It's probably better that we make our own way independent of each other." He managed a smile. "Anyway, I rather think Kate may have plans for you."

"Give that man a kewpie doll," said Kate. "I was about to introduce you to someone, Karen, someone who would like to share some of the things she has been learning herself."

Karen looked with delighted surprise at the figure that appeared beside Kate. "Do I know you?"

"I'm Cynthia." Cynthia smiled at her. "So you're Mr. Prescott's daughter."

"Where have you been, Cynthia? Why did you leave without a word to the rest of us?" Prescott shot the questions at her.

"I've been with Kate and Howard. You called me?" Cynthia asked Kate. At Kate's smiling nod, Cynthia looked at her attentively, then gasped, her eyes sparkling with pleasure. "You mean it? I can help? You think I'm ready?"

"Yes," Kate said with quiet satisfaction.

Karen had been watching them all, wide eyed. "You know Cynthia?" she asked her father.

"She was our copilot," said Prescott.

Karen made a little sound. "Oh, yes. I remember the name from the newspapers." She turned to Cynthia and said softly, "There was a picture of your husband holding your little girl. I'm so sorry."

Cynthia went to Karen and took her hand. "Don't be.

They are being cared for, and while they are on earth, they're in the stream of providence. Meanwhile I have so much to learn while I'm waiting for Rob." She smiled. "And one special thing I'm learning is how to share what I've been given with newcomers like you. We'll have a wonderful time, you and I. You can't imagine how incredible it is here. When I was first shown—not just told but shown so that I understood it—that all good and all truth come from God, it was like . . .," she paused a moment as she thought, "it was like I was in front of a shining curtain that parted to reveal the most beautiful scene in creation." She glanced at Kate and gave a little laugh. "Oh, for pity sake, there I go, babbling again."

"Not exactly what I'd call babbling," said Kate. "All right then, off you go, both of you. Howard and I will expect you to join us at dinner."

Cynthia flashed Kate a look of pure pleasure at the invitation, then took Karen's hand again and half turned away from the two by the desk. And the next moment, Sherwood Prescott was alone with Kate.

He sat heavily in the chair he'd vacated for Karen. "She's an angel already, isn't she?" he asked Kate.

"Cynthia? Yes."

"So soon? So quickly?"

"You still speak of 'soon' and 'quickly'? There is no time here, remember? But to answer your question, Cynthia's state was attuned to heaven from the moment she came from earth. She led a life that, when she came here, allowed her to absorb the truths she was given like a sponge in deep water."

Prescott gave a deep sigh and said, "While I, on the other hand—"

"Oh, come on, Sherwood—stop feeling sorry for yourself. It's not particularly attractive. Think of it; I've just told you some marvelous news about that lovely young woman.

292

Rejoice!"

"Of course, I'm glad to hear about Cynthia." Sherwood Prescott gave Kate a reflective look and rubbed his chin. "But you know, I'd have thought that as an angel you'd be a bit more, ah, sympathetic."

"What do you think an angel would say?" Kate asked him. "A sympathetic angel."

Prescott raised an eyebrow at her tone. "I imagine I thought an angel would have been charitable enough to categorize the emotion she saw in me as regret rather than self-pity."

Kate grinned. "Nice try, Sherwood. Let me give you a heavenly hint; it isn't an act of charity to help someone deceive himself. Think back. Was what you felt really regret?"

Prescott colored. An unwilling smile tugged at the corner of his mouth. "Am I really such a pompous ass?"

They both laughed.

"Not all the time, but you do have your moments. What I'm trying to do is encourage you to admit to your real thoughts and motives," Kate said more gently. "Otherwise, how can you ask God to take them from you? I know you've been doing your best to figure things out on your own, but it doesn't seem to have gotten you very far, has it? The trouble you have asking anyone for help is going to be a real stumbling block unless you work on it." She came from behind her desk and leaned against it, folding her arms across her chest as she regarded him, musing. "Let's see. Who can we find that you'd accept as a mentor? Plato? Aristotle? Or perhaps you'd like someone a little more modern?"

Prescott felt a flush creep over his cheeks again. "I don't think of myself as the sort of person who can't take instruction."

"Don't you?" Kate murmured. The phone on her desk

rang, and the glow that lit Kate's face even before she picked it up increased to a brilliance that forced Prescott to look away. "Yes, Howard?" She listened a moment and then said, "Perfect! You've spoken to him? Right. I think so too." She flashed a smile at Prescott as she replaced the receiver. "I think you'll like the person you're going to meet, Sherwood."

Prescott stared gloomily at the flowered carpet. He was tempted to say he didn't particularly want to meet this mentor Howard had chosen, that he simply didn't want a mentor, however illustrious he might be. But when he looked up, Prescott saw the space Kate had occupied was empty and lounging in the chair behind her desk was a slight, blond man with a pointed beard. The young man raised a languid hand. "I'm Brandon. Seems we'll be working together. Shall I call you Prescott, or would you rather I use your given name?"

"Most people call me Prescott," Prescott said guardedly.

"But then I'm not most people." He looked into Prescott's eyes. His own were an astonishing shade of blue, a changing pale blue-white that reminded Prescott of a sparkling lake washed with sunshine.

Prescott frowned. He'd never seen anyone remotely like this slightly peculiar-looking man, but there was something strikingly familiar about him.

Brandon stood up. "Let's go for a walk. I find it easier to discuss things when I'm walking, don't you?"

Prescott stood too. Brandon's head came barely to Prescott's shoulder, but the man's quietly authoritative presence made Prescott feel like a very junior executive about to be shown the ropes by senior staff. He wasn't completely surprised to find they were no longer in Kate's office, but in a meadow sprinkled with red and pink poppy-like flowers, on a path just wide enough to allow the two men to walk side by side.

"Where are we going?" Prescott asked.

"I thought we'd mosey back to Selveridge House, do some chatting along the way."

"Do I know you?" Prescott said cautiously. "I mean, should I have heard of you? Are you someone famous?"

"No, no, and no." Brandon stooped to pick up a small stone. He tossed it high into the air, looking joyously pleased when it came down and landed perfectly in his outstretched palm. "But I know you. Howard thought that, since you seem to be having a difficult time with your review, it might help if you had someone who knows you well guide you."

"My, ah, review?"

"That's what we've been talking about, isn't it? Reviewing your life?"

"Well, yes—" Prescott thought of the uncomfortable memories he'd been going over before his interview with Kate, one of the most uncomfortable of which was that regrettable incident during the Hovercraft negotiations when certain innuendoes he'd allowed to go unchallenged had caused Dan Morton to lose his job. Prescott felt a spasm of shame. No, it was difficult enough to relive these memories by himself; he wasn't about to have a voyeur along for the ride. "Yes, I have been going over some of my life decisions," he said to Brandon, "but if you don't mind, I'd rather do it privately."

"This is a very public place," Brandon said casually, "concealing past and present sins isn't easy to do here, at least not after you've been here a while. But don't worry, Prescott; none of it's news to me. I was there when it happened."

Prescott stared at him. "What?"

"I was one of your associate spirits while you were on earth—been with you pretty much of late," Brandon sobered, "though not all the time." Then he saw the look on Prescott's face, and his own lit in a mischievous grin. "Not to worry—I'm one of the ones whose job it was to steer you toward good. Not that you always paid attention."

"You were with me? But I had no idea—"

"What if you had? It wouldn't have worked too well, would it? As it is, you were always free to listen to me and my partner. Sometimes you did, and sometimes you chose to listen to your other companions."

Prescott looked about apprehensively.

"They're not with you anymore." When Prescott looked at him in question, Brandon continued. "You don't need us to be with you. That part is done. The decisions you made formed the person you are and will be from now on. It's customary during a certain period after your arrival to go over those decisions to try to discover just what character you've formed." Brandon leaned over a heavily blossomed bush of coral flowerlets and sniffed appreciatively. "It's all pretty standard, y'know; I don't see why you're having such a difficult time with it."

Sherwood Prescott had been a couple of steps ahead when the other man stopped to admire the bush. Prescott halted too. He spoke without looking at Brandon. "What did you mean when you said a minute ago that— Is there no chance—" He struggled to regain his composure. "Do you mean the person I am now is who I will be forever?"

"Didn't say that. I said you formed the essential 'you' when you lived on earth. Didn't say that was it as far as it goes. Angels, for instance, keep learning and growing forever."

"What about . . . about those who don't become angels?"

"They also develop—in their own way. They learn what are the acceptable limits and what they must do to in order to live the way they want to," Brandon said, his easy nonchalance vanished. Prescott noticed the angel could not repress a slight shudder.

"Is there any possibility that I'll be able to . . . to—." Prescott stopped, unable to articulate the question to which he so desperately wanted to know the answer.

"I don't know. That depends on what is seen in your review," Brandon said not unkindly.

"Oh God!" It was a cry. "If I'd known, if only I'd known."

"You'd what?" Brandon said with some asperity, "tried harder?"

"I'd have thought more about things that mattered."

"Good, good, but what would you have done differently?"

Prescott's brow furrowed. "I'd have given more time to Phillipa and Karen," he said at last. Then he added, "But it isn't what I haven't done that's been bothering me." He darted a look at Brandon. "There are things I wish I hadn't done, events I've been going over lately that, frankly, I'd rather not talk about." He fumbled with his tie and looked away. "You spoke of being unable to conceal one's sins here. Does that mean you already know everything I've done?"

"If it's part of my job to know, then I know," Brandon said enigmatically. They had come to a grassy expanse beyond which was a walled estate. Brandon's pace quickened. "Here we are, Selveridge House. Any objection to continuing our conversation in one of the interview rooms?"

Prescott looked as though he had quite a few objections, but he didn't voice them. Instead he examined the imposing brick facade of the building before them and said, puzzled, "It looks different. Wasn't it white stucco?"

"Things change." Brandon opened the gate and indicated that Prescott should go ahead. "Are you saying you don't recognize this as Selveridge House?"

Prescott looked at the English garden backed by high hollyhocks and delphiniums, at the lawn leading up the slope to the dining room. "That's the strange part. It does seem familiar. I know if I went around that corner I'd see Michael and Blossom's Rose Cottage. No, in spite of the differences, I know I'm at Selveridge House."

Brandon nodded, satisfied. "It appears to have changed because you've changed."

"Is that good?" Prescott said, sounding not at all like his confident self.

"Let's go in and talk, and maybe we'll find out."

23

MALVENA STEPPED BACK INTO THE SHADOWS, MAKING SURE the couple coming out of the brightly lit hotel wouldn't see her. Though there was no particular reason for her reluctance to be seen, remaining inconspicuous had become second nature. She looked across the rain-darkened square at the peak-roofed building. It wasn't as large or inviting as Selveridge House, but she didn't want Selveridge House; she didn't want to be with the rest. It was becoming too hard to keep up the pretense.

Malvena shifted to a more comfortable position, flexing her cramped toes against the wet leather of her high-heeled shoes. She had chosen these stupid shoes in order to play the part, but it was no longer really necessary. If she stayed away from the rest of them, who was there to suspect, who indeed, to care? Malvena's shoulders slumped. If, as she was beginning to be forced to accept, the plan had succeeded, why was she still among these infidels? She had expected to be met with gratitude, to be greeted and given untold rewards. No, she would not question. Surely soon enough it would be made known what she should do. Meanwhile, the building ahead promised warmth and food. Malvena stepped into the misting rain. But before she was halfway across the square, she heard raised, angry voices from the direction the couple had taken. A moment later, a woman strode into the pale light of the square, her arms swinging at her sides, her hands balled into fists. Malvena willed herself to continue walking casually, to look unconcerned, disinterested.

The woman cast an impatient glance at Malvena, then stopped. "Oh it's you," she said. "What are you doing here?"

"Who are—?" Malvena's jaw dropped. "Mrs. Jorgenson?"

It wasn't just the fact that, instead of a business suit, Beatrice Jorgenson was wearing a low-cut, black satin dress. Malvena had never seen Beatrice with anything but a dab of lipstick, and the woman before her was expertly, if heavily, made up, her khol-ringed eyes fringed with mascara-laden lashes, her full, scarlet lips generously outlined with a darker red lipstick. If it hadn't been for the voice, Malvena wouldn't have recognized her.

Beatrice gave a brief smile. "Yes, yes, I know. Not quite the way you saw me last." She adjusted a shoulder strap. The satin dress afforded little protection against the night's damp, chill air, and she shivered. "Don't stand there gawking, girl. Let's go inside." She paused a moment, scowling in the direction she and the man had taken, then strode toward the hotel. "That bastard is liable to come and try to have a go again."

"What . . . what did he do?" Malvena unconsciously raised the pitch of her voice, made the words hesitant.

Beatrice cast her a sharp glance. "Still doing the shy little foreigner bit? Why? What's in it for you now we're here?"

"I don't know what you mean."

Beatrice gave a sardonic roll of her eyes but merely shrugged and pushed open the door. Following close behind, Malvena saw they had entered some kind of tavern or pub. The smoky interior was crowded but not noisy. The people who lined the bar or sat at the small, brass-covered tables talked quietly, engrossed in private conversations. Several looked up as the two women made their way across the room; though no one spoke, Malvena had the impression those they passed looked expectant, hopeful that Beatrice would acknowledge them. She did not.

"Here, this will do." The corner booth Beatrice indicated was already occupied, but at Beatrice's gesture, the two girls in it immediately rose, collected their jackets and cigarettes, and slid out of the booth. Both bobbed their heads as they passed Beatrice.

"Who are you?" Malvena said sharply.

"Didn't take long, did it?" Beatrice said with a satisfied smirk. "Came here, investigated the layout, saw what was needed, what would work and what wouldn't, took proper steps to ensure the success of the venture; and here I am, head of what will be the largest concern of its kind in the area."

The barman appeared at the booth carrying a tray laden with a large glass of ale and a pot of tea with a cream pitcher and sugar bowl, a cup and saucer, a plate of biscuits. "Here you are, then. You got rid of the sport okay, B?"

Beatrice gave a disgusted shrug. "Only just. Bugger tried to slip one over on me. Me! Imagine!" She dismissed him and poured the tea for Malvena. "You won't want anything else we offer here, but the tea's all right." She looked up to see Malvena quietly watching her. "You don't have to pretend, you know. A friend of mine told me all about you."

Malvena sat very still. She felt brittle; she felt as though her neck might break if she moved it, her head fall off. How had the stupid woman found out? No, Beatrice wasn't stupid—whatever else she might be, she wasn't stupid. "What did your friend tell you?" she said carefully.

"That's for me to know and you to find out," Beatrice said. Then she sobered. "Look, who you are and what you've done doesn't interest me except as far as it affects my organization." She looked thoughtful. "It's why he should have taken the trouble to tell me about you that intrigues me."

Who is this 'he'? Is there someone here who knows about me? But Malvena didn't say these things aloud. She sipped her tea, hot with a slight flavor of herbs and mint, then took a small bite of sugary biscuit. She must be careful. It was important not to give anything away. Beatrice might not really know much; perhaps she was just fishing for information. "What is this organization you talk about?" she asked Beatrice.

"A business I've recently taken over." Beatrice traced the top edge of her glass with a forefinger. "I've done well, but recently there have been complications. I could use some help, someone who can take orders, carry them out, but who isn't afraid to take initiative when necessary." Her eyes met Malvena's. "I'm not promising anything, but it's possible there might be a job for you."

In spite of herself, Malvena's lip curled. "Thank you, no."

Beatrice was not offended. "Keep it in mind. It looks as though you're going to be around for a while."

"You think I stay here? No, no!"

"Yes, yes." Beatrice smiled. It was not a nice smile. "This is an interesting place, unusual in ways. I think you'll find it's not so easy to leave." Her eyes searched the smoky room and came to rest on a figure in the far corner. "Ask him," she said, nodding at the man who slumped over a small table, his elbows propped on the brass tabletop, his head buried in his hands.

Malvena looked at him. She couldn't see his face, but there was something oddly familiar about what she could see of the lanky figure. As though drawn by her gaze, he raised his head. It was a moment before she recognized the drawn, wasted face, the person behind the bleak eyes. "Oh, the man of God." Malvena did not attempt to hide her disdain.

"Yes, it's Fred Hampton." Beatrice chuckled. "Poor man, he just about collapsed when he found himself here. As you can see, he's still unhappy about it. Can't seem to do anything but sit and pray. Or try to." She raised a hand and beckoned to him. "Come say hello, Fred," she called out. "Come talk to us."

Fred Hampton stared at her dully. He shook his head and returned his gaze to his bony hands, now tightly clasped on the table before him. Beatrice gave an almost imperceptible signal to the barman, and the man went to Fred, leaned over and whispered something. Hampton listened to the barman a long moment, then rose stiffly and shambled to the table where the women sat. "You want me?" he mumbled.

"You bet. Come sit down and tell Malvena what you've learned about this place. She has just come to us."

A glimmer of concern showed in Fred's lean face as he recognized Malvena. "My dear, you can't want to be here. See if you can get a pass to leave."

"Why would I need a pass?" Malvena darted an uneasy glance from Fred to Beatrice.

"She shouldn't be here, Beatrice; she has nothing to do with you or your business. Let her go."

At first, Beatrice seemed pleased by Fred's request, but then she sighed and said regretfully, "I don't decide who leaves and who doesn't. Maybe someday, but right now I have my hands full just finding out just what is and isn't allowed here." A shade of annoyance crossed her sharp-featured face. "They keep changing the rules."

"I don't think the rules change," Fred said wearily, "I think perhaps it's just that you keep pushing the limit until you're punished for going too far." He seemed to have regained something of his composure; at least his haggard face showed a spark of life.

"Who are you to speak to me like that?" A light flashed in Beatrice's eyes like summer lightning. "What do you know about anything? You, a failed priest?" The words sounded like a curse.

Fred looked stricken. "You're right. I am a failed priest . . . a failed man."

"All right, all right, Fred. Don't you think that's about enough self-abasement for the time being? Haven't we done the gloom-and-doom thing pretty thoroughly by now?" The man who stood beside the table regarded Fred with a benign smile. The light emanating from the stranger filled the area about him with such brightness that many of those at nearby tables shied away or raised their hands to protect their faces.

A spark of incredulous hope lit Fred's face. "Are you, are you—?"

"My name is Stephen. I'll be your instructor for your next phase."

"But I thought—Dalrymple said I didn't have a chance. Said my prayers were useless, that when they weren't vain repetition, they were mostly about me. He said I'd spent my life in training to be with him and his like." Fred's voice caught. "I've been going over some . . . incidents, and I'm afraid . . . I'm afraid it's true."

"Dalrymple said a lot of things, but then that's his job, isn't it? As he sees it. To lie, to twist everything in the hope that it will cause unhappiness and bring despair."

"Then I haven't ruined everything?"

"You certainly made a stab at it." Stephen grimaced. "Dalrymple was right about the laziness and your fascination with the sleazy. But then you always fought against it when you took the time to realize you were doing something wrong. And occasionally you did let us win for you." A slight smile flitted across Stephen's face. "Dalrymple and his crew weren't the only ones with you, you know. My associates and I were there too." His voice became gentle. "We were with you when you gave your life for the boy. That was no death-bed repentance; it was the effect of how you'd often tried to live your life."

Fred looked away but not before those at the table saw his tears. "I did what I had to," he said quietly. "Sammy was so young, so frightened."

"Look, if you two want to continue this prayer meeting, could you do it elsewhere?" Beatrice's rasping tone was cocky, but the skin showed gray beneath her make-up; and when Stephen turned to survey her with cool, nonjudgmental eyes, she dropped her gaze and became absorbed in the shimmering images in the brass-topped table.

"Right," he said. "I think it's time we went, Fred."

"Oh, yes," Fred looked at Stephen, his eyes bright. "Yes, please." Then he paused. "What about the girl?" he whispered. "Shouldn't we . . . shouldn't you take Malvena too?"

"Suppose we ask her?" Stephen looked at Malvena. "Would you like to come with us?"

Malvena took her time about answering. "Even if what they say about this place is true, I do not think I want to go with you," she said at last. "Wherever you are going, it cannot be a place where I will find . . . those I wish to see."

Stephen nodded. "Perhaps you'd like to speak to someone about that? I can arrange it."

Malvena regarded him uneasily. "What do you think you know about me?"

"Everything."

Malvena flinched at the quiet finality in Stephen's voice. "You are the friend who told Beatrice about me?"

The corners of Stephen's mouth quirked. "I rather think she was speaking of Dalrymple." He inclined his head in Beatrice's direction. "I haven't met this lady until now."

Malvena felt a chill on the back of her neck. How many people knew? She raised her chin. "No matter what you know, you cannot understand. None of you can," she said.

"Actually I do understand. Quite well." A flash of sadness crossed Stephen's face. "You have permission to leave this place," he said. "If you want, you may continue your journey."

"Now wait a minute," Beatrice sat up straight. "I was just about to give her a job offer. She should have time to consider it."

"When you wish guidance," he continued to Malvena as though Beatrice had not spoken, "you have only to ask."

Malvena tossed her head at this. Who was this stranger to suggest she needed guidance? The idea of getting away from this place, however, had an undeniable appeal. Her eyes darted about the smoky room. The little group at the corner booth was being studiously ignored by the rest of the pub's inmates. "You will give me something, this pass they speak of, to tell these people I am allowed to go?" she asked.

Stephen seemed to find this amusing. "You don't need a pass—unless you stay here too long," he said. He put a hand on Fred's shoulder. "Ready?"

Fred had been hovering at Stephen's side, all but dancing in his anxiety to be gone. He cleared his throat. His head bobbed up and down. "Yes. Yes, certainly."

Stephen's light touch turned Fred around, and at the same time he also turned about. And they were gone.

Not only Beatrice, but Malvena and those sitting at the nearby tables relaxed perceptibly at the sudden lessening of light. A quiet, murmuring buzz of conversations resumed. Malvena slid to the end of the bench.

"Now just a minute," Beatrice reached out to stop her. "Don't just go tearing out of here. Give my offer some thought."

"He said I could leave," Malvena said coldly. She shook her arm free of Beatrice's grip. "You can't stop me."

"No one's trying to stop you. I'm just saying take your time, think it over. You might find you like it here."

"You think I would want to work for you? Like one of these frightened girls who tremble when you frown? No, thank you."

"Not like them," Beatrice said quickly. "I don't need more of those. I need someone with steel in her backbone; and from what I hear, you've an ample supply." Her tone grew coaxing, "Why not give it a try? That Stephen person didn't say you couldn't stay a little while."

Malvena hesitated; though she wasn't tempted by the offer, the older woman's obvious respect was flattering.

"As I said, I know you wouldn't want to do what the girls do," Beatrice went on, "but I'm pretty sure we could find something to accommodate you if you decided to join us." She gave Malvena a sly smile. "I have you pegged as a watcher, right?"

Malvena colored. "I see you know nothing about me," she snapped, "nothing. I will leave now."

Beatrice realized her mistake; her jaw tightened in frustration. "Wait! Aren't you hungry? Stay and have something to eat. How about a snack while I fill you in about the organization? I'll have the barman put it on my tab."

"No." Malvena stood up and gave Beatrice an abrupt nod before she marched off, her high heels clicking against the slate floor. A few of the couples at the small tables and some at the bar looked at Malvena as she passed, but no one made a move to stop her. She pushed against the heavy oak door and for a heart-stopping moment thought it was locked. But it gave, swinging open with a scraping rasp, and Malvena stumbled into the misty night.

❧

Talia sniffled, dabbing at her nose with a handkerchief. "But why? Why should he have to stay like this? It's not fair. Jeff never did anything terribly wrong; he didn't have time to." She drew the coverlet over Jeff's sleeping form, careful not to touch the puffy hand that twitched as the light wool touched it. "Sure, he lived in his own world, and sure, he could be a stinker. In high school everyone knew you crossed Jeff at your peril. But most of the time, he was just fun to be with." She looked up at Kate, her lips trembling. "We both were just getting started with our lives."

"Jeff was an adult when he came here."

"Barely," Talia said bitterly.

"He is what he is now because of decisions he made as an adult," Kate said patiently. A sadness shadowed her lovely face. "And not just a few isolated incidents like shoving Sammy from the floating debris the child was clinging to. It's because that's the way Jeff led his life—thinking only of himself."

But Talia hadn't heard. She was peering gloomily at the strand of blond, none-too-clean hair she'd wound about her finger. "It's not fair," she said again. She gave a start as

Jeff moaned.

He batted the air above him and the moan became a frightened wail.

Kate quickly moved to the chaise lounge, put a slender hand on Jeff's forehead and stroked his bulbous face, lightly touching his red-veined cheeks. Jeff sighed, as though Kate's touch had cooled his fevered fantasies and chased away his dream gremlins. He snuggled into the cocoon of his wool coverlet, a smile on his swollen, glistening lips.

"He'd hate the way he looks now," Talia whispered.

"He doesn't know how he looks," Kate said sadly. "And he's quite content in his dream world—most of the time."

"What will happen to him? Will he always be this way?" Talia could not conceal her horror at the thought.

"I don't know what's in store for your friend, but I do know that, though he chose to be like this, everyone here must do something useful, even those who don't want to."

"How could Jeff have chosen to be like this?"

"When he was shown his book of life, it was a strange amalgam of the life Jeff imagined and the life he actually led. In both, however, he was the only one who mattered. His dream world existed only for his pleasure, and as far as he was concerned, the real world did too. He despised anyone who didn't fit in with his plans of his overall view of what he wanted."

"He was always amusing to be around." It was weak, and Talia knew it. But she wasn't really paying attention, occupied by a thought that had suddenly occurred to her. Aside from the fact that she didn't live in a dream world, was she so very different from Jeff?

"He liked having you around because it made him look good," Kate was saying. "You're beautiful and smart. He collected people like you, people who could reinforce his immense sense of self-worth."

Talia ran her hand through her mane of hair and then looked at her fingers, disgusted. "People like me. Sure."

"You'd like to freshen up?"

Talia grimaced. "Oh, what I'd give for a shower, a bar of soap, some shampoo."

"Then go on. Have at it."

For a moment, Talia looked hopeful; then she shook her head. "Every time I go looking for the bathroom, I can't find it," she confessed. "I can find a place with a toilet and a teensy little sink, but that's it." She looked at her wrinkled shirt. "I don't know how long it has been since I've found anything clean in my closet, but it feels like ages." Talia glanced at Kate and then looked away, shamefaced. "I'm not a complete idiot," she said quietly. "I've seen how things work around here. Nothing happens by accident; everything means something. So, if one day there are beautifully decorated bathrooms all over Selveridge House and the next I can't find a single one— well, it's pretty obvious that I'm not going to be able to get clean until I . . ." she gave a brittle laugh, "until I come clean." She straightened and made herself look at Kate. "Having a few chats with Lorraine just isn't going to hack it, and besides she has taken on Brad and his insecurities as her latest girl-scout project. That's why I asked for you."

"So you did. But first things first." Kate stepped into the adjoining room. Talia heard brisk footsteps, and a moment later Kate reappeared carrying two fluffy aqua towels and a washcloth. "You'll find a door next to your closet," she said. "Try it."

Talia took the towels gratefully. She knew there had been no door beside her bedroom closet; she also knew she'd find one there now. "Thanks," she said. "Thanks a lot." Then she stopped, worry creasing her lovely face. "You're sure it's okay if

I leave? I mean, I'm supposed to be talking with you about . . . stuff."

"Go." Kate's hands made a scooting motion. "When you're ready, I'll be here. Until then I have other things to do. And frankly I'd rather do them than be with a young woman so . . . so obviously in need of soap and water."

Talia gave a hoot of laughter. Funny, she wasn't at all offended by the gentle jibe. Was this what was meant by having a sense of humor about yourself? But she didn't take time to ponder. The thought of the fresh, hot water, the piles of soap suds awaiting erased everything but spiraling, joyous anticipation. Still, as Talia stepped past Jeff's sleeping figure she paused. "I don't know how long he has been responsible for those adult decisions you were talking about, but it couldn't have been very long," she said to Kate.

"No. And I don't know what the future would have held for him," Kate said quietly. "But consider this; the Lord bends all that happens to us to the best possible outcome, all the while leaving each person free to do what he or she choses. It could be that, if Jeff had remained on earth, his future decisions would have made him into something too horrendous to contemplate. If so, divine mercy could have allowed his passage into this world before that was possible." She looked at Talia. "Do you understand?"

Talia stilled a small shiver. "I'm not sure." She took a quick breath. "But I guess that's one of the things we're going to talk about later, right?"

"If you like, but don't get the idea that I'm going to feed you information for you to regurgitate the way your university lecturers did." She smiled briefly at Talia's shocked surprise. "I can say that because I was one. Anyway, though I will be your teacher, you have to understand that what I know is microscopically small compared to what there is to know. I've been learning ever since I came, and I'm astonished to have an occasional glimmer of how little I truly comprehend." Kate's face lit. "You can't imagine how exciting it is to be able to look forward to a continual unfolding of truth, of things that will help me live a truly useful life." Then she recollected herself. "But that's another matter. Go on, off with you."

Talia didn't wait for a further invitation. For one thing, she didn't quite know how to react to Kate's exalted paean to learning. Was she supposed to be excited about something like an eternity of graduate school? Please. Not that she'd ever say as much to Kate, but Phi Beta Kappa or not, the idea sounded a whole lot more like hell than heaven.

A half smile twitched Kate's lips as she watched Talia hurry off. The smile disappeared when she went to the chaise lounge and stood looking down at the sleeping Jeff Edwards. "You've been extremely useful today whether you know it or not, my poor young man," she said. "Now it's time you were on your way."

She nodded to the two men in white uniforms who appeared in the doorway. "You can take him now." She stood aside as they unfolded a gurney, picked up the swaddled bundle from the chaise and carefully transferred it onto the cart.

One of the men tipped his cap to Kate. "Got anyone else for us then?"

"No," Kate gave a sigh that contained so much in it—gradations of relief, pleasure, thoughtfulness—she had no need to complete the rest, though she did. "There might have been, but fortunately it appears not."

24

BRAD NELSON TUCKED HIS SHIRT INTO HIS PANTS AND patted his stomach. Not bad. Even if sports clothes were the only things he found in his closet nowadays (what kind of uniform had he worn? His mental picture of it was hazy) at least he looked pretty good in them, wasn't ballooning out at the waist anymore. Brad looked in the mirror and grinned. But then his pleased complacency changed to alarm. "Didn't mean it," he mumbled earnestly. "Didn't mean to be thinking of my looks. Doin' my best to concentrate on what's really important."

He shook his head, exasperated. This was going to be harder than he'd thought if he couldn't even feel pleased at the evidence of some progress. After all, was it so bad to be happy about how you looked? Hadn't Lorraine told him that Kwan, that mentor of hers, had been head over tin cups excited when Lorraine told about her restored face? Nah, it must be okay to be concerned with how you looked—if you didn't overdo it. And he wouldn't.

Brad ran a hand through his thickening hair and, despite his resolution, felt a jolt of pleasure. How long had it been since he could do that and not feel exposed scalp beneath his fingers? He reached for his sports jacket, hooked the collar with his forefinger and slung it over his shoulder, heading for the door. Would Lorraine be in the downstairs sitting room, or was she still in one of the assignment rooms having a session with Kwan? Brad's mounting anticipation was immediately pricked with a twinge of sheepishness. Might think he was a teenager, for G—for Pete's sake.

But as Brad approached the hall, his step quickened.

She was there. Seated on the chintz-covered couch, knees together, feet properly flat on the rug, Lorraine was reading in a notebook. With her hair brushed back into a roll and her neatly pressed blouse tucked into a tan skirt, she looked like a studious graduate student, Brad thought.

"Where'd the pooch come from?" Brad snapped his fingers at the tan-and-white spaniel that lay curled at Lorraine's feet. The dog, though she didn't get up, wagged her tail amiably.

Lorraine looked up and gave him a guilty grin. "I found her." She reached down to scratch the dog's ears. "Really. Bess was outside my door when I went back to my rooms after breakfast. She might as well have had a red ribbon tied around her neck with a gift card attached because she sat there looking at me and I knew she was mine. I've always wanted a dog, but I didn't know anything about taking care of one, and anyway I told myself having a dog in the city simply wasn't practical."

"You never had a dog? Not even when you were a kid?"

"Mom had enough on her hands working two jobs to get enough to pay the rent and feed us without shelling out for dog food." She shrugged. "And then when Mom and I were both working and money wasn't so tight, what with my traveling and Mom's crazy hours, there wasn't anyone home to take care of a dog."

She saw Brad's face and added quickly, "I'm not complaining; Mom did the best she could. Better than a lot of single moms." Then she added softly, "I've been reviewing my life, and Kwan has helped me to see things from different angles, helped me to see the trials and hardships of some of the people in my life from their points of view."

"And?"

"I guess understanding is the first step to forgiving."

"That sounds like a quotation."

"You could say so." Lorraine ducked her head in the old, familiar gesture dating from the days of her scarred face. "Sorry. I don't mean to bore you, going on about my life story."

"You're not! I mean, I'm not." Brad sat on the couch beside her. "Go on. I want to hear about your life. You've told me what happened in Africa, but not much else." He scratched Bess's ears, and the spaniel's eyes half closed in ecstasy. "How'd you get there anyway?"

"How did I get to Africa?" Lorraine paused. For a moment Brad thought she wouldn't continue, but then she said, "Like anything else, it seemed pure chance, but in retrospect I'm not so sure. I had good grades in high school, and I wanted desperately to go on, but college was out of the question. Mom wasn't well and couldn't keep up her hours at Taco Bell and the neighborhood dry cleaners, so I had to get a full-time job. So I did, and it was great. Got a job that let me travel. I'd always loved the idea of traveling, mostly because I wanted to get away from the places I'd grown up in, but some of it was just wanting to see what was over the next hill. I'm efficient and found I had a facility for languages, so working for a travel agency was a natural. I got to accompany several tours to

Europe, but the safari was the first time I'd been to Africa." Lorraine looked off into the distance. "I liked being on my own, self-sufficient and totally in charge, or at least I thought I was," she paused. "I was twenty-five when the accident happened." Lorraine gave a tiny shake of her head. "But I've already told you about that."

"Only because I pried it out of you, and then just the bare minimum. You said that you were terribly scarred and after several operations you came home, that you got a secretarial job and stayed there." Brad appraised her shrewdly. "You pretty much stopped living after the accident, didn't you?"

Lorraine regarded the closed notebook in her hands. "What a waste. I know now that I should have done more with my life." She bit her lip. "But I also know regrets don't do any good. I'm just glad that at least I kept on working, doing the best I could with whatever I was handed. My job kept me from thinking about myself, forced me, at least sometimes, to think of others—and that let the angels who were with me do the rest." She saw Brad's look of utter incomprehension and said quickly, "Don't worry; it's just another quote."

Brad gave her a rueful smile that reminded Lorraine of a preschooler in need of comforting.

"I guess it's obvious I'm not up on that type of thing," he said. "I haven't had Kwan's coaching. Matter of fact, I haven't had anyone to clue me in on what the guidelines are here."

"You'll have your own instructor soon," Lorraine said quickly. "I'm sure of it."

"How?" Brad's face was glum.

"Because I can feel that you're essentially a good person—and because you came back to us from where you were with Stuart."

He flushed and looked at his hands. "Wish I hadn't told you about that."

"I'm glad you did." Lorraine got up and Bess, alerted, bounced to her feet too, tail wagging furiously. "Yes, I'll take you for a walk," Lorraine said to the spaniel. She looked down at Brad. "If you . . . that is . . . would you like to come with us?" she said.

When Brad, still contemplating his hands, did not answer immediately, Lorraine leaned over to give Bess an awkward pat. "Of course, if you'd rather not—"

Brad came to with a start. "Oh sure, sure, I'd like that. Where are we going?"

Lorraine's usually serious expression was almost mischievous. "You'll have to come along to find out, won't you?"

※

Prescott rested his hands on the deck railing and watched the soaring scarlet of a flight of macaws, their piercing color slashing against the lush green of the valley below. He never tired of coming back to his room and watching the now-familiar yet ever-changing scene. Especially after a session like the one he'd just been though. Not that he didn't enjoy the time spent with his mentor in the interview room. Afterward, however, he always felt as though he'd just completed a twelve-hour endurance race and come in last. Afterward he needed this.

He thought of his grandparents, of the beautiful woman who had been his grandmother. He'd been so terribly stung by her gentle warning about his blind spots! At the time, he hadn't known the half of it, hadn't yet begun to realize how his pompous self-righteousness had held him back from being the kind of man he wanted to be, the sort of person he'd thought he was.

Prescott straightened. You don't stand here and whine; you get on with the job at hand. Which was learning, which was attempting as well as one was able, to prepare for what lay ahead. Prescott raised his face to the sun's warm rays and sudden contentment flooded him. He didn't deserve it, but thanks be to God, he'd been told there was a place prepared for him. He had only to find it. Would he go from here to search for it? Be given instructions? Don't push it, Prescott told himself. At the proper time, he'd know what to do.

His thoughts shifted to Karen. How was she faring with Cynthia? How could Karen manage to cope if her preparation was even half as difficult as his? Perhaps he could help her, coach her in some way? As Prescott stood thinking, he heard a sound like the rustling of a bird alighting on a branch, and Karen was standing beside him.

"Dad, you make such hard work of things." Karen's eyes were teasing. At Prescott's hurt look, she covered his hand with hers. "Don't be that way, Dad; really, it has been a snap. Cynthia was right—it's like a curtain being opened to show you the most wonderful things. And the great thing is it all makes such perfect sense!" She studied him. "This isn't what you wanted to hear, is it?"

It took a moment, but at last Prescott gave a weak guffaw. He took his hand from the railing beneath hers and patted his daughter's. "Of course it is. Stands to reason it's easier for you. I have a lot of baggage you don't. So you and Cynthia have been getting along, have you? She's a very nice young woman."

Karen regarded him anxiously. "Cynthia isn't with me anymore. Is it going to upset you to know she has moved to another community? Kate said it was at another level, one where she'll be able to fully develop her abilities."

"What possible reason could I have to be upset?" Prescott said more sharply than he'd intended.

Karen's face fell.

"Oh, my dear, I'm so sorry." Prescott found he'd put more meaning into those words than he could have imagined. Despite his very real sorrow, the analytical part of Prescott's mind, working as always, was struck by this new ability.

His daughter's expression lightened as she heard him, but all she said was, "For a moment there, it was beginning to sound like some of those conversations we used to have."

"Unfortunately." There it was again; Prescott heard the world of regret he'd been able to put into the half-humorously spoken word. He was struck by the tremendous difference it made in communication—with his daughter, and with, he supposed, anyone attuned to it.

"You never said you were sorry before," Karen said softly. "Oh, I don't mean you never said the words, but you never meant it."

"I thought fathers shouldn't have to apologize to their children," Prescott said. "I thought it was a sign of weakness."

"And you earned your living negotiating?" Again her tone was teasing.

"That was work; you were family." Prescott put a hand on Karen's shoulder. "You've come to say goodbye, haven't you?" he said quietly.

"Yes." Her face shone. "I've been welcomed to my home. It's a marvelous city beside the ocean—you know how I've always loved the ocean—and the buildings are all blue and pearl white. My apartment's right on the beach, and on top of everything, I have the most wonderful job. I'm—" she stopped. "This is going too fast for you, isn't it Dad?" She looked at him anxiously. "But it's all so wonderful, I can't help it. And there's someone I want you to meet. Not now I think, but in a while, when . . . you're able."

"Is this someone male?"

"For sure." Karen gave a happy laugh. "He looked at me, and I just knew. And the marvelous thing is, so did he." She put her hands in her back jeans pockets. "So it's okay if I go? You're doing okay here?"

"I haven't progressed at your speed, but I think I'm getting there," Prescott said dryly. "Gradually."

"That's so great."

And of course, now Prescott heard in her words the myriad facets of his daughter's joy. Her happiness for him and for herself, her bubbling joy at the thought of what lay ahead, were in her every tone, in the brilliance of her smile.

"Your mother would be proud of you," Prescott said softly.

"She still grieves for us," Karen told him, "but it's gotten easier. There's so much she doesn't understand, but the comfort she feels when she's able to think of us here together helps. I think it's one of the things that is preparing her for when she'll join us."

Prescott looked at his only child in wonder. "How did you become so wise?"

"Good genes," she said with a grin. "Absolutely terrific genes." She reached up and gave Prescott a kiss. "Gotta go. I'll be in touch, okay?"

"Okay," Prescott said. "Definitely okay."

The next moment he was alone on the deck. Looking out over the treetops, Prescott saw the flight of macaws return, wheeling on the thermals. He watched, feeling a vast content followed by a rush of gratitude. "Thank you," he murmured. "My Lord and my God, I thank you. It's good to be alive."

Malvena picked her way through the brittle, tangled shrubbery. At the sound of heavy trucks in the distance, she scuttled to crouch in the roadside ditch. After a moment, she raised her head to peer down the dusty road. Another convoy? The truckloads of men with guns could have been either troops or paramilitary; but whichever, she knew better than to let them see her. She sneezed and wiped dust from her nose with the tail of her headscarf. What was she doing here by the side of a desert road, alone and afraid? Afraid? No, she was afraid of nothing, not even death. She'd proved that. Malvena straightened her shoulders. She should be in the Garden of Allah, served fruits and sweet pastries as others praised her heroic deeds.

"Bringing pain to the innocent is not heroic, my child." The calm voice came from behind her.

Malvena shot upright and whipped around to gape at the turbaned man. "What do you mean?" Then she paused as the roar of oncoming trucks grew louder. "You'd better come hide, Imam. Soldiers are coming."

"They will not harm me." He dismissed the trucks with a wave of his hand. "Nor you when you're with me, so let us sit." He adjusted his robes and settled into one of the two heavily carved chairs that appeared beneath the shade of one of the taller shrubs.

Malvena stared, first at the handsome man sitting in the chair, then at the clouds of dust rising in the distance. "You're sure it will be all right?" she said hesitantly.

The imam indicated the other chair with a long finger. "Sit."

Malvena sat. The convoy, now in plain sight, bore down on them, and the first truck thundered past. Malvena nervously pressed her fingers to the waist of her dust-covered dress, smoothing the folds of her skirt. She looked from the impassive imam to the trucks. A few of the men in them tried to shout conversations over the noise, one laughed uproariously and fired his gun in the air; no one so much as glanced in the direction of the two by the side of the road.

"They didn't see us?" Malvena said after the convoy passed.

"No." The imam's keen eyes assessed her. "But then you are used to not being seen, aren't you? I imagine, however, it is becoming more difficult to hide yourself from others as effectively as you once did. Ah yes, I see by your expression that it is so." He took a small cup from a tray on the table that appeared at his elbow. "This is a dusty, dirty place; a cup of tea will refresh you," he said, handing it to her.

Malvena took the cup, but looked mistrustfully at the reddish brown liquid in it.

"You have nothing to fear from me, my child."

Something in the mildly reproachful words made Malvena look up sharply. "From you. Do you mean I am right to be afraid . . . of something else?"

"Have you given thought—any thought at all—to the devastation you caused? Have you considered the desolation you brought to the lives of those who mourn the ones you took with you?"

"I did what I had to do." Malvena sat up straight. "I gave my life willingly."

"Ah. So you haven't allowed yourself to consider the consequences." The imam sighed. "Have you not thought even of the mother of the child?"

For a moment, Malvena looked puzzled. Then she twitched her shoulders. "He was my cousin's. She is a simpleton and knows nothing but making babies. She has other children and undoubtedly will have more." When the imam greeted this with silence, she lifted her chin and said, "It was necessary. I could not afford to arouse any suspicion. My checked bag passed the scanner, but I couldn't risk having it opened for inspection."

"Why did you do this terrible thing?"

"For Allah," Malvena said promptly. "For the holy jihad."

The imam simply looked at her until Malvena glanced away. But once again her chin jutted out, and she repeated, "I did it for A—for—," but she could not say the name she had begun to pronounce. "I also did it for revenge," she snarled. "To avenge the death of my brother."

"Oh?" the imam said.

The road beside them disappeared. In its place, Malvena saw a small room with unpainted cement walls, a room lit by a single, uncovered bulb. Three people crowded about a worktable piled with wires and electrical devices and several small plastic bags. Malvena saw herself come to the doorway carrying a cardboard box.

"I have news," said the Malvena in the doorway.

One of the men looked up and frowned. "Put the box in that corner and leave us. This is no place for women."

"But you said I could help. You promised."

The Malvena sitting with the imam heard the icy, barely contained anger in the other Malvena's voice.

"I only said that because you tired me with your continual whining." The bearded man gave an impatient gesture. "I've changed my mind, sister. It is not right that you should be part of something as dangerous as this." The two men with him nodded in agreement, and the Malvena in the doorway, seeing this, came into the room and carefully deposited the box on the floor.

"I will not tell you what I heard at the market then." The petulance in her voice had changed to something more dangerous.

"We are not interested in market gossip," said her brother.

Malvena lowered her head; a small noise came from deep within her throat. The gesture was submissive, but the sound was not. Still, she stayed. She indicated the box in the corner. "What do you think is in the box?"

"Why should it concern you?" Then he relented. "Only supplies we ordered."

"Are you sure?"

"Of course. Go, woman. Leave us."

His sister tossed her head. "As you wish."

Something in Malvena's tone made her brother look up sharply, but then he shrugged and went back to his work.

The Malvena seated beside the imam held her hand to her mouth. "Stop!"

The room and the figures vanished.

"You knew," growled a tall, bearded man beside Malvena's chair. "You knew the box contained explosives."

Malvena twisted in her chair to look up at him. "Perhaps I suspected the box might be dangerous, but—" Her eyes widened. "Daron?" she said. Her voice quavered.

The man's teeth flashed in an unpleasant grin. "Do you not know me, my sister?" He reached into the folds of his loose-fitting shirt.

"Enough!"

The tall man recoiled at the imam's sharp command. "She betrayed me and my friends, Imam," he protested. "I must be allowed my revenge."

"No, you must not," the imam said. He held the other's gaze until the bearded man shuffled his feet and glanced away. "You have performed your task. You may leave us."

"But I . . . I—" The man's glance darted from the imam to Malvena. He sucked in a breath. "Yes, Imam," he mumbled. And he was gone.

Malvena relaxed from her spring-coiled position. "I would have told him about the rumors that there might be explosives if he had let me. And I didn't know of a certainty that the box contained a bomb; if I had, I would have run from the house instead of staying in the kitchen."

"You were regarded as a heroine when you survived, weren't you?" said the imam. "How pleased you were when your suggestion that you take your brother's place was accepted."

"I knew I could carry out the plan as well as he. And I did." Then Malvena's bravado disappeared. "He always does what he threatens," she whimpered. "He will search until he finds me, and when he does—"

"There are those wronged in their natural life who, when they arrive here, seek out the people who harmed them," said the imam. "It can be very unpleasant."

Despite the desert heat, Malvena shivered. She rubbed her arms. "But you will help me, won't you, Imam?" she said softly. "You won't let anything bad happen to me."

"My child, I am only a humble servant of the Almighty; I cannot change what is and what will be." The imam's expression was somber. "I am afraid you have put yourself beyond the protection of the forces for good. You must make your way to your home, the one you prepared for yourself while on earth."

Malvena shrank back. "Perhaps I don't want to go there."

"Where do you want to go?"

She thought a moment and said, "With you, Imam, with you." She'd meant to give him a shy, submissive smile; but instead Malvena felt her lips curl in a sneer. She covered her mouth with her hand. "Please, Imam, I tell you I hold you in the highest regard—" she began, but her mouth puckered, contorted in pain.

"Say nothing, my child. To say nothing is better than to lie. You do not hold me in any regard whatever. You despise me just as you despise all in authority."

Malvena snapped shut her mouth, her teeth making an audible click.

"I must leave," said the imam, "and you must continue your journey."

Malvena's jaw worked. She jumped to her feet in a violent motion that sent her heavy chair backward into the ditch. Then she strode off across the road into the desert. After fifty feet or so, she looked back. The ornately carved legs of Malvena's overturned chair poked in the air above the ditch; where the imam had been sitting there was no imam and no chair, nothing but dusty ground. Malvena let her fury bubble to the surface, let her face contort into a murderous scowl. She snarled a curse. It felt good, deliciously good, to unleash the fullness of her rage. It felt so good that Malvena gave a surprised chuckle. She went on her way, her step buoyant.

25

BLOSSOM PLACED THE LAST OF THE TRAYS ON THE CART AND pushed it down the sparkling white hallway. Usually she loved this early morning part of the day, when she got to serve breakfast, greet the newcomers, and assuage any worries they might have. Today, however, she couldn't shake a vague feeling of malaise. It was missing Michael, of course.

Blossom stopped in the middle of the hall; her knuckles gripped the cart's handle. "Dear Lord," she whispered, "I know you're taking care of the both of us and I'm trying to be patient; but Lord, please can't we be together? I've tried to just concentrate on learning what I must and doin' the best job I can here, but I miss him so much." Blossom wiped a tear from her smooth, unlined cheek with the back of her hand. Then she gave a short, determined sniff, took a tray from the cart, and entered the first room. She was unaware of the two who watched from the end of the hall.

"Oh Howard, why can't she be with Michael?" Kate said, her own eyes moist.

Her husband caught her hand and kissed it. "Is this my hard-headed, logical Kate?" he said. "You know very well there must be a good and valid reason for this separation." He sobered. "My love, I don't like to see Blossom's unhappiness any more than you, but this must be best for them both." He paused. "You're really troubled, aren't you? Would you like me to ask Petros about it? He'll know."

Kate shook her head. "No. If Blossom can wait, I can too." She brightened. "It helps to concentrate on so many in this group who have come through well. Of course, our star has to be Cynthia; she reminds me of one or two students I had when I was teaching, you know the ones, those you knew had the chance to make a difference, to win a Pulitzer or a Nobel."

"You had *two* of those?" Howard teased her, but he nodded. "It was a real privilege to be able to teach Cynthia, even though she was with us so little before she grew beyond us."

Kate smiled. "She definitely gave us as much and more than we were able to give her." She followed her husband back inside the office and shut the door. "Do you suppose we'll be allowed to help her Rob when he arrives? I hope so. It would be so wonderful to be a part of their happiness." She leaned against the door, her hands behind her back. "But aside from Cynthia, some of the others have been doing pretty well too. Have you seen Sherwood Prescott lately—and Fred?"

"I haven't talked with Prescott since we decided he was ready for another mentor," Howard said, "but you're right—I hear he's coming along nicely. And after a conspicuously inauspicious start, I think Fred's beginning to have a clue. I caught him coming from his first session with Stephen, and he looked as though dawn had finally broken and he wanted to paint the sunrise."

"It's so marvelous to see someone like that come out of his struggles—and he did have quite a struggle, didn't he? And then there's Lorraine, who with Kwan's help has opened like a flower," Kate said, counting on her fingers, "and Brad, and even our Talia seems to be headed in the right direction."

"The girl's a piece of work. But you're right: all in all it's been a good group," Howard agreed. He glanced at Kate and sobered. "With notable exceptions."

Kate closed her eyes a moment. She held her hand against her stomach, as though quelling a sharp pain. "Poor Stuart. You know, he still doesn't get it? He's just happily lapping up the life he has chosen with no concept that what he calls freedom is the most abject slavery."

"And Beatrice," Howard said quietly. "Time and again she has been told there are boundaries she has to observe, but it's obvious she can't stop herself. And now she's left the inn and gone to the next town."

Kate shuddered. "The woman's heading for disaster, but I suppose she hasn't tumbled to the new companions she has chosen yet."

"Of course not," Howard's tone was dry. "It will take her completely by surprise because she has no concept of anyone's feelings or any interest in them, except for how they impact on herself."

"Like Jeff and Malvena." Kate lowered her head into her hands. "Oh, Howard."

"Enough." The word was infinitely gentle. "They will be cared for even as the others, even as we are." He took a seat at one of the two desks facing each other in the center of the room. "On another subject, did I see something going on between Lorraine and Brad?"

Kate followed his lead gratefully, slipping into the seat at the other desk. "If you didn't, there's something terribly wrong with your eyes," she said, smiling. "Of course, there something's going on, and it's delightful."

"Thought there might be a spark there, but keeping up with that sort of thing is your job. And while we're at it, how about Delion and Jessie? Did Blossom's little ploy produce anything?"

Kate shook her head, exasperated. "Delion took one look at Jessie and was a goner, but that fast-talking young man has a lot of work before he'll be in a position to do anything about it." She turned on her computer. "Our small-time crook thinks he can sweet-talk his way into and out of anything, and I'm afraid he's going to have a terrible time breaking the habit."

"That's not the only habit Delion's going to have to break," Howard said with some asperity. But his annoyance quickly disappeared, and he said, "I have to admit that, despite an appalling background and the fact that Delion thoroughly enjoys having a facade that scares people silly, as far as he was able, the boy lived a good life. Didn't hurt those weaker than himself and however misguided his peculiar code of honor, he pretty much lived according to it."

Kate's mouth quirked. "That sounds rather like damning with faint praise."

Howard tilted his head as though he had glasses on, and looked at Kate over imaginary lenses. "Tut tut, such unangelic speech."

"Look who's talking! I'd say I don't have a corner on that."

"Ah, but with me it's merely giving the appropriate name to inappropriate behavior, dear heart." Howard stared intently at his screen. "Have you seen our message?"

Kate examined her screen and looked up, her smile brilliant. "We've been assigned another group!"

"That we have. Looks like a family of seven."

"No, no, look. It's a family and two neighbors. I'll prepare the packages, and you can go through their files." Kate opened a desk drawer and rummaging through it, pulled out paper and manila envelopes. The office settled into a companionable silence.

Blossom took the next-to-last tray from the cart and shouldered open the door of the next-to-last room. She came to an abrupt halt as she stepped passed the threshold. There was no bed in the room. A comfortable, upholstered couch with a couple of end tables sat along one wall and two wingback chairs flanked the window, a low coffee table between them. A man sitting in one of the wingback chairs glanced up at her.

"You're not a patient." Blossom took a firm grip on the wobbling breakfast tray.

The man folded the paper he'd been reading and tossed it aside. "Correct," he said. "Do sit down, Blossom." He indicated the chair opposite him, "Have a cup of coffee."

Blossom told herself it was silly to be bothered by the man's penetrating gray eyes, but she had trouble quieting her shaking hands as she placed the tray on the table between the chairs and took a seat. There was a moment's silence as he poured the coffee.

Blossom cleared her throat. "I don't mean to be rude, but . . . who are you?"

"My name is Yannish," said the gray-eyed man. "I've come to see if I can help explain some of the things that are troubling you and seem to be keeping you from being able to move on."

Blossom's cup rattled against the saucer. "How do you know what troubles me?" she said, lifting her jaw an inch.

"I research my assignments before I meet them." Yannish smiled. "In your case, I had a head start because of the person I've been tutoring."

Blossom put down the cup and saucer and clasped her hands. "I know I have a lot to learn," she said humbly. "I've found I don't know much of anything. Always been more of a doer than a thinker. Matter of fact, I'm beginning to realize I never paid much attention to anything important, certainly not to religion, other than spending Sunday mornings in church." She took a breath. "But I've been doing a lot of it lately. Thinking, that is." She gave Yannish a twisted smile. "Okay, you're right, I am troubled. And one of the things that troubles me most it that I'm not sure exactly what it is I believe. I've always believed in God. And I believe in a life after death, of course. I'm here, aren't I? And I want to go to heaven and serve God and love him. I do." Despair swept Blossom's face; she turned away. "But when it comes right down to it, that's all just words, isn't it? Just empty words. I say I love God, but how can I know if I really do?"

Yannish leaned forward and laid a hand on her shoulder. He waited until Blossom's agitation calmed. "That's an easy one. Remember the joy you felt in the presence of Cynthia's goodness, when you saw Jessie's courage?"

Blossom looked confused, but she nodded.

"You sensed the good that was in them and loved it. It was the good in both those women that you loved."

Blossom nodded again. "I guess so."

"That was loving the Lord."

"What?"

"All good comes from God; there is no other source. So when we love the good in another person, we love God," Yannish explained patiently. "When you loved the good you saw reflected in Jessie and Cynthia, you were loving our Lord."

Blossom still looked doubtful. "But that's so simple."

"Yes, isn't it?"

"That can't be all there is to it. It can't."

"It isn't. You say you've been doing a lot of thinking about your life. When were you truly happy?" When Blossom hesitated, Yannish answered for her. "When you were helping others, my dear Blossom. Your fulfillment came from making others happy, and not just your family, though they always held first place in your life; you loved helping just about everyone with whom you came in contact. That's why, despite the fact that you miss Michael so much, you've been reasonably happy here at the hospital. You enjoy being of service to other people."

Blossom's face was glum. "We're cutting to the chase now, aren't we? Okay, I have been thinking about that, about all my superwoman and supermom role-playing. Sure, I loved it. Question is, how much of all that stuff did I do just because I wanted to feel good about myself?"

Yannish gave a hoot of laughter. "You want to be perfect, don't you?" His smile became gentle. "Sometimes you had selfish motives, and sometimes you didn't. A great many times you weren't being selfish at all."

"You think?"

"I do."

Blossom looked down at her hands. "I'd just about come to the conclusion that I'm the reason Michael and I aren't allowed to be together."

"No, no, not completely," Yannish said quickly. "Michael has things to learn just as you do, but it was better that he tackle them by himself."

"Why?" Blossom's voice cracked.

"Ever notice you have a problem with control, Blossom?"

She flushed, her eyes darting to his and away again.

"You like calling the shots, especially with Michael," he said gently. "I'm afraid you've gotten into the habit of deciding what Michael should do and when he should do it."

"But I never insist—" Blossom stopped.

"You don't need to."

"Look, I know I tend to be manipulative; it's one of the things I've been working on since I came here. But you have to understand, sometimes Michael needs someone—needs me—to keep at him." She met Yannish's gray eyes and gave a sheepish grin. "Or maybe not."

"Maybe not," Yannish agreed. "You're a quick learner, Blossom," he said. He got up. "I don't see that there's much work left for you to do here—and Michael's been an apt pupil too. He's also ready to move on." Yannish answered the quickening hope in her face. "Yes," he said with a smile, "you will be together."

"Yes!" Blossom was on her feet. Then she looked around. "Where is he? Why isn't he here?"

"Calm yourself, child. Perhaps there are some duties you must finish?"

An impatient frown creased Blossom's forehead, but she gave a brief nod. "I'm delivering breakfast, and I have one more room. I can do that."

"I'm sure you can."

"Then can I be with Michael?"

"I'd like to see anyone try to stop you."

A grin lit her face. "Are you laughing at me, mister?"

"I wouldn't dare." Yannish held out a hand. As she took it, he murmured, "May your blessings be unending."

"Thank you," Blossom said, humbly. And then she was out the door, pushing the cart toward the room at the end of the hall.

"Time for breakfast; rise and shine," she sang out. She stopped and peered at the comforter-covered figure in the bed. "You come from Antarctica or something?" she asked the lump beneath the covers.

The lump stirred. "I was tryin' to get some sleep, that is, I was until someone arrives uninvited and—"

"Michael?" Blossom's voice quavered.

The comforter was pushed aside, and Michael erupted from the bedclothes. "Woman, is that you?" he shouted.

"No, it's your fairy godmother." Blossom shied back as Michael exploded from the bed. She unpursed her lips but had no chance to say anything before she was enfolded in Michael's arms, her face buried against her husband's chest. And when at last she did speak, the words were unintelligible.

"Hush now, hush now," Michael whispered. "I knew it wouldn't be long before we'd be together. I knew they couldn't keep us apart."

Blossom leaned back her head to look at her husband. "Michael, oh, Michael," she murmured.

They both started at a knock on the door. The door opened enough for a young woman to stick in her head.

"Well, come in, Jessie, come in," said Blossom.

But Jessie, though she opened the door wider, simply stood on the threshold and stared.

"What is it, girl?" Blossom asked without moving from her position within Michael's arms.

"Your . . . your faces," Jessie stammered.

"What about 'em?" Michael asked.

"It's like . . . like there's sunshine around you—sunshine coming from your eyes, from your skin."

His eyebrow raised, Michael looked at Blossom. "I see a little rain," he said, gently brushing his wife's cheek, "but yes, I think you may be right, young lady. I do believe I can see the sunshine too."

Questions for Disccussion

1. *The Arrivals* presents an unusual view of the afterlife. Discuss the unusual aspects of this depiction and how you responded to it. Overall, did you find this depiction of the afterlife satisfying or troubling?

2. The story posits that angels are human beings who have lived on earth and have made choices that have led them to a life of love and usefulness in heaven. How does this idea differ from previous depictions of angels you are familiar with? What other aspects of angelic life, as portrayed in this story, did you find intriguing or objectionable?

3. Each character must undergo self-examination before proceeding onto the next phrase of the journey. Did you feel that any character was particularly hard on him- or herself? Did you feel that any character was given an unfair judgment at the end of the story?

4. How is Fred Hampton's ultimate redemption foreshadowed early in the novel? Why do you think he had such a hard time coming to grips with his past? Was his earthly occupation a hindrance to him in the afterlife?

5. Beatrice Jorgenson ends up using her business skills in an unusual way. Discuss why, within the world of the book, her end was inevitable.

6. Did the fact that Kate and Howard were married surprise you? Do you believe that people who truly love each other in this world will be reunited in the next?

7. The world of spirits seems very much like a place on earth, yet there are subtle differences. What seemed similar and what seemed different? How do you feel about the idea that a spirit awaking in the afterlife might need time to adjust to his or her new situation?

8. Two young characters in the novel, Jeff Edwards and Talia Innes, are both self-centered and self-satisfied, yet their eventual end is quite different. What was the main difference between them? Was Talia's intellect and mental acuity very important in her new life?

9. The mothers in the novel are allowed to see their children, yet not to influence their decisions. Discuss how this affected you.

10. Blossom is a good woman who has lived a moral life. Did you feel that she should have had an easier time in her move toward angelhood? Why do you think she had such a long period of self-examination during her move toward becoming angelic?

11. Children who have died are treated especially well in this depiction of the afterlife, including growing to adulthood and becoming angels, as Yussef explains to Lorraine VanDyck. What are your thoughts on this conception of children in the afterlife?

12. What was the basic difference between the characters of Malvena Blatska and Jackson Delion?

13. Why was Jackson physically punished for using foul language when other characters occasionally did so with no repercussions?

14. Several characters in the novel—Beatrice Jorgenson, Sherwood Prescott, and Blossom O'Meara—are "take-charge" personalities. This seems to be one of their problems in the afterlife. Why is Beatrice's final destination so different from that of Prescott and Blossom?

15. There are physical changes in all the characters. Some are positive, as when the old become young and the disfigured are made whole. Yet some characters gain weight or become increasingly dirtier. What does this tell you about spiritual states?

16. Did you feel that the group was in danger at any point? Discuss some reasons that some characters were chased or beaten by thugs, while others were unmolested.

17. How did the physical surroundings change according to a character's thoughts or inner personality? Could you tell which characters would eventually be heaven-bound and which would be going to hell by either the company they kept or by the places they frequented?

18. Various spirits and guides appear to the arrivals. Discuss why they were necessary for the character's understanding of his or her situation. What were your reactions to Dalrymple?

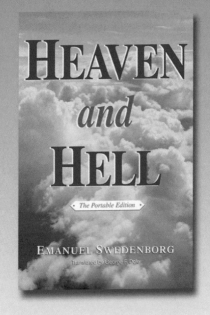

ABOUT THE AUTHOR

Naomi Gladish Smith was born in England to American parents and attended college in Bryn Athyn, Pennsylvania. A former teacher, she is married, the mother of four children, and grandmother of numerous grandchildren. She currently lives in Glenview, Illinois, and Lake Worth, Florida. Among her publications are a novel *Buried Remembrance* (1977); numerous essays and short stories that have been published in the annual anthology THE CHRYSALIS READER, *The Christian Science Monitor*, and *Interludes Magazine*. She also has been a regular contributor to WBEZ, the National Public Radio station in Chicago, Illinois.